SANDRA BROWN

WHITE HOT

D0036388

$9.99 U.S.
$12.99 CAN.

ISBN 978-1-9821-3216-3 **$9.99 U.S./**$12.99 Can.

50999

"Full of steamy sex, intrigue, and greedy secret plots."
—*The Washington Post*

"A thriller with more twists and turns than a Cowboys wide receiver trying to lose his marker . . . Great story, well told."

—*Herald Sun*

RICOCHET

"No one does steamy suspense like Brown, as shown by this expert mix of spicy romance and sharply crafted crime drama. . . . Tight plotting, a hot love story with some nice twists, and a credible ending help make this a standout thriller."
—*Publishers Weekly* (starred review)

"A great, entertaining read, with lots of surprising twists and turns, credibly flawed characters, and a love affair that's as steamy as a Savannah summer."
—*The Washington Post*

"[A] taut Southern thriller . . . delectable."
—*Life* magazine

"Gripping and absorbing . . . a must-read."
—*Booklist*

CHILL FACTOR

"Races along with the passion and verve that are the hallmarks of a Brown novel."
—*Orlando Sentinel*

"Compelling characters, sexual tension, and stunning plot twists . . . a page-turner that will keep readers guessing until the end."
—*The Sunday Oklahoman*

"Virtuoso plot twists . . . Brown's thriller engages the primal senses."

—*Kirkus Reviews*

SANDRA BROWN

WHITE HOT

POCKET BOOKS

New York   London   Toronto   Sydney   New Delhi

Pocket Books
An Imprint of Simon & Schuster, Inc.
1230 Avenue of the Americas
New York, NY 10020

This Pocket Books paperback edition December 2020

POCKET and colophon are registered trademarks of Simon & Schuster, Inc.

For information about special discounts for bulk purchases, please contact Simon & Schuster Special Sales at 1-866-506-1949 or business@simonandschuster.com.

The Simon & Schuster Speakers Bureau can bring authors to your live event. For more information or to book an event, contact the Simon & Schuster Speakers Bureau at 1-866-248-3049 or visit our website at www.simonspeakers.com.

Manufactured in the United States of America

10 9 8 7 6 5 4 3 2 1

ISBN 978-1-9821-3216-3
ISBN 978-0-7432-7347-3 (ebook)

Dedicated to the memory of Mark W. Smith.

He lived with grace, died with dignity, and is now healed.

WHITE HOT

prologue

Some said that if he was going to kill himself, he couldn't have picked a better day for it.

Life was hardly worth living that particular Sunday afternoon, and most organisms were doing a half-assed job of it. The atmosphere was as thick and hot as breakfast grits. It sucked the energy right out of every living thing, be it plant or animal.

Clouds evaporated under the ferocity of the sun. Moving from indoors to out was like stepping into a blast furnace like those in the Hoyles' foundry. At the family's fishing camp on Bayou Bosquet—so named because of the island of cypress trees in the middle of the creek's slow-moving current—a stuffed, six-foot gator basked in the heat of the yard. His glass eyes reflected the glare of the hot sky. The Louisiana state flag hung furled and limp upon its pole.

Cicadas were too indolent to make their grating music, although one industrious insect occasionally disturbed the somnolent atmosphere with an attempt that was halfhearted at best. Fish remained well below the surface of the water and its opaque green blanket of duckweed. They kept to the shadowy, murky depths, their only sign of life being the periodic pulsing of gills. A water moccasin lay inert on the bank, menacing but motionless.

The swamp was a natural aviary, but today every species of fowl seemed to be napping in its nest, with the exception of a single hawk. He was perched at the top of a tree that had been killed by a lightning strike decades before. The elements had left its branches as naked and white as bones picked clean.

The winged hunter eyed the cabin below. Perhaps he spied the mouse skittering among the pilings that supported the fishing pier. More likely, animal instinct alerted him to imminent peril.

The crack of the gunshot wasn't as loud as one might expect. The air, dense as a goose-down pillow, smothered the sound waves. The shot created barely a ripple of reaction in the swamp. The flag remained furled. The stuffed gator didn't flinch. Making only a small splash, the water moccasin slithered into the bayou, not alarmed, but piqued that his Sunday slumber had been disturbed.

The hawk took flight, spiraling on air currents with a minimum of effort, on the lookout for prey more appealing than the small mouse darting among the pilings.

To the dead man inside the cabin, the hawk gave no thought at all.

chapter 1

"Do you remember Slap Watkins?"

"Who?"

"The guy who was spouting off in the bar."

"Can you be more specific? What bar? When?"

"The night you came to town."

"That was three years ago."

"Yeah, but you should remember." Chris Hoyle sat forward in an attempt to goose his friend's powers of recall. "The loudmouth who caused the fight? Face that would stop a clock. Big ears."

"Oh, that guy. Right. With the . . ." Beck held his hands at the sides of his head to indicate large ears.

"That's how he got the nickname Slap," Chris said.

Beck raised an eyebrow.

"Whenever the wind blew, his ears—"

"Slapped against his head," Beck finished.

"Like shutters in a gale." Grinning, Chris tilted his beer bottle in a silent toast.

The window blinds in the den of the Hoyles'

home were drawn to block out the shimmering heat of a late-afternoon sun. The closed blinds also made the room agreeably dim for better TV viewing. A Braves game was being televised. Top of the ninth and Atlanta needed a miracle. But despite the unfavorable score, there were worse ways to spend a stifling Sunday afternoon than inside a semidark, air-conditioned den, sipping cold brews.

Chris Hoyle and Beck Merchant had idled away many hours in this room. It was the perfect male playroom, with its fifty-inch TV screen and surround-sound speakers. It had a fully stocked bar with a built-in ice maker, a refrigerator filled with soft drinks and beer, a billiards table, a dartboard, and a round game table with six leather chairs as soft and cushy as the bosom of the cover girl on this month's issue of *Maxim*. The room was paneled with stained walnut and furnished with substantial pieces that wore well and required little maintenance. It smelled of tobacco smoke and reeked of testosterone.

Beck uncapped another bottle of beer. "So what about this Slap?"

"He's back."

"I didn't know he was gone. In fact, I don't think I've seen him since that night, and then I was looking at him through swelling eyes."

Chris smiled at the memory. "As barroom brawls go, that was a fairly good one. You caught several of Slap's well-placed punches. He was always handy with his fists. He had to be because he shot off his mouth all the time."

"Probably defending against cruel cracks about his ears."

"No doubt. Anyway, that smart mouth of his kept him on everybody's fighting side. Soon after our altercation with him, he got into a feud with his sister's ex-husband. Over a lawn mower, I think it was. Things came to a head one night at a crawfish boil, and Slap went after his ex-brother-in-law with a knife."

"Killed him?"

"Flesh wound. But it was right across the guy's belly and drew enough blood to warrant an assault with a deadly weapon charge and probably should have been attempted murder. Slap's own sister testified against him. He's been in Angola for the past three years, now out on parole."

"Lucky us."

Chris frowned. "Not really. Slap's got it in for us. At least that's what he said that night three years ago when he was being hauled away in a squad car. He thought it unfair that he was being arrested and we weren't. Screamed invectives and threats that made my blood run cold."

"I don't remember that."

"That may have been when you were in the men's room nursing your wounds. Anyhow," Chris continued, "Slap is an unstable and untrustworthy ne'er-do-well, a trailer trash Bubba whose only talent is holding grudges, and in that, he excels. We humiliated him that night, and even drunk as he was, I doubt he's forgiven and forgotten. Keep an eye out for him."

"I consider myself warned." Beck glanced over

his shoulder in the general direction of the kitchen. "Am I invited to dinner?"

"Standing invitation."

Beck settled even more comfortably into the sofa on which he was sprawled. "Good. Whatever's baking in there is making my mouth water."

"Coconut cream pie. Nobody can make a better pie than Selma."

"You'll get no argument from me, Chris."

Chris's father, Huff Hoyle, strode in, fanning his ruddy face with his straw hat. "Get me one of those longnecks. I'm so damn thirsty, I couldn't work up a spit if my dick was on fire."

He hung his hat on a coat tree, then plopped down heavily in his recliner, swiping his sleeve across his forehead. "Damn, it's a scorcher today." With a sigh, he sank into the cool leather cushions of the chair. "Thanks, Son." He took the chilled bottle of beer Chris had opened for him and pointed it toward the TV. "Who's winning this ball game?"

"Not the Braves. In fact it's over." Beck muted the sound as the commentators began their postmortem of the game. "We don't need to hear why they lost. The score says it all."

Huff grunted in agreement. "Their season was over the minute they let those high-paid, non-English-speaking, prima donna players start telling the owners how to run the show. Big mistake. Could have told them that." He took a long swig of the beer, nearly draining the bottle.

"Have you been playing golf all afternoon?" Chris asked.

"Too hot," Huff said as he lit a cigarette. "We played three holes, then said screw this and went back to the clubhouse to play gin rummy."

"How much did you fleece them of today?"

The question wasn't whether Huff had won or lost. He always won.

"Couple of hundred."

"Nice going," Chris said.

"Ain't worth playing if you don't win." He winked at his son, then at Beck. He finished his beer in a gulp. "Either of you heard from Danny today?"

"He'll show up here in a while," Chris said. "That is if he can work us in between Sunday morning worship and Sunday night vespers."

Huff scowled. "Don't get me in a bad mood by talking about *that*. I don't want to spoil my dinner."

The gospel according to Huff was that preaching, praying, and hymn singing were for women and men who might just as well be women. He equated organized religion to organized crime, except that churches had impunity and tax advantages, and he had about as much intolerance for Holy Joes as he did for homosexuals and laborers with union cards.

Chris tactfully steered the conversation away from his younger brother and his recent preoccupation with spiritual matters. "I was just telling Beck that Slap Watkins is out on parole."

"White trash," Huff muttered as he toed off his shoes. "That whole bunch, starting with Slap's granddaddy, who was the lowest reprobate ever to draw breath. They found him dead in a ditch with a broken whiskey bottle jammed in his throat. He must have crossed somebody one time too many. There's bound to have been some inbreeding in that family. Down to the last one of them they're ugly as sin and dumber than stumps."

Beck laughed. "Maybe. But I owe Slap a debt of gratitude. If it hadn't been for him, I wouldn't be here sharing Sunday dinner."

Huff looked across at him with as much affection as he showed his own sons. "No, Beck, you were meant to become one of us, by hook or by crook. Finding you made that whole Gene Iverson mess worthwhile. You were the only good thing to come out of it."

"That and a hung jury," Chris said. "Let's not forget those twelve. If it weren't for them, I wouldn't be here sharing Sunday dinner. Instead I could be sharing a cell with the likes of Slap Watkins."

Chris often made light of having been put on trial for the murder of Gene Iverson. His joking dismissal of the incident never failed to make Beck uncomfortable, as it did now. He changed the subject. "I hate to bring up a business matter when it isn't even a workday."

"In my book, every day's a workday," Huff said.

Chris groaned. "Not in my book, it's not. Is it bad news, Beck?"

"Potentially."

"Then can't it wait till after supper?"

"Sure, if you'd rather."

"Nope," Huff said. "You know my rule about

bad news. I want to hear it sooner rather than later. I sure as hell don't want to wait through dinner. So, what's up, Beck? Don't tell me that we've been slapped with another fine by the EPA over those cooling ponds—"

"No, it's not that. Not directly."

"Then what?"

"Hold on. I'm going to pour a drink first," Chris said to Huff. "You like to hear bad news early, I like to hear it with a glass of bourbon in my hand. Want one?"

"Lots of ice, no water."

"Beck?"

"I'm fine, thanks."

Chris moved to the bar and reached for a decanter and two glasses. Then, leaning closer to the window, he peered through the slats of the blinds and twirled the wand to open them wider. "What have we got here?"

"What is it?" Huff asked.

"Sheriff's car just pulled up."

"Well, what do you think he wants? It's payday."

Chris, still looking through the blinds, said, "I don't think so, Huff. He's got somebody with him."

"Who?"

"I don't know. Never saw him before."

Chris finished pouring the drinks and brought one of them to his father, but the three said nothing more as they listened to Selma making her way from the kitchen at the back of the house to the front door to answer the bell. The housekeeper greeted the callers, but the exchange was too softly spoken for individual words to be understood.

Footfalls approached the den. Selma appeared ahead of the guests.

"Mr. Hoyle, Sheriff Harper is here to see you."

Huff motioned for her to usher him in.

Sheriff Red Harper had been elected to the office thirty years before, his campaign substantially boosted and his win guaranteed by Huff's pocketbook. He had remained in office by the same means.

His hair, which had been fiery in his youth, had dulled, as though it had rusted on his head. He stood well over six feet tall but was so thin that the thick leather gun belt with the accoutrements of his job attached looked like an inner tube hanging on a fence post.

He looked wilted, and not only because of the heat index outside. His face was long and gaunt, as though three decades of corruption had weighted it down with guilt. His woebegone demeanor was that of a man who had sold his soul to the devil far too cheaply. Never jolly, he seemed particularly downcast as he shuffled into the room and removed his hat.

By contrast, the younger officer with him, a stranger to them, seemed to have been dipped in a vat of starch along with his uniform. He was so closely shaven, his cheeks were rosy with razor burn. He looked as tense and alert as a sprinter in the blocks waiting for the starting gun.

Red Harper acknowledged Beck with a slight nod. Then the sheriff looked toward Chris, who was standing beside Huff's chair. Finally his bleak eyes moved to Huff, who had remained seated in his recliner.

"Evening, Red."

"Huff." Instead of looking directly at Huff, he focused on the brim of his hat, which he was feeding through his fingers.

"Drink?"

"No thanks."

It wasn't Huff's habit to stand up for anyone. That was a show of respect reserved for Huff Hoyle alone, and everybody in the parish knew it. But, impatient with the suspense, he pushed down the footrest of his recliner and came to his feet.

"What's going on? Who's this?" He gave the sheriff's spit-and-polish companion a once-over.

Red cleared his throat. He lowered his hat to his side and nervously tapped it against his thigh. He waited a long time before looking Huff in the eye. All of which signaled to Beck that the sheriff's errand was much more consequential than picking up this month's graft.

"It's about Danny . . ." he began.

chapter 2

*T*he highway was barely recognizable. Countless times, Sayre Lynch had driven this stretch of road between New Orleans International Airport and Destiny. But traveling it today was like doing so for the first time.

In the name of progress, landmarks that had made the area distinct had been obscured or obliterated. Rural Louisiana's charm had been sacrificed to gaudy commercialism. Little that was quaint or picturesque had survived the onslaught. She could have been in Anywhere, USA.

Fast-food franchises now occupied the spots where once had been mom-and-pop cafes. Homemade meat pies and muffaletta sandwiches had been replaced with buckets of wings and Value Meals. Hand-painted signs had given way to neon. Menus scribbled daily on chalkboards had been supplanted by disembodied voices at drive-through windows.

During the ten years she had been away, trees

draped with Spanish moss had been bulldozed to allow for additional highway construction. This expansion had diminished the vastness and mystery of the swamps that flanked the road. The dense marshes were now ribboned with entrance and exit ramps jammed with semis and minivans.

Until now Sayre hadn't realized the depth of her homesickness. But these substantial changes in the landscape made her nostalgic for the way things had been. She longed for the mingled aromas of cayenne and filé. She would like to hear again the patois of the people who served up Cajun dishes that took more than three minutes to prepare.

While superhighways made for faster travel, she wished for the roadway she had known, the one lined with trees that grew so close to it the branches overlapped to cover it like a canopy and cast lacy patterns of shadow on the asphalt.

She longed for the times she could drive with the windows down and, rather than choking on motor exhaust, inhale the soft air that was perfumed with honeysuckle and magnolia and the seminal scent of the swamp.

The changes that had come about in the past decade were jarring to her senses and an affront to her memories of the place in which she'd grown up. But then, she supposed that the changes in herself were equally drastic, although perhaps not as apparent.

The last time she'd driven this road, she'd been traveling in the opposite direction, away from Destiny. That day, the farther she got from home, the lighter she felt, as though she were molting layers of negativity along the way. Today she was returning, and her dread was as heavy as chain mail.

Homesickness for the area, no matter how acute, would never have brought her back. Only her brother Danny's death could have compelled her to return. Apparently he had withstood Huff and Chris for as long as he could and had escaped them in the only manner he'd felt was open to him.

Fittingly, as she approached the outskirts of Destiny, she saw the smokestacks first. They jutted belligerently above the town, large and black and ugly. Smoke billowed from them today as on every other day of the year. It would have been too costly and inefficient to have shut down the furnaces, even in observance of Danny's demise. Knowing Huff, it probably hadn't even occurred to him to make this concession to his youngest child.

The billboard marking the city limit read "Welcome to Destiny, Home of Hoyle Enterprises." *As though that's something to boast,* she thought. Quite the contrary. Iron pipe casting had made Huff rich, but it was a bloodstained wealth.

She navigated the streets of town which she had first explored on bicycle. Later she'd learned to drive on them. Then as a teen she had cruised them with her friends, looking for action, boys, and whatever amusements they could scare up.

While still a block away from the First United Methodist Church, she heard the organ music. The pipe organ had been a gift to the church from her mother, Laurel Lynch Hoyle. It bore a brass plaque in her memory. It was the small congregation's pride and joy, being the only pipe organ in Destiny. None of the Catholic churches had one, and Destiny was predominantly Catholic. Her mother's gift had been generous and sincere, but it was yet another symbol of how the Hoyles lorded over their town and everyone in it and refused to be outdone.

How heartbreaking that the organ was playing a dirge for one of Laurel Hoyle's children, who had died fifty years too soon, and by his own hand.

Sayre had received the news Sunday afternoon upon returning to her office from a meeting with a client. Ordinarily she wouldn't have worked on a Sunday, but that was the only day this particular client was free for an appointment. Julia Miller had recently celebrated her fifth year as Sayre's assistant. She wouldn't let Sayre work on a weekend without working herself. While Sayre was with the client, Julia had been catching up on paperwork.

When Sayre returned, Julia passed her a pink memo slip. "This gentleman has called three times, Ms. Lynch. I wouldn't give him your cell number, although he demanded it."

Sayre glanced at the area code, then wadded up the memo and tossed it into the wastepaper basket. "I don't wish to speak to anyone in my family."

"He's not family. He says he works for the family. It's imperative that he reach you as soon as possible."

"I won't talk to anybody who works for my family either. Any other messages? By any chance has Mr. Taylor called? He promised those valances by tomorrow."

"It's your brother," Julia blurted out. "He's dead."

Sayre stopped short of her private office. For a long moment she stared through the wall of windows toward the Golden Gate Bridge. Only the very tops of the orange supports were visible above a solid blanket of fog. The water in the bay looked gray, cold, and angry. Foreboding.

Without turning around, she asked, "Which one?"

"Which—"

"Brother."

"Danny."

Danny, who had called her twice in the last several days. Danny, whose calls she had refused to take.

Sayre turned to face her assistant, who was regarding her sympathetically. She said gently, "Your brother Danny died earlier today, Sayre. I thought you should be told in person, not over a cell phone."

Sayre released a long breath through her mouth. "How?"

"I think you should speak with this Mr. Merchant."

"Julia, please. How did Danny die?"

Gently she said, "It appears he killed himself. I'm sorry." Then after a moment, she added, "That's all the information Mr. Merchant would give me."

Sayre then retreated to her private office and closed the door. She heard the phone in the anteroom ring several times, but Julia didn't put the calls through, realizing that she needed time alone to assimilate the news.

Had Danny been calling to tell her good-bye? If so, how would she live with the guilt of having refused to speak to him?

After about an hour, Julia knocked tentatively on the door. "Come in," Sayre called. When Julia stepped inside, Sayre said, "There's no point in your staying, Julia. Go home. I'll be fine."

The assistant laid a sheet of paper on her desk. "I've still got work to do. Buzz me if you need me. Can I bring you anything?"

Sayre shook her head no. Julia withdrew and closed the door. On the sheet of paper she'd brought in she'd written down the time and place of the funeral. Tuesday morning, eleven o'clock.

Sayre hadn't been surprised that it was scheduled so soon. Huff always acted with dispatch. He and Chris would be impatient to put this behind them, to bury Danny and get on with their lives as soon as possible.

However, the timeliness of the funeral had probably worked to her advantage, too. It prevented a lengthy internal debate on whether to attend. She couldn't languish in indecision but had been forced to make up her mind quickly.

Yesterday morning she'd caught a flight to New Orleans via Dallas–Fort Worth and had arrived in the late afternoon. She'd taken a walk through the French Quarter, eaten dinner at a gumbo shop, then spent the night at the Windsor Court.

For all the comfort the luxury hotel afforded,

she'd had a virtually sleepless night. She did not want to go back to Destiny. She *did not*. Silly as it was, she feared walking into some kind of snare that would trap her there, keep her in Huff's clutches forever.

Daybreak hadn't lessened her dread. She'd gotten up, dressed for the funeral, and set out for Destiny, planning to arrive just in time for the service and to leave immediately thereafter.

The church parking lot was already overflowing into the surrounding neighborhood streets. She had to park several blocks away from the picture-book church with the stained-glass windows and tall white steeple. Just as she stepped onto the columned porch, the bell chimed the hour of eleven.

The vestibule was cool compared to outdoors, but Sayre noticed that many in the sanctuary were waving paper fans to supplement the inadequate air-conditioning. As she slipped into the back row, the choir finished singing the opening hymn and the pastor stepped up to the pulpit.

While everyone else bowed their heads for prayer, Sayre looked at the casket in front of the chancel rail. It was simple, silver, and sealed. She was glad of that. She didn't think she could bear her last image of Danny to be his lying like a wax doll in a satin-lined coffin. To prevent thoughts of that, she concentrated on the elegant purity of the arrangement of white calla lilies on top of the casket.

She couldn't see either Huff or Chris for the crowd, but she supposed they were seated in the front pew, looking appropriately bereaved. The hypocrisy of it all made her nauseated.

She was named among the surviving family members. "A sister, Sayre Hoyle of San Francisco," the minister intoned.

She wanted to stand up and shout that Hoyle was no longer her name. After her second divorce, she had begun using her middle name, which had been her mother's maiden name. She'd had her name legally changed to Lynch. That was the name on her college degree, her business stationery, her California driver's license, and her passport.

She wasn't a Hoyle any longer, but she had no doubt that whoever had supplied the minister with the information had intentionally given him the incorrect name.

The homily was straight out of a clerical textbook, delivered by a shiny-faced minister who looked too young to vote. His remarks were directed toward mankind in general. There was very little mention of Danny as an individual, nothing poignant or personal, which seemed particularly sad since his own sister had refused his telephone calls.

As the service concluded with the singing of "Amazing Grace," there were sniffles among the congregation. The pallbearers were Chris, a fair-haired man she didn't know, and four others whom she recognized as executives of Hoyle Enterprises. They carried the casket up the center aisle of the church.

It was slow going, giving her time to study her brother Chris. He was as trim and handsome as

ever, with the suavity of a 1930s matinee idol.
The only thing missing was a thin mustache. His
hair was still as black as a raven's wing, but he
was wearing it shorter than he used to. It was
spiked up in front with gel, a rather hip look for a
man in his late thirties, but nonetheless the style
suited Chris. His eyes were disconcerting because
the pupils were indistinguishable from the dark
irises.

Huff followed the casket. Even on this occasion
he carried himself with an air of superiority. His
shoulders were back, his head high. Each footstep
was firmly planted, as though he were a conqueror
with the sovereign right to claim the ground beneath him.

His lips were set in the hard, thin, resolute line
that she remembered well. His eyes glittered like the
black bead eyes of a stuffed toy. They were dry and
clear; he hadn't cried for Danny. Since she'd last
seen him, his hair had turned from salt-and-pepper
to solid white, but he still wore it in a flattop of
military preciseness. He had put on a few pounds
around his midsection but appeared as robust as
she remembered.

Fortunately neither Chris nor Huff saw her.

To avoid the crowd and risk of being recognized,
she slipped out a side door. Her car was last in the
procession to the cemetery. She parked quite a distance from the tent that had been set up over the
newly dug grave.

In somber groups and singly, people made their
way up the slight rise for the graveside service. For
the most part, they were dressed in their Sunday

best, although armholes had sweat rings and hat-
bands were stained with perspiration. They walked
in shoes that were too tight from infrequent wear.

Sayre recognized and remembered many of these
people by name. They were townsfolk who had
lived in Destiny all their lives. Some owned small
businesses, but most worked for the Hoyles in one
capacity or another.

She spotted several faculty members from the
public school system. Her mother's fondest desire
had been to send her children to the most exclu-
sive private schools in the South, but Huff had
been adamant. He wanted them to grow up tough
and under his tutelage. Whenever the argument re-
curred, he would say, "A sissy prep school isn't
the place to learn about life and how to muscle
your way through it." As in all their arguments,
her mother had conceded with a relinquishing
sigh.

Sayre remained in her car with the motor idling.
The service was mercifully brief. As soon as it concluded, the crowd returned to their cars, making an
effort to conceal their haste.

Huff and Chris were the last to leave the tent
after shaking hands with the minister. Sayre
watched them make their way to the waiting limou-
sine provided by Weir's Funeral Home. The ancient
Mr. Weir was still plying his trade although he was
way past due going to his own reward.

He opened the limo door for Chris and Huff, then
stood at a discreet distance while they conducted a
short conversation with the blond-haired pallbearer.
When the conversation concluded, they climbed into

the limo, the man waved them off, Mr. Weir got behind the wheel and chauffeured them away. Sayre was glad to see them go.

She waited another ten minutes, until the last of the mourners had left. Only then did she kill her engine and get out of her car.

"I've been asked by your family to escort you to the house for the wake."

Startled, she spun around so quickly that her shoes sent up a shower of dusty gravel.

He was leaning against the rear fender of her car. He'd taken off his suit jacket and folded it over his arm. His necktie was askew, and the collar button of his shirt was undone, shirtsleeves rolled up to his elbows. He'd put on a pair of dark sunglasses.

"I'm Beck Merchant."

"I guessed."

She had only seen his name in print and had wondered if he used the French pronunciation. He didn't. And his appearance was as American as apple pie, from his dark blond hair, through his easy smile and straight teeth, to the Ralph Lauren cut of his trousers.

Giving no heed to her ungracious tone, he said, "Pleased to meet you, Ms. Hoyle."

"Lynch."

"I stand corrected." He spoke with utmost courtesy, but his smile mocked her.

"Does delivering messages fall into your job description? I thought you were their lawyer," she said.

"Lawyer, errand boy—"

"Henchman."

He laid his hand over his heart and flashed an even wider grin. "You give me far too much credit."

"I doubt it." She slammed shut her car door. "You've extended their invitation. Tell them I decline. Now, I would appreciate some time alone to say good-bye to Danny." She turned and headed up the rise.

"Take your time. I'll wait for you."

She came back around. "I'm not going to their damn wake. As soon as I'm done here, I'm returning to New Orleans and catching a flight back to San Francisco."

"You could do that. Or you could do the decent thing and attend your brother's wake. Then later this evening, Hoyle Enterprises' corporate jet could whisk you back to San Francisco without all the hassle of commercial flight."

"I can charter my own jet."

"Even better."

She'd walked right into that one and hated herself for it. She had been back in Destiny barely an hour, and already she was reverting to old habits. But she had learned how to recognize the traps and avoid them.

"No thank you. Good-bye, Mr. Merchant." Once again she started up the rise toward the grave.

"Do you believe Danny killed himself?"

Of all the things he could have said, she didn't expect that. She turned to face him again. He was no longer leaning indolently against the car fender but had taken a few steps toward her, as though not only to hear her answer but to gauge her reaction to his surprising question.

"Don't you?" she asked.

"Doesn't matter what I believe," he said. "It's the sheriff's office that's questioning the suicide."

chapter 3

"This'll start you off, Mr. Chris," Selma said, offering him a plate of food.

"Thank you."

"Anything for you, Mr. Hoyle?" Although the housekeeper wasn't supposed to be working today, she had put an apron on over her black dress. Incongruous with the apron, she still had on the hat she'd worn to the funeral.

"I'll wait awhile, Selma."

"Not hungry?"

"It's too hot to eat."

The balcony above the gallery provided shade along its entire width, but even that was insufficient against the inescapable heat. Ceiling fans circulated, but they only stirred hot air. Huff frequently had to wipe his sweating face with a handkerchief. Inside, the AC was keeping the house comfortably cool, but Huff felt it only proper for him and Chris to greet their guests as they arrived and personally accept their condolences before they went in.

"You need anything, sir, you just holler and I'll fetch it." Dabbing her tearful eyes, Selma went back into the house through the wide front door, over which she had draped black crepe bunting.

She had balked at hiring a caterer for the wake because she disliked having anyone else in her kitchen. But Huff had insisted. Selma wasn't up to throwing a party. Since receiving the news about Danny, she'd been given to bouts of loud weeping, to falling to her knees and, with her hands clasped, calling on Jesus for mercy.

She had worked for the Hoyles since Huff had carried Laurel over the threshold as a bride, nearly forty years ago. Laurel had grown up with domestics, so it was natural for her to relinquish the management of her own household to Selma. The black woman had seemed middle-aged and maternal then; her age now was anybody's guess. She couldn't weigh more than a hundred pounds, if that, but she was as strong and resilient as a willow sapling.

After the children came along, Selma had acted as their nanny. When Laurel died, Danny, as the youngest, was also the neediest. Selma had mothered him, and consequently they'd had a special bond. She was taking his death hard.

"I saw the buffet in the dining room," Chris remarked. He sat the plate Selma had given him, untouched, on a wicker side table. "There's a vulgar abundance of food and liquor in there, don't you think?"

"Since you have never known a day of hunger in your life, I'd say you are no authority on how much food is too much."

Privately, Huff conceded that perhaps he had gone a little overboard. But he'd worked like the devil to provide the best for his children. He wasn't about to skimp on his youngest boy's wake.

"Are you going to remind me how ungrateful I am for all I have, how I don't know what it's like to go without the basic necessities of life like you did?"

"I'm glad I had to go without. Going without made me determined never to go without again. It made me who I am. And you're who you are because of me."

"Relax, Huff." Chris sat down in one of the rockers on the porch. "I know all the lessons by heart. I was suckled and weaned on them. We don't have to rehash them today."

Huff felt his blood pressure receding to a safer level. "No, we don't. Stand up, though, here comes more company."

Chris was beside him once again as a couple approached and started up the gallery steps toward them. "How do, George? Lila. Thank you for coming," Huff said.

George Robson pressed Huff's right hand between his own. They were moist, fleshy, and pale. *Like all of George,* Huff thought with repugnance.

"Danny was a fine young man, Huff. Nobody finer."

"You're right about that, George." He reclaimed his hand, barely curbing the impulse to wipe it dry on the leg of his trousers. "I sure appreciate you saying so."

"It's a tragic thing."

"Yes, it is."

George's much younger second wife said nothing, but Huff intercepted the sly glance she cast at Chris, who smiled at her and said, "Better get this pretty lady inside and out of this heat, George. She looks sweet enough to melt. Help yourselves to the buffet."

"Plenty of gin in there, George," Huff said. "Have one of those bartenders make you a tall one, light on the tonic."

The man seemed pleased that Huff remembered his drink of choice and quickly ushered his wife inside. Once they were out of earshot, Huff turned to Chris. "How long has Lila been one of yours?"

"As of last Saturday afternoon while George was out fishing with his son by his first marriage." Smiling, he added, "Second wives are advantageous that way. There's usually an offspring that keeps their husbands occupied at least two weekends a month."

Huff scowled at him. "Speaking of wives, between diddling Lila Robson, have you talked to Mary Beth?"

"For about five seconds."

"You told her about Danny?"

"As soon as she said hello, I said, 'Mary Beth, Danny killed himself.' And her response was 'Then my share just got bigger.' "

Huff's blood pressure soared again. "Her share, my ass. That gal won't see one red cent of my money. Not unless she does right by you and gives you a divorce. And I don't mean in her own sweet time. I mean *now*. Did you ask about those divorce papers we sent down there?"

"Not specifically. But Mary Beth isn't going to sign any divorce papers."

"Then get her back here and get her pregnant."

"I can't."

"You won't."

"I *can't*."

Attuned to Chris's dark tone, Huff narrowed his eyes. "How come? Is there something you're not telling me, something I don't know?"

"We'll talk about it later."

"We'll talk about it now."

"This isn't the time, Huff," Chris said, straining the words. "Besides, you're getting red in the face, and we know what that means in terms of your blood pressure." He headed for the front door. "I'm going to get a drink."

"Hold on. Look at this."

Huff directed Chris's gaze toward the lane in front of the house, where Beck was approaching a car that had just pulled to a stop. He opened the driver's door and extended his hand down.

Sayre alighted, but without any assistance from Beck. In fact she looked ready to hiss at him if he touched her.

"We'll I'll be damned," Chris said.

He and Huff watched as the two came across the yard and started up the walkway. About halfway, Sayre tilted her head back and looked up from beneath the wide brim of her black straw hat. When she saw him and Chris there on the gallery, she changed her direction and angled off toward the side of the house and the footpath that led to the rear.

Huff watched her until she disappeared around the corner. He hadn't known what to expect upon seeing his daughter for the first time in ten years, but he was proud of what he saw. Sayre Hoyle—that name-changing business was horseshit—was a fine-looking woman. Damn fine. To his mind, she couldn't have turned out any better.

Beck climbed the steps to join them.

"I'm impressed," Chris said. "I figured she'd tell you to fuck off."

"Close."

"What happened?"

"Just as you thought, Huff, she was planning to leave without seeing you."

"So how'd you get her here?"

"I appealed to her sense of family loyalty and decency."

Chris made a scoffing sound.

"Has she always been that snotty?" Beck asked.

Chris answered yes at the same time Huff said, "She's always been a little high-strung."

"That's a nice way of saying that she's a pain in the ass." Chris scanned the yard. "I think everybody who's coming is here. Let's go inside and give Danny his due."

The house was jammed with people, which didn't surprise Beck. Anyone even remotely connected to or acquainted with the Hoyles would turn out to pay respects to one who died.

Top- and middle-management personnel from the plant were there with their wives. Only a few laborers were there, men Beck knew had been employees since they were old enough to work. They stood apart from everyone else, wearing clip-on neckties with their short-sleeve shirts, looking ill at ease inside Huff Hoyle's house, awkwardly balancing plates of food and trying to avoid a spill.

Then there were the ass-kissers who were always eager to stay on the Hoyles' good side because their livelihoods depended on it. The local politicians, bankers, educators, retailers, and physicians all operated under Huff's largesse. If one got crosswise with him, he was soon out of business. It wasn't a written law, but it was etched into the stone of common knowledge. Each made certain to sign the guest register so that, in the unlikely event they didn't speak to Huff personally, he would at least know they had paid homage.

The fewest in number were the people who were actually there for Danny, standouts because of their expressions of genuine grief. For the most part, they stayed clustered together, talking sadly among themselves, but having little to say to him, Chris, or Huff, out of either indifference or intimidation. As soon as they had stayed for a polite length of time, they left.

Beck mingled, accepting condolences like a bona fide member of the family.

Sayre mingled, too, but only with guests. Him, Chris, and Huff she avoided, ignoring them as though they weren't there. People kept their distance from her unless she approached them, he noticed. These were simple, small-town folk. Sayre was anything but. She made herself accessible, but many seemed shy of her sophistication.

He succeeded in making eye contact with her

only once. Her arm was linked with Selma's as they made their way along the central hallway. Sayre was consoling the housekeeper, who was sobbing onto her shoulder. She spotted him watching them but looked straight through him.

Two hours elapsed before the crowd began to thin out. He joined Chris, who was grazing at the buffet. "Where's Huff?"

"Having a smoke in the den. Ham's good. Have you eaten?"

"I will later. Is Huff all right?"

"Tired, I think. The last couple of days have been a strain."

"How about you?"

Chris shrugged. "Danny and I had our differences, you know. But he was still my brother."

"I'll go check on Huff and leave you to play host."

"Thanks for nothing," Chris muttered.

"It can't be that bad. I see Lila Robson over there." Chris had boasted of his latest conquest, confirming what Beck had always suspected—that Lila's husband was a schmuck. "She looks a little forlorn, like she could use some company."

"No, she's sulking."

"Why's that?"

"She thinks I'm using her just for sex."

"Now why would she think that?" Beck asked sarcastically.

"Beats me. She started whining about it right after she gave me a blow job in the upstairs bathroom." Chris checked his wristwatch. "About ten minutes ago."

Beck looked at him. "You're not serious."

Chris's shrug neither denied nor confirmed. "Go check on Huff. I'll try to keep these yahoos from walking out with the family sterling."

Beck found Huff in his recliner, smoking. He closed the door behind himself. "Mind if I sit with you for a while?"

"Who sent you, Chris or Selma? I know it wasn't Sayre. She wouldn't waste any worry on me."

"I can't speak for her." Beck sat down on the sofa. "But *I'm* worried about you."

"I'm fine." He blew a gust of smoke toward the ceiling.

"You're putting up a brave front, but you just lost your son and that's gotta be tough."

The older man smoked in silence for several moments, then said, "You know, I think Danny would have been Laurel's favorite."

Beck leaned forward and propped his forearms on his knees. "Because . . . ? "

"Because he was like her." He shot Beck a glance. "I ever tell you about Laurel?"

"I've picked up things here and there."

"She was exactly what I wanted, Beck. Not particularly bright. But hell, who wants that? Laurel was soft and sweet and pretty."

Beck nodded. The oil portrait that dominated the staircase landing depicted a woman who was soft, sweet, and pretty. But he couldn't help but think that part of Laurel Lynch's attraction had been the metal pipe casting factory that her daddy had owned and where Huff had been an employee.

"I was rough and uncouth, foul talking. She was a refined lady. Knew which fork to use."

"So how did you talk her into marrying you?"

"I bowled her over," he said, chuckling at the memory. "I said, 'Laurel, you're going to be my wife,' and she said all right. She'd been courted by men who walked on eggshells around her. I guess she liked my brass."

He contemplated the smoke rising from the tip of his cigarette. "You may not believe this, Beck, but I was faithful to her. Never strayed. Not once. I didn't go to another woman until she had been dead a respectable amount of time, either. I figured I owed her that."

After a moment of reflection, he continued. "When she got pregnant, I busted my buttons with pride. I knew the baby would be a boy. Had to be. Chris was mine from the second they pulled him out of her and handed him to me. Back then, delivery rooms were off-limits to fathers. But I bribed the staff with a huge donation and they agreed quick enough to let me come in. I wanted my face to be the first one my son saw when he entered this world.

"Anyhow, I claimed Chris from the start, and from then on, he was mine. As the trade-off, it was easy to leave Sayre to Laurel. Sayre was her little doll to put in ruffled dresses, and to throw tea parties for, give English riding lessons to. Bullshit like that. But if Laurel had lived, she and Sayre would have wound up fighting tooth and toenail. Sayre isn't exactly the tea party type, is she?"

Beck doubted that she was.

"Sayre wouldn't have cared a flip about anything that was important to Laurel," Huff continued. "But Danny now, his mother would have doted on him. He is—he *was*—a gentleman. Like Laurel, he was born about a century too late. He should have been born in a time when everybody dressed in white clothes and knocked around croquet balls and had clean fingernails all the time. Sipped champagne cocktails on the gallery. When leisure was an art form."

He looked across at Beck, and the tender expression brought on by his reverie disappeared. "Danny wasn't cut out for business. Especially our business. It's too dirty. Not clean enough for the likes of him."

"He did his job well, Huff. The workers loved him."

"They're not supposed to love us. They're supposed to be scared shitless of us. We appear, their knees should start knocking."

"Yes, but Danny served as a buffer. He was proof to them that we're human. At least to some extent."

Huff shook his head. "Naw, Danny was too tenderhearted to be a good businessman. Wishy-washy. Always agreeing with the last speaker. He could be swayed too easily."

"A trait that you frequently relied on," Beck reminded him.

He snuffled an agreement. "Hell, I admit that. He wanted to make everybody happy. I knew that about him, and I used it to my advantage. What Danny never figured out was that you can't make everybody happy. If you try, you're whipped before you begin.

"Unfortunately, I wasn't the only person he listened to. I hate to speak ill of him, but I've always called a spade a spade. I can be honest about the natures of my own children, and Danny was weak."

Although he didn't argue the point, Beck wouldn't have used *weak* as the adjective to sum up Danny's character. Granted, he didn't go for the jugular like his father and brother—or like Beck himself, for that matter. But gentleness had its advantages, too. It didn't necessarily make one weak. Indeed, Danny had been steadfast in his view of where one should draw the line between right and wrong.

Beck wondered if his strict moral code was the reason he'd had to die.

Huff took one final pull on the cigarette, then ground it out. "I should get back to the party."

As they stood, Beck said, "Last night I put a folder on the desk in your bedroom. You probably haven't had a chance to look at it."

"No. What's in it?"

"I just wanted to bring it to your attention. We can talk about it later."

"Give me a hint."

Beck knew that Huff's mind was never far from his business, even on the day he buried his son. "Ever heard of a man named Charles Nielson?"

"Don't think so. Who is he?"

"A labor advocate."

"Bastard."

"Synonyms for sure," Beck said with a wry smile. "He's written us a letter. A copy of it is in the folder. I need to know how you want me to respond. It's not urgent business, but it needs to be addressed, so don't wait too long to give it a look."

Together they moved toward the door. "Is he good, this Nielson?"

Beck hesitated, and when Huff picked up on it, he made a hand gesture that said, "Give it to me." "He's building a reputation in other parts of the country," Beck said. "But we can handle him."

Huff slapped him on the back. "I have every confidence in you. Whoever the son of a bitch is, or *thinks* he is, he'll be a flyspeck when you get through with him."

He opened the den door. Across the wide hallway they could see into the informal parlor, which Laurel had designated a conservatory because of its expansive windows. She had filled it with ferns, orchids, violets, and other tropical plants. The room had been her pride and joy, as well as that of the Destiny Garden Club, of which she had been president for several consecutive years.

After she died, Huff had hired an indoor plant service in New Orleans to come to Destiny once a week to tend the plants. He paid them a hefty retainer but had also threatened them with a lawsuit if the plants died. The room remained the prettiest one in the house, also the most infrequently used. The men who lived there seldom went into it.

It was presently occupied, however. Sayre was

seated at the baby grand piano, her back to them, her head bent over the keyboard.

"Can you get her to speak to me, Beck?"

"I could barely get her to speak to *me.*"

Huff nudged him forward. "Use your powers of persuasion."

chapter 4

"*D*o you play?"

Sayre turned. Beck Merchant strolled into the room, his hands in his pants pockets. When he reached the end of the piano bench, he acted as though he expected her to scoot over and make room for him. She didn't respond to the hint and, instead, remained firmly fixed.

"I'm curious, Mr. Merchant."

"So am I. I'm curious to know why you don't call me Beck."

"How did Huff know I was at the funeral? Did he get advance notice that I was coming?"

"He hoped you'd come but had no guarantee that you would. All of us were on the lookout for you."

"In the church, neither he nor Chris gave any indication they knew I was there."

"They knew."

"Something in the air?"

"Something like that, I guess. Bloodline vibes." He paused as though waiting for her to laugh.

When she didn't, he said, "Realistically, did you think the dark sunglasses and hat would conceal your identity?"

"I knew there would be a crowd attending the funeral. I had hoped to get lost in it."

Again he paused before saying quietly, "I don't think you could get lost in any crowd, Sayre."

The compliment was subtle, rife with insinuation and suggestiveness. She hadn't invited, nor did she welcome, the flattery, so if he was expecting a simpering thank-you, he was in for a disappointment.

"If you hadn't worn the hat, Huff and Chris would have spotted you immediately," he said. "I would have, and I don't even know you."

Her hat had begun to give her a headache, so she had removed it. She'd also unclasped her hair and let it hang free. The humidity had encouraged the natural curl that she controlled every morning with her blow-dryer and straightening device. When she'd happened to catch her reflection in a hallway mirror a short while ago, she'd noted that her hair had reverted to the disobedient mane it had been in her youth.

The sunlight streaming through the tall windows of her mother's conservatory was catching each strand and setting it ablaze. The manner in which Beck Merchant was watching the play of sunlight on her hair made her wish for shade.

She also didn't like having to tilt her head back in order to look up at him. The alternative was to address his belt buckle. Either way, she was at a distinct disadvantage. With the intention of leaving, she slid toward the end of the bench. "Excuse me."

"Interesting name."

She stopped and looked at him over her shoulder. "Pardon?"

"Sayre. Who named you that?"

"My mother."

"Family name?"

"Her paternal grandmother."

"I like it."

"Thank you. So do I."

"For the longest time, after I came to work for your family, I wasn't sure how it was pronounced."

"Like it's spelled."

"Wouldn't that be S-a-y-*e-r* instead of r-e?"

"Does it really matter?"

"Obviously not."

She made to leave again, but he forestalled her. "You didn't answer my original question, Sayre with an *r-e*."

This time, she swiveled all the way around to face him. "Are you trying to be cute?"

"No, only conversational. But I can't seem to say a damn thing, no matter how inconsequential, that doesn't irritate you. Why is that?"

She released an audible sigh and folded her arms across her middle. "I don't recall a question."

He nodded down at the piano. "Do you play?"

"No, regrettably. Mother enrolled me in piano lessons when I was eight and mandated an hour of practice every day. 'Because every young lady should know how to play a musical instrument,' she said."

Sayre smiled at remembered reprimands for her failure to practice. "Mother tried to curb my wild streak but eventually gave up on me, declaring me a lost cause. Piano required musical talent and self-discipline, neither of which I had."

"Really?" He sat down beside her, crowding her, with his back to the keyboard so that they were sitting hip to thigh, and face-to-face. "You lack self-discipline?"

"I did when I was eight," she said, making her voice crisp. "I've cultivated some since then."

"I hope not at the expense of that wild streak. Restraint in a redhead would be a shameful waste of natural impulses."

She didn't give him the satisfaction of a reaction, except to say, "You're living up to my preconceptions of you. I would expect you to be insulting."

"Insulting? I was trying to pay you a compliment."

"Perhaps you should consult your dictionary."

"What for?"

"The definition of a compliment."

She slid off the opposite end of the bench and strode across the room, making it only as far as the portiere that separated the conservatory from the central foyer, which was crowded with a group of people about to leave. Several of them paused to offer her a murmured expression of sympathy.

In the midst of this group was Sheriff Red Harper. His face had grown longer and thinner in the past ten years, but she would have known him anywhere. Before he left, she saw him shake hands and exchange whispered words with Huff and Chris. Witnessing this hushed conversation reminded her of why she had returned to this house she had sworn never to enter again.

Beck Merchant had moved up behind her. She sensed him standing close. Speaking softly, but loud enough for him to hear, she said, "Red Harper doubts that Danny's death was a suicide?"

"Let's go outside."

He cupped her elbow, but as she turned to face him, she pulled it away. "Let's stay here."

He looked annoyed at her rebuff but kept his voice low. "Are you sure you want to talk about this where we might be overheard?"

Their long stare amounted to a war of wills, but eventually she left the room and headed toward the back of the house, trusting that he would follow her. As they moved through the kitchen, Selma, who was loading the dishwasher, asked if they'd had anything to eat yet.

"I'll get something later," Sayre told her.

"Same here," Beck said.

As they went through the back door, she called after them, "Y'all need to eat something. You need your strength."

Without having to think about her destination, Sayre walked across the manicured lawn in the direction of the bayou. The muddy creek bank behind the house had been her special retreat when she was a girl. She had come here to pout when things didn't go her way, or to escape the charged atmosphere of the house when Huff was displeased, or to seek refuge from Chris, whose favorite pastime had been to torment and tease her.

She would lie for hours beneath the branches of

the cypress and live oak trees, nursing whatever emotion was governing her life on that particular occasion. She made grand, ambitious plans for her future. Sometimes she plotted retribution for a slight. Often she dared to dream of a home life where family members laughed more and blustered less, where there were more hugs than hostility, where parents and children truly loved one another.

Now, as she neared the familiar spot, she was disappointed to see that the dense shrubbery under which she used to hide had been replaced by a bed of begonias. They were pretty, but they wouldn't provide concealment for a little girl seeking solace.

However, the old wood swing was still there, hanging from a stout horizontal branch of one of the oaks. The ropes from which it was suspended were as big around as her wrists. It had weathered, but it hadn't been removed and she was glad of that.

She ran her finger up and down the prickly rope. "I can't believe it's still here."

"Was this your swing?" Beck had moved to the opposite side of it.

"Old Mitchell . . . that's the only name I knew him by . . . did our gardening. He put up this swing for me. He told me that the ropes had come off a ghost ship that had been sunk just off the coastline of Terrebonne Parish. It was a pirate ship, dashed by the worst hurricane in history. Everyone onboard had perished.

"But the spirits of the pirates liked Looz-ana so much that they opted to stay rather than to go on to heaven. They probably wouldn't have got very good positions in heaven anyway because of their evil deeds on earth, Old Mitchell said. So they elected to stay put. And once a month, on the night of the full moon, the ghosts came out to barter with anyone who was brave enough to do business with them."

"And Old Mitchell was?"

"To hear him tell it," she said, smiling. "In exchange for a pint of rum, he got a gold bracelet that he melted down to cap his teeth." She laughed. "I envied his gold teeth and wanted some for myself. I threw a temper tantrum because Huff and Chris laughed at me when I demanded them. Mother just became distressed."

"Fortunately they didn't let you have your way."

"Fortunately. Anyway, in exchange for the rum, Old Mitchell got the bracelet and a coil of rope. He said he told the captain of the ship, the most fearsome pirate of the lot, that the rope was going to be used to make Miss Sayre a swing. And because it was for me, the pirate threw in a piece of the ship's plank for him to make the seat out of." She gave the swing a gentle push.

"He told you quite a tale."

"I believed every word of it. He had me convinced of his magical powers. He said he learned them from a one-eyed voodoo priestess who lived with a panther in the swamp. He wore a leather pouch around his neck with his gris-gris in it. He never would show it to me, and Selma threatened to knock him senseless if he did.

"He would get mad at me when he was fishing.

He'd tell me to hush up or I'd scare the fish away. Once he caught me up in that tree," she said, pointing. "He told me to get down before I fell out and broke my neck and had to spend the rest of my days in a wheelchair.

"Despite the scoldings, I thought of him as my best friend, which horrified my mother and scandalized Selma. Sometimes when he was finished with his work for the day, he would let me ride in the wheelbarrow as he pushed it back toward the toolshed. It's odd," she said upon reflection, "that I didn't spot Old Mitchell at the funeral. I would have thought he'd be there."

"Sit down. I'll push you."

Beck Merchant's offer roused her from her nostalgic reverie and made her feel silly for having engaged in it. "No thanks."

"Okay, then you can push me."

He sat down in the swing and took hold of the ropes. He smiled up at her, his eyes squinting against the sunlight. Bottle-green eyes, she noticed. Besides being attractive, they were also intelligent and intuitive, and she didn't know which attribute annoyed her most.

Snubbing him and his smiling eyes, she walked past the swing toward the channel of water that moved slowly but inexorably toward the Gulf. The muddy current already gave off a briny scent. A pelican on the opposite shore rose with a perturbed flap of wings.

A light breeze stirred the feathery branches of the cypress trees and caused an occasional flutter of the Spanish moss, but it wasn't strong enough even to disturb the more substantive foliage of the live oaks.

The heels of her shoes sank into the spongy ground, so she slipped the shoes off and carried them by the narrow heel straps. The mud felt cool against the soles of her feet. If not for her companion, she might have lain down in it.

"Was it something I said?" he asked.

She turned toward him. "Stop with the charm, all right? It's wasted on me. I grew up with charming men. I know firsthand just how false it can be. In any case, Mr. Merchant, it lost its allure a long time ago."

"Call me Beck. And what is it exactly that you don't like? Charm or men?"

The swing wasn't moving in a very wide arc, but he was actually swinging, and it irritated her no end. "I don't like you."

"You don't know me."

She gave a bitter laugh. "I know you. I know you because you're just like them," she said, motioning in the direction of the house.

"How so?"

"You're unscrupulous, unethical, greedy, and smug. Shall I go on?"

"I don't think my ego could withstand any more," he said dryly. "What I'd like to know is how you formed such a low opinion of me so quickly. We've just met."

"I've formed it over time. I read the company reports that have continued to be sent to me even though I've repeatedly requested that I be dropped from the mailing list."

"Then why do you read them?"

"Because I'm staggered by the lengths to which my family will go to make a buck for Hoyle Enterprises."

"You're a partner of Hoyle Enterprises."

"I don't want to be," she said, raising her voice. "I spent a year of my time and thousands of dollars in attorney's fees trying to extricate myself. Your crafty machinations prevented me from pulling out."

"Those machinations were legal."

"Barely."

"Barely counts."

He left the swing rocking upon its ropes and walked toward her. "I work for Huff. He wanted you to remain a partner in the family business and told me to pull out all the stops to make certain you did. I only did what he paid me to do."

"Then we know what that makes you, don't we?"

"You're calling me a whore?" Dropping his voice to a lower pitch, he said, "I don't think you want to go *there,* do you, Sayre?"

The implication stung, but she was more angry than hurt. She no longer empowered anyone with the ability to hurt her. "You even fight dirty like they do."

"I fight to win."

"Of course you do."

"What do you fight for?"

"Survival," she fired back.

Then willfully getting a grip on her temper, she took a deep breath. Realizing that her hands were clenched into fists at her sides, she relaxed them. She shook back her hair and wet her lips.

When she was steadied, she said, "I fought to survive them. And I did. The only conceivable circumstance that could have brought me back here was to bury my brother Danny. Although I mourn his death, and will always—" She stopped herself from telling him that she would always be haunted by those two telephone calls she didn't take from him. "I'm grateful that at least he's finally escaped them. I hope he's found peace. But I'd like to know—"

She stopped abruptly when he raised his hand to her cheek and brushed it with the back of his fingers. Startled into silence, she gaped at him.

"Mosquito."

"Oh." She touched her cheek where his fingers had been. "Thank you."

"You're welcome."

Seconds ticked past before she refocused on the subject. "I'd like to know how Danny died. Give me the details."

"I would have told you everything on Sunday. I made several calls to your office. You wouldn't talk to me."

"I wasn't prepared to hear about it then."

That wasn't the reason she had refused to speak with him and he knew it. Nevertheless he didn't dispute her. Instead, he said quietly, "He was killed by one gunshot to the head. There was no . . . Well, he wouldn't have felt a thing. Death would have been instantaneous."

She could do without any more description than that. That was bad enough. "Who found him?"

"Fishermen on the bayou. Their outboard had started smoking. They stopped at the fishing camp to see if they could borrow some oil. Danny's car was parked out front, so they assumed someone was there. When they went inside the cabin, they found him."

She tried not to think about the scene that would have greeted the fishermen. "It was ruled a suicide."

"Initially."

"But Red Harper is having second thoughts?"

"Not Red. There's a new detective in his department, a younger man named Wayne Scott. Red assigned him to investigate the scene. He thought it would be routine. A form to be filled out, rubber-stamped, and filed. End of case and Danny becomes a statistic. But Scott came back from the fishing camp with more questions than answers."

"Such as? Does he think it could have been an accident?"

"He's not sure. As I said, he has more questions than—"

"You're hedging, Mr. Merchant," she said impatiently. "I'm a grown-up. Don't talk down to me."

"Deputy Scott hasn't revealed his hand to me. I swear it," he said when she looked at him skeptically. "I just have a gut feeling that he's not one hundred percent convinced that the coroner's ruling is correct."

He leaned against the tree trunk behind him, bending one knee and planting that foot flat against the bark. He turned his head away from her to gaze out across the channel and reflexively whisked away a bead of sweat that was trickling down his temple.

He said, "For a brief time, before I realized that criminal law was not my forte, I worked in a prosecutor's office. From that experience, I learned how cops think. And the first thing they always think is foul play. They rule that out first.

"I don't know Wayne Scott or what makes him tick. I don't know how adept he is at investigating crime scenes, or how much experience and training he's had. I only met him on Sunday evening when he and Red came to the house with the news. He looks wet behind the ears, but strikes me as being eager and aggressive.

"Maybe he's just trying to play the big shot or impress his new boss. Maybe he's looking for clues to support the theory that Danny didn't take his own life simply because that would make for a juicier investigation."

Sayre had listened carefully, read his body language, and realized where he was going with this verbal meandering. She also understood his reluctance to say it outright, because the alternative to a suicide or accidental death was unthinkable.

"Are you saying that this detective thinks Danny was murdered?"

His gaze moved back to her. "He hasn't said that directly."

"Why else would he be looking for clues and asking questions?"

He shrugged. "He's new in town. He's been on the job only a few weeks. He doesn't know—"

"He doesn't know that his boss takes graft from my family and then looks the other way whenever they break the law?"

"Huff subsidizes Red's insufficient salary."

"He bribes him."

"Huff's subsidies make for more money in the parish till," he said tightly. "Which prevents a tax increase."

"Oh, right. It's for the taxpayers' benefit that Huff bribes local law officials."

"Everybody benefits from his generosity, Sayre."

"Including you."

"And *you*." He pushed himself away from the tree trunk and walked toward her. "Tell me, would you have rather spent the night in jail those times Red caught you driving drunk. Or skinny-dipping. Or making out on a city park picnic table. Or drag racing down Evangeline Street?

"On those occasions—and I've only scratched the surface of what I've heard about your adventurous youth—weren't you glad that Huff slipped the sheriff a few bills each month so your indiscretions would go overlooked and unpunished? Never mind answering. The answer is obvious. Try looking at the big picture for a change and you'll see—"

"What I see, Mr. Merchant, is how neatly you've rationalized your corruption. Is that how you manage to sleep at night?"

He stepped close enough for his pants legs to brush against her shins. As on the piano bench, he was crowding her. She had to either tilt her head back to look into his face or fall back several steps, which she wasn't about to do. She wasn't going to give an inch of ground.

He spoke in a rough whisper. "For the last time, Sayre, call me Beck. And if you want to know how

I sleep, consider this an invitation to find out. Anytime."

Before she struck him, which she was sorely tempted to do, she turned away and began walking toward the house.

"He died."

Stopping, she looked back.

"Old Mitchell," he said. "A couple years ago, they found him in his house. He'd been dead for several days."

Following the departure of the last guests, Huff went upstairs to his bedroom to exchange his dark suit and dress shirt for more comfortable clothes.

In the hallway, when he came even with Danny's room, he paused, but didn't open the door. Selma had closed off the room, leaving it as Danny had on Sunday morning when he went to church. She would probably wait for a signal from him on when to reopen the room, sort through Danny's things, decide what to keep and what to give away to charity. That task would fall to her. He wasn't sure he could look at or touch anything that had belonged to Danny, ever again.

He wasn't without regret, but what was done was done. Dwelling on it would be a waste of time and energy, and Huff never squandered either.

On his way back downstairs, he glanced out the double French doors adjacent to Laurel's portrait on the landing. The doors opened onto the second-floor balcony. He spotted Sayre and Beck standing on the bank of the bayou in the shade beneath a grove of trees.

Amused, he anchored his cigarette between his lips, placed his hands on his hips, and stood there to watch. Beck was carrying out his latest assignment and, as usual, was applying himself. Sayre just might have met her match.

She was a double handful of hotheaded, short-tempered, outspoken female, but Beck had the tenacity of a pit bull. He hadn't retreated yet, where a lesser man would have waved the white flag after just one of Sayre's acid put-downs.

In her whole life, the girl had never done anything without putting up an argument about it first. Even her birth had been a battle royal. Laurel was in labor for twelve hours, twice as long as she'd been with the boys.

Sayre, her temperament already in keeping with the color of her hair, had emerged from her mother's body red in the face with anger and screaming in rebellion over the trauma of—or maybe the delay of—her birth. She'd been giving those around her a hard time ever since.

No doubt she was giving hell to Beck now, although Huff wondered what Beck was saying to her to have kept her in place for even this long. Sayre wasn't one to stand and listen when what was being said was something she didn't choose to hear. But they were standing practically toe-to-toe and seemed to be deeply engrossed in their conversation or . . .

Deeply engrossed in each other.

That thought gave him pause. He looked at the two with a fresh perspective, and damned if they didn't make quite a pair.

Sayre had a smart mouth on her. She never approached anything with less than absolute passion. But Huff assumed that her passion for issues would carry over into areas that would make a man extremely happy, at least content enough to put up with her less desirable traits.

As for Beck . . . If you were a young woman, what wasn't there to like about Beck?

Through the French doors, Huff watched as Beck stepped up closer to Sayre. She was taller than the average woman even in her stocking feet, but Beck still towered over her. They were drawn up tighter than a pair of bowstrings on the verge of snapping, and for a moment Huff thought Beck was going to grab her and plant one on her.

But Sayre spun away from him and aimed for the house. She hadn't gotten far, however, before Beck said something that caused her to turn around. Whatever he said must've pissed her off good, because when she turned once again in the direction of the house, she was practically marching.

"This ought to be fun." Chuckling to himself, Huff continued downstairs and was there to intercept Sayre in the central hallway when she angrily pushed through the kitchen doors. Selma was right behind her, urging her to sit down and have a plate of food.

But Sayre didn't address Selma's nagging. She drew up short when she saw Huff. Selma, ever attuned to the goings-on of the family she served, disappeared back into the kitchen.

Huff assumed his most intimidating scowl as he looked his daughter up and down. He could tell by the fit of her black dress that her figure hadn't suffered in the ten years she'd been away. Maturity had chiseled away some fullness in her face. She looked like a woman now, not a girl.

At the funeral, gussied up in her wide-brimmed hat and dark glasses, she'd looked like a grieving movie star or the bereaved widow of a head of state. She had acquired the classiness that Laurel had always wanted her to have, but she had kept the haughty air she'd been born with. It provoked as well as amused him.

"Hello, Sayre."

"Huff."

"You always did call me Huff, didn't you?"

"That and a lot worse."

He removed the cigarette from his mouth and laughed. "You came up with some doozies, as I recall. Were you going to leave without even speaking to me?"

"What I had to say to you, I said before I left. Ten years hasn't changed my mind about anything."

"Out of respect for Danny, you could have paid me the courtesy of asking how I'm getting on, how I'm dealing with my grief."

"I don't owe you any courtesy. I don't respect you. As for your grief, you didn't even shut down the furnaces today. Danny's death was tragic, but it doesn't change the character of this family."

"*Your* family."

"I've rejected my family. I want nothing to do with you or Chris or your foundry. I came to Destiny to say a personal and private good-bye to

Danny at his grave. I was prevented from doing that when you sent your lackey after me."

"Beck didn't toss you over his shoulder and carry you here."

"No, but he cleverly baited me with something he knew I couldn't ignore. The ploy worked. I came. But now, I've done my duty. I'm going to the cemetery, then I'm going home."

"You *are* home, Sayre."

She laughed, but not with humor. "You never give up, do you, Huff?"

"No. Never."

"Well do yourself a favor this once. Face up to the reality that you have zero influence over me." She formed a circle with her thumb and fingers. "Zero. I will not heed a single thing you say to me. And don't bother threatening me. You couldn't possibly do anything to me that would be worse than what you've already done. I'm no longer afraid of you."

"Is that right?"

"That's right."

He crossed to the door of the den and pushed it open. "Prove it."

chapter 5

He had issued a challenge from which she couldn't back down, just as Beck Merchant had done earlier. It wasn't within her to stand down. She had inherited some traits from her father, like it or not.

Acknowledging that she was probably playing right into his hands, she followed him into the den. She had said she was no longer afraid of him. He probably didn't believe that, but whether he did or not wasn't important. What was important was that *she* believe it. She didn't need to prove her fearlessness to him. But she needed to prove it to herself.

From over two thousand miles away, it was easy to boast about recovery and indifference. However, the only valid test of one's mettle was to come face-to-face with the enemy who had dealt you near-fatal blows. Only by doing so would she be wholly convinced that her fear of Huff was long past and that he no longer held sway over her.

So she followed him into the den. With the exception of the large-screen TV, it looked much the same as she remembered. As she looked about, she tried to recall one pleasant memory associated with this room. There wasn't one. For her Huff's den evoked only painful memories.

She'd been banished from it when she was a little girl having to compete for Huff's attention. Chris and Danny had been allowed, even welcomed, into this inner sanctum, but rarely had she been, and it was an exclusion based solely on her gender.

It was in this room that Huff had explained to her and her brothers how sick their mother was. Acting as spokesperson, she had asked if Laurel was going to die. When he told them yes, she and Danny began to cry. Huff had no patience for tears. He told them to buck up, to behave like grown-ups, like Hoyles. Hoyles never cried, he told them, and he held Chris up as their example. *You don't see him crying, do you?*

But she had cried in this room on one other occasion. She had cried copiously, hysterically, begging Huff not to do what he had ultimately done. That was the night she couldn't forgive. That was the night she had come to hate him.

His footsteps sounded heavy on the hardwood floor as he crossed to the bar and offered her a drink.

"No, thank you."

He poured a whiskey for himself. "Want me to have Selma get you something to eat? She's itching to feed you."

"I'm not hungry."

"And even if you were starving, you wouldn't

eat food paid for by Hoyle Enterprises. Isn't that
right?" He sank into his recliner and looked at her
over the rim of his glass as he took a sip of bourbon.

"Is that your opening volley, Huff? Do you want
to see which of us can score the most points against
the other? Batter each other with words until one of
us concedes? Because if that's what you have in
mind, I don't want to play. I'll never play any of
your damn games again."

"Your mother would not have approved of that
kind of language."

She leveled a condemning stare on him. "My
mother would not have approved of a lot of things.
Should we talk about some of those?"

"Still sassing me, I see. Well, I can't say as I'm
surprised. In fact, I think I'd have been disappointed if you'd lost that sass." He reclined his
chair, reached for a box of matches on the side
table, and lit a cigarette. "Sit down. Tell me about
your business."

She sat down on one of two matching sofas that
faced each other, separated by a coffee table. "It's
doing well."

"One thing I can't stomach, Sayre, is false mod-
esty. If you've done it, you've earned the right to
brag about it. I read that piece about you in the
Chronicle. It was quite a spread. Pictures and everything. Said you were the decorator of choice for San
Francisco's wealthy and elite."

She didn't ask him how he'd learned about the
newspaper feature story. He was capable of anything, even spying. He probably knew more about

her life in California than she even suspected. Beck Merchant probably gathered information for him.

"What did you have to pay that old queen to buy out his business?" he asked. "Bet you paid too much."

"That 'old queen' was my mentor and dear friend."

She had interned for the renowned decorator while attending classes to earn her degree. Upon her graduation, he'd made her a full-fledged employee. But she was more than just someone who earned a commission on anything she sold from his home design studio. From the outset, he had groomed her to take over his business.

He had sent her on shopping expeditions for fabrics in Hong Kong and antiques in France, implicitly trusting her instincts, her business acumen, and her taste. He had forty years of experience along with a directory of valuable contacts; Sayre contributed fresh and innovative ideas. They had made a great team.

"When he decided to retire," she continued, "he made the terms of sale very easy for me." Under her management, the business had grown. She had paid off her debt within three years, half the anticipated time. But she didn't tell Huff that, considering that her financial affairs were none of his business.

"Hanging window curtains makes you quite a chunk of change."

He was deliberately belittling her business, but she didn't take the bait. "I love my work. I would almost do it for free. Fortunately, it's turned out to be lucrative as well as enjoyable."

"You've earned back your investment several times over." He rattled the ice cubes in his glass. "So those marriages of yours weren't so terrible after all, were they? If it wasn't for the cash settlements I insisted on in the prenups, you wouldn't have been able to buy out that fairy and do the work you love so much."

In order to speak, she had to relax her clenched jaw. "I earned those cash settlements, Huff."

"And there are worse ways to make a living," Chris remarked as he sauntered into the room. "Making a career of divorcing rich men has its perks." He sat on the opposite sofa and smiled at her across the coffee table. "Not a bad career path at all."

Her inclination was to get up and storm out, but she knew that would only amuse him. Giving her older brother that satisfaction would be worse than enduring his snide grin. "You're as insufferable as ever, Chris. But you're right about the perks of divorcing rich men. I'm sure your ex-wife would agree."

His grin slipped a little, but he said smoothly, "You've got your facts wrong, Sayre. Mary Beth refuses to divorce me."

She had assumed that the noticeable absence of Chris's wife from the family fold indicated that her brother's turbulent marriage had finally come to an end. "Why isn't she here?"

"She lives in Mexico now. In a house overlooking the blue Pacific. We were vacationing down there. I imbibed a few too many margaritas on the beach one afternoon. Mary Beth has an uncanny knack for seizing an advantage. I woke up the next day a hungover homeowner. All according to her plan. She got the house with the servants first, then announced that she wanted a separation. Indefinitely," he added, shooting Huff a glance.

Sayre hadn't known her sister-in-law because Chris had married after she left, but she reasoned that, for putting up with him, his missus probably deserved a staffed house on the Pacific coast. She doubted that marriage had put a stop to his countless affairs.

During Chris's explanation of his wife's absence, Huff had remained reclined in his chair, puffing on his cigarette. But he wasn't relaxed. He was vexed. Sayre noticed now that he was holding his highball glass so tightly his thick fingers had turned white. Huff was unhappy over Chris's marital status, and suddenly Sayre realized the reason for his displeasure.

"No children."

Huff swiveled his head like an owl, switching his baleful gaze from Chris to her. "Not yet. But it's not over."

Chris's strained expression turned into a smile as he glanced beyond her. "Come on in, Beck."

"I don't want to interrupt." He spoke from behind Sayre, near the door. She didn't turn around.

"Please do," Chris said. "I welcome the reprieve. This family is yet to have a gathering that would leave any of us with a warm fuzzy."

Sayre heard Beck approach. He rounded the end of the sofa and said, "Red's here, Huff."

"He left an hour ago."

"He's back, and this time it's in an official capacity. Wayne Scott is with him. They want to talk to us."

"What about?"

Beck looked at him, and his frown said, *What do you think?*

"How long will it take?" Chris asked. "I'm tired of the funeral atmosphere and hoped to go out for a while."

Sayre was dismayed by his self-absorption, although she shouldn't have been. He had always thought about Chris first. He was interested in something only insofar as it affected him, his plans, his wishes. His selfishness, which had been honed by Huff's indulgence of him, knew no bounds, extending even to the day he had buried his brother.

Unable to bear his company any longer, she stood up. "I'll go now and leave you to your meeting with Red." Looking at Huff, she said, "Danny was unarguably the best of us. I deeply regret the loss."

Looking down at her surviving brother, she said, "Chris . . ." Beyond that, she could think of nothing to say to him that wouldn't have been hypocritical. "Good-bye." She turned toward Beck Merchant. For him she had only a curt nod.

But as she tried to go around him, he touched her arm. "Red would like for you to stay."

Before Sayre could recover from her surprise enough to speak, Chris asked, "Why her?"

"He didn't say."

"He must have said something," she argued.

Beck looked down at her with asperity. "He said

just what I told you. He'd like for you to stick around. Should I show them in, Huff?"

"This is a damn bother. Like Chris, I've had it up to here with thinking and talking about death. I'm sick of it. But we'd just as well get this over. Bring them in, Beck."

Sayre had no intention of staying and would tell Red Harper as much. Beck disappeared only long enough to escort the veteran sheriff and a younger man into the room.

She went on the offensive immediately. "Sheriff Harper, I'm trying to make a late flight out of New Orleans. I'm already pressed for time."

Red Harper was still wearing the shiny black suit he'd worn to the funeral. The deputy with him was in standard uniform, although he had removed his hat. He was looking about, taking in the details of the room, as bouncy as a racehorse in the starting gate, appearing as eager as Beck Merchant had described him.

The sheriff said, "I hate to hold you up, Sayre, but Deputy Scott here wanted to ask y'all some questions."

"I appreciate your thoroughness," she said, speaking directly to the younger officer. "I admire your sense of duty. But I don't have any information for you. I don't live here and hadn't had any contact with Danny for more than a decade."

"Yes, ma'am, but you might know more than you think." His twang sounded more Texan than Louisianan. "You mind staying just a while? This will be short, I promise."

Reluctantly she returned to her place on the sofa.

"Beck, pull two chairs away from the game table for the lawmen," Huff directed from the comfort of his recliner. "You can sit there by Sayre."

The sheriff and his deputy sat in the chairs Beck dragged forward for them. Beck sat down next to Sayre. She glanced at Huff and saw a familiar gleam of devilment in his eyes as he fanned out another match and dropped it into an ashtray.

He said, "Well, Red, you called this meeting. You've got our attention. What's on your mind?"

The sheriff cleared his throat. "You know, I hired Wayne to serve as a detective for the department." He said it almost as an apology.

"So?"

"So, he's been doing some detective work out at your fishing camp, Huff, and there are facts relating to Danny's suicide that aren't sitting right with him."

Huff shifted his gaze to the young deputy. "Like what?"

Wayne Scott scooted forward in his seat until he was practically perched on the edge of it, as though he'd been anxiously awaiting his turn to speak. "The shotgun that killed him—"

"Shotgun?" Sayre exclaimed.

When Beck told her that Danny had died of a gunshot wound to the head, she had assumed it was a handgun. She didn't have an encyclopedic knowledge of firearms, but she definitely knew the difference between a pistol and a shotgun, as well as the damage each was capable of inflicting.

Depending on the caliber and trajectory, a bullet fired point-blank from a pistol into a person's head would be lethal and certainly messy. But nothing compared to the damage to a human skull that a shotgun shell would cause.

"Yes, ma'am," the detective said solemnly. "He didn't stand a chance of surviving."

Beck said tersely, "Maybe you should get to the point."

"Well, Mr. Merchant, my point is this. The victim still had his shoes on."

For several moments they all continued to stare at him with misapprehension. Huff reacted first. "I don't know what the hell you're up to, but—"

"Hold on." Beck raised his hand to silence Huff, but he was looking at Scott. "I think I understand Deputy Scott's confusion."

Chris, tugging on his lower lip, nodded. "He's wondering how Danny pulled the trigger."

Scott vigorously bobbed his head. "That's correct. I investigated a suicide by shotgun one time over in Carthage. East Texas? Anyhow, the man pulled the trigger with his big toe." He glanced contritely at Sayre. "Forgive me, Ms. Hoyle, for talking so straightforward about—"

"I'm not going to faint. And by the way, my name is Lynch."

"Oh, sorry. I thought—"

"That's all right. Please go on."

His eyes darted around the circle of faces watching him. "Well, I was about to say that everything with Mr. Hoyle's apparent suicide is consistent with that other case. Except it keeps nagging at me how he managed to pull the trigger.

"It'd be a real trick to do, considering the length of the barrels and— Oh, that's another thing that's got me stumped. This weapon was a side-by-side double-barrel, and both barrels were loaded. Now, if you're planning to shoot yourself in the head with a shotgun, why would you bother to load both barrels? You'd hardly need that second shell."

No one ventured a comment or an answer. Red Harper cleared his throat again. "Do you recall the last time you saw that particular shotgun, Huff? I don't see an empty space in your gun cabinet there."

He nodded toward the corner cabinet with the glass doors. Huff owned an array of firearms, including several handguns, deer rifles, and a shotgun used for bird hunting. All were on display.

"That was an old gun. None of us liked it. We retired it, so to speak. Kept it out at the fishing camp for emergencies. I don't know when it was last fired."

"I do."

Everyone's attention shifted to Chris. Judging by his characteristic insouciance, they could have been discussing anything—a missing glove, or the weather. Nothing as significant as the weapon that had killed his brother.

"One weekend—it was about three months ago, wasn't it, Beck?" Beck nodded. "The two of us spent the night out there. Late that night, Frito started going crazy. We went outside to see what had stirred him up and spotted a bobcat. Beck fired the shotgun into the air twice just to scare it off. The cat hightailed it into the woods."

Beck took up the story from there. "The next morning I cleaned and oiled the shotgun and put it back in the rack above the door."

"Did you reload it?" Sheriff Harper asked.

"No."

"Well, somebody did," Scott said.

"Have you checked it for fingerprints?"

He replied to Sayre's question with a polite "Yes, ma'am. Your brother's—Danny's—are all over it, along with some others. One of the latent prints will probably turn out to be yours," he said to Beck.

"So you know that Danny handled the shotgun," Sayre said.

"Yes, ma'am. I just don't know when."

"Is his fingerprint on the trigger?"

"We didn't lift any distinct prints off the trigger," Red Harper said. "Which is also a bit confounding. I mean, if Danny was the last one to touch it . . ." He left the thought unfinished.

Huff seemed to reach the limit of his patience. He came out of his recliner, rounded it, and took a bead on Wayne Scott. But he addressed Red Harper. "Why in hell are you letting this new detective of yours drag us through all this? To earn his crisp new uniform? Is that it? If so, let me give him something better to do, like patrolling the shop floor at my foundry and knocking heads with anybody who starts talking about unionizing. Now *that* would be putting his duty time to good use.

"As it is, he's wasting my time and keeping me thinking about things I don't want to think about anymore. Danny is dead. We buried him. That's the end of it." He shook a fresh cigarette from the pack.

"Excuse me, Mr. Hoyle, but that's not the end of it."

Huff glared at Scott as he lit the cigarette.

Bravely, the young man continued. "It's not just the position of the shotgun on Mr. Hoyle's body that raises questions. Or the contortions he'd have had to go through to pull the trigger with his finger while the barrels were in his mouth. There's more to it that puzzles me."

The new detective's face had turned red, whether with embarrassment or with fervor, Sayre didn't know. But he was standing up for himself before the mighty Huff Hoyle, and she commended him for that, even though she guessed that, after tonight, his days in the sheriff's employ were numbered.

"Well, let's hear what's got you bumfuzzled," Huff said.

"It was your son's newfound religion."

The surprises just kept coming. Sayre glanced at Chris and then at Huff to see if they were laughing over the bizarre notion of a Hoyle with religion. But they remained stone-faced. If anything, Huff's frown deepened.

She turned toward Beck, who evidently sensed her bewilderment. "Danny had recently joined a congregation of—"

"Bible thumpers," Huff snarled.

"He had embraced their beliefs and became very devout," Beck continued.

"How recently?"

"For about a year. He never missed a Sunday service or Wednesday night prayer meeting."

"He became a real bore," Chris added. "He stopped drinking. Got upset if we took the Lord's name in vain. He'd become a real Jesus freak."

"What brought it on?"

Chris shrugged.

"You never asked?"

"Yes, Sayre, we asked," he replied snidely. "Danny refused to discuss it."

Beck said, "We couldn't trace his sudden involvement back to a particular incident, like a near-death experience or anything like that. Suffice it to say, he became a different person the last few months of his life. He changed completely."

"For better or worse?"

In answer to her question, Huff said, "That's a matter of opinion." His scowl expressed his opinion of Danny's religious conversion.

She turned back to the young deputy. "How do you think this relates to his suicide?"

"I've questioned his pastor and members of the congregation who talked to Danny Sunday morning. Without exception, everybody said he was upbeat and happy. Left the services on fire for God and telling everybody he would see them that night at evening vespers." He made eye contact with everyone in the room before adding, "It seems peculiar that a man in that mood, on a spiritual high so to speak, would go off and shoot himself."

"Are you saying it was staged to look like a suicide?" Sayre asked.

"Now, don't go putting words in Wayne's mouth, Sayre," Red Harper said, casting an uneasy glance in Huff's direction. "All he's saying—"

"What I'm saying is that the circumstances surrounding Danny Hoyle's death warrant further investigation."

"The parish medical examiner didn't equivocate when he ruled it a suicide."

"That's right, Mr. Merchant, but the cause of death was obvious." He glanced at Sayre. "I'll spare you the graphic terminology that was in the ME's written autopsy report." Then to Beck he said, "It's the method of death that, in my opinion, remains undetermined."

"The method of death," Beck repeated, his eyes narrowing on the detective. "The barrels of the shotgun were still in Danny's mouth, indicating that he did not pull the trigger."

"Right," Scott said, nodding somberly. "Otherwise the weapon would have been knocked away from the body by the recoil. It's pretty much a foregone conclusion that someone held the muzzle inside Danny's mouth. It was a homicide."

Red Harper winced as though in pain. "Which brings me to the question I've got to ask. Do y'all know anybody who would have wanted Danny dead?"

chapter 6

The afternoon heat had taken its toll on the floral arrangements that covered the new grave. Blossoms had withered. Petals had turned brown, curling downward upon their stems as though in total defeat.

Because there was no breeze to disperse it, the smoke from the blast furnaces of the foundry had formed a gray cloud bank above the cemetery. It hung there, an ugly pall.

Sayre thought of it as Danny's shroud. She'd gone to the cemetery in the hope of finding some measure of peace, but after the session with Deputy Scott, she thought it unlikely that Danny's death could be that easily reconciled.

Of Huff's three children, Danny had been the least like him. He'd been mild-mannered, soft-spoken, and to her knowledge had never committed a spiteful act or harbored any malice toward anyone.

When they were kids, Danny had always deferred to her and Chris, putting up token resistance if he was wronged, but eventually yielding, especially to Chris, who was the undisputed bully of the three. Chris was also devious and knew how to manipulate his younger brother. Danny invariably fell for Chris's tricks, which were often cruel.

She'd had the fiercest temper. Whenever she unleashed it on Danny over some real or perceived affront, he bore her tirade with grace and didn't hold a grudge later for the hateful things she had screamed at him.

Once, during one of her most vicious tantrums, she had thrown his favorite toy truck into the bayou. He had cried, and called her names, and ordered her to dive in and retrieve it. Of course she had refused and, instead, had described to him in tortuous detail how his shiny truck would rust and erode even before it reached the Gulf of Mexico.

Danny had wailed for hours, then lapsed into a funk that lasted for days. When Laurel demanded to know why he was so blue, he declined to tattle on Sayre. He never told what she'd done. If he had, she would have felt justified for having done it. But he had let her get away with it, which made her deeply remorseful for her meanness to him.

Their mother had doted on Danny because he was the baby of the family. Sayre remembered Huff saying often that Laurel was going to make a mealymouthed sissy out of the boy if she didn't stop coddling him. Yet, despite their mother's obvious favoritism, ironically it was Huff's approval that Danny craved most.

Chris had automatically gained it by being the firstborn. His temperament and interests also mirrored Huff's. It fed Huff's ego to have Chris near him because he was a mini-personification of Huff himself.

Sayre was regarded as the rather useless but decorative princess of the clan and treated accordingly. She was a brat who constantly demanded her way, and when she didn't get it, she pitched tantrums. While her mother looked upon these fits of temper as improper behavior for a young lady, her father thought they were amusing. The more infuriated she became, the harder he laughed.

Because Danny was self-effacing and well-behaved, he was last in line for Huff's attention.

Growing up, Sayre had sensed this family dynamic but lacked the intellect and insight to analyze it. Now, as an adult, she realized how hurtful it must have been for Danny always to be Huff's afterthought, the far distant second son.

The family had been operating under the same dynamic when Danny died. Chris was the indulged, anointed heir apparent who could do no wrong in Huff's eyes. Sayre was the thorn in his side, the one who had rejected him. That left Danny to be the obedient child, who did as he was told and never voiced a contrary opinion, the one to be counted on but rarely acknowledged.

Was it that feeling of invisibility that had prompted Danny to kill himself?

If he had killed himself.

She pinched a dying rose off one of the sprays and twirled it against her lips. A tear slid down her cheek. It was unfair that the sweetest, most harmless of them had died young and violently. And, if

Wayne Scott's intuitions proved correct, he hadn't died voluntarily.

"Ms. Lynch?"

Sayre spun about to see a young woman standing not two yards away from her.

"I didn't mean to startle you," she said with apology. "I thought you would have heard me."

Sayre shook her head. Finally able to find her voice, she said, "I was lost in thought."

"I don't want to disturb you. I can come back later. I wanted to come . . . wanted to come and say good night to him." The woman was about her age, possibly a few years younger, and she was struggling not to cry. Sayre remembered seeing her at the wake but hadn't had an opportunity to meet her.

"I'm Sayre Lynch." She extended her hand, and the young woman shook it.

"I know who you are. I saw you at the wake. Somebody pointed you out to me, but I had already recognized you from photographs."

"The photographs in the house are all old. I've changed."

"Yes, but your hair is the same. And Danny had showed me a recent newspaper article about you. He was very proud of your accomplishments." She laughed, and Sayre was impressed by the musical quality of the sound. "When I remarked on how glamorous and sophisticated you are, Danny said that looks could be deceiving and that you were actually a hellion. But he meant it affectionately."

"What's your name?"

"I'm sorry. Jessica DeBlance. I am . . . I was Danny's friend."

"Please." Sayre motioned toward a concrete bench beneath a tree a short distance from the grave.

Together they walked toward it. Jessica was wearing a tastefully cut linen dress. Her hair was light and fell into soft waves to her shoulders. She was petite and wholesomely pretty.

They sat down on the bench. By tacit agreement they shared a long moment looking toward the grave without speaking. Jessica sniffled into a tissue. Acting on instinct, Sayre placed her arm across the woman's thin shoulders. At her touch, Jessica began to tremble with weeping.

There were dozens of questions Sayre wanted to ask her, but she refrained from saying anything until Jessica's crying had subsided and she mumbled a gruff apology.

"Don't apologize. I'm glad my younger brother had someone who cared enough to cry for him in front of a perfect stranger. Apparently you were very good friends."

"Actually, we were going to be married." Jessica extended her left hand, and Sayre stared speechlessly at the round diamond solitaire on a narrow platinum band.

"It's lovely."

And because the understated ring embodied a simple declaration of love, the quiet kind of profession that Danny would make, she was engulfed in pity for the young woman. She was also furious at Chris and Huff. Danny's fiancée should have been included in their family observances. It was a glaring snub.

"I'm sorry I didn't make it a point to speak to you at the house, Jessica. I didn't know Danny was engaged. No one told me." Maybe Danny had tried. Maybe that was what he'd been calling to tell her.

"No one knew about our engagement," Jessica said. "No one in your family. Danny didn't want your father or brother to know about me until after we were married."

Although she felt she already knew the answer, Sayre asked the obvious question. "Why?"

"He didn't want them to interfere. He knew they probably wouldn't have approved of me."

"That's ridiculous. Why wouldn't they?"

Again the woman laughed, but with sadness. "I don't come from money, Ms. Lynch."

"Please call me Sayre."

"My daddy works at the Tabasco plant in New Iberia, and my mother is a homemaker. They scraped together enough money to send me and my sister to college. We're their pride and joy because we're both elementary school teachers."

"They have every right to be proud, and I don't mean that to sound condescending. How did you meet Danny?"

"I teach third grade, but I also work as a volunteer in the public library. He came in one night to browse and got interested in a book. It got time to close. I roused him and asked him to leave. He looked up at me, and kept on looking for the longest time. Then he said, 'I'll go quietly, but only if you'll join me for a cup of coffee.' " She touched her cheek with the back of her hand as though the memory of their meeting had caused her to blush.

"Did you?"

"Go for coffee? Yes," she said with a soft laugh. "I shouldn't have. It wasn't like me to go somewhere with a man I'd just met, but I did." She returned her gaze to the flower-banked grave. "We talked for hours. Before we said good night, he asked me for a date the following weekend. By the time Saturday rolled around, I had learned that he was Huff Hoyle's son. That scared me. I started to beg off, but I liked Danny so much that I kept the date.

"We went to dinner at a place between here and New Orleans. Danny said he wanted to take me there because it was such an excellent restaurant, and it was. But I understood even then the reason for the secrecy. I didn't mind. I didn't particularly want to get involved with your family." Turning her head quickly, she said, "I hope you're not offended."

"Not at all. I dislike being involved with us myself. I know better than you how rotten we are."

Jessica smiled sadly. "Danny wasn't rotten."

"No, not him."

"He worked at the foundry and did his job there well, but his heart wasn't in it. He disagreed with your father and brother's management philosophies. He disagreed with them about a lot of things. It was just hard for him to stand up to them, lifetime habits being difficult to break. Although he was getting more courageous."

Sayre tucked away that statement to think about later. How had Danny demonstrated his newly acquired courage, she wondered.

"How long had you been engaged?"

"Two weeks."

"Two weeks?" Sayre exclaimed.

"That's right." Jessica shook her head adamantly. "They're saying Danny killed himself. He didn't. I know he didn't. We were making plans about where to live and what we wanted to do. We'd chosen names for our future children. Danny did not commit suicide. He would have considered it a sin."

The word *sin* triggered Sayre's next question. "Do you attend Danny's church?"

"Yes. After our second date, I invited him to go with me. I was singing a solo that Sunday in the worship service."

So she was a vocal soloist. That accounted for her lilting laugh.

"Danny was reluctant to go. He said Huff—that's usually what he called your father—scorned religion. But I told Danny I couldn't continue seeing him if he couldn't believe as I do. And I meant it."

She smiled shyly. "He cared enough to go with me that Sunday. After that first time, he realized that it was God's love that had been missing from his life. He discovered it and became a new person."

On that point Huff, Chris, and Beck Merchant agreed with her, although they attributed Danny's personality change to a lapse in reason rather than to a religion-based renewal. They saw it as a negative change, not a positive one.

"I think you must have been very good for my brother, Jessica. I'm glad he knew you. I'm grateful to you for loving him."

"I can't accept any gratitude for that." Her voice cracked, and she held the tissue to her eyes as tears began to flow again. "I loved him with all my heart. How am I going to endure this?"

As Jessica wept, Sayre hugged her against her shoulder. Tears filled her own eyes, but they were as much for Jessica as for Danny. Danny was beyond feeling, while this young woman's heart was breaking and there would be no surcease except the passage of time.

There were events in your life that you didn't think you could survive . . . and weren't sure you wanted to. Things happened that were so painful, you'd rather die of them than go on living with the agony of surviving. Sayre knew what that was like. She remembered what it felt like to have a heartache so severe she wanted to die. Nothing short of death would relieve the pain. But the survival instinct is a miraculous thing. One's heart goes on beating even after the will to live is lost. One takes another breath even when the desire to breathe has been crushed. One lives on.

She didn't blame Danny's fiancée for her bitter grief. Nor did she try to console her with banalities. She merely held her and would have continued holding her all night if necessary, because when she'd gone through her personal hell, there had been no one to hold her.

Eventually Jessica stopped crying. "Danny wouldn't want me to do this." She blotted her eyes and blew her nose. When she was more composed, she said, "I do not accept the coroner's ruling."

"It may give you some comfort to know that you're not alone. Hard questions are already being asked." Sayre told her about the meeting with Sheriff Harper and Wayne Scott. She gave her as detailed an account as she could remember.

When she was finished, Jessica mulled it over for several moments, then said, "This detective works for Red Harper?"

"I know what you're thinking. That Red Harper is on Huff's payroll. Nevertheless, Deputy Scott seems determined to continue his investigation."

The young woman thoughtfully gnawed on her lower lip. "Danny had been troubled by something lately. Every time I asked him about it, he made a joke, said he was worried about how he was going to support me, or what if I got fat and sloppy after he married me, or if he lost all his hair would I still love him. That kind of thing. I'd begun to wonder if I was imagining it, but I don't think so. I knew him so well."

"He never gave you a hint about what was troubling him?"

"No, but something definitely was."

"Something weighty enough to cause him to take his own life?" Sayre asked gently.

"He wouldn't hurt me like that," Jessica insisted. "He wouldn't leave me with a lifetime of asking myself why he did it and what I could have done or said to prevent it. He wouldn't burden me with that kind of self-doubt. No, Sayre. I'll never believe he shot himself."

After a pause she said, "But I'll admit that the alternative is just as unthinkable. Danny was so guileless. Even foundry workers who don't think too kindly of the other Hoyles liked Danny."

"Not entirely, Jessica. He was director of human resources, in charge of hiring and firing, insurance claims, salary. Issues like that can create ill will."

"Danny only implemented Huff's policies, which are feudalistic, and I think the employees were aware of that."

Maybe, thought Sayre. But someone with a bent toward revenge might not have made that distinction. "When Deputy Scott asked us who might have wanted to kill Danny, Beck Merchant— I'm sure Danny had mentioned him to you."

"I know who he is. Everybody does. He's a top dog at the foundry. He and Chris are thick as thieves."

"Are they that good of friends?"

"Practically inseparable."

Sayre tucked away that tidbit of information to think about later, too. Anything said to Beck might go straight to Chris.

To Jessica she said, "When Sheriff Harper asked if we knew who might have wanted to see Danny dead, Mr. Merchant answered for all of us, saying what I believe we were all thinking. The Hoyles have cultivated a lot of enemies over the years, for various reasons. If someone wanted vengeance, Danny would be an easy target because he kept the lowest profile and was the most defenseless."

Jessica thought it over for a moment before saying softly, "I suppose. But it hurts to think that he lost his life because someone had a grudge against the family over something that was none of Danny's doing."

"I agree." Sayre hesitated, then asked, "Do you plan to tell Huff and Chris about your secret engagement?"

"No. Absolutely not. My parents knew, because Danny asked my father for my hand. They and my sister are the only ones. Not even the faculty at my school knew. We always met away from town. Even at church, we were always careful to be part of a group, never alone.

"I see no reason to announce it now. It would only cause a brouhaha with your brother and father that, frankly, I don't have the desire, or the strength, to engage in. I want to concentrate all my thoughts on Danny, not them. I want each memory of our time together to be sweet. They would say or do something to taint it."

"Sadly, I agree with you," Sayre said. "I think that's a very wise decision. Don't give them the opportunity to hurt you any more than you're already hurting. Although it's their great loss that they won't know you." Sayre reached for Jessica's hand and squeezed it. "I'm glad you and I met. It's made this easier, knowing that Danny was happy the last year of his life."

She decided to leave so that Jessica would have time alone at the grave. They exchanged telephone numbers before saying good-bye. Sayre promised to keep Jessica apprised of developments in the investigation.

Out of keeping with her fragile appearance, Jessica said stubbornly, "No matter what conclusion that Deputy Scott reaches, I know that Danny didn't commit suicide. He wouldn't have left me. Somebody killed him."

chapter 7

The Destiny Diner had undergone a renovation since Sayre had last been there. The chrome stools along the counter now had turquoise vinyl seats where once they had been red. New Formica table-tops had been installed in the booths. These were also turquoise, probably intended to complement the hot-pink tufted benches.

Apparently the owners had thought this Miami Beach color scheme was an imitation of a classic 1950s diner. But all they had accomplished was to turn the real thing into a tacky parody of itself.

Compact discs had replaced 45s in the Wurlitzer, but at least the jukebox was still there. And, although the decor had changed, the current unrepentantly high-caloric, artery-clogging menu was virtually the same as the original.

Sayre placed her order, then relaxed against the padded pink vinyl of the booth to sip her vanilla-spiked Coke and to ask herself for the umpteenth time what she was doing here, why she hadn't driven back to New Orleans tonight so she could

take the first connecting flight to San Francisco tomorrow morning.

Instead, upon leaving the cemetery, she had
driven to the better of the two motels in Destiny,
which wasn't much of a boast, and checked into a
room. Then, deciding that she was hungry, or perhaps just restless, she left for the diner.

On this weeknight, well after the dinnertime
rush, she almost had the place to herself, which
suited her frame of mind. She needed time to reflect
on all that had happened today.

Her timing for going to the cemetery had been
fortuitous. Had she arrived a half hour sooner or
later, she might never have known that Jessica De-
Blance existed, or about Danny's happiness with
her. Talking with the woman who had loved him
had been like receiving a consolation gift.

But, more important, his recent engagement was
the most compelling argument against the suicide
ruling. Now that Sayre was equipped with that
information, she wondered what she should do
with it.

It also made the reason Danny had called her
after a ten-year silence an even more puzzling question. Had he been going to share the news of his engagement, or put closure on their relationship prior
to his suicide, or ask her advice on the problem he
was confronting? Not knowing would torment her
forever.

"Hiya, Red."

Roused from her thoughts, Sayre glanced
around, expecting to see someone addressing Sheriff Red Harper. But the man standing at the end of

her booth was grinning down at her and had obviously called her Red because of her hair. Did he actually think he was being original? Apparently so, because his smile seemed to be self-congratulatory.

He nodded toward her glass of Coke. "Drinking alone?"

"And I prefer it that way." She faced forward again, hoping he would take the hint and go away. He didn't.

"How do you know? You ain't tried drinking with me yet."

"Nor will I."

"Nor will I," he repeated, imitating her. "You sure picked up some highfalutin ways out in San Francisco."

She looked at him sharply.

"Ha! Wondering how I know you? I know you, Miss Sayre Hoyle. Couldn't forget that hair, or . . ." His eyes slid over her in what he probably thought was a sexy come-hither. "The way you're put together. You've acquired a few bad habits out in California. All them fags out there talk fancy, I guess, so I can't say as I blame you."

Leaning in closer, he lowered his voice to a whisper. "But I bet your ass is still as sweet as it was when you were a sixteen-year-old cheerleader bouncing all over the football field, turning cartwheels and such. Gave me a charge every Friday night to see you do those high kicks. Looked forward to it all week."

"Charming," she said, giving him a drop-dead look. "Now will you please get lost?"

Instead, he slid into the bench opposite her. She

reached for her handbag, but before she could leave the booth, he clamped his hand over her wrist. She tried to yank it free, saying, "Let go of me."

"I'm just trying to have a friendly conversation," he said in a wheedling voice. "It's not like we're strangers. Don't you remember me?"

She didn't want to have a conversation, friendly or otherwise, with this creep who had long, yellow, lupine teeth, a scraggly yellow goatee, and enormous ears. But she also didn't want to get into an undignified arm wrestling match with him and attract the attention of the few others in the diner.

Besides not wanting to make a spectacle of herself, she would just as soon Huff and Chris think she had returned to New Orleans tonight, according to her plan. It wouldn't take long for news to reach them that she was fighting off a masher in the diner, which would no doubt provide them with a good laugh.

She fixed her frostiest glare on the man. "I don't know who you are, nor do I care to know. If you don't let go of my hand immediately, I'll—"

"What?" he taunted, applying more pressure to her wrist, digging into the tender underside of it with his thumb. "Wha'chu gonna do if I don't let go?"

"She'll break your fucking neck. And if she doesn't, I will."

Her unwanted companion's jaw went slack as he looked up and beyond her. She turned to see Beck Merchant leaning indolently against the back of the booth behind her, in much the same way he'd been leaning against the fender of her car that morning. He was smiling the same casual smile now, too, but only with his mouth. His eyes echoed the threat he had issued.

It caused the other man's confidence to waver, although he tried to brazen it out. "Who're you to be butting in?"

"I'm the guy who's going to break your neck."

"I whipped your ass once, you know. You've obviously forgotten that. But I'll be all too happy to refresh your memory."

He was bluffing. Even Sayre, who was by no means an expert on fistfights, could tell that.

"Let go of her." Emphasizing the two words separately, Beck added, "Right now."

The man hesitated only a moment longer, then released her and slid out of the booth. Sneering down at Sayre, he said, "Just like all the Hoyles, you always did think you was hot shit."

She didn't bother with a comeback but watched him saunter to a booth at the far end of the diner, where his companions began riling him for being shot down. Then she looked at Beck. "I could have handled the situation myself."

"Hold the thought."

Before she could say more, he walked to the door of the diner, pushed it open, and whistled softly. A large dog leapt from the bed of a pickup truck and bounded up to him. "Go on back there and let them feed you."

The golden retriever ran to the double swinging doors that led into the kitchen and nosed his way through them. Sayre heard exclamations of greeting from the staff. Beck rejoined her, sliding into the booth.

"Frito?" she asked.

"How did you know?"

"Chris mentioned him."

"Oh, right. The night at the fishing cabin. The bobcat."

"I assumed Chris was referring to a dog." She glanced toward the diner kitchen. "Apparently Frito is a regular."

"So am I, but I've never seen you here, and frankly I'm shocked. At the house, you were chomping at the bit to be on your way back to California."

"I went to the cemetery. It got late. I decided to stay here tonight and get a fresh start tomorrow."

He assimilated that without comment, then asked, "Have you ordered?"

"A cheeseburger."

He called out to the short-order cook who could be seen through the open space behind the counter. "Grady, double her order, please."

"Coming up."

He settled back into the booth. "Now, what were you saying about handling the situation with Slap Watkins?"

"Watkins," she said with sudden enlightenment. "I remember now. He was a troublemaker, several classes ahead of me in school. I think he had to repeat a couple of grades. He once got suspended for window-peeping into the girls' locker room."

"He's still a troublemaker. I heard from Chris that he's recently been released from prison and is on parole. When I pulled in, I saw you through the window, and it looked to me like you needed some help."

"Insert 'thank you for rescuing me' here?"

He grinned, then looked up at the approaching waitress and winked when she set a glass of Coke in front of him. "You remembered the lemon wedge without my even asking. Thanks."

"You bet," she said, returning his flirtatious smile.

"Do you know Sayre Lynch?"

The two of them exchanged obligatory smiles. Speaking in a low voice, the waitress said, "That Slap Watkins has stunk up the place. Want me to wipe down the table for you, Beck?"

"I think it's okay, but thanks."

"They should have kept him in prison."

"Give him time, he'll go back."

"Until then, I wish he and his buddies would find another place to hang out. Burgers will be ready soon. Nice to meet you," she said to Sayre before turning away. But Sayre questioned her sincerity. In fact she seemed reluctant to leave Sayre alone with Beck Merchant.

The waitress probably wasn't the only heart in Destiny that he kept aflutter, and Sayre could understand why. He had an undeniable sex appeal— the green eyes, the rakish blond hair, the smile that suggested he could talk you into being naughty. He looked as good and as comfortable in the old jeans and chambray shirt he was wearing now as he had in his funeral suit. Altogether, a very attractive package.

But so was Chris. He wore clothes well, too. He was movie star handsome. But many reptiles were as beautiful and alluring as they were poisonous. Chris was a snake who struck even as he charmed.

She trusted Beck Merchant no more than she trusted her older brother, and possibly even less. Chris came by his meanness naturally, whereas Beck was paid to be mean.

"Selma would be heartbroken to learn that we'd come here to eat after she tried all day to feed us," he remarked.

"She loves us. Always has. Much more than we deserve to be loved."

Folding his arms on the table, he leaned forward. "Why don't you think you deserve to be loved?"

"You're a lawyer, Mr. Merchant, not a psychoanalyst."

"I'm only making casual conversation."

"I believe Slap Watkins used that same line."

He laughed out loud. "Then my technique needs some work." He twirled the straw in his glass for several moments. "Sayre," he said slowly, "I apologize." He looked up, met her gaze. "For telling you about Old Mitchell like that. It was a cheap shot. Even when I'm angry, I usually play more fairly than that."

Disliking her own mistrust of what appeared to be a sincere apology, she said nothing, merely raised one shoulder in a half shrug of acknowledgment.

The waitress arrived with their orders. The burgers and fries were everything they should have been—greasy, hot, and delicious. For several minutes, they ate in silence, but she was keenly aware of him watching her. Finally she said, "What is it, Mr. Merchant?"

"What?"

"You keep staring at me."

"Hm, sorry. I was just thinking, would it have killed you to thank me?"

"For what?"

"For fending off Watkins."

He nodded through the plate-glass window. She turned to see the man climbing onto a motorcycle. He stomped the starter, then peeled out of the parking lot. Just before roaring onto the highway, he raised his middle finger at them.

"That sums up what he thinks of us, doesn't it?" Then, looking across the booth, she said, "I could have handled the situation, but probably not without making a scene and becoming the talk of the town tomorrow. So, thank you."

"Glad to oblige."

"He said he had whipped your ass before. True?"

"That's his version." He finished his burger and pulled two paper napkins from the dispenser to wipe his hands. "Chris and I were reunited because of Slap Watkins. Two coffees," he told the waitress, who had returned to take away their plates. "If Frito is in your way, send him out here." She told him the dog was snoozing and went to get their coffee, which Sayre was glad he had ordered. It would be the perfect chaser for the rich food.

"Chris and I met at LSU when I pledged the same fraternity. He was a senior. We had a passing acquaintance before he graduated. We didn't see each other again until three years ago."

He acknowledged the arrival of their coffees with another smile for the waitress, then as Sayre raised the steaming cup to her lips, he warned, "It's caffeinated chicory coffee."

"I drank it from my baby bottle and still have it shipped to me in San Francisco." She took a sip, then asked, "What happened three years ago to re-unite you?"

"The Gene Iverson case. Indirectly anyway. How much do you know about that?"

"Only what I read in the company newsletters."

"Those newsletters that you don't want sent to you, but which you read anyway?"

On that point he had her, although she would never admit it. She faithfully read the newsletters, not because she cared about Huff and Chris's welfare but because she cared about the men and women who worked for them and about the fu-ture of the town. Without Hoyle Enterprises, there would be no local economy. Hundreds of families would be without income. Even though she didn't want to profit from the foundry, she felt a moral responsibility to keep a close eye on it, warts and all.

She said, "The information in the newsletters is filtered through Huff and Chris, particularly if it's even fractionally negative. In other words, my source on the Iverson case was biased and unreli-able. What can you tell me about it?"

He leaned back and studied her for a moment. "Your brother was indicted for murder, yet you never bothered to learn the facts of the case. Doesn't your concern come a little late?"

"I'm not concerned, I'm curious. I don't give a damn about Chris and what he does. I feel the same about Huff. I wrote them off ten years ago, and if that sounds harsh and unfeeling, that's just too damn bad."

"Where did Danny rate?"

"Danny," she said, made sad again at the mention of his name. "Whatever Huff and Chris dished out, he took lying down. I'm sure you witnessed his subordination to them every day. Danny never stood up for himself."

"But you did."

Not until ten years ago, she thought. Not until she had struck rock bottom. Not until she had determined that, in order to survive, she had to leave her family and their town and never return.

"I got lucky," she said. "I finally found the wherewithal to defy Huff and leave. But Danny didn't."

Beck hesitated, then said, "Maybe he took his leave in another way, Sayre."

"Maybe."

"But when you left here ten years ago, you didn't think too well of him for being such a pushover."

"No, I didn't."

In fact she had left hating them all. But after years of therapy her feelings toward Danny had softened—just not enough to take a phone call from him that had come out of the blue.

Thoughtfully she sipped her coffee, but when she replaced the cup in the saucer, she realized that

Beck Merchant was looking at her with disconcerting interest. She berated herself for talking to him about issues so personal that until now she had confided them only to her therapist.

"We were talking about the Gene Iverson case."

"Right." He sat up straighter and cleared his throat. "What do you want to know?"

"Did Chris kill him?"

His left eyebrow shot up. "You don't mince words."

"Did he?"

"The evidence against Chris was purely circumstantial."

"That's not an answer," she said. "No, allow me to rephrase. That's a *lawyer's* answer."

"The prosecution's case was weak enough to deadlock a jury."

"And it was never retried."

"It shouldn't have been tried in the first place."

"No body, no murder?" That had been at the crux of the articles she had read. Gene Iverson's body had never been found. He had disappeared without a trace.

"If I were a prosecuting attorney," he said, "I would never go into a murder trial without a dead body, no matter how compelling the circumstantial evidence was."

"How did you become involved?"

"I'd read about the trial. Thought it was a bum rap for reasons I've expressed. I came down here to lend support to my fraternity brother, assist him any way I could. But by the time I got here, the trial was over. I found Chris and Danny celebrating in that old honky-tonk out on the highway. You know the place?"

"The Razorback?"

"That's the one. Chris was buying drinks for everybody to celebrate the outcome of his trial. Slap Watkins was there. He started spouting off about money buying justice, and rich people never serving time, and so forth. Didn't set well with Chris. Or Danny. In fact, he threw the first punch in defense of his older brother. All hell broke loose. I plunged in and, despite Watkins's claim of victory, tilted the odds in the brothers' favor. We mopped the floor with him."

"So you've rescued all three of us from the ugly clutches of Slap Watkins."

"So it would seem," he said, smiling. "I'm a handy man to have around."

"Huff and Chris certainly think so."

He propped his forearms on the table and leaned forward. "Right now I'm interested in what you think."

The statement was deceptively simple. She sensed an underlying meaning that was more complex. "I think it's time I said good-bye."

When she opened her handbag, he said, "I'll cover your dinner. I have a tab here."

"Thanks anyway."

"Afraid of being indebted to me?"

She tucked a twenty-dollar bill beneath the sugar dispenser, then looked straight into his teasing eyes. "I'm not afraid of anything, Mr. Merchant."

He left the booth when she did and followed her to the door. "Dogs?"

"What?"

He whistled sharply. "Are you afraid of dogs?"

He barely had time to complete the question before Frito shot through the swinging double doors. He was a beautiful animal—golden fur with white feathering on his underside. He wagged his tail so exuberantly that Sayre was forced to dodge it or risk being knocked down.

He greeted his owner with such enthusiasm it could have been months rather than minutes since he had last seen him. Then he turned his unbridled affection onto Sayre. He danced around her feet and bathed her hands with happy licks, only settling down when told to "be nice!" He obeyed and squatted on his haunches but quivered with uncontrollable energy and implored Sayre with large brown eyes to pet him.

Which she did. "He's wonderful. How long have you had him?"

"Couple of years. Since he was seven weeks old. One of the workers brought a litter to the foundry. I took one look inside the box and was suckered into taking him home." He scrubbed his knuckles across the top of the dog's head. "We had several clashes when it came to housebreaking, but now I don't know what I'd do without him."

As she watched him shower affection on his dog, Sayre conceded that Beck Merchant had sexy eyes, an engaging grin, and a cute pet. One could easily be taken in. But she rejected the notion that he was a nice guy. At the end of the day, he was still Huff Hoyle's chief legal adviser, capable of corporate treachery and God only knew what else. She would put nothing past him, not even faking this love for his dog in an effort to disarm her.

They stepped outside, where it felt like a steam room compared to the air-conditioned diner. The sultry air engulfed her, for a moment robbing her of breath. She grew dizzy. Her ears began to buzz.

He touched her elbow. "Are you all right?"

She pressed her hand against her struggling lungs and inhaled deeply through her nose, exhaled through her mouth. The dizziness subsided. The buzzing in her ears, she realized with chagrin, was one of the neon tubes in the window spelling out the fare of the diner. "I'm not quite acclimatized."

"It takes a while." Looking down at her, he said, "But you won't be here long enough for that, will you?"

"No. Not that long."

He nodded, but he didn't move away from her and his gaze remained on her face.

"Before I go," she said, "I wanted to ask— Ouch!"

"What?"

"Frito stepped on my foot."

The dog had been trying to nudge his way between them when one of his paws landed hard on her instep.

"I'm sorry." He opened the cab of his pickup and motioned Frito inside. The retriever leapt in as though he'd done it a thousand times, then poked his head through the open passenger window, his tongue lolling out the side of his mouth, looking adorably guileless.

Sayre hobbled to the bed of the pickup and supported herself there while she checked her foot.

"Any permanent damage?"

"No. It's all right."

"I'm terribly sorry. He thinks he's a lapdog."

Although her foot was throbbing, she said, "It startled me more than hurt."

"What were you about to ask?"

It took her a second to remember. "How you got from assisting my brothers in a brawl to becoming chief counsel for Hoyle Enterprises. After the night at the Razorback, how long before Huff hired you?"

"As soon as I recovered from my hangover." He chuckled. "Actually, Chris invited me to stay for a few days, go fishing, hang out. Over the course of the visit, it became clear to him that I was unhappy with the law firm I was in. By the end of my stay, Huff had made me an offer I couldn't refuse. Relocation was no problem for me. I hadn't come to Destiny intending to stay, but ultimately the decision was a no-brainer."

He had sunk his fingers into Frito's dense pelt and was idly rubbing the back of his neck. The dog's eyes were closed. He looked drunk with pleasure.

Snapping her attention back to the subject, Sayre asked him what had happened to Calvin McGraw. He had been Huff's lawyer for as far back as Sayre could remember. Beck Merchant had replaced him.

"Mr. McGraw retired."

"Or Huff retired him," she countered.

"I don't know what their arrangement was. I'm

sure Huff offered him an attractive retirement package."

"Oh, I'm sure of that, too. Ensuring McGraw's silence would have been expensive."

"His silence?"

"About bribing the jury during Chris's murder trial."

Beck's fingers stopped their mindless movement, and gradually he withdrew his hand from the nape of Frito's neck. The dog whined a complaint, but his owner seemed not to notice. His attention was focused on Sayre. Purposefully he walked toward her and didn't stop until he was standing directly in front of her, effectively trapping her between him and the truck.

She recoiled. "Back up."

"Not yet."

"What are you doing?"

"Confessing. I lied to you."

"I would expect that. You'll have to be more specific."

"The mosquito."

She stared up at him with incomprehension.

"This afternoon, down at the bayou, when I brushed the mosquito off your cheek? There was no mosquito, Sayre. I just wanted to touch your face."

He wasn't touching her now, except with his eyes, and their touch was almost as effective as fingertips. He shouldn't have been standing this close to her. It was an inappropriate distance between strangers. Furthermore it was physically uncomfortable. It was too sultry for two people to be standing this close, close enough to feel each other's body heat, forced to share the inadequate air.

"I don't remember that," she lied. Pushing him aside, she headed for her car, which was parked a short distance away. By the time she reached it, he had caught up with her. Hooking her elbow, he brought her around.

"First of all, the hell you don't remember. Second, you've been tossing out some mighty bold allegations tonight. You intimated that Chris got away with murder, then accused your father of jury tampering. Those are serious crimes."

"So is tampering with evidence."

He raised his shoulders. "You've lost me."

"Yellow mud." She pointed toward the pickup truck. "Your tires are caked with it. So are your boots." Simultaneously, they looked down at the muddy boots poking out from beneath the stringy hems of his worn jeans. Looking into his face again, she said, "There's only one place in the parish where the soil is that ocher color. On Bayou Bosquet. Where the fishing camp is."

His jaw bunched. "Your point?"

"You went out there tonight, didn't you? Don't bother lying. I know you did. I just wonder what you did while you were there."

"You know," he said, "if your design business ever tanks, maybe you could sign on with the FBI."

"Deputy Scott told us that until further notice the cabin at the camp was considered a crime scene. He said it had been cordoned off."

"With bright yellow tape."

"Which you ignored."

"Did you know that dogs are color-blind? Frito didn't realize it was crime scene tape. He charged right past it. I had to go get him."

"Even though he immediately responds to hand gestures, verbal commands, and whistles?"

A weighty silence yawned between them. He knew he'd been caught.

chapter 8

*H*e was pudgy and pink.

No two ways about it, George Robson thought.

The full-length, well-lighted three-way mirror in his bathroom unmercifully revealed all his physical flaws. He didn't like what he saw. Each day it seemed there was less hair growing on his head and more on his back. His breasts sagged, his stomach was flabby. Beneath it, his penis looked no bigger than a thumb.

Less time on the golf course and more time in a gym would help the pecs and abs. There wasn't much he could do about the other. That was what had him worried. He had a beautiful, young wife to satisfy, and unfortunately, this was the equipment he had to do it with.

Modestly, he put on a pair of undershorts before joining Lila in the bedroom. She was propped up in bed looking through one of her fashion magazines. He crawled in beside her. "You're prettier than any of the models in that magazine." He wasn't just saying so. In his estimation it was true. Lila was the most beautiful woman he'd ever seen.

"Hm."

"No, really. I mean it." She was wearing one of the slip-type nightgowns he liked. Short. Skinny straps. One had slid off her shoulder. He reached over and pushed it down farther, then stroked her breast.

She brushed his hand aside. "It's too hot tonight."

"Not in here, honey. I set the AC down to sixty-eight, just where you like it."

"Feels hotter."

He lay beside her quiescently and let her peruse her magazine without further interruption. He gazed at her face, her lovely hair, that incredible body, and tried to fend off his fear. Was it warranted? He didn't want to know, but he *had* to know because not knowing was driving him crazy.

"Nice funeral today," he remarked, as casually as possible.

Her expression didn't change. "I almost fell asleep in the church. *Bor*-ing."

"Huff threw quite a wake."

"It was okay."

"Where'd you disappear to?"

"Disappear to?" She thumbed to another page. "When?"

"There for a while, in the house, I couldn't find you."

She looked over at him. "I went to pee."

"I checked the powder room."

"There was a line. I went upstairs. Is that all

right with you? Or should I have held it until I got home?"

"Don't get mad, honey. I just—"

"Oh, forget it." She tossed the magazine to the floor. "It's too hot to argue over something as stupid as my going to the bathroom."

She began to fluff the pillows behind her head. She had bought the embroidered silk pillowcases at a specialty shop in New Orleans. They'd cost a freaking fortune. He had hit the ceiling when he discovered the charge on their credit card statement.

"You spent this on pillowcases?" he'd said incredulously.

She'd told him she would return them, but she had been so unhappy for the next several days, he'd relented and said she could keep the damn things. She had tearfully thanked him and said he was the best husband ever. He had basked in her affection.

"Thank you for going with me today," he said, laying a hand on the curve of her hip. "It was important that we go."

"Of course we had to go. You work for them."

"Safety director is a very important job, you know. I have lots of responsibility, Lila. Without me, the Hoyles—"

"Did you feed the cat?"

"I mixed dry food with canned just like you asked me to. Anyway, my work at the plant is just as vital as what Chris does. Maybe more so."

She stopped fiddling with the lace-trimmed pillowcases and looked at him. "No one doubts that you're a top man at that foundry, George. I'm the first to know all the long hours you give that place." Pouting, she said, "I know, because every hour you're there, you're not here with me."

Smiling, she pulled her nightgown over her head, then teasingly dragged it across his chest. His small penis stretched with excitement. "Got something for Lila tonight, George? Hm?" she purred.

Sliding her hand into the fly of his shorts, she applied herself to pleasing him, and she knew how. When he caressed her in turn, she moaned as though deriving as much pleasure from their foreplay as he.

Maybe he was wrong. Maybe he was just being paranoid and imagining things, picking up clues and catching vibes that weren't really there. He was short, pudgy, and pink; Chris Hoyle was tall, dark, and handsome. He had a reputation for taking whatever woman he wanted.

George knew several men at the plant whose marriages had either suffered or ended over the wives' infidelity with Chris. Naturally a man would feel a little insecure whenever his wife was around such a notorious womanizer.

He had worked for the Hoyles over twenty years. He'd given them so much of himself—time, integrity, pride. But the more you gave them, the more they took. They fed on people, on lives, on a man's soul. George had accepted that a long time ago. He was willing to be a yes-man.

But, by God, the line had to be drawn somewhere. And with George Robson, it was his wife.

Wearing only his boxer shorts and an old-fashioned, ribbed cotton undershirt, Huff descended the wide staircase. He tried to tread lightly, but several of the stairs squeaked anyway, and sure enough, by the time he reached the ground floor, Selma was already there wrapped in a robe that was too thick and fuzzy for the season.

"Do you need something, Mr. Hoyle?"

"Some privacy in my own goddamn house would be nice. Do you keep your ear to the floor?"

"Well excuse me for being worried about you."

"I told you a thousand times today that I'm fine."

"You're not fine, you just don't let on."

"Can we save this conversation for some other time? I'm in my drawers."

"I have to pick up and wash those drawers. You think seeing you in them is going to put me in a swoon? Besides that, it ain't a'tall a pretty sight."

"Go back to bed before I fire you."

With the hauteur of a prima ballerina, she did a pirouette on her terry-cloth scuffs and retreated into the darkness at the back of the house.

For a while Huff had lain in bed, wakeful and alert. Although, even when he was asleep, his brain didn't shut down entirely. Like the furnaces in his foundry, his mind burned just as hotly through the night as it did by day. Some of his knottiest problems had unraveled while he was asleep. He would go to bed with a dilemma and wake up the following morning with a solution worked out for him by his active subconscious.

But tonight's problems were particularly disturbing, and sleep had eluded him completely. Every time he closed his eyes, he would see an image of

Danny's fresh grave. Even dressed up with flowers, a grave was a hole in the ground, and there was nothing dignified about that.

The walls of his bedroom had seemed to be closing in on him, like the walls of earth inside Danny's grave, like the satin lining of his casket. Huff had never been claustrophobic before, especially not in his own house. Even though the air-conditioning vents were directed toward his bed, the linens were damp with his sweat, so clingy that even though he'd thrashed his legs he couldn't kick off the sheets.

He had a bad case of heartburn to boot. So rather than lie there and nurse these miseries until dawn, he'd decided to get up and go outside. Perhaps the tranquillity of the countryside at night would calm him enough to bring on sleepiness.

He pulled open the front door. There was no alarm system in his house, and the doors were rarely locked. Who would dream of stealing from Huff Hoyle? The thief would have to be either extraordinarily courageous or downright crazy.

Huff despised Arabs—just as he did Jews, Latinos, blacks, Asians, and any ethnicity other than his own—but he admired the swift justice that was meted out in Islamic nations. If he caught somebody stealing from him, he'd cut off the culprit's hand and only then turn him over to the sluggish legal system, which these days was less concerned about punishing the wrongdoer than it was about safeguarding his goddamn civil rights.

Just thinking about that sad state of affairs fanned his heartburn. He belched sourly.

Huff eased himself into his favorite rocking chair and lit a cigarette. He puffed in contentment as he gazed at the portion of the horizon that was aglow with the lights of the foundry. The smokestacks had created a thin layer of cloud above the town. He might be momentarily at rest, but his work never was.

In the summertime, the gallery ceiling fans were kept on around the clock, because often, like tonight, they provided the only breeze to be had. Huff leaned back and enjoyed the caress of the soft air against his clammy skin. Closing his eyes, he thought back to the first time he'd ever seen a ceiling fan. He remembered it like it was yesterday.

He'd gone into a drugstore with his daddy, who'd been looking for work. The Drugstore Man wore a bow tie and wide suspenders. Hat in hand, head lowered, Huff's daddy meekly offered to push the oiled dust mop around the hardwood floors of the store, or burn trash in the big barrels out back, or do any other menial tasks the proprietor might want to delegate to someone not afraid of hard labor. For instance, he'd noticed a few dirt dauber nests up under the eaves as he was coming in. Wouldn't Drugstore Man like those knocked down?

While the two men negotiated the terms of his daddy's temporary employment, young Huff stood staring at the circulating blades of the overhead fan, marveling over the fabulous machine that stirred his hair with cool air and dried the sweat off his sunburned face.

All that day his daddy stocked shelves and swept floors and washed windows. He burned trash in the blazing sun and told Huff to help him be on the lookout for flyaway sparks. Huff became entranced by the licking flames and the heat waves that shimmied up out of the barrels.

His daddy hauled and fetched and carried for Drugstore Man until his back was bent and his face was lined with exhaustion. Huff got to eat that night, though. A pimento cheese sandwich, a leftover from Drugstore Man's soda fountain. Nothing had ever tasted so good, although he felt guilty for eating it in front of his daddy, who'd said he wasn't hungry.

Huff wished that Drugstore Man would offer to make him an ice cream cone, like he'd been watching him make for folks all day, piling the scoops so high that Huff didn't know how they stayed on the cone.

But Drugstore Man didn't offer to make him one, and as soon as Huff had eaten his sandwich, making it last as long as he could, the man said it was time for him and his daddy to "move along now," which was something they heard often.

Headlights swept a bright arc across the front lawn. Huff, roused from his reverie, rubbed his hands over his face as though to wash away the memory and the embarrassment it would cause him if anyone knew of it.

Chris's shiny Porsche Carrera came to a stop, and he climbed out. He jogged up the walkway and was almost to the gallery before he noticed Huff.

"What are you doing out here this time of night?"

"What does it look like I'm doing?"

"Nice outfit," Chris remarked with amusement as he dropped into the other rocking chair and stretched his arms high above his head. "I'm so tired, I might sleep straight through tomorrow."

"You've got work tomorrow."

"I'll call in sick. Who's gonna fire me?"

Huff harrumphed. "What kept you out so late?"

"George's mom came down with a stomach virus. She called at a most inopportune time. Poor George had just got it up when he had to go see about Mama, leaving Lila alone and lonely."

"That girl is trouble."

"Granted. That's what makes it stimulating."

Huff expelled a gust of smoke. "Are you going to waste your best years diddling frustrated house-wives? Or are you going to get your wife back into your bed and make her pregnant?"

Chris pressed the heels of his hands into his eye sockets as though they suddenly pained him. "I'm not going to talk about this tonight."

"We'll talk about this when I say we talk about this," Huff said. "You've been dodging the subject of Mary Beth for weeks. I want to know what's going on."

"All right." Chris rested his head on the back of his chair and took a deep breath. "She refuses to sign the divorce document. Beck consulted the best divorce lawyer in New Orleans. This one favors the men, not their money-grabbing, whining exes. He's as tough as they come.

"He drew up the document, and Beck went over every word of it. In his opinion, it was the best pos-sible deal for me and still very generous to Mary

Beth." He stopped rocking his chair and leaned across the distance separating them, bringing his face close to Huff's. "She won't sign."

"Then there's hope for a reconciliation."

Chris gave a short laugh and returned to his original position. "Mary Beth isn't refusing the divorce because she wants to stay with me. She's refusing out of spite. She hates me, hates you, hates this town, the foundry. She despises everything about us."

"Hell, boy, she's only a woman. A *woman*. Stop screwing Lila and get yourself down to Mexico. Woo your wife. Do what you have to do—flowers, jewelry, a new automobile, new tits if she wants them.

"Win her back with gifts and romance. Eat some crow if you have to. It won't kill you. Hose her enough times to get her pregnant, then lock her up until the kid is born. Once we've got the kid, we'll claim her an unfit mother, send her packing without a penny."

Chris shook his head. "It's not going to happen, Huff." He held up his hand to stave off Huff's arguments. "Even if I was inclined to seduce the bitch into my bed again, which I'm not, and even if I hosed her, as you so romantically put it, a thousand times, it wouldn't take."

"Wouldn't take? What the hell are you talking about?"

"She had her tubes tied."

Huff felt his blood pressure skyrocket. In a matter of seconds, his heartburn had grown from a low ember to a wildfire that was searing its way through his diaphragm and up into his esophagus.

Chris said, "The last time I made a pitch for reconciliation, she laughed at me. She said she knew I only wanted to patch things up so I could provide you and myself with an heir. Did I think she was stupid?" He looked across at Huff. "She's a lot of things, but stupid isn't one of them.

"Then she dashed our hopes for good by informing me that she'd had a tubal ligation. She said birth control pills were making her fat. And that much is true—her butt is getting as broad as a barn. She's wearing thong bikinis now, so she can't afford any extra poundage or fluid retention. That's a quote direct from her. So she had the procedure.

"Now she can screw her Mexican pool boy nine ways from Sunday, or she can come back here and be my loving, devoted wife, or she can join a convent, but the one thing she is not going to do is conceive a baby." He sighed. "That's what I've been dreading to tell you, and I can honestly say I'm glad it's finally off my chest."

Huff smoked his cigarette down to a nub while he contemplated this unwelcome piece of news. His silly, shallow daughter-in-law—a title too elevated to apply to the conniving shrew—had made herself barren. All right. That left Chris with only one option: to obtain a divorce from her and marry a woman who would bear him children.

Huff relaxed again. At least they wouldn't have to play any more guessing games about what they should do with Mary Beth. She had eliminated herself from the decision-making process, and Huff could almost thank her for it. Now that the new goal had been set for them, he and Chris could go full throttle toward achieving it.

"Have you told Beck?" he asked.

"Nobody," Chris replied. "I only told him that I'd given up on the marriage completely and wanted out as soon as possible."

"And he thinks this lawyer in New Orleans is the best?"

"He's expensive, but his clients don't leave the courtroom completely fleeced, carrying their balls in a paper sack."

Huff laughed and reached across to pat Chris's knee. "Try and hang on to those. You're going to need them."

Chris smiled, but he was still dejected. "I should've listened to you and got Mary Beth pregnant as soon as the marriage vows were spoken. Instead, I went along with her and agreed to hold off until she had 'settled into the family,' as she put it."

Chris didn't know this, but Huff hadn't left the decision to the newlyweds. He had gone to Doc Caroe and told him to replace Mary Beth's birth control pills with sugar placebos. The doctor had done it . . . for a hefty fee, of course.

It had turned out to be a bad investment. Months went by, but to his consternation Mary Beth didn't conceive. Even that soon into the marriage, she and Chris were fighting more often than they were having sex.

"That's water under the bridge now, Son," he said. "No sense in wasting energy on regret. We need to concentrate on getting you a speedy divorce. If she's screwing her pool man, we can cite adultery."

"She would only counter by listing my affairs,

most of which were with her good friends. We've got to think of something else."

Huff patted his son's knee again, then stood up. "This New Orleans lawyer sounds like a good man to have on our side, and even if we can't rely on him to get the job done, we can rely on Beck. Let's go to bed."

"Long day," Chris observed as they entered the silent house. "It seems like ages since we left to go to the funeral, doesn't it?"

"Hm." Huff absently rubbed the bonfire still raging inside his chest.

"What did you think of Sayre? We haven't had a chance to talk about her."

"Still prissy."

"Prissy?" Chris scoffed as they climbed the stairs. "That's like calling Osama bin Laden a troublemaker."

"She didn't leave town like she said she was going to. The manager of The Lodge called me. She booked a room for tonight."

"Why?"

"Maybe she was as tired as we are, or didn't want to make the drive to New Orleans in the dark."

Chris looked at him skeptically. "If she wanted to leave badly enough, she would have crawled out of town. She thinks no more kindly of us and Destiny than Mary Beth does. Possibly even less."

"Damn women. Who knows why they do anything?" Huff grumbled. "At least Beck was with her part of the evening."

"Still on assignment for you?"

"Actually no. He saved her from Slap Watkins."

Chris stopped on the landing. "Come again?"

Huff turned, grinning and shaking his head. "That's what I said. Beck went to the diner to grab a burger, saw Sayre sitting inside, which was astonishing enough. But there was Slap, big ears and all, trying to pick her up."

Huff recounted for Chris what Beck had told him. When he finished, Chris was shaking his head with a mix of amusement and bewilderment. "What in the world would Slap Watkins have to say to Sayre?"

"The last thing he said was insulting to the family." He frowned. "I'm glad Beck came along when he did. No telling what that white trash was up to. Beck called me as soon as he and Sayre parted company. He was following her back to the motel. He watched until she was inside her room. She knew he was following her and probably knew he was talking to me the whole time. He said if looks could kill he'd be dead."

"I'll bet."

"She told Beck she was spending the night so she could get a fresh start in the morning, but I'm not convinced that's her only reason. I think she regrets not being around when her family needed her."

"You give her more credit than I do," Chris said. "I don't think she gives a damn about us."

"Don't be so sure. Beck said she wanted to know about that Iverson mess."

"How nice of her to finally get around to asking."

He smiled at Chris's sarcasm. "I think your sister feels guilty for not being here for you when you needed her, and probably for not being here for Danny."

"What could dear Sayre have done for him that we didn't?"

Standing now in the shadowed hallway, Huff looked at the closed door to Danny's room. "Nothing, probably. Hell, I never could figure out that boy. I think that losing his mama at such an early age must have taken something out of him that he never got back."

Chris laid his hand on Huff's shoulder. "I hope he's got it now, Huff. I hope he's at peace."

With that they said good night and went into their respective rooms. Huff, who was rarely even tired, was exhausted tonight. But he didn't go to bed. He sat in an armchair in front of the wide windows that overlooked the rear lawn and the bayou beyond it.

The disturbing thoughts he had hoped to leave out on the gallery had returned inside with him, and Chris had contributed to them with the update on the Mary Beth situation. Then there was Sayre. Brimming with malice toward him. *Him,* her own daddy.

He didn't blame Laurel for dying, but she had left him with three children to rear. He'd done what he thought best for all three, but Chris was the only one who'd turned out to his liking.

Life was complicated. Of course, it beat the alternative.

Huff didn't believe in an afterlife. Preachers could say what they wanted about laying up treasures in heaven, but when it was over, it was over.

That was all she wrote, mister. Dead was just that—dead. He hadn't contradicted Chris's comforting sentiment about Danny's finding peace, but he didn't agree with it.

Danny hadn't found peace any more than he'd found a host of angels waiting to welcome him at the pearly gates with a star-studded crown and a set of wings. He'd been swallowed into a void. Eternal dark nothingness. That was death.

That was why you had to make the most of life. The only rewards you got were those you stockpiled for yourself while you were alive. That was why he scraped and clawed and grabbed and did whatever else it took to be the best, the biggest, the baddest. And fuck anybody who condemned his methods. Huff Hoyle answered to no one.

If his way of life didn't allow for much tranquillity, fine. There were worse things to live without.

chapter 9

Sayre entered the sheriff's office and approached the reception desk. The uniformed deputy seated behind it grunted an unintelligible reply when she told him good morning. He kept his big feet on the corner of the desk and continued paring his fingernails with a pocketknife.

"I'm here to see Deputy Wayne Scott."

His surly expression remained in place, and if performing the public service he was paid to perform involved removing his feet from the desk, bringing his chair upright, and saving this personal hygiene project for a more appropriate time, he was disinclined and disinterested. "Scott's out."

"Sheriff Harper then."

"He's got a full schedule today."

"Is he here or not?"

"He's here, but you—"

She sailed past his desk and marched down the short hallway. He lumbered after her, shouting, "Hey!" which she ignored and without knocking first pushed open the door to Red Harper's private office.

He was seated behind his desk, apparently dealing with the stack of paperwork in front of him.

"Sorry, Red," the deputy said from behind her. "She just come barging in here like she was somebody."

"She *is* somebody, Pat. It's okay. I'll holler if I need you."

"Want the door closed?"

He had addressed the question to Red, but Sayre replied, "Yes."

He gave her a nasty look as he withdrew, pulling the door closed behind him. Coming back around to the sheriff, she asked, "Is he the best you could do?"

"Pat can get cranky sometimes."

"Which is no excuse for rudeness."

"You're right. It's not." Red Harper motioned for her to take a seat in the chair facing his desk. "Can I get you some coffee or something?"

"No, thank you."

He took a moment to look her over. "California's treated you favorably, Sayre. You look good."

"Thank you." Unfortunately she couldn't return the compliment. He looked even more haggard this morning than he had yesterday, as though he'd gotten little rest in the meantime.

He eased back in his chair. "It's good to see you, but I hate like hell the reason you came home. I always liked Danny."

"A lot of people did."

"He was a likable guy." He paused for several

seconds, as though paying proper respect to the recently deceased. Finally he asked, "What can I do for you this morning?"

"More to the point, there's something I can do for you. I have information pertinent to Deputy Scott's investigation."

Registering surprise, he signaled for her to continue.

"Beck Merchant and I happened to be at the diner last night at the same time. Around ten o'clock."

"Um-huh," Red said, apparently unsure where this was going.

"As we left, I noticed that the tires of his pickup truck, as well as his boots, were caked with yellow mud. The kind that surrounds the fishing camp. I accused him of going out there and compromising the crime scene, possibly even tampering with evidence. He admitted that he was there. He went after the meeting at the house, where we were told that the cabin was considered a crime scene and that the entire camp was currently off-limits."

"Right."

"Right?"

"Beck was out there last night at my request."

It was as though he'd taken hold of the fringe of the rug on which she was standing. "Your request?"

"I asked him to meet me and Deputy Scott out there."

He yanked the rug out from under her.

Red continued, "I wanted somebody from the family—"

"He's not family."

"That's the reason I asked him to go out there, Sayre. Scott and I wanted someone from the family to walk through the cabin, see if there was anything that didn't belong, anything out of kilter, maybe something noticeably missing.

"I didn't have the heart to ask Chris or Huff to do it. It's still . . . well, it's a bloody mess, speaking frankly. There are companies that specialize in that kind of cleanup, but as long as we're still gathering evidence—"

"I think I understand," she said thickly.

"I didn't want to put Huff or Chris through an ordeal like that, but we needed somebody familiar with the cabin to take a look around, check for anything unusual or out of place."

Feeling like a complete fool, she murmured, "That makes sense."

She hadn't slept for wanting to report Beck Merchant's activity, which had seemed suspicious at best, and possibly criminal. Instead he had spared her family from a horrible chore, and for that she supposed she should be grateful.

His deceit, however, was another matter. When she'd challenged him about the mud on his tires and boots, he could easily have explained the situation to her, told her that he had granted the sheriff a favor that couldn't have been pleasant. He had deliberately set her up to look like an idiot.

"Did he?" she asked.

"Pardon?"

"Did Mr. Merchant find anything unusual, out of place, or missing?"

"I can't discuss the particulars of a criminal investigation while it's ongoing, Sayre. I'm sure you understand."

She understood perfectly. He was stonewalling her. "You're calling it a criminal investigation. Does that mean you're no longer convinced that Danny's death was a suicide?"

"Suicide is a crime, and as such must be investigated." Leaning forward, he said gently, "We're being thorough, is all. We want to be one hundred percent certain that at some point while he was fishing in Bayou Bosquet, Danny decided, for whatever reason, to take his own life. We'll probably never know all the answers."

"Did he leave a note?"

"Not that we've found."

Perhaps Danny had figured that if he wasn't important enough to take a call from, he needn't bother with writing a farewell note. Nevertheless, she said, "Don't you think it's odd that he didn't?"

"In at least half the suicides I've investigated, the person didn't leave a note." Looking at her kindly, he said, "The truth is, someone in that frame of mind can't explain even to himself why he's doing it. In such cases, we who are left behind are forced to accept the unacceptable."

It was a pretty speech, but if he'd been patting her on the head when he made it, he couldn't have sounded more patronizing. He was a member in good standing of the good ol' boys club, and even though she was a Hoyle by blood, she was, after all, only a female.

"What about the fishermen who discovered the body?"

"If you're implying foul play, they've been cleared of all suspicion. Their wives were with them, and those ladies were shaken up by what they saw in that cabin, believe me. We've got no reason to think they were anything other than passersby, and unlucky ones at that."

"Tell me about Gene Iverson," she said.

"Huh?"

Abruptly shifting the subject had been intentional. She'd wanted to see what kind of reaction she would get at the mention of the name, and she got one. The sheriff had gone whey-faced.

"I went to the library as soon as it opened this morning and got on the microfiche," she said. "The local newspaper's accounts were laughably slanted and incomplete, so I read the *Times-Picayune* coverage of Iverson's disappearance, Chris's arrest, and the eventual trial."

She now had a better grasp of the facts surrounding her brother's indictment. Eugene Iverson had been an employee of Hoyle Enterprises. Almost from his first day on the job, he had lobbied to organize a chapter of the ironworkers union. Although he performed his job without fault, he antagonized management personnel by rallying other disgruntled workers.

Eventually he threatened to organize a strike unless working conditions improved and safety measures as mandated by the Occupational Safety and Health Administration were implemented and enforced.

The threat of a strike agitated workers loyal to— or cowed by—the Hoyles. Many of the employees didn't welcome union interference and resisted mandatory membership. This fission of opinion caused friction in the workplace that hampered production.

Huff, wanting to prevent adverse publicity, OSHA's attention, and unionization, called a meeting between Iverson and upper management to see if they could reach an agreement they could all live with.

During that meeting Iverson denounced the lame concessions that Huff proposed. He said he couldn't be bought with a piddling pay increase and empty promises for improvements. He pledged that he would continue his efforts until Hoyle Enterprises was a union shop.

Iverson left the meeting and was never seen again.

"After Iverson stormed out, my brother made a remark about shutting up the agitator for good," Sayre said.

"That was testified to at his trial by the men who heard him say it. Under cross-examination by McGraw, they also testified that Chris said it in a joking manner." Red grinned wryly. "It was also cited that if you're planning to kill somebody, you don't announce it to a room full of people."

"You might if you're a Hoyle."

Sheriff Harper gave her a reproving look.

Sayre pressed on. "Iverson was trying to make my family accountable for all the work-related accidents at the foundry."

"They've been held accountable."

Now Sayre was the one to give him a look of reproof. "Their accountability is a joke. If they're caught violating a safety regulation that caused a maiming accident—and two deaths that I recall— Hoyle Enterprises pays a fine and considers it a cost of doing business. They get a slap on the hand, and that's the end of it until the next accident.

"And every time OSHA inspectors come, they clean up their act only long enough to pass inspection, then it's right back to business as usual. That foundry is a menace, and you know it, Red Harper.

"Iverson was an agitator," she continued. "He may have been the most obnoxious individual on the planet. I didn't know him, and I probably wouldn't have liked him if I had, but I admired what he was trying to do. Huff and Chris would not."

"Hundreds of workers didn't like what he was doing, Sayre. He was threatening their livelihoods. If they don't work, their families don't eat. Maybe Iverson could've afforded to strike, but they couldn't. Any number of them would have liked to see him dead."

"But no one did, see him dead, I mean. That's how Chris got off."

"Chris got off because the jury thought he was innocent."

"Only half of them."

It was a good shot, but it didn't dent the sheriff's armor. She hadn't really expected it to. She could sit here all day and fire verbal volleys at him and it would be a waste of time. Red Harper would go to his own grave covering for the Hoyles because they owned him body and soul.

She doubted his unflagging loyalty to them was founded on affection or allegiance or even avarice for the graft he took from them. Rather, it had become a habit he couldn't break. He was like a chain smoker who doesn't even realize when he's lighting up. Red had lied for her family for so long that it was a conditioned reflex, no longer a matter of conscience and choice.

And quite possibly he wasn't covering for them this time. Chris may have been unfairly accused, indicted by an ambitious prosecutor trying to make a name for himself by bagging a high-profile person with enviable wealth. In fact, that had been the theme of a newspaper editorial she'd read that morning. Her brother may have been a convenient celebrity scapegoat for a mystery that remained unsolved.

If he was innocent of the crime for which he'd stood trial, then her lingering suspicion was unfair. But if he had gotten away with murder, she wasn't going to hear it from Red Harper.

She gathered her handbag and stood up. "Thank you for seeing me without an appointment."

"You're welcome anytime, Sayre." He came from around his desk and ushered her toward the door. "Are you staying in town for a while?"

"I'm leaving this afternoon."

"Well, you take care out there. Lots of weirdos in San Francisco from what I hear." He stretched his droopy lips into what passed for a smile. "Deputy Scott has got all your phone numbers. I think he'll have his investigation wrapped up by tomorrow at the latest. I'll make sure he calls you when we make our official ruling."

"I would appreciate that." As she was leaving, she remembered Jessica DeBlance, and that caused her to hesitate. Danny's secret engagement could be relevant. But Red was on Huff's payroll. Anything said to him would go straight to Huff, and Jessica had said she didn't want Huff to know about their plans to marry.

Sayre wasn't even sure she would trust Wayne Scott with the information, because he would feel obligated to share it with his new boss. Until she had cleared it with Jessica, she decided to say nothing.

Something else was niggling at her, but she couldn't quite put her finger on it. Then, just as she reached the end of the hallway, she realized what it was. "Sheriff Harper?"

By now he had stepped back into his office. He poked his head out the door and looked at her inquisitively.

"Earlier you said that at some point while he was fishing Danny decided to take his own life."

"That's my best guess."

"I find that hard to accept."

"We've been through that, Sayre."

"I'm not talking about the suicide. It's the fishing I don't accept. Danny loathed fishing."

The moment Beck walked into Huff's office, he could tell the old man was upset. Before he could even say good morning, Huff picked up what appeared to be an enclosure card from a stack of similar cards on his desk and waved it at Beck. "This pisses me off."

Some would consider it unseemly that he and Chris had returned to work the day following Danny's funeral. The correct protocol probably would have been for them to take the rest of the week off. But Huff had never stood on ceremony, and his credo was that every day was a workday. In his book, there was no such thing as a holiday.

"What is it?"

Huff handed Beck the card. He sat down on the short sofa adjacent to Huff's desk. On the far side of the office was a wall of windows that overlooked the shop floor, which was a scenic view only if you were someone who profited from the grimy ugliness of iron pipe casting. It was dark, clamorous, hot.

Beck had a similar office down the hall, as did Chris and Danny. Chris had stumbled in a short while ago. The door to Danny's office remained closed this morning.

Beck looked at the card Huff had given him. "With deepest sympathy, Charles Nielson," he read. Then, looking across at Huff, he laughed shortly. "He sent flowers to Danny's funeral?"

"Can you believe the gall of that son of a bitch? Sally is going to send acknowledgments for me," he said, referring to his executive assistant. "I wanted to go through the cards before turning them over to her. Came across this one. Can't believe he would use my son's death as a means of pricking with me."

"The man has got guts. Have you had a chance to look through the file I left you?"

"I read enough to know that Nielson is only trying to build a name for himself. Those newspaper articles read like press releases he wrote."

"I tend to agree," Beck said. "But they're being published. He's a grandstander who thumps his own chest, but people are sitting up and taking notice. So far he's targeted only smaller shops, but he's been one hundred percent successful in bringing the union into those companies or winning extraordinary concessions from management. Now he's feeling flush with success. What I'm afraid of is that he's looking for a bigger bull's-eye that would place him in the media limelight."

"And you're afraid Hoyle Enterprises might be that target."

"We'd be a natural, Huff. We're a captive shop. Our castings are our product. We don't do castings for other manufacturers. So if only one aspect of the melting or casting process is affected—"

"Production suffers, we can't fill orders, and our business goes to crap."

"I'm sure Nielson realizes that. And, unfortunately, we've had some work-related accidents and deaths."

Huff came out of his chair with a heartfelt "Shit!" and went to stand at the window. Looking down, he said angrily, "You know how many men have worked here who never had a serious accident or injury? Huh?"

He came back around. "Hundreds. Do they write about that? Do these labor agitators paint picket signs with that statistic on it? Hell, no. But one worker bleeds a little and it makes news."

"Bleeds a little" was a gross understatement for the bloodletting involved when one's leg is crushed by pipes sliding off an unguarded vibrating conveyor, or the loss of a digit in a machine without a kill switch, or a burn that literally melted flesh off the bone. But Beck kept silent. Huff was too wound up to reason with.

"*Network* news, mind you," he ranted on. "Like somebody in New York City or Washington, D.C., knows anything about the way we do things down here. Bunch of bleeding-heart liberal, communist muckrakers." He sneered.

"An accident on the shop floor makes news, and next thing you know, I'm up to my ass in government inspectors. They parade in here with their clipboards and their sympathetic ears, and record every little gripe of those whiners." He waved his cigarette hand to encompass the men working below.

"When I was a kid, do you know how grateful I'd have been to have a job like theirs? Do you know how grateful my daddy would've been to have a regular paycheck?"

"You're preaching to the choir, Huff," Beck said softly. "Settle down before you stroke out."

"Bullshit is what it is," Huff muttered as he returned to his desk. He settled heavily into his chair. His color was high, and he was breathing hard.

"Are you taking your blood pressure medication?"

"No. I take that, my dick won't stay stiff."

It was no secret to anyone that at least once a week he visited a woman who lived on the outskirts of

town. As far as Beck knew, Huff was her only customer, and she was probably well compensated for
keeping it that way.

"Between high blood pressure and a limp dick,
I'll take high blood pressure, thank you."

"Hear, hear," said Chris, strolling in.

As always, he was immaculately groomed and
dressed. Not a hair out of place, not a single wrin-
kle. Beck often wondered how he managed that
when the temperature reached ninety degrees before noon.

"It sounds like I'm missing a very interesting
conversation. What's up? Pun intended."

While Huff poured himself a glass of water from
a carafe on his desk, Beck summarized for Chris
their discussion about Charles Nielson.

Chris dismissed the threat he posed. "We know
his type. These provocateurs come on strong and
then fade into obscurity. We just have to wait him
out."

"This one is distinguishing himself. I don't think
he'll fade that quickly."

"You're always the prophet of doom, Beck."

"That's what we pay him to be," Huff said
sharply. "Beck looks after these little problems so
they don't become big problems."

"I appreciate the vote of confidence," Beck said.
"How do you want me to respond to Nielson?"

"What do you recommend?"

"Ignore him."

Both Hoyles were startled by his terse suggestion. Beck gave them time to comment, but when
neither did, he outlined his reasons. "Sending flow-

ers to the funeral was a test. He knew it was in poor taste and did it only to see how you would react.

"I could send him a letter of denunciation, but that would signal anger or fear, and Nielson could use either of those reactions as ammunition against us. By ignoring him we're saying he's not even worthy of a response. He's insignificant. That's the strongest message we could send."

Huff tugged on his lips thoughtfully. "Chris?"

"I was going to suggest we burn his house down. Beck's approach is subtler." They all shared a laugh, then Chris asked, "Where's he from anyway?"

"He commutes between several offices scattered all over the county. One is in New Orleans. That proximity is probably how we came to his attention."

They mulled it over in silence for several moments. Finally Beck said, "I could draft a brief letter. Tell him—"

"No, I like the first option better," Huff said decisively. He struck a match and stood up as he lit a cigarette. "Let's sit back and wait, see what he does next, let the son of a bitch sweat over what we're thinking, not the other way around."

"Good," Beck said.

The telephone on Huff's desk rang. "Get that, will you, Chris? I gotta take a leak," he said as he crossed the room toward his private toilet.

Chris went to the desk and depressed the blinking button on the phone. "Sally, it's Chris. Did you need Huff?"

The nasally voice of Huff's long-suffering assistant could be heard through the speakerphone. "I know y'all are in a meeting, but I thought Mr. Hoyle—well, all y'all—would want to be interrupted for this."

"For what?"

"Your sister is downstairs, and she's raising Cain."

chapter 10

"Sayre is here?" Chris asked in shock.

On his way to the bathroom, Huff did an about-face.

Beck launched himself off the sofa and went to the wall of windows. He didn't see anything out of the ordinary on the shop floor. Everyone was going about his business.

"She came in through the employee entrance," Sally was saying, "not the visitors' entrance. The guard there is relatively new. He didn't recognize her. He's detained her, but she's demanding to be let inside the shop."

"Did she say what for?" Huff asked.

Sally hesitated, then said, "She says because she owns the place. But he was afraid to let her in without getting authorization first."

"Tell the guard to keep her there," Chris said. "We'll get back to him."

"She's giving him hell, and those are his words."

"Tell him I'm going to give him hell if he doesn't do his bloody job," Chris said before disconnecting.

Huff laughed through a fog of cigarette smoke. "Well, boys, it appears that our absentee partner has taken a sudden interest in the business."

Chris didn't seem to think Sayre's appearance was that funny. "I wonder why."

"Like she said, she owns the place," Huff said expansively. "She's got every right to be here."

"That's true," Beck said. "In every legal regard, she's a partner. But are you even considering letting her out onto the floor?"

"Absolutely not," Chris said.

"Why not?" Huff asked.

"For one thing it's dangerous."

Huff shot Beck a sly grin. "For years, we've been denying the potential hazards to the OSHA inspectors. If I would let my own daughter out there, I must be confident that it's as safe as a nursery. Right?"

It was typical of Huff to find an advantage, to use even an undesirable situation to suit his purposes. Beck had to admit that the slant he was giving this one wasn't without merit. But he still had misgivings, and apparently Chris was of the same mind.

As he moved toward the door, he said, "This is a bad idea, and I don't mind telling her so. After all, I'm the director of operations. If I say she can't go out there, she can't go."

"Wait a minute, Chris." Huff raised his hand. "If you take that kind of stance with her, she'll think we've got something to hide."

Beck could see the wheels of Huff's shrewd mind turning as he rolled the cigarette from one side of his mouth to the other. Then he looked across at Beck. "You go. Feel her out. Hear what she has to say. I trust your instincts. If you think it's best to escort her out, do that and lock the door behind her. But if you think our purposes would be better served by letting her take a look inside, give her the nickel tour."

Beck glanced at Chris. Operations was Chris's department, and Chris was territorial. He didn't look pleased, but he didn't countermand Huff. And possibly he would just as soon not have to hassle with Sayre.

Beck didn't particularly look forward to it.

Hoyle Enterprises had nearly six hundred employees, but only several dozen of them were women. They worked in clerical capacities in annex offices. Except for the executives' assistants like Sally, the production area of the plant was exclusively male.

The men reported to work and punched in their time cards in what they called the Center. It was one main room about the size of a modest convention center and was distinctly unattractive. The floor was concrete, the ceiling a network of exposed air ducts, electrical wiring, and water pipes.

Rows of army-green metal lockers took up almost half the square footage. Each employee was assigned a locker with a padlock where he could store his hard hat, safety glasses, gloves, lunch box, and other personal belongings. Signs alerted the workers that Hoyle Enterprises was not responsible for theft or loss, which were frequent because among the workforce were ex-cons and parolees desperate to find a job that would keep their parole officers satisfied.

Restroom facilities were located behind the lockers. The fixtures were the originals and looked it. Mismatched tables and chairs with chrome legs were scattered across the remainder of the open area to form the lunchroom. One wall was lined with vending machines and microwave ovens stained with the spatters of ten thousand meals.

A first-aid station had been sectioned off by a set of portable walls. It was unstaffed, leaving it up to the injured man to tend to himself with the limited inventory of medications and bandages.

The Center was where hardworking men took their breaks, swapped jokes, talked sports and women. Fifty or so were presently taking their morning break. Few of them had ever been this close to a woman of Sayre Lynch's caste and would have been no more surprised if a unicorn had appeared in their midst.

When Beck strode in, she was attempting to converse with a group of five seated around one of the tables. It appeared she was having limited success. In spite of having dressed down in a pair of jeans and a simple cotton T-shirt, she wasn't exactly blending into this blue-collar environment.

The men kept their heads bent and mumbled monosyllabic answers to her questions, casting furtive glaces up at her or at one another, evidently mystified by her presence and even more wary of her desire to chat.

As he approached, Beck forced himself to smile

warmly and to say for the benefit of their audience, "This is an unexpected pleasure."

Her smile was as phony as his. "I'm glad you're here, Mr. Merchant. You can explain to this gentleman that I need a hard hat for my tour of the foundry."

The "gentleman" to whom she referred was one of the security guards who manned the employee entrance. He'd been standing apart, as though afraid to get too close to Sayre. Now he rushed forward. His face was shiny with nervous perspiration. "Mr. Merchant, I didn't know if I should—"

"Thank you. You acted according to protocol. I'll escort Ms. Lynch from here." Beck gripped her elbow in a way that brooked no resistance and turned her around. "Come with me, Ms. Lynch. We keep hard hats for visitors over here."

"It was nice speaking to you," she said over her shoulder to the men she'd been trying to engage in conversation.

Beck propelled her through the maze of tables and chairs and into a supply room, which, fortunately, at the moment was vacant. As soon as he shut the door, she rounded on him. "They didn't want me talking to the workers, did they? They sent you to get rid of me."

"Not at all," he replied evenly. "Huff and Chris are pleased by your interest. But if you want to talk to someone about our operation here, ask me, not those men out there. Even in this new bargain basement outfit, you're too glamorous. You make them tongue-tied."

"They're not shy of me, they're cowed by and suspicious of anybody named Hoyle."

"Then why place them in such an awkward position?"

Rethinking it, she could see that he was right. "Perhaps that was unthoughtful of me. I'll find out much more by going on the shop floor anyway," she said. "Where's my hard hat?"

"You can see most of it from the windows in our offices upstairs."

"Those nice, clean, safe, air-conditioned offices? Not a fair representation at all, is it? I want to experience what the workers do."

"That isn't a good idea, Sayre," he stated firmly. "Chris oversees operations. That comes directly from him."

"Didn't he have the courage to come and tell me himself?"

"He was relying on my diplomacy."

"Exercise all the diplomacy you like. It won't change my mind."

"Then I'll be blunt." Placing his hands on his hips, he moved in closer. "What the hell are you doing here?"

"As you reminded me yesterday, I'm a partner of Hoyle Enterprises."

"Why today, when you've never shown one iota of interest in the business before?"

Unwilling to disabuse him of the misconception, she said, "It's time I got interested."

"Again, why? Is it because you weren't welcome here when you were a little girl? Chris and Danny got to spend time here, but I've been told it was off-limits to you. Did you resent not being one of the boys?"

Her eyes glittered dangerously. "Don't use that penis-envy bullshit on me. I don't have to explain my reasons to you."

He hitched his chin toward the door behind her. "To get through that door, you damn sure do."

"You're an employee, Mr. Merchant. Ergo, you work for me, don't you? I'm your boss."

Her haughty condescension infuriated him. It also aroused him, unreasonably but urgently. He wanted very badly to kiss her, to show her that not in all aspects was she boss.

Tamping down the impulse, he asked, "What do you hope to achieve?"

"I want to see if this place is as dangerous as it's reputed to be. Have the allegations of hazardous working conditions been exaggerated or, as I suspect, understated?"

"Of course it's hazardous, Sayre. It's a foundry. We melt metal. The business is rife with danger."

"Don't talk down to me," she said angrily. "I know it's inherently dangerous. All the more reason why every conceivable precaution should be taken to protect the men who do the work. I think Hoyle Enterprises has been grossly negligent in that regard."

"Our policy is—"

"Policy? As written by Chris and Huff and executed by George Robson, the toady of all toadies? You and I both know that policy and practice are too often strangers. Unless Huff has changed his tune in the past ten years—which I seriously doubt—his motto is 'Production at all costs.' Nothing stops production. Proof of that was yesterday, when he didn't even shut down for his own son's funeral." She paused to take a breath. "Now, please give me a hard hat."

Her truculent expression told him that she couldn't be talked out of this. The more he tried to dissuade her, the more determined she would become and, as Huff had surmised, the more suspicious that they had something to hide. Beck hoped, if he indulged this whim, she would have her curiosity satisfied and go on her way before causing any real damage.

Nevertheless, he gave it one last try. Pointing back toward the door, he said, "Did you see those men in there, Sayre? Did you look at them closely? Nearly all bear scars of one kind or another. The machinery can cut, burn, pinch, crush."

"I don't intend to get that close to any moving parts."

"No matter how careful you are, there are a thousand ways to get hurt."

"My point exactly."

Acknowledging that he was being baited, he removed two hard hats from the shelves behind him and thrust one at her. "Safety glasses, too." He passed her a pair. "Nothing I can do about your feet. Those are hardly steel-toed," he said of her shoes.

She put on the glasses first, then set the hard hat on her head.

"Not good enough." Before she could stop him, he removed the hard hat, gathered her hair and piled it on top of her head, then worked the hard hat down over it. The strands that escaped, he tucked beneath the hat. And not haphazardly, either. He took his time, standing close.

"Don't bother," she said. "I think that's fine."

"No loose strands, Sayre. I'd hate to see your hair singed by a flying spark or caught in a machine and ripped out by the roots. It could also be a distraction to the workers."

She tipped her head up. He looked past the glasses into her eyes. "As long as I've been here, there's never been a woman on the shop floor. There sure as hell has never been one who looked like you. They'll be checking out your breasts and your butt. There's nothing I can do to stop that. But I'd hate for a guy to get hurt because he was looking at your hair and imagining it sweeping across his stomach." He held her stare for several seconds, then put on his glasses and hard hat. "Let's go."

He opened a trapdoor into hell.

That was Sayre's first impression. The immensity of the heat struck her full force, like a wide hand pressing against the center of her chest and holding her on the threshold.

Beck was already several steps down the metal staircase leading to the shop floor. Sensing that she was hesitating, he looked back. "Changed your mind?" he shouted above the racket.

She shook her head and motioned for him to continue. He led her down the staircase. The treads felt so hot beneath the soles of her shoes, she was afraid the leather would dissolve.

It was a realm of noise and darkness and heat. The vastness of it amazed her. The space seemed infinite. She couldn't see the far end of it. Only blackness and more blackness relieved by showers of sparks and bubbling vats of liquid fire. Molten metal glowed white hot in giant ladles as they rocked along the overhead monorail. Metal clanged against metal, conveyor belts rolled, machinery clanked and clattered and churned.

The racket was incessant. The darkness encompassing. But the heat was inescapable. Once inhaled, it became one with you.

The Vulcans of this underworld were men with sweating faces behind safety glasses, who regarded Beck and her with a mix of deference and wariness. They were in constant motion, some operating several machines at once. There was no sitting down on this job. One had to be always watchful for a spark, a spill, a fall, a slip, because life and limb depended on it.

"You don't have to do this, Sayre," Beck said, speaking directly into her ear. "You don't have to prove anything to anyone."

The hell I don't. She looked up at the row of lighted windows high above them. As expected, there was Huff, the despot of this hell, standing with his feet widely spread, puffing a cigarette, the tip of it a smoldering red.

Turning away from the smug challenge she saw in his eyes, she said to Beck, "Show me more."

As they moved along, he said, "We cast a ferrous alloy of predominantly iron, some carbon and silicon."

She nodded but didn't even try to respond.

"Hoyle Enterprises collects scrap iron. We have sources in several states who ship it to us by rail. It comes in here by the ton."

Sayre supposed that unsightly mountain of scrap iron on the back side of the foundry was a necessary evil, although she remembered her mother asking Huff if there wasn't something he could build, a wall or fence of some sort, to conceal it from the highway.

He wouldn't even consider it because of the expense. He'd said, "If it weren't for that pile of junk, as you call it, you wouldn't have a mink coat and new Cadillac."

"The scrap iron," Beck continued, "is melted in furnaces called cupolas. The molten metal is poured into either a spin machine, which casts by using centrifugal force, or a sand-casting mold."

She watched as a ladle of molten metal was poured into one of the molds. She was impressed by the technology but staggered by the danger to the men operating the machinery and coming into such close contact with liquid fire and hot, rapidly moving parts.

"What's on his hands?" she asked, nodding toward one worker.

Beck hesitated, then said, "Duct tape. To make the gloves we provide thicker so his hands won't get burned."

"Why not just provide thicker gloves?"

"They're more expensive," he said brusquely, then nudged her around a puddle of molten metal that was bubbling on the floor. She glanced up to see it dripping from one of the ladles. The man overseeing the ladle was standing on a platform with no guardrails, she noted.

Beck went on to explain the process. "Once the metal has solidified inside the sand molds, they go through what we call shakeout. A vibrating conveyor literally shakes the sand away."

He nodded her toward an exit door. As he held it for her, he summarized as though talking to a fourth-grader on a class field trip. "Once the castings have been removed, the pipe goes through cleaning and inspection. We do a metallurgical check for metal quality and chemical content. Any defective product is recycled and goes back to the furnace. What began as scrap metal ultimately leaves the foundry in one of our trucks in the form of a pipe with a wide variety of uses. Any questions?"

She removed her safety glasses and hard hat and shook out her hair. "How hot does it get in there?"

"In the summer up to a hundred and thirty degrees. Not that bad during the winter months." He ushered her toward an elevator and pushed the up button.

Once they were inside the elevator, they both fixed their eyes on the light panel. She said, "One of the machines . . ."

"Yes?"

"Had a white cross painted on it."

He continued staring at the numbers above the elevator doors and took so long to respond that she thought he was going to ignore her. Finally he said, "A man died there."

She wanted to ask more, but when the elevator doors slid open, Chris was waiting to greet them. He smiled disarmingly. "Hello, Sayre. This is a new look for you, isn't it?" he said of the clothes she'd purchased in a store on the town square just before coming here. "Can't say I like it much. How was your tour?"

"Very informative."

"I'm glad you enjoyed it."

"I didn't say I enjoyed it."

Beck's cell phone rang. "Excuse me," he said, and stepped away from them to take the call.

Sayre said to Chris, "I saw nothing on the shop floor to dispel the allegations of safety and environmental violations for which you've been cited. What was the odor?"

"It's from the sand, Sayre," he said with exaggerated patience. "It has chemicals in it. Mixed with heat, those chemicals can give off an odor, which is sometimes unpleasant."

"And potentially harmful?"

"Name me an industry that doesn't have some occupational hazards."

"But there are modern ventilation systems that—"

"Are exorbitantly expensive. However, we're constantly looking into ways to improve our work environment."

"Speaking of the environment, I remember that we were heavily fined for polluting public water a few years ago. Runoff from cooling ponds, I believe."

His smile remained, but it had become fixed.

"We go out of our way to protect the local environment, too."

Patiently skeptical, she said, "Tell it to the EPA, Chris."

Beck ended his call and rejoined them. "You'll have to excuse me. A matter has come up that needs my immediate attention." He reached for the safety equipment Sayre had worn. "Can you find your way out?"

"It can't be that difficult."

Chris said, "It's a shame I can't take you to lunch before you leave town, but I also have business to attend to." He leaned forward and kissed her cheek. His eyes mocked her as he pulled away. "Have a nice flight, Sayre."

Together Beck and Chris watched her walk down the corridor and disappear around a corner. "Well, that's that."

"Not quite, Chris."

He turned to Beck. "You think she'll start bugging us about safety, environment, and so forth?"

"That remains to be seen. But she's been an awfully busy young lady this morning."

Chris arched his eyebrow. "Oh? Doing what?"

"For one thing, she talked to Red Harper. That was him on the phone. He's asked that you come to his office and address some questions."

Sayre didn't leave town immediately. Instead she drove through a neighborhood that lay practically in the shadow of Hoyle Enterprises' smokestacks. At one time, when she'd been young and naïve, when anything had seemed possible and the future had looked bright, just turning onto this residential street had made her giddy with joy. This house in the middle of this lower-middle-class neighborhood had been the center of her universe. It had signified hope, happiness, security, and love.

Today, seeing it filled her with despair.

The whole neighborhood had declined in the past ten years. But this house in particular had fallen into disrepair. The run-down condition of the place made her think that surely she had made a mistake, taken a wrong turn, had the wrong address.

But of course she hadn't. Despite the house's appearance, she recognized it. And if she doubted her memory at all, she had only to read the name on the mailbox to know she had the right one.

The front yard was littered with children's toys, many of them broken and seemingly abandoned. A few shrubs clung to life near the house, and they were in sad need of pruning. What grass there was grew in scattered patches. A metal glider sat rusting on the front porch. The paint on the exterior walls was blistered and peeling.

Although she told herself that she had come here on a whim, the truth was she had been toying with the idea of driving past this house ever since she arrived in Destiny. Now that she was here, she was stricken with a rare case of butterflies.

Before she could summon the courage to get out of her car, her cell phone rang. Recognizing Jessica DeBlance's number on the caller ID, she answered.

After they exchanged hellos, Danny's fiancée

said, "I don't want to bother you. I just called to ask if there had been any developments in Deputy Scott's investigation."

"I talked to Sheriff Harper this morning." Sayre told her that he, Deputy Scott, and Beck Merchant had conducted a careful search of the cabin the night before. "I gather they found nothing untoward because he said that Deputy Scott would conclude the investigation no later than tomorrow."

Dispiritedly, Jessica said, "Well, that's what I expected."

"Do you want me to mention the engagement to them?"

"No. It would get back to the Hoyles. They would probably blame me for Danny's suicide, like I was pressuring him into marrying me and drove him to it."

Unfortunately Sayre agreed. "I feel like I'm letting you down, Jessica." Like she had let Danny down by not speaking to him when he'd called her last week. "I wish I could do more."

"Your willingness to help me already has." After a short pause, she said, "Maybe I just need to accept that Danny wasn't as happy as I thought, that he had reasons unknown to me for wanting to end his life. He was deeply troubled by something. I suppose he couldn't live with it, whatever *it* was. Now, I'll never know."

"I'm sorry." This young woman's heart had been broken in two, and that lame platitude was all Sayre could say to her. It seemed woefully inadequate. However, she did promise to notify her when she heard anything from the sheriff's office.

They hung up just as the screen door of the house was pushed open and a man came out onto the narrow gallery. He was shirtless and barefoot, dressed only in a pair of stained blue jeans.

His manner was suspicious and belligerent as he called out, "Can I help you with something?"

chapter 11

Sayre realized she couldn't see who was inside the car because of the tinted windows. Feeling guilty for being caught spying, she was tempted to drive away. But she'd come this far, she might just as well go through with it. She lowered the window. "Hello, Clark."

The instant he recognized her, his lips formed her name, then his face broke into the smile that had melted hearts at Destiny High School when he was the star quarterback on the football team, president of the student body, the senior voted class favorite and most likely to succeed.

Clark Daly jogged down the front steps as she got out of the car. They met at the halfway point of the cracked walkway leading up to the house. They didn't hug, but he reached for her hand and tightly clasped it between his.

"I can't believe it." His eyes moved over her face, down her body, back up again. "You look just the same, only better."

"Thank you."

He looked neither the same nor better. His

athlete's body, always lean and hard, was now so thin that each rib was discernible. He had several days' growth of beard, and it wasn't a fashionable scruff—he had neglected to shave. His dark hair had thinned, making his forehead and brow seem more pronounced than she remembered. His eyes were bloodshot. And unless she was mistaken, there was alcohol on his breath.

He let go of her hand and took a step back, as though suddenly aware of how changed he must look to her. "I guess I shouldn't be all that surprised to see you," he said. "Did you come in for Danny's funeral?"

"Yes. I arrived yesterday morning just in time for it, and I'm on my way out now."

"I'm sorry I couldn't make it to the funeral. It's just, you know . . ." He waved his hand toward the house as though that would explain his failure to attend the services for Danny.

"That's all right. I understand."

There the conversation lapsed. She had a hard time looking him in the eye. Shyness was a typical reaction to seeing an old flame for the first time in years, but there were more profound reasons for the awkwardness between the two of them.

Injecting her voice with an artificial brightness, she asked, "So, what are you doing these days?"

"Working at the foundry."

She gasped with disbelief. "Huff's foundry?"

He laughed shortly. "That's the only one we've got."

"Doing what?"

He shrugged self-consciously. "Charging the furnace. Graveyard shift."

At first she thought he must be making a bad joke. But as she gazed into his sunken eyes, she saw a bleakness that was deep and absolute.

Her father had succeeded in ruining this man's life as thoroughly as if he'd shot him dead, as he had threatened to do.

"It's a living," he said, forcing a grin. "You want to come in, have some coffee?"

She lowered her head so he wouldn't see her dismay. "No, I have a flight to catch. Thanks, though." She was sure he hadn't really expected her to accept his invitation. It had been extended half-heartedly, out of obligatory politeness.

After another awkward silence, he asked softly, "Are you happy out there in California, Sayre?"

"How did you know that's where I live now?"

"Come on. You know what the grapevine around here is like. You've got a decorating business out there, right?"

"Home interiors."

"You'd be good at that. Do you have a . . . a family?"

She shook her head. "My marriages didn't last."

"I'm on my second."

"I didn't know."

"Four kids. Three of them hers. We've got one together. A boy."

"That's wonderful, Clark. I'm happy for you."

He ducked his head, slid his hands into the rear pockets of his jeans, and looked down at his bare feet. "Yeah, well, we all do the best we can, I guess. Play the cards that are dealt us."

She hesitated, then asked the pressing question.

"Why didn't you go into electrical engineering like you planned?"

"I couldn't."

"Why not?"

"Didn't you know? I never got to go to school. My scholarship was revoked."

"What?" she exclaimed. "Why?"

"I never was told why. Just one day I got a letter that said, basically, don't bother enrolling unless you can pay your own tuition because your academic scholarship has been rescinded. I tried for an athletic scholarship, but even the smaller colleges wouldn't grant me one because of that knee injury.

"Mom and Dad couldn't afford to send me to school, so I decided to work for a couple of years, save enough money to put myself through. But . . . well, things happened. Mom got cancer, and Dad needed help taking care of her. You know how it goes."

They both knew the reason his scholarship had been rescinded—Huff. He had pulled strings that probably had large amounts of money attached to them. He had vowed to ruin Clark Daly and he had. You could always trust Huff to keep his word. Clark was now on his payroll, doing backbreaking labor, and that must have given Huff tremendous satisfaction. He probably derived a daily chuckle or two out of it.

"I guess you're disappointed in me." With a self-deprecating laugh, Clark added, "Hell, *I'm* disappointed in me."

"I'm sorry things didn't turn out better for you.

There were extenuating circumstances you couldn't overcome. Namely Huff Hoyle."

"You didn't exactly have an easy time of it yourself, did you?"

"I survived, and survival was all my life felt like for years."

"Danny must have felt that survival alone wasn't good enough."

"I suppose."

"How are Huff and Chris reacting to his suicide?"

She motioned toward the smokestacks that dominated the town's skyline. "Nothing stops production. They're back at work today. Beck Merchant—I gather you know who he is."

His lips compressed into a hard line of dislike. "I know who he is, all right. Steer clear of him. He's—"

"Clark?"

A woman who appeared to be in her late twenties had come out onto the gallery. She was blond and pretty. Or would have been if not for her surly expression. A child about a year old, wearing only a diaper, was propped on her hip.

"Hey, Luce, this is Sayre Hoyle. Sayre, my wife, Luce."

"How do you do?" Sayre said pleasantly.

"Hi."

Her notable lack of friendliness seemed to embarrass Clark, who said quickly, "That's Clark Jr."

"He looks like a fine boy." Sayre divided a smile between the parents.

"He can be a handful," Clark said. "He skipped

walking and went straight from crawling to running."

"I'm going to be late for work," Luce announced ungraciously. The screened door slammed shut behind her as she reentered the house.

Clark came back around to face Sayre. "During summer break, I have to keep the kids while Luce works. She has a job at the hospital. In the records office, filing insurance claims, things like that."

"You work at night and babysit during the day? When do you sleep?"

"I manage." He shot her a smile, but it gradually faded. "Don't blame Luce for being rude. She's not mad at you. I'm the one who's put that chip on her shoulder. I'm not the most reliable husband." Lowering his voice, he said, "The truth is, Sayre, I'm a drunk. Ask around about me, that's the first thing folks will tell you."

"I would never pay attention to gossip, Clark. Especially about you."

"Well, the gossips would be right." He turned his head aside and gazed off into the distance for several moments. "After . . . You know . . ."

Yes, she did know.

"After all that, I got off track," he said.

"We both did."

His eyes moved back to her. "But you got back on. And look at you. Wow. You're something." He gave another humorless laugh directed toward himself. "Then there's me. I never got back on track. I went into a downward spiral and never saw much point in trying to pull myself back up. I didn't see the point in much of anything."

"I'm sorry." There they were again, those two words, heartfelt but utterly ineffective.

"Luce has stuck with me longer than she should have. She's given me more chances than I deserve to get my act together. I'll do all right for a while, then . . ." His voice trailed off, and he looked deeply into her eyes. His were filled with desperation. "I've got to find some purpose in life, Sayre. I've got to do right by my son."

"I'm sure you will. You'll regain your footing and go on. Just as I did."

She reached out and touched his arm in encouragement. He glanced down at her hand where it rested, then looked at her, and they smiled at each other, but their smiles were rueful expressions of regret over what might have been.

"I won't keep you," she said hoarsely, letting her hand fall away. "I should have called before I came by. Or maybe I shouldn't have bothered you at all."

"I wouldn't trade for seeing you, Sayre."

"Take care of yourself."

"You too."

Close to tears, she turned and walked quickly to her car. As she drove away, she glanced back at him. He was standing on the gallery, watching her. He raised his hand in farewell.

She drove two blocks before bringing her car to a stop in the shade of a railroad overpass, then reclined her head on the back of the seat and sobbed, crying like she hadn't cried over the loss of her own brother.

The Clark Daly she had known, that talented and smart, sweet and sensitive, promising and ambitious boy she had known and loved was, today, just as dead as Danny.

Red Harper had made the request sound innocuous, but Beck was convinced that it was neither optional nor unimportant.

Casual though Red wanted it to appear, Chris's being called into the sheriff's office to answer questions amounted to an interrogation. Beck hadn't used that term with Chris, though. With more offhandedness than he felt, he'd said, "Apparently there are some loose ends that need tying up."

"Why does Red need me to tie up his loose ends?"

"I guess we'll find out when we get there."

Beck hadn't planned on telling Huff about the meeting at all—not until he knew the substance of it. But as luck would have it, Huff intercepted them on their way out. As with Chris, Beck downplayed the sheriff's request. "I'm sure it's just a formality and shouldn't take more than half an hour, if that."

"What do you think it's about?" Huff asked.

"I think it's about Red humoring his ambitious new detective, Deputy Scott." The three of them laughed. Beck promised to give Huff a briefing as soon as they returned.

But now, as they were ushered into his office, the sheriff's bearing confirmed the seriousness of the meeting. He greeted them with a dour "Thanks for stopping by" and motioned them into chairs.

Wayne Scott moved to stand beside Red, who was seated behind his desk, so that both officers were facing Chris and Beck.

Before either Red or his detective had an opportunity to speak, Beck went on the offensive. "First off, I'd like to know in what capacity I'm here."

"Capacity?" Scott's puzzlement seemed feigned, and Beck was immediately mistrustful of it.

"Am I here to answer questions, or am I here as Chris's attorney, or—"

"Attorney?" Chris said. "Why would I need an attorney?"

With a look, Beck told him to shut up. "As I was saying, why was I asked here? Do you suspect me of some wrongdoing? In which case, I want my own lawyer present."

"Now, Beck," Red said with an uneasy laugh, "you're jumping the gun. There's no need for you to go all legal on us."

"I think there is, Red. Before we go any further, I'd like to know the nature of this meeting and the questions you intend to pose to Chris. Are you simply ironing out the details of Danny's suicide? Or do you have reason to believe that his death was a homicide?"

Scott avoided giving a direct answer. "It's just that a couple of things don't add up. I believe Mr. Hoyle might clarify them for us."

Beck glanced at Chris, who shrugged indolently. "I've got nothing to hide."

"All right," Beck said to Scott. "Ask your questions, but at any time, I may instruct my client not to answer."

"Fine." Scott consulted a small spiral notebook. "How often did the deceased go out to your family's fishing camp, Mr. Hoyle?"

"I don't know. Danny and I kept separate schedules. The last person there was responsible for cleaning up, turning out the lights, and replacing anything he'd used. Beer, toilet paper, necessities. That was the understanding. So it was difficult to tell when someone had been there." He looked at Red. "Is that important?"

"Could be," he replied with a noncommittal shrug. "Did Danny fish much?"

"I have no idea."

"This morning, your sister said—"

"My sister? You called me in here to verify or deny something that Sayre told you? What did she say?"

Beck held up his hand to silence Chris, then asked the detective, "Are you seriously basing this interrogation on something said by someone who hasn't even lived in Destiny for more than a decade and hasn't spoken to any member of her family in all that time?"

"She told Sheriff Harper that Danny loathed fishing. Her word, right, Sheriff? Loathed?"

"That's right."

Chris looked over at Beck and started to laugh. "What are they getting at? That somebody took a shotgun to Danny because he bad-mouthed fishing?"

"This isn't a joke," Scott snapped.

"Really?" Chris looked at him coldly. "I think you're hilarious."

Beck tried to improve the climate in the room. "What was Danny doing out at the fishing camp when he didn't like to fish? That's what you're trying to reconcile, correct?"

"Correct." Scott, who was still smarting from Chris's insult, looked toward him for an explanation.

"How the hell should I know?" Chris said. "Maybe he had decided to give fishing another try. Or maybe the last thing on his mind was fishing. He could have gone out there to pray. Or to take a nap. Or to jerk off. Or to do exactly what he did, which was to blow his brains out. The fishing camp afforded him privacy."

"Fishing gear was found on the pier."

"There you go," Chris said with an idle wave of his hand. "Danny was going to give fishing another try, test his loathing for it."

"Without bait? Tackle box, rod, everything was assembled there on the pier, but there wasn't any bait."

Chris gave each of them a look in turn, then raised his shoulders in a shrug. "I can't help you."

"It just looked sort of staged, you know?" Scott said. "Like somebody wanted us to think he'd gone there to fish, changed his mind, killed himself instead."

Chris snapped his fingers. "I think you're on to something, Deputy Scott. He forgot to buy bait, so he shot himself."

"Chris."

If Sheriff Harper hadn't reproved him for that remark, Beck would have. His sarcasm was inappropriate and certainly wasn't helping relations with the deputy.

"I apologize," he said, looking like he meant it. "I meant no disrespect to my brother. But these questions are asinine. Danny's reason for being at the camp is obvious. He went out there to kill himself, and he did." Fixing his dark gaze on Wayne Scott, he said, "Anything else?"

"When did you last see him?"

"Saturday. At the country club. We played several sets of tennis that morning. We quit around noon because of the heat. I stayed to swim for a while. Danny left right after our match."

"You didn't see him on Sunday?"

"Chris answered your question," Beck said. "He last saw Danny on Saturday morning. They parted company around noon."

"Where were you on Sunday?" Scott asked Chris.

"Home. All day. I slept late. Lounged around. Read the *Times-Picayune*. Beck came over in the afternoon, and we watched a Braves game on TV. Our housekeeper can vouch for me. Is this necessary?" he asked, suddenly turning to the sheriff. "What's this about, Red?"

"I'd like to know, too," Beck said.

"Indulge us just a little longer," Red said. "Hurry it along, will you, Wayne?"

The deputy consulted his spiral notebook again, but Beck figured that was window dressing. Scott seemed to have a direction already. "Where were you on Saturday night?"

"What difference does it make?" Chris countered impatiently. "Danny wasn't there."

"Where were you?" Scott repeated.

Chris held the detective's stare, rocking slightly back and forth in his chair, clearly furious over having to answer to someone he felt was inferior. Eventually he said tightly, "I went to a new nightclub in Breaux Bridge. It had a great band. Pretty cocktail waitresses. You should try it, Deputy. Let it be my treat."

But Deputy Scott was unimpressed with the offer. "Do you smoke, Mr. Hoyle?"

"Not habitually. Sometimes when I'm out."

"Did you smoke on Saturday night at the new club in Breaux Bridge?"

Beck jumped in before Chris had time to answer. "Nothing more from Chris until I know where this is going."

Scott looked down at Red Harper, whose hangdog face seemed to have stretched another several inches since the interrogation began. With apparent reluctance, he opened one of his desk drawers and withdrew a brown paper sack, like the ones they used for collected crime scene evidence. He handed it to the deputy, who made a production of opening it and shaking out the contents onto Red's desk.

chapter 12

"Beck—"

"Not until we get outside."

"But this is—"

"Not until we get outside," Beck repeated with emphasis. Ignoring the startled staff, he pushed Chris down the hallway, through the anteroom, and then out the door of the sheriff's office.

He didn't allow Chris to speak until they were inside his pickup, which felt like a convection oven cooking them from all directions. He started the motor and set the air conditioner on high, then turned to his friend, who it now appeared was a suspect in a homicide investigation.

"Tell me."

"There's nothing to tell," Chris said with remarkable calm. "Just like I told Red and that . . . that deputy." He spoke the word like an insult. "Regardless of what he found at the fishing camp, he can't link it to me. I was not there on Sunday. Selma knows I didn't leave the house all day. You yourself were with me for several hours. I did not see or talk to Danny after Saturday morning at the country club."

"Where the two of you were overheard having a heated argument."

"Over a baseline call. Who doesn't argue over tennis? Jesus."

"Him, too."

"What? Oh." Chris directed the vent in the dashboard toward himself so he could catch the blast of air that was finally beginning to turn cool. "True enough. According to Danny I blasphemed and said some derogatory things about his Holy Roller church. He was my brother. I saw my brother taking a wrong path. I was entitled to my opinion."

"But did that entitle you to ridicule?"

Chris sighed. "Huff had asked me to see if I could talk sense into Danny, turn him around. If I got a little sarcastic—"

"You came down on him pretty hard, if those witnesses that Scott talked to heard correctly. Did they?"

"I don't remember exactly what I said."

" 'I don't remember what I said.' Not a very solid defense to take into court, Chris."

Chris looked at him sharply. "Court?"

"Haven't you caught on yet? They're trying to put you at the scene. They're this close to placing you at the spot where a shotgun blasted Danny's head all to hell."

"They can't place me there because I *wasn't* there."

Beck looked at him hard. "You cannot lie to me,

Chris. If this thing turns ugly, I don't want any surprises sprung on me."

"What do I have to do? Cross my heart and hope to die?"

"Fine. Be funny. This is all a huge gotcha joke."

Chris relaxed his smirk. "Look, I realize you're in lawyer mode now. Like Huff said, you're paid to worry, so we don't have to. But I don't know what else I can say to convince you that I wasn't at the fishing camp this weekend.

"The last time I was there was that night several months ago with you. And the last time I saw Danny, he was headed for the locker room at the country club on Saturday morning. He'd gone round the bend with that religion nonsense. He was supersensitive to criticism of it. I made some irreverent cracks about it, so, yes, he left a little hot under the collar."

"What about you? What was your mood when you separated? Danny was always so tractable. Suddenly he's developed a stubborn streak. How did that sit with you?"

"I admit I was upset with him for making such a fool of himself in front of those Bible beaters. A lot of them work for us. We can't have them thinking we're pussies, for the Lord or anything else. I was angry.

"To cool myself off, I did laps in the pool, then went to Lila's house as soon as she called me with the all-clear, and spent the rest of the afternoon between her strong thighs. It's amazing how much frustration you can work off having sex with a rough and rowdy partner like Lila. Her creativity knows no bounds."

"Spare me the details."

"Your loss, friend. Anyway, I left her house around five, went home to change, then drove to Breaux Bridge. That's it. There's nothing more to tell." Spreading his hands, palms up, he looked at Beck imploringly. "Besides, give me one good reason why I would want to kill Danny."

"We have that going for us," Beck said. "Lack of motive. But they're trying to place you out there, and that eager young detective is going to be digging for a motive. If there's something I don't know—"

"There isn't."

"You'd better tell me now, Chris. Don't lie to me. Should I be soliciting a trial lawyer, putting a criminal defense attorney on the payroll?"

"No."

Beck's cell phone rang. He checked the caller ID. "It's Huff."

Chris covered his eyes with his hand. "Fuck."

Beck answered. "Hey, Huff, we're leaving now and should be back in five minutes. Want a Blizzard? We could swing past the Dairy Queen. You sure? Okay then. Yes, I'll fill you in the minute we get there." He clicked off and said to Chris, "We're not to stop for anything on the way back. He's waiting for us."

"How much should we tell him?"

"Everything. If we don't, he'll get it from Red. Outside of Wayne Scott's hearing, of course."

"That's the other thing I've got going for me," Chris said. "Good ol' reliable Red Harper. He's not going to let me get hit with another bogus murder rap."

*　　　*　　　*

Sayre didn't make the drive back to New Orleans. Following her visit to the foundry, her conversation with Clark, and the resultant crying jag, she was physically and emotionally whipped. Driving for two hours, then having to contend with the inconveniences of modern air travel held no appeal whatsoever.

One of her clients in San Francisco was president of a jet charter service. He owed her a favor for redecorating his Russian Hill town house under a ridiculously short deadline. She placed a call to him. He lent a sympathetic ear and then asked for five minutes to make the arrangements. He called her back in four. "Luckily we had an available plane in Houston. It's on its way to you now."

"Can the runway here accommodate a private jet?"

"That was the first thing I checked. There's some big outfit in Destiny, a metal pipe manufacturer. They have a company jet."

She remembered now Beck mentioning that, but she didn't tell her client that she was a partner in that "big outfit."

"Leave your rental car keys with the airfield personnel," he told her. "Someone will pick the car up later and drive it back to New Orleans."

The royal service was a rare luxury for her, but she could afford it. And if it got her out of Destiny sooner rather than later, it would be well worth the cost.

When she reached the airfield, she parked the rental car in the designated space and retrieved her overnight bag from the backseat. As she entered the compact building, a middle-aged woman approached her. "Are you Ms. Lynch?"

"That's right."

"Your plane's coming in now, honey. Have you got car keys for me?"

The concrete tarmac was like a broiler when Sayre walked out to greet the distinguished-looking gray-haired pilot who stepped out of the small, sleek jet that had taxied to within twenty yards of the building.

"Ms. Lynch?"

"Hello."

"I'll be your captain on this flight." He introduced himself, and they shook hands. Once they were aboard, he introduced his copilot, who waved at her from the cockpit. Then the captain pointed out the emergency exits and showed her where drinks and snacks were stored. "Make yourself at home."

She thanked him, and he went forward to take his seat in the cockpit. Relieved to be under way and grateful to relinquish control to someone else, Sayre rested her head against the cool leather upholstery of her seat and closed her eyes. Within minutes, the plane began its taxi to the end of the runway.

She was dozing by the time it turned and positioned itself for takeoff.

But rather than the engines revving as she expected, they gradually whined to a stop. She opened her eyes to see the captain squeezing himself out of the cockpit. "Sit tight, Ms. Lynch. We've got a situation here, but I'll take care of it and then we'll be on our way." He spoke politely and calmly, but she could tell that he was hopping mad about whatever had held them up.

He released the lock on the door, pushed it open, and rushed down the steps. "What the hell do you think you're doing?" he demanded.

"I need to see your passenger."

Sayre unfastened her seat belt and moved toward the door. The pilot's back was to her. He was reading the riot act to Beck Merchant, who seemed unfazed.

"I tried to get the lady in the terminal to radio you not to take off, but she refused," he explained. "She said I had no authority. I didn't know how else to stop you."

Sayre climbed down the steps. When Beck saw her, he motioned toward his pickup truck, which was idling in the center of the runway directly in front of the jet. "Get in."

"Have you lost your mind?"

"Huff's had a heart attack."

Beck glanced at his passenger. "Aren't you the least bit curious to know what happened?"

Sayre hadn't spoken a word since he boosted her into the cab of his truck. She turned her head toward him now. Her expression was impassive, but at least she was looking at him.

"Huff was in his office," he said. "Sally, his assistant, heard him cry out. She rushed in, found him slumped over his desk, clutching his chest. Her quick thinking may have saved his life. She pushed an aspirin tablet into his mouth and then called nine-one-one.

"Chris and I got to the hospital right behind the ambulance. We were there maybe half an hour—although it seemed longer—before they allowed Chris to see him. They only let him stay in the ICU about five minutes. He said they were trying to get Huff stabilized but he was fighting them. He was extremely agitated and asking for you. I was dispatched to locate you and bring you back."

"Did they give Chris a prognosis?"

"Not yet. They're still trying to assess the severity of the attack. All I can tell you is that when I left the hospital, Huff was still alive. I told Chris to call me on my cell if there was some drastic change. He hasn't."

"How did you know where to find me?"

"The car rental company. I called the branch office in New Orleans to see if you'd turned in your car yet. I was told you were leaving it at the airfield here to be picked up later. I raced out there." After a pause, he said, "I offered you the company jet."

"And I declined the offer. I wouldn't avail myself of the company jet when the company doesn't provide adequate work gloves to its employees because they're more expensive. How expensive can work gloves be?"

"That's not my department."

She looked at him with contempt. "Right. You're their errand boy. They send you to do their dirty work. You could have caused a catastrophe by driving onto an active runway."

"The captain mentioned that."

"But his words bounced right off you. You pulled an arrogant stunt like that because you knew you could get away with it. No wonder you fit in so well with my family."

Beck's grip on the steering wheel tightened. "You don't approve of my methods? Fine. It's not your approval I'm after. I was asked by my employer to find you and bring you to the hospital, and that's what I'm doing."

"And you always do what they tell you to do. It doesn't matter if it's right or wrong, or how it may affect someone else." Tilting her head slightly, she appraised him. "How far would you go for them, I wonder. Where would you draw the line? Or would you ever?"

"You've already made clear your low opinion of me."

"Last night at the diner, why didn't you tell me that you were at the fishing cabin because Sheriff Harper had asked you to be there?"

"And spoil your fun? You wanted to think the worst of me, and I handed you an opportunity to do so."

She turned her head away and stared out the passenger window. Anger was radiating off her like the heat rising out of the hot asphalt. Her hair shimmered like flame in the glaring sunlight. Her skin looked feverish; it would be hot to the touch. *Better not to think about touching her.* Although it did no good to tell himself that. He had thought about little else since seeing her for the first time.

Yesterday at the cemetery, when he'd come face-to-face with Huff's daughter, he'd had a hard time concealing his shock. Naturally, he'd seen pictures of her, but they were pale representations of the real thing. In the flesh, she made a stunning physical impact that could never be captured two-dimensionally.

He'd thought, This is Chris's younger sister about whom I've heard so many wild tales? This is the femme fatale of Destiny, the Lolita, the little sister of vicious tongue and vile temper fame?

He had expected her to be loud and vulgar. He'd expected a flashy dresser who flaunted a voluptuous figure, not a sophisticated fashion plate with impeccable taste. She'd made understated elegance sexy and tantalizing.

She'd been described to him as a firebrand, a spoiled brat, a pain in the ass, a harridan. All of which he was certain she could be. But Chris had failed to mention that his sister was a woman of alluring mystery. Because incongruent with the appropriate clothing and air of cool condescension was a restlessness that hinted at a latent passion, an unmined lode of sensuality that flowed far beneath the surface of her hauteur.

Of course Chris, being her brother, wouldn't have noticed all that, especially the sexual aspects of the inner Sayre. Beck reasoned that she counted on that shortsightedness. She didn't want anyone to see past that off-putting manner she had affected to safeguard the real her.

But Beck had seen beyond it. He'd caught only a few glimpses of what she would be like if that referenced wild streak asserted itself, and they had excited him. The thought had made his belly jump with expectation and his skin tighten with the strain of concealing it. He'd seen her lips part in astonishment over his bold statement about her hair as he was tucking it under the hard hat. He'd imagined gently biting her full lower lip, for starters. And then he'd fantasized beyond that first taste of her. He'd imagined tapping into that underlying vein of sensuality. His life would be much easier right now if he hadn't.

As he sped toward the hospital, she continued to ignore him, which was damned annoying. He would rather she do anything other than pretend he wasn't there. "Are you comfortable?"

She looked across the seat at him. "What?"

"The air conditioner. Too much? Not enough?"

"It's okay."

"You may pick up some of Frito's shed hair on that seat. I apologize for that. He likes to ride—"

"If the heart attack was so severe that Huff is asking to see his children before he dies, shouldn't he be helicoptered to a hospital in New Orleans, where there's a cardiac center?"

He didn't mind being interrupted. At least she was talking now. "I suppose that could be an option once they determine the seriousness of his condition."

"Before today, has he shown any symptoms of a heart ailment?"

"High blood pressure. He's supposed to take medication for it, but he doesn't like the side effects. He smokes constantly, sometimes I think out of sheer defiance of the warnings against it. His only form of exercise is rocking in his rocking chair.

He makes his café au lait with half-and-half. He threatened to fire Selma if she ever again substituted turkey bacon for the real thing. He was probably a heart attack or stroke waiting to happen."

"Do you think Danny's death contributed?"

"No doubt. Losing his son, especially under those circumstances, coupled with the repercussions, has been stressful."

"What repercussions?" she asked.

"Here we are."

He parked in the hospital parking lot and alighted from the truck before she could ask him again about the repercussions of Danny's death. Did she really need to know that Huff had suffered his heart attack less than an hour after he and Chris had recapped for him their unsettling meeting with Red Harper and Deputy Scott?

With typical cocksureness, Chris had told Huff that it was nothing to worry about, that Wayne Scott had rattled sabers just to impress everybody with how big and bad he was, that the so-called evidence they had was so flimsy it was funny.

"He's justifying his employment at my expense," Chris had said. "That's all there is to it. Beck will make mincemeat of him and his investigation. Mark my words, in a couple of days, we'll be having a good laugh over this."

Beck had said something similarly dismissive, but apparently it had stressed Huff past endurance to think that one of his sons would even be considered capable of fratricide.

Beck saw no advantage to discussing that with Sayre and instead went around to open the passenger door for her. By the time he reached it, she was stepping from the cab and declined the hand he offered. When she turned back to get her overnight bag, he said, "Leave it. I'll lock the truck."

She hesitated, then gave a curt nod, and together they walked toward the hospital entrance. He allowed her to go ahead of him through the revolving door. When it emptied him into the lobby, he bumped into Sayre, who had barely cleared the door before coming to a dead stop.

Almost knocking her down and losing his own balance, he took her lightly by the shoulders and caught her up against him, their bodies making accidental intimate contact in a way that at any other time would have stopped his breath. It would have now, except for his puzzlement over why she'd stopped so suddenly.

Dr. Tom Caroe was coming toward them from across the lobby. He was a short man, who carried his narrow shoulders in a perpetual stoop. The poor posture made him appear even more diminutive. His clothes always looked several sizes too large, as though he had shrunk after putting them on. His sparse hair was dyed unnaturally black in an attempt to conceal his advanced years, which the lines on his face gave away.

As he reached them, he said hello to Sayre and extended his right hand. But when she made no move to take it, he quickly let it drop to his side. To cover his embarrassment, he said, "Thank you for bringing her so soon, Beck."

"No problem. How is he?"

Sayre, overcoming her shock—or whatever it

was that had caused her to become transfixed—
shrugged his hands off her shoulders and moved to
stand at his side.

"He's stable," Dr. Caroe told them. "I need him
that way before conducting any more tests."

Speaking for the first time, Sayre issued a direct
challenge to the family physician's competence.
"Are you qualified to make a diagnosis? Shouldn't
a cardiac specialist be consulted?"

"Yes, I think one should be," he replied evenly.
"But Huff doesn't. He was quite insistent about it."

"Maybe I can convince him otherwise." Beck
nudged Sayre toward the elevator. "What floor?"

"Second. He's in ICU," the doctor said. "Your visits will be limited to a few minutes per hour. He needs
absolute rest." Focusing on Sayre, he added, "He particularly wanted to see you, which, frankly, I think is
inadvisable. But if you do speak with him, keep in
mind his condition and don't say anything that's likely
to upset him. Another arrest could kill him."

Chris looked up when the elevator doors opened
and she and Beck stepped out. "Well, well, Sayre.
Thank you for troubling yourself to come back."

She ignored him, which was one's best defense
against Chris.

"We ran into Tom Caroe downstairs," Beck told
him.

"Then you know as much as I do." Chris looked
at her. "Huff's been asking for you."

"Do you know why?" she asked.

"Haven't the faintest. I thought you might be
able to shed some light."

"No."

"Maybe it has something to do with your sudden interest in our operation."

"As I said, Chris, I don't know."

That ended the conversation. They took seats in the waiting room and tried to avoid making eye contact. Eventually, Beck stood up and announced that he was going in search of a vending machine. Sayre declined his offer to bring her back a soft drink.

"I'll go with you," Chris said, and followed Beck from the waiting room, leaving her alone to dread the visit with Huff.

It was impossible to envision a repentant Huff, but he had never faced his mortality before. As he stood looking into the abyss, was he fearing the hell he had repudiated? Faced with the probability of spending eternity there, was he wanting to beg her forgiveness and make atonement?

If so, he would be wasting his dying breath. She would never forgive him.

She was still alone in the waiting room when a nurse informed her that she could go in. Sayre followed her to where Huff lay connected to machines that blipped and bleeped with reassuring regularity. A cannula was feeding oxygen into his nostrils. His eyes were closed. The nurse silently withdrew.

Staring into his face, Sayre marveled at how completely the man to whom she owed her life had destroyed her love for him. She remembered being a young girl and looking forward to his coming home from work each evening. He announced his arrival in a voice that boomed through the hallways of the house, filling it with a vitality it lacked when he wasn't there. He was the heart that pumped life—be it good or bad—into the family.

She remembered when his slightest notice of her was better than the gifts she received on Christmas morning. She had treasured his miserly approval. Even though he frightened her at times, she remembered loving him with wholehearted and unqualified devotion.

But then, she had been seeing him through the eyes of a child, which were blind to his depravity. When her eyes were opened and she was made to see it, it was the most painful, disillusioning experience of her life.

She stood at his bedside for several moments before he became aware of her. When he opened his eyes and saw her, he smiled and spoke her name.

"Are you comfortable?" she asked.

"Now that they've got me doped up."

"You're stabilized. Blood pressure. Heart rate. All that."

He nodded absently, barely listening. His eyes were roving over her face. "I fought your mother on naming you Sayre. I thought it was a silly name. Why not Jane or Mary or Susan? But she insisted, and now I'm glad she did. It suits you."

She refused to walk hand in hand with him down memory lane. It would be shamefully hypocritical. She brought the subject back to his condition. "It must have been a mild attack or you wouldn't be feeling this well. The damage to your heart couldn't be too severe."

"So you're a cardiac specialist now?" he asked caustically.

"No, but I've had a lot of experience with damaged hearts."

He tipped his head as though to say, *Nice shot.* "You're a hard, unfeeling creature, Sayre."

"I learned by example."

"Referring to me, I suppose. Your mother—"

"Please don't invoke Mother, especially in order to make me feel guilty for standing up to you. No, I'm not the sweet, compliant lady she was, but I don't think she would like the way any of us turned out."

"You're probably right. Danny, maybe. I think she would've liked him. I'm glad she wasn't here to see him dead and buried."

"I'm glad of that, too. No mother should have to bury her child."

His eyes narrowed. "You probably don't believe this, Sayre, but I grieve for Danny. I do."

"Who are you trying to convince, Huff? Me or yourself?"

"Okay, don't believe me. But I've had plenty to be upset about. First Danny. Now Chris coming under suspicion."

"Chris . . . What? What do you mean?"

"Ms. Hoyle?"

It was the nurse, coming to remind her to keep the visit short. She nodded, not bothering to correct the name.

"Don't mind her," Huff said after the nurse withdrew. "She wouldn't dare throw you out."

The sad fact was, Sayre couldn't wait to leave him. "You'll recover, Huff. I don't think even the devil is ready for you."

One side of his mouth tilted up in a grin. "He wouldn't appreciate the competition."

"The devil is no competition for you."

"I think you mean that."

"Oh, I do."

"Mighty harsh words to lay on a man who could have died a few hours ago. You've harbored this grudge for years. Isn't it time you stopped being so goddamn angry with me?"

"I'm not angry at you, Huff. Anger is an emotion. I don't feel anything for you. Nothing."

"Is that so?"

"Yes, that's so."

"Then why did you rush back here to see your poor ol' daddy one last time before he cashed in?"

"Why did you send for me?"

He grinned craftily, then laughed out loud. "To prove that you'd come running. And lookee here, Sayre. Here you are."

chapter 13

"What do you think they're talking about?"

Beck looked across at Chris, shrugged, and continued to thumb through the outdated *People* magazine. "What's the problem between them?"

"It goes back to when Sayre was a teenager. She was high school sweethearts with Clark Daly."

Beck looked at him pointedly.

"Yes, that's the one," Chris said.

Beck knew Clark Daly from the foundry. Several times his foreman had sent him home for reporting to work drunk. He was even caught with a flask of whiskey in his lunch box. It was surprising to learn that Sayre had been involved with him.

"For a while Huff was okay with their little romance," Chris continued. "It seemed harmless enough. But when it looked like the puppy love was growing more serious, he put a halt to it."

"Did he have a drinking problem back then?"

"Nothing worse than sneaking a beer every now and then. He was a star athlete, student leader."

"Then what was the problem?"

"I don't know the details. I was already at LSU. I wasn't interested in Sayre's affairs and didn't follow the courtship closely. I only know that Huff wasn't too keen on having Clark Daly as his son-in-law. As soon as they graduated high school, he stepped in and put a stop to the romance."

"How did Sayre react?"

Chris gave a crooked smile. "How do you think? With fireworks on the scale of Vesuvius. Or so I've been told. When her tantrums didn't make an impact on Huff, she went into a deep funk, lost a lot of weight, moved around the house like a ghost. Who's that character in the book, traipses around in her moldy wedding gown?"

"Miss Havisham?"

"Right. I remember coming home one weekend and barely recognizing Sayre. She looked like hell. She wasn't attending college, wasn't working, wasn't doing anything, and never left the house. When I asked Selma about it, she started crying, told me Sayre had turned into a 'poor little haint, bless her heart.' Danny said she hadn't spoken to Huff for months, avoided being in the same room with him."

Chris paused to take a sip of his canned soft drink. Beck wanted to know the rest of the story but didn't prod Chris to continue. He didn't want to appear overly interested. Fortunately, Chris continued without being prompted.

"This went on for months. Finally Huff had his fill of it. He told her to stop sulking and get it together, or he was going to send her to a psychiatric hospital."

"That was Huff's cure for a teenage broken heart? He threatened to commit her?"

"It sounds severe, doesn't it? But it worked. Because when Huff picked out a guy and insisted she marry him, she went willingly enough to the altar. I guess she figured marriage was better than the loony bin."

Beck stared thoughtfully at the closed double doors that led into the ICU. "That's a long time to hold a grudge against Huff for coming between her and her high school sweetheart."

"That's Sayre. Even when she was a little kid, she always had a burr up her butt over something. She's still like that. Takes every little thing so damn seriously." He stood up and stretched his back, then moved to the window.

For a long time, he stood there silently, staring out, seemingly at nothing. Eventually Beck asked, "Something on your mind, Chris?"

He raised his shoulders with an indifference that Beck knew was feigned. "That business today."

"It's been an eventful day. Which business?"

"In the sheriff's office. Will they arrest me, do you think?"

"No."

"I didn't like jail the first time, Beck. Huff bailed me out within hours, but it's not a place where I want to spend any amount of time."

"They're not going to arrest you. They don't have enough evidence yet."

Chris came around. "*Yet?*"

"Is there more for them to find, Chris? I need to know."

His dark eyes flashed. "If my own lawyer doesn't believe me, who will?"

"I believe you. But you have to admit that, right now, it's not looking very good for you."

Chris relaxed his stance. "Right, it's not. I've been giving this a lot of thought, and I've come to a conclusion." He paused, then said, "Somebody's framing me."

"Framing you?"

"You sound skeptical."

"I am."

Chris returned to his chair and leaned across the narrow space separating them. "Think about it, Beck. Because of that Iverson case, which is still on the books as an unsolved missing person and possible homicide, wouldn't I make an ideal fall guy?"

"For whom?"

"Slap Watkins."

Beck laughed shortly. "Slap Watkins?"

"Hear me out," Chris said irritably. "He resents the Hoyle brothers. You, too, for that matter. He's got an ax to grind."

"Over a barroom brawl that took place three years ago?"

"But he hasn't forgotten it. You told Huff he mentioned it to you in the diner last night."

"Okay, but—"

"It's not just that. On a hunch, I had Danny's secretary check the job applications we've received over the last few weeks, and guess what turned up?" He withdrew a folded sheet of paper from his trousers pocket and waved it at Beck. "Slap Watkins filled one out."

"He applied for a job at the foundry?"

"Danny rejected his application. Slap has another reason to dislike the Hoyles."

"Enough to murder Danny?"

"A guy like that, it wouldn't take much provocation."

"I suppose it's feasible," Beck said thoughtfully. "Certainly worth checking into."

"Have you mentioned this to Red?"

"Not yet. I'd just seen the rejected application when Huff had his heart attack. I haven't had a chance to talk to anybody about it."

Beck thought for another moment, then shook his head. "There's a problem with it, Chris."

"What?"

"How did Watkins get Danny out to the fishing camp?"

Chris considered the question for several seconds before admitting that he didn't know. "But he was a cagey bastard to start with, and he had three years' coaching in prison." Glancing up, he saw Sayre emerge from the ICU. "We can talk about it later."

They stood up as she approached. "He's fine," she declared. "Hardly on the brink of departing this world."

"Then why was he so adamant about seeing you?"

"No cause for alarm, Chris. He didn't change his will and appoint me his sole heir, if that's what you're worried about. He called me back for his own entertainment." Turning to Beck, she said, "Will you please go outside and unlock your pickup so I can get my bag?"

"Are you flying out tonight?"

"I dismissed the jet because I didn't know when I would be leaving. But I hope the rental car . . . What?" she asked, when Beck started shaking his head.

"It's already been picked up. I took the liberty of calling for you to check."

"Well, I planned on spending the night at The Lodge anyway. I'll get another car tomorrow." Beck offered to drive her to the motel, but she said, "I'll call a taxi."

Chris informed her that Destiny's only taxi company was no longer in service. "It folded years ago."

It was clear to Beck that she wanted to remove herself from them as swiftly as possible and was irritated by these roadblocks to her escape. "All right," she said with resignation. "If it's not too far out of your way, I would appreciate a ride to the motel."

"No trouble at all. Chris, are you staying here?"

"I'll hang around until Doc Caroe comes back for his evening rounds. If he thinks Huff is out of immediate danger, I'll leave."

They agreed to keep their cell phones handy in case one needed to notify the other of a change in Huff's condition and said their good-byes.

On their way to the ground floor, Beck asked for a more detailed assessment of Huff's condition. "If meanness equates to longevity," she said, "he'll outlive us all."

Then she pushed through the revolving door. He wanted to pick up the conversation outside, but reading her body language, he thought better of asking her to recount what she and Huff had said to each other.

"You look tired," he said as he gave her a hand up into the cab of the truck.

"Encounters with Huff always leave me feeling tired."

He went around and got in. As he turned the ignition key, he apologized for the heat inside the cab. "I should have left the windows open an inch or so."

"I don't mind it." She laid her head on the back of her seat and closed her eyes. "When it's fifty degrees in July in San Francisco, I miss the real summertime. I actually like the heat."

"I would guess that about you."

She opened her eyes and looked across at him. Their gazes held, causing the temperature in the truck to rise. At least Beck's temperature went up significantly. Semireclined as she was, she looked defenseless and altogether feminine. Fine strands at her hairline had curled in defiance of the chemical control she imposed on them, lending her a softness she would disclaim. Her cheeks were flushed, and again he imagined that her skin would be hot to the touch.

He ached to find out, but he didn't risk it, afraid that if he touched her, he would upset some delicate balance that had been struck, and that it wouldn't tilt in his favor. Instead he said, "Hungry, Sayre?"

She lifted her head from the headrest. Her eyes looked foggy with misapprehension. "What?"

"Hungry?"

"Oh." Shaking her head slightly, she said, "No."

"Bet you are."

He continued staring at her for several moments before engaging the gears of the pickup. Leaving the hospital parking lot, he headed in the direction opposite that of the motel.

She said, "The Lodge is on the other side of town."

"Trust me."

"Not as far as I could throw you."

He merely grinned. She said nothing else, which he took as her consent to go along with whatever he had in mind. Just beyond the outskirts of town, he turned off the main highway onto a rutted gravel road that wound through dense forest. He followed it to its dead end, where there was a clearing on the elevated bank of a wide bayou. Several vehicles were parked around a small building that seemed on the verge of collapse.

Sayre turned to him. "You know this place?"

"You sound surprised."

"I thought it was a secret known only to us natives."

"I'm not that much of an outsider anymore."

The drive-up fish shack had been owned and operated by the same family since the early 1930s, when bootleg liquor was their actual drawing card. The building was constructed of corrugated tin that had fallen victim to rust decades ago. It listed several degrees. It was only ten feet wide, and all of it was kitchen.

Through a narrow window were served oysters on the half shell with a red sauce hot enough to make your eyes water, a dense gumbo flavored with filé and okra, and a crawfish étouffée so delicious you used a chunk of French bread to clean the paper plate. Everything from alligator meat to dill pickles could be had batter-dipped and deep-fried.

Beck ordered them cups of gumbo and fried shrimp po'boy sandwiches. While their order was being prepared, he went to the water trough at the side of the shack and worked his hand through the chipped ice until he found two longneck bottles of beer. He opened them by using the church key that dangled from a dirty string nailed to a tree.

"It's cold," he warned Sayre as he passed her one of the frosted bottles. "Want a glass?"

"They would be insulted."

She tilted the bottle to her mouth like a pro. He smiled down at her. "That upped your approval rating."

"I'm not gunning for your approval."

His grin stretched wider. "That's a damn shame. It's off the charts."

When their order was ready, they carried the paper boats of food to a weathered picnic table beneath an umbrella of live oaks. Strands of colored Christmas lights had been ineptly strung from the lower branches and through the Spanish moss. Another customer had tuned the radio in his car to a station that played zydeco, which added to the ambience.

They ate their cups of gumbo first, then Beck watched Sayre unwrap the tissue paper around her sandwich. The home-baked roll was hot, buttery, and crusty on the outside, soft in the center. It was piled high with fat, breaded shrimp straight out of the frying grease, shredded lettuce, and rémoulade sauce. To this she added a liberal sprinkling of Tabasco from the bottle on the table.

She took a large bite. "Delicious," she said when she had swallowed. "San Francisco has incredible food, but this tastes like . . ."

"What?"

"Home." She smiled, but it was a sad, wistful expression.

He concentrated on her as much as on his meal, and he sensed that she was concentrating on him concentrating on her. His unwavering attention made her uncomfortable, though she tried to appear nonchalant.

Finally, she frowned at him. "Do I have sauce on my face or something?"

"No."

"Then why do you keep staring at me?"

His gaze challenged her to take a wild guess, but of course she didn't. They resumed eating. After a time he said, "Do you ever sweat?"

She looked across at him and blinked. "I beg your pardon?"

"It's hotter than hell out here. There's no breeze. The humidity must be ninety-nine percent. You're eating red pepper sauce practically by the tablespoon. But you're not sweating. Your skin isn't even dewy. How is that possible?"

"You're not sweating either."

He blotted his forehead with his sleeve, then extended his arm to show her the damp spot. "Pints of it are rolling down my trunk and pooling at my waist." That was somewhat of an exaggeration, but it got a genuine smile out of her.

"I sweat. Not often," she admitted. "I have to really exert myself."

"Ahh, good to know," he said. "I was beginning to think you might be an alien with no sweat glands."

When they finished their meal, he gathered up the trash and threw it in one of the oil drums used for that purpose. When he returned to the table, he sat on it and placed his feet on the bench beside her. He took a sip of beer, then looked down at her. "What have you got against Doc Caroe?"

She carefully set down her bottle of beer and wiped the condensation from her palm with a paper napkin. "Was my dislike that obvious?"

"Very. Given a choice between shaking hands with him or being held against me . . ." He paused and waited until she had looked up at him before finishing. "You preferred not to shake hands with Caroe. Knowing of your dislike for me, I'd say you must really despise that man."

She averted her head and looked at a group of people who were eating at one of the other tables. There was a burst of laughter, as though one of them had just delivered a good punch line. Their children were chasing lightning bugs through the trees, squealing delight each time they caught one.

"They're having a good time, aren't they?"

"Seems like," he said. Then he nudged her thigh with the toe of his shoe. "Why don't you like Doc Caroe?"

Her gaze moved back up to him. "He's a peacock. That ridiculous hair. He has a Napoleonic complex. He's a menace to anyone who goes to him for healing because he's incompetent, and either too stupid or too vain to accept his limitations. He should have had his license revoked years ago."

"Other than that, what have you got against him?"

Picking up on his teasing tone, she ducked her head and laughed softly. "I got carried away. Sorry."

"Don't be. I like you better when you get carried away. I don't think you let yourself get carried away nearly often enough."

"You enjoy psychoanalyzing me, don't you?"

"Doc Caroe?"

Her smile gradually retreated. "He was my mother's doctor when she got stomach cancer."

"Chris told me about that. It was tough for all of you."

"Once she was diagnosed, it was probably too far advanced for any treatment to have worked. But I couldn't accept that Dr. Caroe was doing everything he could to save her."

"You were a little girl, Sayre. You wanted a quick fix. Then when Laurel died, you needed someone to blame."

"I'm sure you're right."

"I felt the same when my dad died." She raised her head and looked up at him. "I was about the same age you were when you lost your mother."

"That must have been awful for you."

For a moment she let all her defenses down. Her expression was soft, her eyes were unguarded, and she spoke with more sincerity than she had since they'd met.

"It was a long time ago," he said, "but I remember how angry I was. I stayed angry for a long time, which made the situation even harder for my mom."

Propping her chin on her hand, she asked, "What did you do when you first heard that your father was gone? The very first thing."

"I took my baseball bat to the outside wall of our garage." He didn't even have to search his memory. It was that fresh. "I knocked the hell out of it again and again until the wood splintered. Don't ask me why. I guess I wanted to hurt something as badly as I was hurting."

He eased himself down onto the bench beside her, keeping his back to the table, assuming the same juxtaposition they'd had on the piano bench. This picnic table bench was much longer, but he sat just as close to her now as then.

"What did you do when you learned your mother had died?"

"I went into her bedroom," she said. "It always smelled good, like the talcum powder she put on every night after her bath. I'll remember until the day I die how she smelled every night when she came to my bedroom to tuck me in and kiss me good night. She would take my face between her hands, which always felt so cool."

Putting words to action, she cupped her face between her hands. Lost in the recollection, she remained that way for several moments, then slowly lowered her hands. "Anyway, when Huff came home from the hospital and told us that she had died, I went into her bedroom. It was Huff's room, too, but it was feminine and frilly, like her. I lay down on her side of the bed, and buried my face in her pillow and cried my heart out.

"Eventually Selma found me there. She bathed my face with a cold washcloth and told me that I was the lady of the house now, that my mother was looking down on me from heaven, and did I want to disappoint her by carrying on like that? So I stopped crying."

"And became the lady of the house."

When she laughed, she shook back her hair. "I think we've covered that subject. I never acted much like a lady. But that's when I developed a dislike for the doctor who couldn't make my mother well, and I've disliked him ever since."

"Understandably."

"Is your mother still living?"

"Yes. She managed to survive Daddy's death and me."

Nodding, she said, "I'll bet you were a demon growing up."

"And still am?"

She studied him for a moment, then said quietly, "Some say you are."

"Who says that?"

Uneasy with the question, she avoided answering it and finished her beer. "I'd better go check in. The Lodge may have had a run on rooms tonight."

He placed his hand beneath her elbow, guiding her over the uneven ground as they walked back to the truck. For once, she didn't recoil. "Whether or not the motel has a vacancy depends on the bowling league," he told her.

"The bowling league?"

"On the nights the men bowl, the wives have their affairs. Not a room to be had on those nights."

Standing within the wedge of space between the door he had opened for her and the cab of the truck, she turned to face him. "What about the nights the women bowl?"

"Same thing. All the rooms are booked because the husbands are entertaining their lady friends. But I think you're safe tonight. Nobody's bowling except the Knights of Columbus."

"Catholic women don't fool around?"

"Yes, but discreetly. They go out of town."

She laughed and climbed up into the truck, unaware of how tightly that big step stretched her skirt across her ass. Luscious curves and no panty line. His mind blared: *thong.* Instantly he was infused with lust. As he walked around the rear of the pickup, he took another swipe of his forehead with his sleeve.

He got in and started the truck. She asked, "How did you come by all this valuable information about the adultery in Destiny?"

"Part of my job." He made a wide turn and redirected the truck onto the narrow road that led back to the highway. On both sides of them, the darkness of the forest was impenetrable.

"I see. You get the goods on people, find out who they're sleeping with, how much they drink, where they're vulnerable. Just in case Huff ever needs leverage against them."

"You make it sound like blackmail."

"Isn't it?"

He looked at her with disappointment. "Here I've treated you to a fine dining experience, and I still can't get into your good graces. I hate for you to leave town tomorrow thinking so poorly of me."

"I'm not leaving tomorrow."

chapter 14

Beck braked so hard the pickup skidded several yards along the gravel road before coming to a complete stop. "Why not?"

"What difference does it make to you?"

"You were ready to rocket out of here this afternoon. What happened to change your mind?"

"Chris came under suspicion in connection to Danny's death."

"Who told you about that?"

"Huff."

Beck assimilated that, then removed his foot from the brake and continued driving.

"Was it Huff's medications talking?" she asked.

"No. He was lucid."

"Can you—will you—talk about it?"

He shrugged with more nonchalance than he felt. "Red Harper asked Chris to come to his office to address some questions." He glanced at her. "Apparently your comment about Danny's aversion to fishing got Deputy Scott excited."

"I thought it might be pertinent. Danny hated the fishing camp. He never went there."

"He hadn't been out there as long as I've been around," Beck admitted. "Not to my knowledge anyway."

"Then don't you find it strange that he died there?"

"I don't know, is it?"

By now they had reached the outskirts of town, and he had to stop for a traffic light. She hadn't responded to his question, so he turned to her and repeated it. "Is it strange that he died there? Why didn't Danny like the fishing camp?"

She remained mutinously silent.

"Was he afraid of snakes? Allergic to poison ivy? Why didn't Danny like the camp?"

"Painful childhood memory," she snapped. "All right?"

He backed off instantly. "All right." The light turned green, and he accelerated through the intersection.

He heard Sayre sigh as she leaned her head against the passenger window. "You want to know the story?"

"Only if you want to tell me."

"You would get it from Chris anyway. At least my version won't be sugarcoated. Maybe it'll give you a clearer understanding of what life among the Hoyles was like when we were kids, and give you an unvarnished look into the nature of the man you work for.

"One day not long after our mother died, Huff decided we needed a family outing. A day that just the four of us would spend together. Which was quite a concession for him. As you know, there's rarely a day that he doesn't go to the foundry.

"Anyhow, he took us out to the fishing camp. He set up each of us with a pole and bait and instructed Danny and me on how to go about it. Of course Chris was already a proficient fisherman because Huff had been taking him fishing for years.

"Danny began whining that he didn't want to do it. He didn't like baiting the hook, because he didn't want to hurt the worm. He said he hoped he wouldn't catch a fish because then it would die. He was preoccupied with death, you see, because of Mother. A week earlier he had cried for hours after finding a dead cricket on the gallery.

"Rather than comforting him, talking him through it, or, dammit, just letting it go—because what difference did it make whether Danny caught a fish that day or not?—Huff became furious and told him he couldn't go home until he caught one.

"He made him sit there in that stinking, yellow mud all afternoon, subjecting him to his own father's scorn and his brother's ridicule. And Chris was allowed, even encouraged, to humiliate him.

"The sun had gone down before he finally caught a fish. He blubbered the whole time he was struggling to get it off the hook. But he did it," she finished softly. "He did it. Then in the only act of defiance I ever saw from Danny, he threw the fish back into the bayou and swore that he would never catch another."

Beck had pulled into the motel parking lot and stopped in front of the office. By the time she finished the story, he was turned toward her, his arm stretched along the back of the seat, his fingers within touching distance of her shoulder.

He knew the moment she realized that she had become immersed in the recollection, and that she was the single object of his focus, because she sat up straighter and cleared the huskiness from her throat. "Danny hated that place. It held a terrible memory for him. So why would he choose to go there last Sunday afternoon?"

"Maybe he chose it for that very reason, Sayre. If he was despondent enough to commit suicide, perhaps he masochistically chose the site of a hateful memory in which to do it."

"If it *was* a suicide." Meeting his gaze directly, she said, "Why are they investigating Chris?"

"They're not. He's only being asked—"

"Yes, yes, I know. He's answering questions. But those questions were serious enough to bring on Huff's heart attack."

He turned his head away and looked at the blinking red neon arrow pointing down at the motel office. Through the plate-glass wall, he could see the clerk. He was sitting in a recliner, chewing on a toothpick, and watching TV. He hadn't shown the slightest interest in his potential customers. Apparently it wasn't uncommon for a man and a woman to remain outside the office and discuss whether or not to go inside and register for a room.

"They found something in the cabin that implicates Chris. He says he hasn't been out there since the night Frito chased off the bobcat." Facing her again, he added, "I think he's telling the truth."

"What did they find?"

"A matchbook. From a nightclub in Breaux Bridge."

"That's it? That's not very solid evidence. Anybody could have dropped a matchbook there at any time."

"Ordinarily, yes. But the club's grand opening was last Saturday, the night before Danny died. The matchbooks weren't available until then," he explained. "Chris admits to being at the club and coming home late. He admits to smoking a few cigarettes, so he had reason to have a matchbook."

"I don't suppose Danny was at the club that night, too."

He shook his head. "Not his kind of place. Especially not recently. He never smoked, so it's unlikely he dropped the matchbook. Anyway, where would he have got it between Saturday night and Sunday morning, when he left for church?"

"So Deputy Scott wanted to know how a matchbook that couldn't have been obtained until Saturday night wound up in the cabin on Sunday afternoon. Chris was at the nightclub, making him the most likely culprit."

"That's Deputy Scott's theory."

"But who else could it have been?"

"I don't know, Sayre, but if that's all Scott has got on Chris, a grand jury wouldn't go near it, even if a prosecutor was hot to indict him."

She seemed taken aback by his use of the legal jargon. "You actually think it will go that far?"

"No, I don't. What would be Chris's motive?" He posed it as a rhetorical question, but she took it at face value.

"I don't think Chris requires much motive for doing anything he wants to do."

Beck couldn't dispute the statement because he knew it to be true.

After a short silence, she said, "I've decided to stay in Destiny until it's been resolved."

"What about your business?"

"I spoke with my assistant this afternoon. I don't have any pressing deadlines this week, and she can reschedule the appointments on my calendar. Besides, this is more important. I hadn't had contact with Danny for the past ten years."

Her voice faltered, almost cracked, and he got the distinct impression that she was withholding an important factor in her decision-making process. Whatever it was, she didn't share it with him.

"I can't let his death go unexplained," she said. "Whether he killed himself or otherwise, I need to know why he died, for my own peace of mind if for no other reason.

"I also feel an obligation to my mother. She doted on Danny. Left to Huff and Chris, his death would go practically unnoticed. I couldn't live with myself if I just swept him under the rug like so much dust. That would break Mother's heart. This is the least I can do for her. And for him." She reached for the door handle.

He touched her shoulder. "Sayre?"

She looked at him, but he couldn't think of anything to say. Her reasons for staying were selfless, so what argument could he offer against them? The best thing for her would be to leave Destiny. He just couldn't bring himself to encourage her to go.

The moment stretched out. Finally she said, "Don't bother coming around for the door. Thank you for the dinner. Good night."

He allowed her to get out on her own and retrieve her bag from behind the seat. She didn't even look at him when she shut the door. He heard the bell jingle above the door when she went into the motel office. He watched her transact the business of registering with the clerk.

Beck told himself to drive away, to make a clean break. He even reached for the key in the ignition. The less he had to do with Sayre Lynch the better for everybody, especially him. She didn't like him anyway. What was he hanging around for?

"Dammit!"

When she came out of the office with a room key, he was waiting for her. Reaching for her bag, he asked, "Upstairs or down?"

"You don't have to walk me to the door."

"Huff would never forgive me if something happened to you."

"What could happen to me?"

He wrested the bag from her hand. "It's not up for debate, Sayre."

Resigned, she pointed down the long open-air corridor. "Last room." Then she gave a bitter laugh. "Huff. Don't fool yourself into believing he's concerned about my well-being."

"I take it that you didn't have a sentimental reconciliation in the ICU."

"He was playing one of his sick games, and I
was the pawn."

"He thought he was dying. Maybe you're
wrong."

"I'm not."

"No benefit of the doubt for Huff?"

"None whatsoever."

"Then I guess when he broke up the romance between you and Clark Daly, you—"

"What?" She came to an abrupt stop and
grabbed his arm. "What do you know about that?"

"Only what Chris told me."

"Chris told you about Clark and me? When?"

"While you were in the ICU."

"Why?"

Her fingers were digging into the crook of his
elbow, although he didn't think she was even aware
of it. Her eyes were ablaze. Hoping to defuse her,
he kept his voice even. "I asked Chris what had
started the feud between you and Huff."

"Well, I hope you found the story entertaining."

Letting go of him, she continued down the corridor at a steady clip, and when she reached the last
in the row of identical doors, she shoved the key
into the lock with such force, Beck was surprised it
didn't break. She yanked the bag away from him
and threw it into the room.

"I wouldn't have mentioned it if I'd known it
would upset you like this," he said.

"It upsets me to know that you and Chris were gossiping like two old ladies about my private life. He

had no business discussing it with you or anybody else. Don't you have anything better to talk about?"

"We weren't gossiping. Besides, it's ancient history." Then his eyes narrowed on her. "Isn't it?"

"Why should that interest you?"

"It interests me the same way your two marriages do."

"You discussed my marriages, too?"

"They're part of the family record."

"A family of which you are not a member."

"True. I'm an onlooker. Merely curious."

"About?"

"Two husbands in three years. Huff picked the first, which could explain why the marriage didn't last very long. What happened to break up the second?"

She remained rigid and silent.

"Incompatibility? Alienation of affection? The torch you were still carrying for Daly? I'd bet on that. I understand you two had a hot thing going."

"You understand *nothing*."

"Then explain it to me, Sayre. Lay it all out there, so I'll understand."

She seethed.

"Maybe you thought since you couldn't have the man you wanted, you'd at least go for the goodies."

"Yes," she hissed. "That's exactly what I did. Do you want a sampling?"

She reached up and hooked her hand around the back of his neck, pulled his face down to hers, and stamped a hard, angry, and defiant kiss on his lips. Then she released him so abruptly that his head snapped back.

Turning away, she stepped into the room and was about to slam the door when he reached for her. "I want to sample more than that."

Curving his arm around her waist, he pulled her against him, then walked her backward into the room. He was the one who kicked the door closed as his mouth came down on hers.

He worked her lips apart and thrust his tongue between them. She tried to turn away, but he took her jaw in one hand and held her head in place while he plundered her mouth.

Suddenly her hands were in his hair, her fingers tightly gripping strands of it. But she wasn't pushing him away. She was pulling him closer, now kissing him back, hotly and wetly and with small wanting sounds vibrating up from deep within her throat and driving him a little mad.

Immediately he tempered the violence of the kiss. His hand no longer held her jaw but caressed it. Their tongues still tangled, but sexily not angrily. He turned them so that her back was against the door and he was leaning into her, pressing his middle into the receiving hollow of hers and wishing like hell their clothes would dissolve.

Coming up for air, he rubbed her lips with his. "I knew you were hungry for this."

In breathy stops and starts, she fiercely denied it, but she angled her head to one side, inviting his lips to slide down the column of her throat. He'd been wrong. Her skin had a fine sheen of sweat on it. He opened her suit jacket and kissed her breasts, which were swelling out of a low-cut brassiere.

When he kissed her raised nipple through the

lace, she murmured, "Don't, don't." But he continued and she didn't stop him.

Kissing her mouth again, he put his hands on her
ass and pulled her against him. "Oh God," she
moaned, then turned away to face the door.

Undeterred, he lifted her arms above her head,
planting her hands flat against the wood. He nuzzled the back of her neck while his hands coasted
down the undersides of her arms. He pressed his
palms over her breasts, squeezed them, reshaped
them, then smoothed his hands down her stomach,
hips, her thighs, all the way to her knees.

On their way back up, one hand slipped beneath
her skirt. Fabric gathered against his wrist as his
hand moved higher along the longest, smoothest
thigh a man could imagine.

The thong was a patch of lace. He caressed her
through it, then beneath it, where the hair was soft
and the flesh pliant. His fingers found her center
ready. Awed, thrilled, grateful, he whispered her
name.

He applied the merest pressure, but she reacted
with a start and a soft gasp. Reflexively she rocked
her hips slightly forward and then back. And when
she did that, he groaned with near-unbearable pleasure. He was there, right there, snug against the
cleft of her ass, and she was moving in a mind-
blowing rhythm against him.

When she came, he leaned into her even more,
pressing her firmly between himself and the door.
She rolled her forehead against it, breathing in
rapid pants, until even the smallest shudders ceased,
and the tension ebbed, and she became still.

He removed his hand from beneath her skirt and smoothed it back into place. Then he rested both hands on her waist, giving it occasional squeezes to let her know that he could be patient.

It was a full minute before she turned around to face him. Her hair was a wreath of damp unruliness, the perfect frame for eyes the color of the strongest whiskey ever to make a man drunk, and a mouth that he hadn't had nearly enough of. Fine beads of sweat dotted her upper lip.

Smiling, he wiped off the moisture mustache with his fingertip. "Only when you've really exerted yourself."

"If you touch me again, I'll kill you."

Stunned, he took a step back. "What?"

"I think I made myself clear."

He realized now that the fire in her eyes wasn't arousal but a rage that was almost primal in its intensity, as though if he ignored her threat and touched her, she would indeed go for his throat.

"I mean it," she said. "Do not touch me."

Infuriated by her tone, he said, "You didn't seem to mind my touch a minute ago. Want me to get graphic?"

"I want you to leave."

With a broad sweep of his hand, he motioned her away from the door, exaggerating his efforts not to make physical contact. He yanked open the door, then stopped and looked back at her.

"Who are you really angry at, Sayre? Me or yourself?"

"Get out of here."

"You knew it was going to happen."

"Go."

"The minute we laid eyes on each other, we both knew it was inevitable."

She shook her head furiously.

"You wanted it to happen, and you liked it."

"I did not!"

"No?" He reached out and dabbed her lower lip with his thumb, then showed her the bead of blood on the tip of it, picked up from the spot where she'd bitten herself.

Leaning down close to her face, he left her with one whispered word.

Huff, lying flat on his back in the hospital bed, eyes closed, heard someone enter his ICU. "Who's that?"

"Your gifted physician."

"Took you long enough," Huff grumbled.

"You're not my only patient," Tom Caroe said.

"I'm not your patient at all." Huff swung his bare legs to the side of the bed and sat up. Cursing, he pulled the cannula from his nostrils. "I hate being tethered to all this crap."

The doctor laughed. "Be glad we didn't run a catheter up your pecker."

"Not a chance in hell of that happening. Think you could rustle up some food?"

Tom Caroe reached into the pocket of his baggy trousers and took out a wrapped sandwich. "Peanut butter and grape jelly from my own kitchen."

"What the hell? You said you'd bring dinner."

"Huff, men who have heart attacks at two in the

afternoon don't usually have meat loaf with mashed potatoes and gravy at ten-thirty that night."

Huff snatched the sandwich from him, unwrapped it, and demolished it in three bites. "Get me a Coke," he said through a mouthful.

"No caffeine."

"That nurse, the real ugly one, took my cigarettes."

"Not even the great Huff Hoyle could get away with smoking in an ICU."

"I donated money to this hospital, and I can't smoke in it?"

"There are oxygen tanks all over the place," the doctor pointed out.

"I'll go downstairs to smoke."

"I'd have to take you off the monitors, and that would send everyone running in here with a crash cart." Caroe looked at him shrewdly. "We can't have that, can we?"

Huff shot him a baleful look. "You're enjoying this, aren't you?"

"This was your idea, Huff. So if you have to go without your rich food and smokes, it's your own fault. How long do you plan to drag it out? The nurses are already scratching their heads, wondering why a cardiac patient has such healthy vitals. I can't keep up the pretense for long."

"When could a heart attack victim feasibly make a miraculous recovery?"

"A day or two. I could conduct some tests tomorrow—"

Huff poked him hard in the chest. "Nothing painful or invasive."

"I could tell your family that I found only minimal infarction as a result of this attack, that it was minor, a wake-up call for you to modify your diet, stop smoking, start exercising, et cetera."

"If you throw in that part about diet, Selma will start feeding me shit."

"That's the price you'll have to pay for faking a heart attack."

"What's the alternative?" Huff snarled.

"I could eat crow and say that it wasn't your heart at all, but only a severe case of indigestion and acid reflux, which scared you and fooled the rest of us."

Huff thought it over. "It would be easy to believe that a quack like you had got a diagnosis wrong, but let's stick with the mild heart attack. I'd like one more day in the hospital. Just for show."

"Of all your shenanigans, this one takes the cake. Why're you doing it?"

"What's it matter to you? You're getting paid."

"Cash, don't forget."

"Have I ever?"

Put in his place, the doctor laughed nervously. "I'm not trying to butt into your business, Huff. Just wondering."

"I have my reasons for wanting to look fragile. And you couldn't be more right. Those reasons are none of your goddamn business."

Tom Caroe was as unscrupulous as any man Huff had ever met, and that was saying something. Huff had become the feared man he was by being generous with bribes but stingy with information. He wasn't about to discuss with Caroe his reasons for putting on such an elaborate charade.

"If you're not going to give me anything more to eat, go on, get out of here," Huff ordered him. "Try not to kill any of your patients before you leave for the night."

"I'll see you in the morning."

"Remember, nothing invasive. Nothing up my ass or snaking through a vein. Only X-rays, stuff like that."

On his way out the door, Caroe pointed to his nose. "Don't forget your oxygen."

Huff replaced the cannula, then lay back down and settled his head into the pillow. A low laugh rumbled out of his chest, which he turned into a cough in case a nurse happened to pass by.

Damned if he hadn't pulled it off. He couldn't have done it without Tom Caroe's help, but one phone call had been all it took to get the doctor's cooperation.

Ever since he'd been informed of Danny's death, he'd been nagged by several problems. They'd circled him like buzzards around a carcass, and no attempt at batting them away had been successful. Periodically one would light on him, pluck at his subconscious relentlessly until another swooped down to take its place.

First, naturally, was the loss of his son. Regrettable. Sad. Tragic even. But Danny was gone and there was nothing he could do about it. He would miss Danny, but it was senseless to dwell on a situation he couldn't change.

Then there was the matter of Chris. Huff was thoroughly put out with him over his failed marriage. Where had he been while his wife was down in Mexico humping pool boys and getting her tubes ligated? Humping the likes of Lila Robson.

Huff didn't give a flip about Chris's marriage and, in fact, hadn't given it even odds of lasting as long as it had. But he'd wanted a grandbaby out of it before it collapsed. The crib in the attic remained empty, and that chafed him constantly.

But it had been Sayre's return that had made him sit up and take notice of just how much control he'd lost. He'd once called all the shots. Nobody did anything without his permission. In every situation, he had decided which way the wind was going to blow. He had controlled his family with a tight and inescapable fist.

Somewhere along the way he'd let that control slip. Where Sayre was concerned, he'd lost all control. It was damn past time to regain it. But before he could get control, he had to get her attention, and in a big way. So he had faked a heart attack, and it had worked to keep her in town.

As he lay there, in the quiet of the ICU, he smothered another laugh, thinking of the plans he had for Miss Sayre Lynch Hoyle.

Fortunately, she was playing right into them.

chapter 15

When Beck arrived home, Frito bounded out to greet him and dropped a soggy tennis ball at his feet. "Sorry, boy. I don't feel like playing tonight."

What he needed tonight wasn't a dog but a punching bag that he could pummel with his fists Rocky-style for a couple of hours. Only then—possibly—would he have taken the edge off his frustration.

But Frito was persistent, and Beck decided it was unfair to take his bad mood out on the dog. "Okay, but only a few times."

Fifty fetches later, Beck was worn out. "I'm beat, Frito. Besides, it's past your dinnertime."

At the mention of food, Frito ran up the porch steps ahead of his master. He nudged the screened door open with his nose and went inside. By the time Beck reached the kitchen, Frito was sitting in front of the refrigerator, his luxuriant tail sweeping the floor, his long tongue lolling outside his mouth in anticipation.

Beck went to the pantry instead and opened the

bin where he stored dry dog food. Frito whined. On Sundays and Wednesdays, he got soft scrambled eggs for supper. He looked at Beck as though to say, *Have you forgotten what day this is?*

"Not tonight. Tonight it's kibbles. I'll make it up to you tomorrow." He dumped a healthy portion of food into the large bowl on the floor.

Frito ambled toward it, gave it an unenthusiastic sniff, then looked up at Beck with imploring eyes and whined again.

"We're out of eggs, okay? This is expensive, nutritious, vitamin-enriched food that starving dogs in China would love to have. Now eat it and stop complaining."

Frito, deciding that this was as good as it was going to get, dipped his head into the bowl and began crunching the nuggets. But as Beck opened the refrigerator to get a beer, Frito glanced into it, and when he saw the eggs neatly lined up in the tray in the door, he looked at Beck with reproach.

"You're too smart for your own good."

Beck had the same problem. Sometimes he was too smart for his own good. From Sayre's angry reaction to his and Chris's conversation about her, he deduced that she wasn't over the breakup with Clark Daly. Not entirely. And that was irritating Beck like a pebble in his shoe. It was also baffling. Daly was a burnout, an alcoholic, a disappointment to everyone who'd known him in his glory days. Why was a successful woman like Sayre Lynch still hung up on him?

It was maddening . . . as was just about everything about her.

Frito emptied his water bowl with one last slurp. "Finished? Go take care of your business, and then I'll lock up for the night." Frito went out the back door.

The single-story Acadian house had two bedrooms. The larger of the two had an adjoining bath, so Beck used it as the master bedroom. The other was furnished as a guest room, but he never hosted out-of-town guests, so he rarely went into that room except to get something from the closet where he stored seldom-used items and out-of-season clothing.

The house wasn't fancy by any stretch, but it was comfortable. He liked the friendly creaks of the hardwood floors and the layout of the rooms, which allowed for a lot of open space and large windows. Being no gardener, he retained a lawn service to keep the grounds from reverting to swamp. A lady came twice a week to clean, do his laundry, and stock the kitchen with staples and frozen casseroles she made for him herself.

He lived a bachelor's existence.

He stripped and got in the shower. Bracing his hands against the tile wall behind the faucets, he bowed his head low beneath the nozzle and let the water beat against the back of his neck.

"I never should have touched her."

When Sayre had grabbed him by the neck and given him that defiant kiss, he should have let her have her little victory and walked away. But he couldn't leave it alone. Couldn't leave *her* alone. And what happened after that . . .

Don't think about what happened after that.

But of course he did. About a dozen times. Long after the water in his shower had turned cold, he continued to replay the episode in his mind without overlooking or shortchanging one single erotic detail.

When he finally left the bathroom, Frito was already lying on his rug at the foot of the bed. "All done?" The dog yawned and lay his head on his front paws. "I'll take that for a yes."

Beck secured the house for the night, then got into bed. He was tired but not sleepy. From the darkness, problems popped out at him like jeering clowns in a fun house ride.

Chris and the investigation into Danny's death.

Huff and what impact his heart attack would have on Hoyle Enterprises.

Charles Nielson and all the work to be done before that matter was settled.

Sayre. Sayre. And more Sayre.

He'd only met her yesterday, yet already she'd brought more turmoil into his life than any woman ever had. She spelled bad news to him for reasons too numerous to count. Getting involved with her would jeopardize all the hard work, all the time and effort he had invested in the Hoyles.

But Sayre couldn't mess up his life without his full cooperation. In order for her to damage the groundwork he'd laid, and consequently to wreck his future, he would have to give her an opportunity to do so, and then be a willing participant in bringing about his own downfall.

Therefore the solution was simple: Stay away from her.

But his resolve was a hell of a lot weaker than his desire. Now that he had experienced her passion, how would he be able to stay away from it?

His last thought before falling asleep was *I never should have touched her.*

It was also his first thought when his cell phone rang less than an hour later.

Then, immediately remembering Huff's heart attack, he rolled over to grab the phone off the nightstand. "Hello?"

"Mr. Merchant?"

"Yes? Who's this?"

"Fred Decluette."

He was one of the night foremen at the foundry. Beck jackknifed into a sitting position. This wasn't going to be good news.

For the second time in less than twenty-four hours, he sped to the parish hospital and entered the emergency room at a run.

There to meet him was Fred Decluette, who had worked for Hoyle Enterprises for thirty-something years. He was built like a fire hydrant and was about that sturdy. Tonight he looked nervous and queasy, and had a death grip on the cap he was twisting between his hands.

From his shirt collar to the cuffs of his khaki work pants, his clothes were stiff with drying blood.

"Thanks for coming, Mr. Merchant. I hated like heck to bother you in the middle of the night, but I didn't know who else to call. I figured somebody from upper management should be notified. I couldn't raise Mr. Hoyle, Chris that is, on the emergency number. Got his housekeeper out of bed. He wasn't home, and she didn't know where he's at. And with Mr. Huff being here in the hospital hisself—"

"It's all right, Fred. I'm glad you called me. What happened to Billy Paulik, and how bad is it?" He was hoping against hope that the employee's injury wouldn't be commensurate with the amount of blood on Decluette's clothing.

"Awful bad, Mr. Merchant. I figure Billy's gonna lose his arm."

Beck took a deep breath and exhaled it slowly. "How did it happen?"

"He was operating one of the conveyors for a guy who's on vacation. He was tracking a drive belt that wouldn't stay centered."

"While the machine was running?"

Decluette shifted his feet uneasily. "Well, yes, sir. You know, unless it's a real bad problem, we don't shut a machine down. So it was still moving. Billy's sleeve got caught in the mechanism. He couldn't reach the switch to shut it off. Damn thing pulled his arm right into the track. One of the other men got to the switch and stopped it, but by then . . ." The foundry foreman swallowed with difficulty. "We didn't even wait on the ambulance. Just scooped him up and carried him here ourselves."

He motioned to three other men who were sitting in waiting room chairs, heads down, looking as shaky as their foreman and just as bloody. "Billy's right arm was hanging by a thread from his shoulder. Moe there had to hold it on, else it might've come clean off."

"Awful bad" was an understatement. This was a catastrophe. "Was he conscious?" Beck asked.

"When we first pulled him out, he was screaming something terrible. I'll never forget the sound of it. Like something inhuman. Then I think he must've went into shock. Anyhow he stopped screaming."

"Have you spoken with a doctor?"

"No, sir. They rushed Billy back there, and that's the last we saw of anybody, except that nurse yonder at the desk."

"He has a family, doesn't he?"

"I called Alicia. She ain't got here yet."

Beck placed his hand on the man's shoulder. "You did your best for Billy. I'll take over from here."

"If it's all the same to you, we'd like to stick around, Mr. Merchant. Men came in to cover the rest of the shift for us. We'd like to see if Billy's gonna pull through. He lost a lot of blood."

Beck didn't even want to think about his not pulling through. "I'm sure Billy would appreciate that."

Fred was about to turn away, then on an afterthought asked, "How's Mr. Hoyle faring?"

"He's out of danger for the time being. I think he's going to be all right."

Beck left the four foundry employees talking quietly among themselves and dialed Chris's cell number. It rang six times before it was answered by his voice mail recording. Beck left a message. "I thought we agreed to keep our cell phones handy. Call me. Huff's okay, as far as I know, but we've got another emergency."

The nurse attending the desk declined to tell him anything specific. Annoyed with her deliberate ambiguity, Beck said, "Can you at least tell me if he's alive or dead?"

"You're not family, are you?"

"No, but I'm the one paying the fucking hospital bill. Which I believe entitles me to know whether or not he's going to make it."

"I don't care for your language, sir."

"Well if you care for your job, ma'am, you'd better give me some information. Fast."

She drew herself up taut. Her lips barely moved when she spoke. "I believe the patient is going to be transferred by helicopter to a trauma center in New Orleans. That's all I know."

Hearing a commotion behind him, Beck turned to see a woman rushing in, trailed by five children. All of them were barefoot, wearing pajamas, their faces white with fear. A toddler carried a ragged, one-eyed teddy bear beneath her arm. The woman was on the verge of hysteria.

"Fred!" she cried when he stood up to meet her. Seeing her husband's blood on the other men's clothing, she screamed and collapsed to her knees. "Tell me he's not dead. Please. Tell me he's still alive."

Her husband's coworkers rushed to assist her. Lifting her from the floor, they placed her in a chair.

"He's not dead," Fred told her, "but he's hurt bad, Alicia."

The children were remarkably subdued, probably stupefied by their mother's hysteria.

"I want to see him," she said frantically. "Can I see him?"

"Not yet. They're working on him and won't let anybody back there."

Fred Decluette tried to calm her down and at the same time explain to her the nature of the accident. He could barely make himself heard above her sobbing. Beck turned to the nurse, who was watching the scene impassively.

"Can you give her something to calm her?" he asked.

"Not unless a doctor orders it."

With a distinct edge to his voice he said, "Why don't you go ask?" Looking thoroughly put out, she stamped off.

"His right arm!" Billy's wife shrieked, "He's right-handed. Oh, Lord, what will we do?"

Beck crossed the lobby toward them. When she saw him, her crying ceased immediately, as though someone had flipped a switch. The other men shuffled aside, enabling Beck to crouch directly in front of her.

"Mrs. Paulik, my name is Beck Merchant. What's happened to Billy is tragic, but I want you to rest assured that I'm going to do whatever I can to help you and your family through it.

"I've been told that Billy will be flown by helicopter to a trauma center in New Orleans, where he'll get the best possible medical care. I'm sure they're already assembling a team of vascular surgeons, orthopedic specialists, and so on. Hopefully his arm can be saved. These doctors can work miracles, even on accident injuries as acute as Billy's."

She continued to stare at him without expression, saying nothing. He thought she might be in shock like her husband. He glanced at the five children. The little girl with the teddy bear was sucking her thumb, staring at Beck over her small fist. The others were regarding him somberly.

The oldest of them, a boy, appeared to be about the age he'd been when his father had died. He was standing apart from the others, his expression so wary it bordered on hostile. Beck recognized this as mistrust of anybody who promised that everything was going to be all right when it most definitely was not.

Beck turned back to the boy's mother. Drying tears had left salty tracks on her plump cheeks. "I'll arrange for your transportation to New Orleans so you can be with Billy. I'll find a place for you to stay near the medical facility. If you need help with child care, I'll see that you get it.

"You'll want to file a workmen's compensation insurance claim as soon as possible. Or someone in the human resources department can do it for you tomorrow. In the meantime, I don't want you to be out any personal expense."

He removed his wallet from his pants pocket. "Here are two hundred dollars to cover whatever you may need immediately. This is my business card. I've written my cell phone number on the back of it. Call me anytime for whatever you need. I'm here to help you."

She took the two hundred-dollar bills and the business card from him and then ripped them in half and threw them on the floor.

Fred, shocked, lunged forward. "Alicia!"

But Beck raised his hand, staving him off.

Billy Paulik's wife sneered. "You think I don't know what you're up to? You do the Hoyles' dirty work for them, don't you? Yeah, I've heard about you. You'd wipe their asses if they asked you to. You're here to throw money around and feed me a lot of bullshit about making everything easy and good for Billy, when all you're really doing is making sure the Hoyles don't get sued or written up in the newspaper. Ain't that right, Mr. Merchant?

"Well, *fuck you,* I ain't filing workmen's comp tomorrow or any other time, and I ain't taking your pissant handout, either. You can't buy a clean conscience from me, and you sure as hell can't buy my silence.

"Write this down, Mr. Smooth-talking Ass-kisser with the pretty smile. Write it down in my Billy's blood. I'm gonna make myself heard about what goes on in that stinking foundry. The Hoyles and you are gonna get your comeuppance. Just wait and see if you don't."

Then she spat in his face.

"Have you been calling me?"

"Chris. Where the hell are you?"

"The diner."

"On my way. Order coffee."

Beck had just left the hospital when Chris returned his call. He was headed for home but made a U-turn and arrived at the diner a few minutes later.

"I'm brewing a fresh pot for you, Beck," the waitress called to him as he walked in. "Give it two minutes."

"You're an angel."

"Yeah, yeah, that's what they all say."

He joined Chris in a booth, propped his elbows on the table, and wearily dragged his hands down his face. "Will this day never end?"

"I just called the ICU. Huff's sleeping like a baby. Heart's ticking like a Swiss clock. So what's the big emergency?"

"Why wasn't your cell on?"

"It was. On vibrate. Problem was, the cell wasn't on *me*." Chris smiled lazily. "A gentleman removes not only his boots but his cell phone when he joins a lady in bed. Didn't your mother teach you anything?"

"Billy Paulik nearly had his arm ripped off tonight."

Chris's grin faded. The two men stared across the table at each other while the waitress refreshed Chris's coffee and filled a mug for Beck. "Something to eat, Beck?"

"No thanks."

Sensing by their solemn mood that banter would be inappropriate, she left them.

"On the job, I assume," Chris said.

Beck gave a grim nod.

"Jesus. On top of everything else, this is all we need."

"That's why I feel like this day has lasted a thousand years." Beck then told him what had happened and brought him up to date. "The helicopter lifted off minutes before you called me. They wouldn't let his wife fly with him. Her brother-in-law is driving her to New Orleans as we speak."

He omitted the spitting incident. What purpose would it serve to tell Chris except to make him think badly of Mrs. Paulik? Beck didn't. He sympathized with the fear and anxiety that had led her to do it.

Even upset, she'd had the presence of mind to realize the irreversible impact this night would have on her family. Her husband might not survive. If he did, he would never be the same. Their economic future was in jeopardy. Tonight had changed their lives forever. No wonder she'd felt contempt for the platitudes, the cash, and the one who offered them.

With as much dignity as possible, he had come to his feet and wiped his face with a handkerchief, then moved away from her and her children. Fred Decluette had been mortified by her behavior. "No need to apologize for her, Fred," Beck had told him when he began stammering apologies. "She's scared and upset."

"I just want you to know that not all of us share her opinion, Mr. Merchant. I'd hate for it to get back to the Hoyles that we're ungrateful for y'all's generosity when something like this happens."

Beck had assured the nervous foreman that the incident would be forgotten. So he kept it out of his account to Chris.

"Billy will undergo surgery, but the ER doctor here told me that his arm is so mangled, it would take divine intervention to successfully reattach it, much less make it useful, and that they'd be doing Billy a favor if they didn't even try."

He paused to take a sip of coffee and glanced up as another customer came in. It was Slap Watkins, exuding the same belligerent arrogance as he had the night before. "Is he paying rent here?"

Beck continued to watch Slap as he paused just inside the door and glanced around. When he spotted him and Chris, his chin went back a notch as though surprised to see them there.

"Well, well, Slap Watkins," Chris said easily. "Long time no see. How was prison?"

Slap divided a calculating look between them, then said to Chris, "Anything beats working in your foundry."

"With an attitude like that, I guess it's a good thing my brother didn't hire you."

"Yeah, speaking of your brother . . ." The grin he flashed raised the hair on Beck's arms. "I bet Danny Boy is getting real ripe by now." Raising his nose in the air, he inhaled deeply. "Yep, I can smell that fucking corpse from here."

Chris moved to leave the booth and attack, but Beck laid a restraining hand on his arm. "That's what he wants you to do. Let it go."

"Good advice, Merchant." Fixing his gaze on Beck, Slap leered. "You been in his sister's pants yet? She as hot as she looks?"

It took supreme willpower for Beck to remain where he was.

The waitress came from behind the counter and approached Slap. "I won't stand for dirty talk like that in here. If you want something to eat or drink, take a seat." She handed him a menu.

Slap pushed it aside. "I don't want nothing to eat or drink."

"Then why did you come in?"

"Not that it's any of your concern, but I was supposed to meet a partner here to talk some business."

Unintimidated, she placed her hands on her hips and eyed him up and down, taking in his greasy blue jeans and the ratty tank top that left his arms bare. There was an array of tattoos. All of them were lewd, some outright obscene. Most appeared to be the work of amateurs.

The waitress said, "I can see you're all dressed up for an important business meeting. But we're not keeping this place open so you'll have free office space. Order something or leave."

"Good idea," Chris said tightly.

Slap looked at them with malice. "Coupla fags. Can't even tell which one's the bitch." Then he turned and swaggered out.

Through the window they watched him climb onto his motorcycle and speed out of the parking lot.

"I told you he was trouble, Beck," Chris said.

"Waiting to happen."

"Or already has. You heard what he said about the foundry. Did you see his reaction when I mentioned Danny? His arrogance slipped. Just a fraction and for just a second. I think we should discuss it with Red."

"All right. Tomorrow. But right now we've got an immediate problem. Do you think we should wait a day or two to tell Huff?"

"About Slap Watkins?"

"About Billy Paulik, Chris," Beck said impatiently. "The guy was maimed for life in your foundry tonight. He's got five young kids. He's worked for Hoyle Enterprises since he was seventeen. We don't have any jobs for one-armed men. What's he going to do now?"

"I don't know. Why are you upset with me? I didn't stick his arm into that machine. If he's worked for us since he was seventeen, he's well aware of the dangers and should have been paying better attention to what he was doing."

"Billy was trying to do some minor repair while the conveyor was running."

"He took it upon himself to do a repair he wasn't qualified to do."

"Because it needed to be done. He was thinking of production first, not safety, because that's what he's been ordered to think. The machine should have been stopped before anyone worked on it."

"Take that up with George Robson. He's the safety director. He sets the criteria for shutting down a piece of machinery."

"George does what you and Huff tell him to do."

Chris sat back against the booth and looked at

him closely. "Whose side are you arguing here?"

Beck placed his elbows on the table again, and this time he pressed his thumbs into his burning eye sockets. "You didn't see his blood," he said softly. After a time, he lowered his hands. "Fred Decluette said that Billy was working that machine tonight in place of a guy on vacation. He also said he shouldn't have taken it upon himself to fix the damn thing."

"You see?" Chris said blithely. "We're clear of all blame."

Beck wondered how the hell Chris could be smiling. Then he sighed and said, "Yeah. Right."

"His medical expenses will be covered by workmen's compensation insurance. That's why we pay out the nose for it."

Beck nodded, deciding not to bring up Alicia Paulik's threats. He would save those for another conversation. And perhaps, once Mrs. Paulik had had time to think about it, once she realized the extent of Billy's medical bills, she would change her mind and choose the easier of the two options available to her, which would be to file an insurance claim and, by doing so, forever lose her right to sue Hoyle Enterprises.

"Look, Beck, I know you feel terrible about what happened. So do I. But what else can we do?"

"We could send a bouquet of flowers to his hospital room."

"Absolutely."

Beck laughed, but not with humor. Chris had missed his sarcasm. "I'll see to it."

"Think you can keep it out of the media?"

Remembering the vehemence behind Mrs. Paulik's threats, he hedged. "I'll do my best."

"Which is usually good enough." Chris drained his coffee mug. "I'm bushed. As if being questioned by the sheriff and Huff's heart attack weren't enough excitement for one day, Lila was feeling particularly amorous tonight."

"How did you avoid George?"

"She told him she was visiting a sick friend."

"And he fell for that?"

"She's got him wound around her little finger by a string that's attached to his dick. Besides, he's not the sharpest knife in the drawer."

"No, just our safety director," Beck said under his breath as he and Chris left the booth and moved toward the door.

Before they parted in the parking lot, Chris asked, "Do you think he'll be all right?"

"He won't be *all right,* Chris. Losing a limb—"

"Not Paulik. Huff."

"Oh." Sayre had said that Huff had been playing one of his sick games when he summoned her to his "deathbed." That sounded typical of Huff. "Yes," he told Chris with confidence. "I think he'll be all right."

Thoughtfully, Chris bounced his car keys in his palm. "Do you know what he told me today? I guess he was feeling mellow, thinking that he'd come close to dying. He was a bit maudlin, but sincere. He said he wouldn't know what he'd do without his two sons. I reminded him that he'd lost Danny. But he was referring to you. He said, 'Beck is like another son to me.' "

"I'm flattered."

"Don't be. Being a son of Huff Hoyle comes with a few disadvantages."

"Like what?"

"Like you can be the one who tells him about Billy Paulik."

chapter 16

"Is Jessica DeBlance here?" Sayre spoke in the hushed tone that one reserves for the library.

The gray-haired lady at the desk smiled at her. "Jessica is working today, but she went down the street to get us some muffins from the bakery."

"So she's coming back?"

"Shouldn't be more than five minutes."

Sayre moved to a reading area where a window overlooked a small, landscaped courtyard. Sparrows were splashing in the shallow bowl of a birdbath. Hydrangea bushes were loaded with blue and pink blossoms as large as birthday balloons. Fig vine and lichen clung to the brick wall enclosure. The serenity of it was inviting.

She hadn't enjoyed a moment of tranquillity since she'd ordered Beck Merchant from her motel room last night.

Liar, he'd whispered.

The incriminating word had stung because it was true. She had denied having any intuition that something like that would happen between them. She'd also denied that she had wanted it to. He had canceled her denials with that one word: *liar.*

It echoed in her mind now as it had all through the night, even during her fitful sleep. She woke up still smarting with humiliation, still infuriated with him, but even more so with herself. He'd known that, too.

Liar also applied to her in a way Beck didn't know or couldn't guess. She had explained her reason for staying in Destiny as an obligation to her mother, as wanting to see to what extent if any Chris had been involved in Danny's death. But the underlying reason was her guilty conscience. Days before his death, she had rebuffed Danny. Her guilt over that was as omnipresent as the humid Gulf air. She couldn't escape it. It had brought her to the library this morning.

"Sayre?"

She looked up to find Jessica DeBlance standing beside her chair.

"I seem to have a bad habit of sneaking up on you," Jessica said by way of apology for startling her.

"My fault both times. I've had a lot on my mind."

"I'm surprised to see you. I thought you were leaving town yesterday."

"Change of plans. I tried to call you at home earlier this morning. Then your cell phone. When I couldn't reach you, I remembered that you'd met Danny in the library. I took a chance that you still worked here."

"I heard about Mr. Hoyle's heart attack. Is that why you stayed?"

"That and . . ." Sayre glanced at the other library visitors scattered about. "Is there someplace we can talk privately?"

Jessica led her into a cramped workroom filled with books, some boxed, others piled in uneven towers on the floor and every other flat surface. "Donations," she explained as she removed a stack of books from a chair and motioned for Sayre to sit down. "To most people it's a headache to inventory and catalog the books, so I volunteer for the job. Even in this age of computers, I still enjoy the smell of old books."

"So do I."

The two women smiled at each other as Jessica sat down on a padded stool. "Would you care for a fresh muffin? Some coffee?"

"No thanks."

"Everyone in the bakery was talking about Mr. Hoyle. Is his condition serious?"

"Early indications are that he'll be fine." After a short silence, Sayre said, "Something happened yesterday that I wanted to talk to you about. I don't know how significant it is, but it's one of the reasons I postponed my trip home."

"What happened?"

"Chris was questioned by Sheriff Harper and Deputy Scott in connection to Danny's death." While Jessica sat stunned, Sayre recapped what Beck had told her. "It's nothing more than a matchbook. As Beck pointed out, a defense lawyer could make a dozen cases as to how it got inside the fishing cabin with no help from Chris. It doesn't prove anything."

"But it's made the sheriff's department wonder if Chris was out there with Danny that afternoon."

"I'm wondering that, too. Jessica, do you know if there had been any strife between them recently?"

"Hasn't there always been strife between them? Their personalities and interests couldn't be more dissimilar. Danny knew that Chris was your father's favorite, but he seemed comfortable with that. Chris is Huff made over. Danny wasn't. He knew it, accepted it, even preferred it. He had no desire to be like either of them."

"Did he compete for Huff's attention?"

"Not especially. It didn't seem that important to him. He wasn't jealous of Chris if that's what you're getting at."

"Was Chris jealous of Danny?"

The question took Jessica aback and she laughed. "Why on earth would he be?"

"I don't know. I'm shooting in the dark." Sayre got up and moved to the window, which afforded another view of the pretty courtyard. The sparrows had left, but now bees were buzzing around the pink blossoms on the Rose of Sharon bush. A fat black caterpillar inched across the cracked flagstones. "I don't know what I'm after, Jessica. I thought perhaps Danny had mentioned an argument or some recent disagreement between them."

"Chris is seeing a married woman. Danny disapproved. But from what he told me about your brother, adultery wasn't anything new. Morally, the brothers would always be at opposite poles. Something tells me . . ."

When she stopped, Sayre turned away from the window and looked back at her. "Something tells you what?"

"It's just a feeling I have. I can't be sure."

Sayre returned to her chair and leaned toward the younger woman. "You knew Danny better than anyone. Far better I think than even his own flesh and blood knew him. If you have a feeling about something, I trust that instinct."

"The thing that had been weighing heavily on Danny's mind . . ."

"You think it related to Chris?"

"Not specifically. They didn't have that much interaction."

"They lived in the same house."

"They shared an address but spent very little time at home together. When they did, it was in the company of Huff and often Beck Merchant. They saw each other at work, of course, but they had different responsibilities and they reported to Huff, not to each other.

"They didn't move in the same social circles, especially since Danny became involved in our church." She paused. "And I think that was at the crux of what was bothering Danny. He was struggling with a spiritual matter."

"Like what?"

"I wish I knew, especially if he died because of it. I hated seeing him in that kind of spiritual quandary and urged him to discuss it with me, or our pastor, or someone else he trusted. He refused.

All he would say was that he couldn't be the Christian he should be or was supposed to be."

"His conscience was bothering him."

Jessica nodded. "I told him there was no sin or shortcoming that God wouldn't forgive. He made a joke of it and said that maybe God hadn't met the Hoyles."

"As far as you know, he never reconciled whatever was troubling him?" Sayre's hope was that, after she declined to talk to him, Danny had found a sympathetic ear elsewhere, that someone had counseled him. But Jessica dashed that desperate hope with a slow shake of her head.

"I don't think he could reconcile it. I hate that he died without making peace with it."

"Perhaps he found peace at the end," Sayre said, again hoping in vain that it was true.

Jessica looked over at Sayre and gave her a gentle smile. "Thank you for saying that, but I don't think he did. The more we talked about marriage and our future, the more he seemed to dwell on this problem. I would be guessing, but—"

"Please. Guess."

"Well, he was constantly bothered about the working conditions at the foundry. He wasn't proud of its reputation, violating OSHA standards, all that. Yet he hired people to work there. He placed them in jobs that he knew were dangerous and with only minimum training. Maybe he couldn't live with that any longer."

The lady who'd been manning the desk tapped on the door and after apologizing for the interruption told Jessica that the nursery school class had arrived for story hour. "About twenty of the little darlings are asking for Aunt Jessica," she said. "I don't know how long we can keep them corralled."

As they were leaving the workroom, Sayre asked Jessica for a favor. "I'll do anything that might help us learn what happened to Danny. What do you need?"

"Do you know anyone who works at the courthouse?"

The general mood was as glum, dark, and oppressive as the shop floor itself.

Beck noticed this immediately as he made his way toward the pipe conveyor that had caused the grisly accident the night before. Each worker was going about his job, but with a discernible lack of enthusiasm and in total silence. None made eye contact with him, but he could feel the resentful stares aimed at his back.

George Robson and Fred Decluette were in discussion near the machine and looked surprised when Beck joined them. "Morning, Mr. Merchant," Fred said.

"Fred. George."

"Hell of a thing." George shook his balding head remorsefully, then mopped sweat off it with a handkerchief. "Hell of a thing."

Beck looked down at the grimy floor. Last night there must have been a lake of blood on the spot where he now stood, but someone had made it disappear before the morning shift reported to work.

"We took care of the mess," Fred said, as though

reading his mind. "Bad for morale. No use reminding them of what happened."

"Maybe a reminder would be good," George offered. "Make them more cautious. Not so care-
less."

To keep himself from hitting the insensitive idiot,
Beck moved closer to the machine. "Show me what
happened," he said to Fred.

"He's already gone over it with me."

"I'd like to see it for myself, George. Huff will
want to know the details."

George, he noted, remained at a safe distance as
Fred pointed out the faulty drive belt and explained
what had gone wrong when Paulik tried to repair
it. "We've got somebody coming out tomorrow to
fix it proper," Fred told him.

"I made arrangements for that first thing this
morning," George said.

Beck looked up at the cast pipes moving along
the shaky conveyor overhead. "Is it safe to operate
as it is?" He directed the question to the foreman,
but George answered.

"In my opinion, yes."

Fred looked less convinced, but he nodded. "Mr.
Robson here seems to think so, and he ought to
know."

Beck hesitated, then said, "All right. Just be sure
everyone knows what happened and caution
them—"

"Oh, they already know, Mr. Merchant. Word of
something like that travels fast."

Of course it would. Beck gave George Robson a
cursory nod, then turned and went back the way

he'd come. His shirt was stuck to his back. He could feel rivulets of sweat sliding down his ribs. He'd been on the shop floor less than five minutes and was drenched with perspiration. His lungs were laboring to expel the hot air he inhaled. These men withstood these conditions for eight hours, unless they worked a double shift to earn overtime.

As he walked past the machine with the white cross painted on it, he paused, wondering if George Robson had ever thought to ask what that cross signified. Or if he had ever even noticed it. Sayre had.

Beck slowed his pace and then came to a complete stop. He pondered the emblem for several seconds and thought about the tragedy it commemorated. Then he did an abrupt about-face and quickly retraced his steps to Fred Decluette and the safety director.

"Christ, this will make news." Huff moved his lips as though clamping a cigarette between them. "The media will have a field day just like they did the last time someone got hurt on the job."

From across the ICU room, Chris said, "Beck should have waited a few more days before telling you."

Huff practically snarled. "Of course he should have told me. He should have told me last night, and not waited till this morning. It's my foundry. It's got my name on it. Would you rather me read about it in the newspaper? Hear it on the five o'clock news? I had to know, and Beck realized that."

Chris noted that Beck had remained silent while Huff ranted over the news of Billy Paulik's accident. Although Beck had had to break the bad news to Huff, Huff wasn't ready to shoot the messenger. Rather, Beck had his wholehearted approval and trust, and to Chris that was a bit galling.

"Paulik's medical bills will be through the roof," Huff said. "The premiums on our workmen's comp insurance will go up because of this."

"Mrs. Paulik may not file," Beck said, speaking for the first time. "She told me she wasn't going to."

Huff reeled off a stream of vulgarities. He knew what Alicia Paulik's failure to file an insurance claim portended for Hoyle Enterprises, and so did Chris. He was perturbed with Beck for springing this on them. "Why didn't you tell me this last night?"

"You didn't ask."

"I shouldn't have had to ask, and I resent the omission."

"We were both exhausted, Chris. It had already been a hellish day. I didn't feel like going into it."

Huff cut their argument short by asking, "You think she intends to sue us, Beck?"

"That was her line last night. She may have changed her mind by now. I hope so."

"If she sues, how much do you think it'll cost us?"

"Too early to tell. Our accountants can't begin to estimate the amount of Billy's medical bills until they've consulted the attending physicians and the hospital, and even they can't know the final tally this soon. He'll have a long recovery period. There'll be rehab, a prosthesis."

"It doesn't have to be the Rolls-Royce of prostheses, does it?" Chris asked. "More like a Ford?" His attempted levity fell flat. It seemed everybody close to him had lost his sense of humor.

Beck continued. "Beyond the medical expenses, I think we can safely anticipate Mrs. Paulik to cite things we can't quantify, like the family's pain and suffering, Billy's lost income due to his disability. I'm afraid she plans to hit us from all sides, and the total damages she'll seek could be astronomical."

"How much will it cost to bury this thing?" Huff asked.

"You mean in terms of negative publicity? That'll be expensive, too. She also promised to make a lot of noise."

"Jesus, you're just overflowing with good news today," Chris remarked.

"He asked," Beck fired back at him.

"You didn't have to let him have it all at once."

"I wanted it all at once," Huff barked. "You can't deal with a problem if you don't know but the half of it."

Chris noticed that Huff's cheeks had become flushed. Worried about spiking blood pressure, he glanced at the monitors beside the bed. He aimed for a more optimistic outlook that would calm Huff down. "I think we're all overreacting. We're dreading a backlash that probably won't happen. Let's stop and think about it before we lose our heads. Okay?"

Beck nodded brusquely. Huff grunted what Chris took as a signal to proceed.

"As Beck said, Mrs. Paulik may change her mind. She flipped out in the emergency room. It was a knee-jerk reaction to a traumatic situation. She was probably mimicking a scene she saw on *ER*. But I rather imagine she's feeling a bit overwhelmed this morning. In the cold light of day, reality has set in. She may be more agreeable to a quick settlement.

"Second, Billy Paulik has always been a good employee. He's never given us any trouble. Once he is himself again, he'll explain to his missus that it was his mistake, not ours. He'll be too embarrassed to hold us liable for an accident that was his fault."

Huff considered Chris's observations, then turned to Beck. "You met the wife. What's your read on her? Was it just hysterics talking?"

"I hope Chris is right, but you pay me to look at the worst-case scenario. Last night she made her plans for us and the foundry very clear."

"She's going for our gonads," Huff said.

"I think we should prepare for it, yes. For some harsh public criticism at the very least."

"Then let's head her off," Chris said, still striving for amelioration. "Let's stop her before she starts. Let's demonstrate our goodwill by giving the kids a carte blanche trip to Toys 'R' Us. Let's park a shiny new SUV in their garage. How about paying their rent for one year? That dump they live in can't be very expensive."

"We own that dump," Huff said. "It's one of our rent houses."

"Even better. We can paint it, make repairs, install a backyard grill. After that, I'll bet Mrs. Paulik would think twice about filing suit. Especially if she thought she might lose— And, Beck, you could dazzle her with legalese that would convince her she would—in which case we would evict her from her renovated house and take back the new car and all the other goodies."

Huff looked across at Beck. "What do you think?"

"Worth a try, I suppose. I'll get someone from my office to prepare a goodwill package starting with the SUV."

Chris said, "And to nullify any allegations about unsafe working conditions, I'll order that conveyor to be shut down until it's repaired."

"It's already shut down."

Chris turned to Beck. "Since when?"

"An hour ago."

"On whose authority?"

"Mine."

Chris felt a surge of anger. He was director of operations, but apparently titles meant nothing to Beck.

"I'm sorry if I overstepped my bounds, Chris, but I went on the floor this morning to assess the situation."

"That's what we pay George Robson to do."

"He was there, with his thumb up his butt, completely ineffectual. Any idiot could see that that conveyor should not be in use. And think of the message it was sending the other employees to see it in operation, with no regard being given to what happened to Billy Paulik. George was too gutless, or too stupid, to make the decision, so I took it upon myself."

Stiffly, Chris nodded. "I'm sure you were acting on my behalf."

"Because you had to be here with Huff. I made it clear to George and everyone else that I was speaking for you." He checked his wristwatch. "I've been away too long. Morale is at rock bottom. We should be visible as much as possible. With your permission, I'll post a memo throughout the plant, expressing management's sorrow over what happened to Billy."

"Be sure and throw in something about how we're looking after his family," Huff said.

"Of course." Beck looked at him and smiled grimly. "This couldn't have happened at a worse time, so soon after Danny. I hope the bad news didn't affect your recovery. How are you feeling?"

"One more day in this place and I get to go home. But that's only a precaution. Unnecessary if you ask me. Doc Caroe says I'm sound as a dollar. Those blasted tests of his. I was poked and prodded and hooked up to machines. Had a quart of blood drawn. Peed into a cup too many times to count. All that, only to learn that there was minimal damage done to my heart."

Chris laughed. "Don't sound so disappointed, Huff."

"Far from it. I want to live forever." Looking at Beck, he said, "I know you hated to give me that report. But it's your job to bring me bad news. Don't blame yourself for doing your job."

Beck nodded absently.

Sensing his inattention, Huff asked, "Something still on your mind?"

"If I'd lost my arm," Beck said thoughtfully, "and effectively my livelihood, I'm not sure I could be pacified with a few toys and a coat of paint on my house." Dividing a look between them, he said, "I still think we should brace for the worst."

After he left, Chris went to sit on the end of his father's hospital bed. "You know Beck. He's the prophet of fucking doom. Don't let his pessimism get you down."

"He takes his job seriously. He's looking out after our interests." Huff poked his thigh. "And your inheritance, Son. Don't forget that."

"All right, all right. The man's a gem. Don't send your blood pressure up again."

"I've never heard you get testy with Beck before. What was that about?"

"Since when is it in his job description to shut down a faulty machine?"

"Would you have rather it chew off somebody else's arm first?"

"Of course not."

"Then he did the right thing, didn't he?"

"I didn't say it wasn't right. I suggested it myself. It's just— Oh, hell, can we drop this? The stress has got to me, that's all. We're all under a lot of pressure these days."

"Speaking of pressure, heard any more from Red's office?"

"Not a word."

"I didn't think you would," Huff said with a

negligent wave of his hand. "Red should send out Deputy Scott to round up milk cows that get out of their fences. Shit like that. Not have him fiddle-farting around with you over some minor detail like a goddamn matchbook. What's the news from Mexico?"

"With Mary Beth? I haven't had time to even think about Mary Beth."

"But you've had time to ball that sly little gal George is married to. As recently as last night."

Chris wasn't embarrassed that his father knew, but he was awed and amused. "Your network of informers is amazing, Huff. How do you manage it? Even from a bed in the ICU."

Huff laughed softly. "I'll tell you something amazing. Did you know that your sister and Beck were out at the fish shack last night? Then Beck took Sayre to the motel, got her checked in, walked her to her door, and went inside."

Chris remembered the lethal expression on Beck's face when Slap Watkins had made the vulgar reference to Sayre. But Beck was from the old school and thought of all women as ladies before proven otherwise. He dismissed Huff's insinuation with a derisive snort. "Surely you're not suggesting anything romantic between Beck and Sayre? She despised him on sight because he's one of us."

"Then why isn't she back in San Francisco?"

"Because she thought you were going to die."

"Hm. Maybe." Stacking his hands behind his head, he said, "It would be interesting, though, wouldn't it?"

"What?"

"If Beck and Sayre were to link up."

"I wouldn't hold my breath if I were you. Beck likes women who're soft, sweet, and low maintenance. That hardly describes Sayre."

"I won't go so far as to hold my breath," Huff said, "but I've got to start considering alternative solutions to my problem."

"Which problem is that?"

"Seeing a third-generation Hoyle born before the killer heart attack gets me. If you're going to sire my grandbaby, you'd better get busy on that divorce from Mary Beth. No sense in barking up that tree if she's sterile. Have you got another woman picked out? Lila?"

"Lila? Hell, no."

"Then you'd be smart not to waste your time—and mine, I might add—on her. Just a thought." Huff depressed the button to recline his bed. When he was settled, he closed his eyes.

Chris could take a hint. He left the ICU, and the hospital, but he took with him everything Huff had said, knowing from experience that nothing coming from his father's mouth was random or trivial.

chapter *17*

The house was situated well off the road. A narrow lane of crushed oyster shells led straight to the front steps. The roof was steeply pitched and extended over the deep gallery to provide shade. The front door was directly in the center of the facade, with two tall windows on each side of it. The exterior walls were white, the shutters and front door were dark green.

Sayre turned into the lane and brought the car to a stop at the bottom of the front steps, which were flanked by beds of caladiums and white geraniums. After a day of unrelenting heat, the plants were drooping.

Beck was sitting in a teakwood glider on the gallery, a bottle of beer in one hand, the fingers of the other buried in Frito's thick pelt.

When she opened the car door, the dog growled low in his throat. But as she alighted he must have recognized her because he bolted down the steps to greet her. She became trapped against the car by ninety pounds of exuberance.

Beck whistled sharply, and Frito subsided, but only marginally. He stayed right at her feet, causing her to stumble over him several times as she made her way up the steps.

His owner didn't stand, didn't say anything, just sat there, looking remarkably imposing for a man wearing only a pair of olive khaki shorts. His expression revealed nothing—whether he was surprised, or angry, or completely indifferent to her showing up on his turf and interrupting his cocktail hour.

When she reached the top step, she paused. Frito planted himself beneath her hand and nosed her palm until she rubbed the top of his head. But she never broke eye contact with Beck. Finally she said, "I doubt you know how difficult it was for me to come here and face you."

He took a sip from his bottle of beer but didn't say anything.

"I didn't want to come, and wouldn't be here at all, except that I think there's something we should talk about."

"You want to talk?"

"Yes."

"Talk?"

"*Yes.*"

"Then you're not here to pick up where you left off last night?"

Her cheeks grew hot with embarrassment, as well as anger. "You're not going to be one whit gallant about that, are you?"

"You want gallantry after threatening to kill me if I touched you again? You don't ask for much, do you?"

"That's fair, I suppose."

"You're damn right it is."

She had assumed that whenever she faced him again she would be subjected to his ridicule and had bolstered herself for it. While she wanted to rush back to her car and drive away, blushing cheeks and all, she endured his stare and held her ground.

Finally he snuffled a bitter laugh and scooted over to make room for her on the glider. "Have a seat. Would you like a beer?"

"No thank you." She sat down next to him.

He glanced at the red convertible in which she'd arrived. "Snazzy automobile."

"It was all the rental company had available on short notice."

"They drove it out to you from New Orleans?"

"This morning."

He looked her over, taking in the linen slacks and coordinating silk T-shirt. "More new clothes?"

"I didn't bring much from San Francisco. I needed supplemental wardrobe."

"So you're still planning to stay?"

"Did you think that what happened last night would scare me off? Was it intended to send me packing? Is that why you did it?"

The bottle-green eyes connected with hers, and it was like getting socked lightly in the gut . . . or lower. "Why did *you*?"

Being this close to him would have been uncomfortable had he been fully clothed. But in his half-dressed state, his nearness was discomfiting. It was vexing that he was the one partially undressed, yet she felt exposed.

She looked away from him and turned toward the cypress trees that lined the banks of Bayou Bosquet, which cut across this lot as well as Huff's property. "This was the original house," she said. "Did you know that?"

"I've heard it mentioned."

"Huff lived here while he was building the big house."

"Before he married your mother."

"Yes. Huff didn't want it to fall into ruin, so Old Mitchell was responsible for the upkeep of this place, too. Sometimes when he'd come here to do his chores, he would let me tag along. While he worked outside, I'd play house in the empty rooms. This was the first house I ever decorated. In my imagination, of course."

"I doubt my decor would meet your standards."

She laughed. "Don't be so sure. As I recall I envisioned a crystal chandelier suspended from the living room ceiling on a tasseled cord, Oriental rugs, and walls hung with bright silk drapes. My motif was a cross between a sultan's tent and a French palace."

"Or brothel."

"I didn't know what that was, but that's sort of the look I had in mind." She smiled at him before returning her gaze to the stand of cypresses and the channel of water beyond. "One time, Old Mitchell and I came here via the bayou. He poled us here in a pirogue and warned me to sit still or we'd capsize and the gators would get us. He told me he knew of gators lurking in those very waters that could swallow me whole and not even burp. I sat as still as a mouse and held on for dear life. That was quite an adventure." She smiled in reminiscence. "I didn't know until today that you lived in this house."

"Does my being here sully your fond memories of the place? Like my sitting in the swing Old Mitchell made for you?"

"My fond memories of childhood were sullied long before I met you."

He let that pass without comment, saying instead, "Huff offered me the use of the house at the same time he offered me the job. It was supposed to be a temporary arrangement, only until I could find my own place. But one day he asked me why I would want to pay rent to somebody else when I could live here for free. I asked myself the same question, arrived at the obvious answer, and have been here ever since."

"They truly own you, don't they?"

That struck a chord. He finished his beer and set the empty bottle on the side table with a decisive thunk. "Why did you come here?"

"I heard about the accident at the plant last night. That's all anyone is talking about."

"What's being said?"

"That it was bad, and that Hoyle Enterprises is largely responsible."

"That's what I would expect them to say."

"Is it true?"

"The man's arm couldn't be saved. They amputated it this afternoon. I'd call that bad."

He didn't address whether or not the fault lay with Hoyle Enterprises, and she doubted that his failure to was an oversight. "I heard you went to the hospital after he was brought in."

"You've got reliable sources."

"And that the injured man's wife rejected your offer of help."

"Stop tiptoeing around it, Sayre. You heard that she spat in my face. Is that why you're here? You came to gloat?"

"No."

"Or to remind me of the hazardous working conditions in the foundry?"

"You shouldn't need reminding, should you?"

"The conveyor that injured Billy Paulik has been shut down."

"On your orders. I heard about that, too."

He gave a negligent shrug.

"Why not George Robson?"

"Because he—"

"Because he's a puppet who doesn't do anything before clearing it with Huff."

"Who was in the hospital recovering from a heart attack, or have you forgotten about that?"

"How did he and Chris react upon hearing what you'd done?"

"They endorsed my decision."

"Don't defend them, Beck. Do you think it's a fluke that George Robson is in charge of safety? Huff doesn't want anyone with a conscience or even common sense in that position. George Robson is nothing more than a title to pacify OSHA. Does he even have a staff?"

"A small one."

"A secretary. That's it. He doesn't have trained

personnel making routine checks, and he certainly doesn't do it himself. Does he have a budget? No. Authority? Zero."

"He implemented the lockout-tagout policy."

Sayre knew the term. It meant that a piece of malfunctioning machinery could be locked down and could not be restarted, either accidentally or intentionally, unless a supervisor with a key deemed it functional and safe for operation. "He implemented it only to avoid a stiff fine. Is it enforced?"

He merely looked back at her.

"I didn't think so. Hoyle Enterprises' so-called safety director, Robson, takes up space, and that's all he does."

"You ought to sign up with Charles Nielson."

"Who?"

"Never mind." He gave the glider a hard push with his bare foot. "So you came to talk about the accident?"

"No. I came to ask you about something that's been bothering me."

"On my stomach."

"What?"

"You once asked me how I sleep at night. I never got around to answering you. Generally I sleep on my stomach. And by the way, the invitation still stands if you ever want to find out for yourself."

She was out of the glider like a shot. When she reached the porch railing, she turned to face him. "I think Chris may have murdered Danny. Now make a joke out of that."

He left his seat and crossed the porch in two long strides. "That would make you happy, wouldn't it? It would validate your hatred of Chris and Huff, and you'd have your vengeance on them."

"It's not vengeance I want."

"Don't you?"

"No."

"Then what, Sayre?"

"Justice," she said heatedly. "And as an officer of the court, I would think—hope—that you'd want that, too. Of course, you live rent free in their house."

He made a sound of aggravation. "Which is totally irrelevant. In any case, I can't talk to you about this. I'm their attorney."

"You're not a criminal lawyer."

"Chris doesn't need one."

"Are you sure?"

Their gazes locked and held. He was the first to back down. He ran his hand through his hair and motioned her back into the glider. She remained where she was, but he returned to it and sat down. "Okay, Sayre, let's talk. I don't promise to say anything, but I'm willing to listen."

She wanted an answer to a question that had been plaguing her, but he was bound by attorney-client privilege, and she by her promise not to betray Jessica DeBlance. She took a moment to arrange her thoughts, then asked, "Lately, had Danny and Chris been quarreling about something?"

"About 'something'? You have been away for a long time. They quarreled about everything. From the hourly wage we pay a new employee through the LSU football team to the virtues of Coke over Pepsi."

"I'm not talking about a squabble. This would have been a recurring argument over something consequential."

"Danny's religion," he said without hesitation. "He and Chris quarreled about it at the country club the day before Danny died. Huff had asked Chris to speak to Danny about it, to see if he could straighten him out. Chris was irreverent. Danny took offense. I'm not violating confidentiality, because several people at the country club witnessed the quarrel and told Deputy Scott about it."

"Did any of these witnesses overhear what they said, specifically?"

"Not to my knowledge."

"Did Chris tell you what was said? Strike that," she said with a shake of her head. "I know you couldn't tell me that."

"No, I couldn't. But in fact, he didn't tell me what was said. He admitted that they argued over Danny's newfound faith and that he'd made some remarks which upset Danny. That's as specific as he got."

Frito ambled over to nudge her thigh with his large head. She reached down and stroked his back.

"I'm jealous," Beck said.

"He does seem to like me."

"I'm not jealous of you. I'm jealous of Frito." His voice was as stirring as the way he was looking at her. "How is it that I can be so mad at you one minute, and the next I want to be—"

"Don't."

"What?"

"Don't say whatever you were going to say. Don't flirt with me. It won't distract me from what we're talking about. And, frankly, it's disappointing that you would think I'm that frivolous."

"Frivolous? Sayre, you're about as frivolous as a train wreck."

"That's not very complimentary either."

"I can't win for losing. When I try to compliment you, you accuse me of flirting to distract you. So let's stop this verbal sparring. Why don't you just level with me and tell me what you're thinking?"

"Because I don't trust you."

He raised an eyebrow. "Well, you could hardly get more straightforward than that."

"You could take anything I say and use it for your own purpose."

"What *is* my purpose? Tell me."

"To let Chris get away with murder," she said huskily. "Again."

He held her gaze for a moment, then said, "The state failed to prove that Chris killed Gene Iverson."

"And the defense failed to disprove it. I know from somebody close to Danny—"

"Who?"

"I can't tell you that. But someone who knew him well told me that Danny was wrestling with a personal dilemma. And this individual feels that it was a moral dilemma, a matter of conscience."

"Danny was walking the straight and narrow. Tithing, attending church every time the doors were open. He hadn't even drunk a beer since he joined the congregation. What could he have a guilty conscience about?"

"According to this person, Danny was conflicted about something more serious than drinking a beer. Perhaps it involved something going on at the foundry. Something illegal. Whatever it was, it was eating him alive. I think he wanted to get it off his chest, come clean. Chris was afraid that he would, so he killed him."

Beck stared at her for a moment, then got up and came to stand at the railing. Leaning forward, he braced his arms against the top rail and gazed into the distance. Sayre saw what he did—a pale nimbus above the treetops, formed by the lights of the foundry that came on automatically with the dusk.

The ever-present smoke hovered above the horizon undisturbed because there was no wind. It was like an entity unto itself, a continuous reminder of the Hoyles' dominance and a perpetual threat to anyone who dared to question their right to dominate.

Beck said, "You've really got it in for them, don't you?"

"Do you honestly think I enjoy accusing my brother of murder?"

He straightened up and turned around, propping his hips against the railing and folding his arms across his bare chest. "I think you might."

"I don't. I don't even want to think that Chris is capable of it. But, tragically, I do. Killing runs in our family."

"Like a physical trait?"

"Huff killed a man and got away with it."

"Oh, first Chris. Now Huff." He shook his head with incredulity. "You just don't stop, do you? Well, leave me out of your petty vendettas against your family, all right?"

He went to his front door, opened it, and motioned Frito inside. The screened door slammed shut behind him. Sayre hesitated only a second before going after him.

She followed the clatter of pots and pans and found him in the kitchen lighting a burner on the range. Frito was excitedly dancing around his feet.

"His name was Sonnie Hallser," she said. "He was a foreman at the plant in the mid-seventies. An advocate for unionizing. He and Huff had locked horns over the working conditions and—"

"Look," he said, coming around and facing her, "I know all about it. I don't need any details because I read them for myself. Huff offered me a— Shit!"

The empty skillet on the burner had begun to smoke. He pulled it off the stove and took two eggs from the refrigerator. He cracked them into the skillet, cooked them quickly, then mixed them with kibbles in Frito's bowl. Frito attacked it as soon as Beck set the bowl on the floor.

"Huff offered me a sweet deal," he continued. "It was a lawyer's wet dream. Beyond the challenging job, there was the house, the car allowance, benefits, great salary. You think I'm a whore for accepting his offer? Fine. Think that. But like any good whore, I work my ass off. I earn what I'm paid.

"Also like any smart whore, I checked out my

client before I took his money. I checked him out thoroughly. You think I was oblivious or naïve? No, Sayre. I did my homework. One of the more negative write-ups about Chris's trial hearkened back to all the other Hoyle employees who had died in job-related accidents.

"Sonnie Hallser was named. I did extensive research, learned everything there was to know about the fatal incident. Granted, the circumstances surrounding it were murky, but—"

"Huff is clever enough to make them murky."

"What do you know about it?"

"I lived through it! I was five years old, but it made an indelible impression. My mother stayed locked in her bedroom, crying all the time. Huff was in a constant state of agitation. Red Harper and other men came to our house in the middle of the night and gathered secretively in Huff's den. Tension inside the house was so hot and thick you could cut it with a knife.

"Even as a child, I sensed all this, and it frightened me. I asked Selma what was going on. She told me that some people thought Huff had killed a man and had made it look like an accident. She told me it was a big fat lie and to pay it no mind.

"But I did, Beck. I thought about it a lot and wondered if it was a lie. I'd seen Huff when he was angry enough to kill someone. Long after things had settled down and returned to normal, I continued to think about it. Years later, I did my own research into the matter."

"Then you know there was no basis for an indictment."

"Maybe not from a legal standpoint, but I'm convinced that Huff did precisely what was alleged. The machine with the white cross painted on it, the one I saw yesterday, that's where Sonnie Hallser died, isn't it?"

"That's what they say."

"It's a behemoth, capable of crushing a man. Huff pushed Hallser into it and watched him die."

Propping his hands on his hips, Beck bent slightly at the waist and took several deep breaths. When he straightened up, he said, "The authorities conducted a thorough investigation, Sayre."

"The authorities were bribed."

"No criminal charges were ever filed."

"Which doesn't mean a crime wasn't committed."

"Huff was cleared of all suspicion."

"The case was swept under the rug."

"Because no one could prove any wrongdoing," he shouted. "And whether I like it, or you like it, that's the way the legal system works."

He was breathing hard, his eyes alight with the ferocity of his argument. Frito's whine finally penetrated his anger. He dropped the combative posture and walked to the back door to let the dog out. "Don't go too far. Remember the skunk." Turning back into the room, he said, "Sure you wouldn't like something to drink?"

She declined with a small shake of her head.

His anger had abated. Now he was merely frustrated, and frustration looked good on him. She tried but failed to keep her eyes away from him as he took a canned Coke from the refrigerator and popped the top, tossing the tab onto the tabletop with typical male negligence.

He drank deeply from the can, then placed it on the kitchen table. "Where were we?"

She pulled her gaze away from his bare torso. "Nowhere. We're going around in circles. This was a mistake. I never should have come here."

She made it only as far as the interior door before he laid his hand on her shoulder. "Why did you come, Sayre? Truthfully."

With him standing that close, turning around was a bad idea. She knew that before she did it. But she turned anyway, bringing her eyes on a level with the V of his throat. "Truthfully? To see if you knew what had been bothering Danny."

"I don't know. And I regret that I don't, because if I did, maybe we'd have an explanation for what happened to him. Now, is that the only reason you came?"

"Yes."

"No other?"

"No."

"I don't believe you." When she raised her head and looked up at him, he added, "I think you came here because you wanted to see me. I'm glad you did. I wanted to see you, too. I'm not nearly the villain you think I am."

"But you are, Beck. The tragedy is that you don't even realize it. You may not have started out that way. I don't know. But now you're so steeped in their corruption that you might as well have been born evil like they were.

"They seduced you three years ago, and the seduction was so complete that now you can't distinguish what is right from what is merely expedient. Mrs. Paulik knew it. I know it, too. Your soul belongs to them."

"Okay, let's say you're right. I'm an opportunist. Rotten to the core. If that's so, why would you let me come within ten feet of you?" He took a step closer. "There must be something about me you like."

She tried to move away, but he wouldn't let her.

"Let's talk about last night."

"No, Beck."

"Why not? We're grown-ups."

She gave a low laugh of self-deprecation. "Is that the way grown-ups behave?"

"Sometimes. If they're lucky." Lowering his voice, he added, "Although you got luckier than I did."

To shut out his smile, she closed her eyes.

"What's the worst thing you did, Sayre?" he asked softly. "You surrendered to your natural impulses. Is that so terrible?"

"For me? Yes."

"Forgive yourself for being human. You had been riding an emotional roller coaster all day. Through it all, you didn't scream, you didn't cry, God knows you didn't laugh. You'd had no release. You had kept your cool, maintained rigid self-control, so all those emotions were pent up inside you. They had reached a fever pitch. Sex provided an outlet."

She opened her eyes. "What happened last night was anger driven. It had nothing to do with sex."

He frowned with mild reproach. "I was there, Sayre, remember? It had everything to do with sex."

"I was livid. You only wanted to insult and humiliate me."

"You don't believe that."

"Yes I do."

He shook his head. "If you believed that, you wouldn't be standing here now."

He was right. If this wasn't about sex, it was a damn good imitation. All the sensations she experienced each time she saw him were sexual. The awareness of him, sexual. The hormonal rush, sexual. The sudden need to hold and to be held, sexual. The desire to be taken to a level of arousal and release that disallowed thoughts of anything else, purely sexual.

God, it would be fabulous to give herself over to it, to take advantage of this very attractive man, to lose herself in physical sensation, to use him. But he was Beck Merchant, Chris's best friend, Huff's yesman.

She whispered, "I can't do this, Beck."

"Neither can I. This is all kinds of wrong." He placed his hands on her waist and drew her lower body against his. "But I still want to be all over you."

Then he kissed her. His lips were warm and his tongue was nimble and she surrendered her mouth to both. She actually whimpered a small protest when he pulled back. He touched the split on her lower lip with the knuckle of his index finger.

"Too much pressure?"

"No."

He smiled. "Not enough?"

He touched the delicate spot with the tip of his tongue, kissed it tenderly, then took bold and intimate possession of her mouth. His hand moved from her face to her breast. His palm ground lightly against her nipple, and she felt a responsive tug, like a hunger pang, deep within her.

Oh God, it felt good. Call it desire, or lust, or whatever, it was wonderful and tempting and terrifying, because if she didn't stop this now, she would make another mistake, more disastrous than the one last night.

"I can't do this with you," she said breathlessly. Before he could react, she pushed him aside and rushed through the doorway, only to be brought up short the instant she entered the living room.

Chris was leaning against the back of the sofa, ankles and arms crossed, smiling his most insolent smile. "I would have cleared my throat, but I hated to interrupt." He gave Sayre a smirking once-over, then looked at Beck. "Go take a cold shower. It seems I'm in dire need of my attorney."

chapter 18

Red Harper was pacing along the sidewalk outside the sheriff's office when they arrived. He was smoking a cigarette, but Beck got the impression that the smoke break was only an excuse for him to be outside, waiting to intercept them before they went in.

Red's first statement confirmed his guess. "I just want y'all to know that I had nothing to do with this."

"With what?" Beck asked.

"Scott acted alone. I knew nothing about it beforehand. Chris, you'd better look sharp in there."

Chris thrust his face to within an inch of the sheriff's. "And if you can't manage this asshole, you'd better start looking for another job."

It wasn't an empty threat, and Red knew it. If he didn't protect the Hoyles, he wouldn't have protection against anyone investigating his ethics. He took a final drag on his cigarette. "We'd better go inside."

Spit-and-polish ready, Deputy Wayne Scott was waiting for them inside Red's private office. He acknowledged their arrival with a grave nod and thanked them for coming on such short notice. "I thought it would be best to clear this up right away."

"Exactly what is it that needs clearing up?" Chris asked.

"Let me do the talking, Chris," Beck said.

They sat in the same chairs as before, facing Red across his battered and littered desk, with Deputy Scott practically standing at attention beside him.

Red began by clearing his throat. "This, uh, this needs some explanation, I'm afraid."

He extended to Beck a sheet of paper on which was printed computer gobbledygook.

"I subpoenaed your telephone records, Mr. Hoyle," Scott said. "This is a record of the calls you made from your cell phone the day your brother died. I've highlighted the call that we'd like explained."

Beck saw that a line of data had been marked with a yellow highlighter pen. "This is A.M.?" he asked, noting the time of the call.

"Yes, sir. At seven-oh-four that Sunday morning, Mr. Hoyle placed a call to the victim's cell phone."

It didn't escape Beck's notice that Danny was now being referred to as "the victim."

"Well, you caught me red-handed, Deputy. I called my brother on the telephone. You'd better handcuff me quick before I'm unleashed on an unsuspecting public."

Beck shot Chris a look that warned him to shut

up. Then, putting on his game face, Beck addressed Scott. "Like my client, I fail to see the problem."

"The problem is that Mr. Hoyle told us he'd slept late that morning, till about eleven o'clock. He didn't mention waking up a little after seven to call his brother. And it seems a strange thing to do anyway. Hadn't Danny Hoyle been sleeping in his room down the hall just a little while before that?"

Red, speaking for the first time, said, "We've established that Danny got home shortly before midnight on Saturday. He slept in his bed that night because Selma made it up on Sunday morning. He had a cup of coffee with her in the kitchen between six-thirty and seven, when he left for a men's prayer breakfast the church has every Sunday morning. He'd been away from the house approximately four minutes when you called him on his cell phone," he said to Chris.

Before Chris could respond, Beck said, "Someone else could have used Chris's cell phone. Selma. Huff. Me. We all had access to it."

"Where do you keep your cell phone, Mr. Hoyle?"

Chris glanced at Beck, signaling that he wanted to answer. "I advise you not to say anything until we've had a chance to discuss this," Beck said.

"It doesn't matter. This is bullshit." Ignoring Beck's warning, he turned to the law officers. "Nobody else used my phone Sunday morning. It was on my dresser, along with my wallet and everything else that came out of my pants pockets the night before. I called Danny that morning. I can't deny it.

There's the proof," he said, waving toward the phone record.

"I didn't mention it before because I'd actually forgotten about it, and I'd forgotten about it because it was insignificant. I woke up to go to the bathroom. If you say it was around seven o'clock, then I guess it was around seven o'clock. I didn't know what time it was and didn't care.

"I was on my way back to bed when I heard a car engine starting. I looked through my bedroom window and saw Danny's car driving away. I remembered that Huff wanted Danny at home for dinner that evening, and he didn't care if Saint Peter himself was going to appear in that Holy Roller tabernacle. That's a quote.

"I was hungover and frankly didn't give a damn where my brother would be having dinner that night. But I knew we'd all bear the brunt of Huff's foul mood if Danny wasn't there because I'd forgotten to tell him to be. So while it was fresh on my mind, I called him. If I'd gone back to sleep, I might not have remembered it later. I gave him a heads-up. I told him that unless he wanted Huff on the warpath, he would be at home for dinner that evening.

"Danny promised he would be. I asked him to toss a five into the collection plate for me, to cover the sins I'd committed the night before. He laughed and said a five probably wouldn't come close to covering my transgressions, then he told me to go back to bed, that he would see me at dinner, and hung up."

His smile was pleasant, but it dripped contempt. "Now, Deputy Scott, if you think you can hang a murder rap on me with that, you're even more laughable than I originally thought."

The insult bounced off Scott's starched uniform. "Yes, sir, that would be pretty flimsy in itself. But then there's the matter of the time."

"Time?" Beck glanced at Red, whose flabby jowl was resting on his fist. He appeared to be miserable and wouldn't look him in the eye.

"That's right, Mr. Merchant," Scott said. "Mind if I ask you a question?"

"You can ask. I may not answer."

"What time did you join Mr. Hoyle to watch the baseball game?"

The question seemed harmless enough. "The game started at three. When I got there it was in the second inning, so I would put my arrival at around three-twenty."

"And Mr. Hoyle was at home?"

"In the den."

"And you were with him the rest of the afternoon?"

"Until you and Red came to the house. So what's the issue, Deputy?"

"The issue is the two hours between twelve-thirty and two-thirty, when no one can account for Mr. Hoyle's whereabouts."

Chris drove to the Sonic, which to Beck seemed an unlikely choice given the gravity of their upcoming conversation. On any summer night, cars packed with teenagers cruised endless circles around the place. The kids honked their horns at each other, the boys shouted innuendos to the girls, and the girls shouted back "kiss off" or equivalents. Some congregated around the metal picnic tables that were bolted down to a concrete pad beneath an aluminum awning. They noshed chili-covered French fries and created small dramas for their small-town entertainment.

Above the Beach Boys classic blaring through the outdoor speakers, Beck said, "What are we doing here?"

"I'm thirsty for a slush." Chris pulled his car into a vacant slot and placed an order through the speaker. Then he turned to Beck.

"This had better be good, Chris."

"Deputy Scott is beginning to annoy me."

"You said Selma could vouch that you stayed home all day."

"I didn't know she'd tell them about her afternoon nap."

"Which leaves you unaccountable for two hours. Did you leave the house? And you goddamn well better not lie to me."

"So what if I did leave?"

"If you did, that means you had an opportunity to kill Danny, because the time of his death, as established by the coroner, would fall into that period of time when nobody knows for certain where you were."

The carhop arrived with their lime slushes. Chris paid her and gave her a generous tip. He sipped from his straw and observed to Beck that the only thing wrong with the drink was that it was missing a couple shots of tequila.

Irritated by his friend's cavalier attitude, Beck

said, "Chris, what is it going to take to wake you up to the fact that you are in a serious situation? What was that bullshit about the phone call? Couldn't you come up with a better story than inviting Danny to Sunday dinner? They saw straight through that. And so did I. When Huff joined us that afternoon and asked if we'd heard from Danny, you didn't mention talking to him by phone that morning."

"I forgot."

"You forgot." Beck snorted. "Great. We've already discussed what a solid defense that makes."

"All right, Beck, you want to hear a better story? What if I'd told Red and Deputy Scott that I called Danny to ask him to meet me at the fishing camp that day? That's right," he said, seeing Beck's astonishment. "That was the purpose of the call.

"I didn't mention it to Huff on Sunday afternoon because I had failed in my mission and I was in no mood for one of his tirades. And just how bad would it have looked for me if I'd told our esteemed lawmen the truth? Would you have preferred that?"

Beck expelled a long breath. "No, that would not have been preferable."

Placing his unwanted drink in the cup holder in the dashboard, he stared through the windshield at the distinctive hood. He liked driving a pickup, but Chris favored fast, sleek, sporty, luxurious imports.

"From here on, Chris," he said, turning to him to emphasize his point, "don't say anything to anybody. You've said too much already."

"Scott provokes me."

"He knows that. He baits you, turning your disdain of him to his advantage. You've got to learn to keep your mouth shut."

"You're talking like you think I'm guilty. Beck," he said, looking at him squarely. "I did not kill my brother. I was not at the fishing camp."

"Then why in the name of God did you ask him to meet you out there?"

"Danny and I had argued the day before. I got nowhere with him. I saw him going off to church that morning and thought, Dammit, I didn't make a dent. So I thought if I got him out in the countryside, in total privacy, we could have a calmer and more effective heart-to-heart.

"It would also placate Huff to know that I'd made an earnest attempt to talk to Danny. Huff was seriously worried about the influence this religious nonsense was having on him and he wanted it to stop."

"Danny agreed to meet you out there?"

"No, he didn't," Chris declared. "That's what has me puzzled. He said he wouldn't be caught dead—" He stopped, realizing what he'd said, and placed his hand against his forehead. "Christ."

"I get the idea, go on."

"Well, when Red showed up and told us that Danny had been found dead at the fishing camp, I was dumbfounded. First of all because my brother was dead, which was shocking enough. But second because of where he had died."

"You didn't go out there?"

He gave an adamant shake of his head. "I had

told Danny that I would go, hoping he would change his mind and meet me. He said, 'Don't wait for me, Chris, I won't be coming.' It was so blasted hot that afternoon. I was hungover. Lazy. So I took him at his word and decided to hell with it, and didn't go. But apparently Danny also took me at my word. He went, expecting me to be there."

"I don't think you can sell a jury on the notion that Danny killed himself because you failed to show up."

"Is that meant to be sarcastic?"

"Definitely. But it illustrates how many holes there are in your story."

"I'm well aware of that. Why do you think I've kept it to myself?"

"Even from me?"

"Especially from you."

"Why?"

"Because I knew you'd be pissed that I hadn't told you in the first place."

Beck rested his head against the back of the seat and took a deep breath. Arguing with Chris over a fait accompli would be counterproductive. He now had to focus on damage control.

"Give me your best guess as to what happened to Danny when he got out there."

"You shot down my best guess," Chris said.

"That somebody's trying to frame you?"

"That's what I think. Have you talked to Red about Slap Watkins?"

"This afternoon, obviously before Scott obtained the phone records. I told him about our confrontation with Watkins last night in the diner, told him that Danny had recently rejected his job application, and what Watkins had said to us, as well as what he'd said to Sayre and me."

"And Red's reaction was . . . ?"

"That it was thin, but that he wouldn't put anything past Slap Watkins. He said he would look into it and keep an eye on him."

Chris frowned. "That's not much of a commitment, but it's something, I suppose."

"How could Watkins or anyone else have framed you, Chris? Who else would have known about the phone call to Danny arranging a meeting?"

"No one. But somebody following Danny, looking for an opportunity to kill him, would seize it when he was alone, in a remote spot like the fishing camp."

"And he would use a shotgun owned by the family?"

"He would if he wanted to pin the murder on a member of that family," Chris returned angrily. "He could have somehow restrained Danny, then taken down the shotgun and shot him in the mouth. Every fishing camp I know of has some kind of firearm around."

Beck thought about it as Buddy Holly waxed poetic about Peggy Sue. "I didn't reload the shotgun before replacing it above the door when we were there. The killer would have had to find the shotgun shells, and only those of us who go there would know where they're kept. The place was dusted for prints. None except mine and those of family members were found."

"That's easy. He would know to wear gloves."

Which brought up another sensitive topic. "Chris, what were you wearing?"

Before they'd left the sheriff's office, Deputy Scott had asked Chris to produce the clothes and shoes he'd been wearing on Sunday afternoon. Chris claimed not to remember what he'd had on. But the point was moot anyway, he said. Anything he'd worn on Sunday, Selma would already have laundered or taken to the dry cleaner.

"Like I told Scott, I don't remember," he said now. "Slacks, a golf shirt. I don't remember."

"When I got to the house, you were wearing a striped shirt with a button-down collar and a pair of black Dockers."

Chris gave Beck an arch look. "You're noticing my wardrobe now? Have you gone queer on me?" Then he laughed. "No, you haven't gone queer. Given the way your tongue was mating with Sayre's tonsils."

Beck refused to be diverted. "I remember what you were wearing because when I got to your house, I was on the verge of melting. The back of my shirt was damp, just from the short drive over. I noticed the difference in us. You looked like you'd stepped out of a bandbox. You had just cleaned up, hadn't you?"

"What difference does it make?"

"It'll make a difference if Selma is put on the witness stand and has to testify under oath what she found, or didn't find, in your clothes hamper between Saturday afternoon after you left for Breaux Bridge and Sunday afternoon. She'll have to testify that you took a shower in the vicinity of three o'clock, after Danny was shot in the head sometime between one and two-thirty." Beck looked at him hard. "Did you leave the house on Sunday?"

Chris stared at Beck with an unwavering gaze, then relented with a drawn-out sigh. He raised his hands in surrender. "Guilty."

Beck felt a weight as solid as an anchor land against his chest, but he tried to keep his anxiety under control and his voice even. "Where did you go, Chris? And why did you have to shower and change clothes shortly before I got to the house?"

"Remember that nasty incriminating evidence on Monica Lewinsky's dress?" He spread his hands wide and grinned. "Caught without a condom. Can you believe it? At my age. I had to pull out before I came."

"Who were you with?"

"Lila. I knew George was playing golf with Huff. So I went over to her place for some afternoon delight."

"For chrissake, why didn't you tell me this? When you were first questioned about how you spent your Sunday afternoon, why didn't you say you were with someone? Lila is your alibi."

"That'll go over real well with the sheriff."

It took Beck a moment to connect the dots; then he groaned, "Oh, shit."

"Right. Lila is Red's sister's daughter. I couldn't have been killing my brother because I was going down on our sheriff's niece. I'd rather avoid telling him that, although right now I'm not feeling too kindly toward him."

"If you're forced to produce an alibi, can we count on her to back you up?"

"I'd rather not involve her," Chris said with a slight wince. "Besides being Red's niece, I don't know that she would jeopardize her marriage to George by owning up to an affair. She makes fun of him constantly, but he's spoiled her rotten, buys her anything she wants. He's besotted, and as long as she puts out occasionally it's an arrangement that makes them both happy. She would probably lie to protect that feather bed she's made for herself."

"You were with her for two hours?"

"Well, I wasn't watching the clock, but that sounds about right."

"Did anybody see you at their house?"

"We take great pains to prevent that."

"All right. We'll hold Lila in abeyance, to be used only if absolutely necessary."

"It won't be necessary," Chris said. "They've got nothing but circumstantial evidence. I know from experience, having been falsely accused of murder before, that that isn't enough."

"This time is different, Chris. This time they've got a body."

"Right. The body. I try not to think about that. I'm glad that Red could identify Danny, instead of one of us having to. But you saw the inside of the cabin. It was a mess, wasn't it?"

"That's why they wanted to see your clothing. The shooter would have been spattered with—"

"Beck, enough. Okay?"

"Don't get queasy yet. If it goes to trial, they'll show crime scene photos."

"It won't go to trial. Or if it does, it won't be *my* trial."

They were quiet for a while and let the last chorus of—and this was ironically chilling to Beck— "Jailhouse Rock" play out. Chris finished his drink, then out of nowhere asked, "Have you fucked Sayre yet?"

"I beg your pardon."

"Look at the man's expression. Surprise. Innocence. Righteous indignation. Why, the idea never entered his mind." He laughed. "Have you?"

"You've got more than that to worry about," Beck said tightly.

"I'm not the only one who has noticed some electricity there. Huff remarked on it, too."

"There is no 'it.' "

"Hm. I guess the steam rising off the two of you there in your kitchen was due to the barometric pressure."

Beck gave him a baleful look.

"If it's not you that's keeping her here, then what is?" Chris persisted. "She hates Destiny and everybody in it, especially if his name is Hoyle."

Beck didn't tell him that Sayre suspected him of killing their younger brother. Surely that would bother Chris as much as it bothered him. He was also concerned about what Sayre might do to try to prove herself right. She wasn't easily intimidated, and just from the short time he'd known her, it had become evident to him that once she set her mind

on something, she was damned and determined to
see it through.

"Your dick is your business," Chris said.

"Thank you."

"But I'd be less than a friend if I didn't offer you
a word of caution. Sayre is—"

"Look, don't go there. All right?"

Chris shot him a wry grin. "Beck, my friend, you
took the words right out of my mouth."

chapter 19

*I*t was hot.

That was one thing you could say about coastal Mississippi in the summertime, and the summer of 1945 was no exception. It was so hot that even grasshoppers died of heatstroke. Tomatoes ripened and burst open on their vines before they could be picked.

Although one time, when Huff and his daddy were really hungry, they'd gathered up some busted tomatoes from off the ground of somebody's garden, dusted the dirt and ants off them, and ate them for supper.

Huff was eight years old that summer. Everybody you met was carrying on about the victory over the Germans. Whipping the Japs was only a matter of time. There were parades in the streets of nearly every town they traveled through. People waved flags, not the usual Stars and Bars, but the U.S. flag.

Huff didn't understand what all the fuss was about. The war hadn't affected him and his daddy much. His daddy hadn't been in the armed services. Huff didn't know why that was, because most men his daddy's age wore a uniform of one sort or another. Passenger trains were packed full of soldiers and sailors, and on one occasion he and his daddy shared a freight car with two black men in uniform. Huff hadn't liked that. His daddy hadn't either, and ordinarily he would have told them to get the hell out and find themselves another freight car. But his daddy had said it was all right this once because those boys were fighting for their country.

If the Army would take niggers, Huff couldn't understand why they hadn't wanted his daddy. He figured it was because of him. What would have happened to him if his daddy had been sent away to kill Nazis and Japs? They moved around so much, never living in any one place for long, that maybe the Army didn't even know his daddy's name. Or maybe the Army was just like everybody else—they flat didn't want his daddy, thinking him no'ccount, or dim-witted, rather than just poor and uneducated.

His daddy had lived through the Great Depression. Huff wasn't sure what that was, but he knew it was bad. His daddy had tried to explain it, and from what he said, Huff gathered that the Depression had been like a war, because it affected the whole country, but the enemy had been poverty. His daddy's family had lost that war.

But they'd always been poor. That was why his daddy didn't have but three years of schooling. He'd had to work in cotton fields alongside his own daddy, and sometimes even his ma. "Her hands a-bleedin' and with a baby or two hanging on her tit," he would say, looking downcast.

His daddy's folks were dead now, like Huff's own mother. When Huff asked what had killed them, his daddy had said, "Being poor, I reckon."

That summer of '45, jobs were even harder to come by because so many soldiers were returning from the war, looking for work. There wasn't enough to go around. So it was like a miracle when Mr. J. D. Humphrey hired his daddy to work in an auto salvage yard.

It was hot, dirty work, but his daddy was grateful for the job and put his back to it. When somebody came to J. D. Humphrey's place looking for a spare part for an early model car, his daddy would forage through acres of junked autos until he found what the customer needed.

At the end of every day, he'd be covered with filth, smeared with grease, bleeding from mean scratches made by rusty metal, his muscles aching from pulling motors from stubborn chassis. But he was so glad to have steady work, he never complained.

Huff hung around the junkyard with him. He was small for his age and shy about talking to anybody except his daddy. He would be allowed to do odd jobs, like fetching a needed tool from the shed or stacking retread tires. Mr. J. D. Humphrey even gave him a cast-off inner tube that had been patched so many times it wasn't worth anything. He played with it in the dusty yard while his daddy worked from sunup to sundown every day except Sunday.

His daddy told him that if things kept up, he might be able to go to school when it commenced in the fall. He was a little late starting, his daddy told him, but he was sure he could catch up to the other kids in no time.

Huff couldn't wait to go to school like other boys. Many times, he'd watched them from a distance as they laughed and horsed around in the school yard, tossing a ball to each other or chasing girls who squealed and giggled and wore ribbons in their hair.

That summer their home was an abandoned shack. The folks who had lived there before had left a lot of trash behind, but also a cotton mattress on the floor and a few pieces of rickety furniture. He and his daddy kicked the varmints out and moved in.

The night that changed Huff's life forever was typically hot, but even more humid than usual. Sweat didn't evaporate but rolled along your skin, leaving muddy trails until it finally dripped off, landing in the dust and making damp little craters like first raindrops. It was hard to take a deep breath because the air was so thick and oppressive. On their walk home from the junkyard, his daddy had remarked on how hot and still it was and predicted a storm before morning.

They had just sat down to eat their evening meal of cold bacon, corn bread, and wild plums that they'd picked from trees along the road when they heard a car approaching the shack.

No one ever came to visit them, so who could it be?

Huff's heart clenched up like a fist, and he had to push down a swallow of dry corn bread. It must be the owner of the shack, wanting to know just what the hell they were doing in his house, sleeping on his mattress, eating off his three-legged table. He would kick them out, and they wouldn't have a place to stay anymore.

What if they couldn't find another place to live before school started the Tuesday after Labor Day? Huff had been living for the Tuesday after Labor Day. His daddy had marked it for him on the calendar with the picture of the naked lady that hung in Mr. J. D. Humphrey's office. That was when he could join the rest of the kids on the school playground and maybe learn to play their games.

His heart in his throat, Huff joined his daddy at the empty window frame and saw a shiny black-and-white car with a red light on top of it. Sitting inside the car with the lawman was Mr. J. D. Humphrey. But he wasn't smiling like he'd been when he'd given Huff the inner tube. And when they got out and headed toward the shack, the peace officer was smacking a billy club against his hard, wide palm.

His daddy told Huff to stay inside and went out to greet the visitors. "Evenin', Mr. Humphrey."

"I don't want any trouble from you."

"Sir?"

"Hand it over."

"Hand what over, Mr. Humphrey?"

"Don't play dumb with us, boy," the lawman barked. "J.D. knows you took it."

"I didn't take nothing."

"That cigar box, where I keep all the cash?"

"Yes, sir."

"Well, it's gone missing. Now who else coulda taken it?"

"I don't know, sir, but it wasn't me."

"You dumb piece o' white trash, you think I believe that?"

Huff peered over the window ledge. Mr. Humphrey's face had turned real red. The law officer was smiling, but he sure didn't look very friendly. He passed his billy club to Mr. Humphrey. "Maybe this'll put some smarts into him."

"Mr. Humphrey, I—"

That was all his daddy had a chance to say before Mr. Humphrey struck him with the club. It caught his daddy on the shoulder and must have hurt something terrible because he went down on one knee. "I swear, I wouldn't steal—"

Mr. Humphrey hit him again, this time in the head, and it sounded like an ax splitting a stick of firewood lengthwise. His daddy keeled over onto the ground. He lay real still and didn't make a sound.

Huff stood rooted to his spot at the window. He was breathing hard, with disbelief, with terror.

"Jesus, J.D., you whacked him right good." The lawman chuckled, bending down over his daddy.

"That'll teach him to steal from me."

"Won't teach him nothing." The lawman straightened up and withdrew a handkerchief from his back pocket. He used it to wipe blood off his fingers. "He's dead."

"You shittin' me?"

"Dead as a hammer."

Mr. Humphrey hefted the club as though weighing it. "Has this thing got an iron rod in it?"

"Good for nigger-knocking." The lawman nudged Huff's daddy with the toe of his boot. "What was his name?"

Mr. J. D. Humphrey told him. But he didn't get the name quite right. "He was just a white trash drifter. You try and do the Christian thing, give a down-and-outer a helping hand, and he winds up biting it."

"Ain't that the gospel truth?" The lawman shook his head over the sorrow of it. "Well, I'll get the undertaker out here tomorrow. I guess the county'll have to pay for the burial."

"I heard the medical school up to the university can always use spare cadavers."

"There's a thought."

"I reckon he stashed your money somewhere inside this rathole."

The two entered the shack and spotted Huff hunkered down beneath the window, cowering against the wall that was insulated with old editions of the Biloxi newspaper. "Oh, hell. Forgot about his boy."

The lawman tilted back his hat, propped his hands on his hips, and frowned down at Huff. "Scrawny little puke, ain't he?"

"Trailed his sorry daddy everywhere. Ask me, I think he's a bit backward."

"What's his name?"

"I don't know his real name," Mr. J. D. Humphrey replied. "All's I ever heard his daddy call him was Huff."

*   *   *

"Huff?"

"Huff?"

Eventually he realized that his name wasn't coming to him from out of that hot evening in the summer of 1945.

He suffered the inexpressible sense of loss that he always did upon emerging from this recurring dream. He was always glad to dream it because it was like having a visit with his daddy. But it never ended happily. When he woke up, his daddy was always dead and he was left alone.

He opened his eyes. Chris and Beck were standing on either side of his hospital bed. Chris smiled. "Welcome back. You were in la-la land."

Embarrassed by the soundness of his slumber and the sentimentality his dream always conjured, Huff sat up and swung his legs over the side of the bed. "Just catching a little catnap."

"Catnap?" Chris said, laughing. "You were practically comatose. I didn't think we were going to wake you up. You were talking in your sleep, too. Saying something about not getting a name right. What were you dreaming?"

"Damned if I remember," he grumbled.

"We came to help you get ready for your trip home," Beck said, "but obviously we're too late to be of much use."

He'd been up and dressed since before daylight. He'd never been one to lie about in bed, and being in the hospital hadn't changed that habit. "I'm ready to get out of here."

"We're past ready to see you go." Dr. Caroe

breezed in, his lab coat snapping like a sail behind him. "The staff has had their fill of your foul disposition."

"Then sign me out. I'm already late for work."

"Don't even think about it, Huff. You're going home," the doctor said.

"I'm needed at the foundry."

"You need more rest before you resume normal activity."

"Bullshit. I've been doing nothing but lying on my ass for two days."

Eventually they compromised. He would go home today and rest, and if he was feeling well enough tomorrow, he could return to work for a few hours, gradually building back up to his previous schedule. This quarrel was all part of the grand charade, of course, performed for the benefit of Beck and Chris.

Caroe, the son of a bitch, was making like Al Pacino in the role of caring physician. He would give Huff the green light on returning to work when Huff gave him the greenbacks for helping him convincingly fake a heart attack.

The dismissal paperwork put a huge strain on his patience, as did having to leave the building in a wheelchair. By the time they finally got him home, he was in a high snit.

"He's meaner than a snake," Chris said to Selma. "Beware."

Unmindful of the warning, she fluttered around Huff, settled him into the den with a glass of iced tea and a lap blanket, which he threw off, bellowing, "I'm not a goddamn invalid and it's ninety fucking degrees outside! If you want to be working here tomorrow, don't ever tuck me into this chair with a blanket!"

"I'm not deaf so you don't have to yell. And mind your tongue, too." With characteristic aplomb, she picked up the blanket and refolded it. "What do you want for lunch?"

"Fried chicken."

"Well you're having grilled fish and steamed vegetables." That was her parting shot as she left the room, soundly closing the door behind her.

"Selma's the only one who can get away with talking back to you," Chris said from across the room. He was throwing darts, but with a notable lack of inspiration.

Beck was seated on the sofa, one ankle propped on the opposite knee, arms stretched along the back cushion.

Huff put a match to his second cigarette since leaving the hospital. "You're doing a damn lousy job of it."

"Damn lousy job of what?" Beck asked.

"Pretending that you don't have a care in the world." Fanning out the match, he said, "Drop the playacting and tell me what's going on."

"Dr. Caroe told you not to smoke."

"Screw him," Huff said to Chris. "And don't change the subject. I want to know what's going on. Who's gonna be the one to tell me?"

Chris took a seat on the vacant sofa. "Wayne Scott is making a nuisance of himself again."

"What now?"

"He's still probing," Beck said. "And all his probes are in Chris's direction."

Huff drew on his cigarette, wondering where the

likes of this pain in the ass detective had been when his daddy was murdered in cold blood. Nobody had asked a single question about how he came to have his head cracked open wide enough for part of his brain to ooze out. Huff wasn't even sure if his daddy had been buried, or if his corpse had been turned over to the university medical school to be mutilated by a group of bungling students.

He had been taken to the jail to spend the night because they didn't know what else to do with him. Mr. J. D. Humphrey had told the lawman on the ride into town that his wife would have a hissy fit if he took Huff home with him. "He's probably got head lice. She'd never let me hear the end of it if our kids turned up with nits."

That night, while he lay crying on the cot in the jail cell, he heard the lawman tell another lawman, who'd been put in charge of keeping an eye on him, that it had been Mrs. Humphrey, J.D.'s wife, who'd taken the cigar box of money, which a search of the shack had failed to produce.

"There was a big sale on textiles at the dry goods store. She was low on cash, so she stopped by the salvage yard and helped herself without bothering to tell J.D."

"Well, if that don't beat all," the other man had said.

They'd had a good laugh over the misunderstanding.

The following morning, Huff had been given a biscuit and sausage patty sandwich for breakfast, then the lawman ordered him to sit and wait and not to give anybody any sass.

Which was what he did until the arrival of a

skinny man wearing a seersucker suit and wire-rimmed spectacles. He told Huff he'd come to take him to an orphanage. As they drove away from the jail, he said, "I'm not gonna have any trouble out of you, am I, boy?"

He'd had no idea of the hell about to be rained down on him and the institution he oversaw. He would live to rue the day that he'd picked up young Huff Hoyle from the jailhouse.

For the next five years Huff had lived—more like existed—in a home for orphaned children run by people who preached Jesus' love but who would beat the living daylights out of you with a leather strop if you looked at them crosswise, which Huff Hoyle often did.

When he was thirteen, he escaped. He left with only one regret—that the bastard in the seersucker suit didn't know it was Huff who'd killed him. He should have woken him up and given him a chance to put on his spectacles before covering his face with the pillow.

He'd made no such mistake with Mr. J. D. Humphrey. He made sure his daddy's murderer saw him and heard the name he whispered close to his ear before he smothered him in his own bed while his fat wife snored peacefully in the twin bed not three feet away.

The lawman saved him the trouble of having to kill him. Huff asked around town until he heard about him coming between two niggers who were arguing over a hunting dog. One of them had a knife, which wound up buried to the hilt in the lawman's gut. It was said he died screaming.

Since the night his daddy died, he'd maintained a low opinion of men who wore a badge, and that contempt showed now. "What has Deputy Scott got his drawers in a wad about this time?"

Beck told him about the interrogation that had taken place the night before. Now and then Chris would interrupt with a droll denial or an acerbic quip about the deputy.

When Beck finished, Huff said, "Chris, your explanation of the phone call should've squelched Scott's excitement. Especially since I did ask you to stay after Danny about that church. But Scott is dogged and he's ambitious, and that's worrisome. Sounds to me like he's not going to give up and drop this nonsense."

"I'm afraid you're right, Huff," Beck said.

"I don't understand what's going on with Red," Chris complained. "Both times I've been called in, he hands the reins over to Scott. I've had to sit there and take crap from that yokel without a peep from Red. Is he holding out for more money? If so, let's give him a few bills and be done with this. Either that, or let's get proactive and do the police work ourselves."

"Police work?" Huff looked from Chris to Beck. "What's he talking about?"

"Chris thinks that someone killed Danny and deliberately made it appear that he had."

"Somebody is framing me, Huff."

Huff shifted in his recliner to find a more comfortable spot. "Framing you, huh? What do you think of that theory, Beck?"

"It's feasible. You've made some powerful enemies over the years. I suppose if someone wanted to get you where it really hurts, they'd go after one of your children. It would be a double coup to have another child blamed for it."

"Any ideas who this individual might be?"

"Slap Watkins," Chris declared.

Huff looked at him for several moments, then a laugh rumbled up from deep inside his chest. "Slap Watkins? He hasn't got sense enough to kill a june bug and get away with it."

"Hear me out, Huff. He is bad news."

"Of course he is. All those Watkinses are degenerates. But I've never known them to be killers."

"They're fighters. They're violent. After three years in Angola, Slap could have graduated to homicide." Chris scooted forward, balancing on the edge of the sofa cushion. "As soon as he was released from prison—mad at the world, I'm sure— he applied for a job at the foundry. Danny didn't hire him. Slap knew as well as anyone that we hire a lot of parolees because they work cheap. Danny, who was rich, who represented everything that Slap hates and blames for his misfortunes, turned him down. Couple that with the fight we had with him three years ago, and I think it adds up to a good motive for murder for revenge."

Beck picked it up from there. "Watkins may have been watching Danny, waiting for an opportunity to strike. Sunday afternoon, he followed Danny out to the fishing camp." Summarizing, he spread his hands. "That's the hypothesis."

"Slap is just stupid enough to have forgotten the bait when he staged a scene to make it look like

Danny had gone there to actually fish," Chris added. "Nor would he know about Danny's aversion to fishing."

Huff got out of his recliner and made a turn around the room, enjoying the sight of his possessions, savoring the burning tobacco taste on his tongue. Finally he said, "Sounds neat and tidy, all right, but it's all speculation. You've got nothing to back up this hunch."

"We've got Slap himself," Chris said. "He's become extremely smug. Why else would he approach Sayre in the diner? He would never have made a move on her before. And he insulted the whole family the other night. Beck heard him."

Huff looked at Beck, who nodded. "He did. Other people heard him, too."

"What's Red's take on it?"

"I've only mentioned it to him once," Beck said.

"He didn't seize on it," Chris said, clearly annoyed with the sheriff's seeming indifference. "Don't you agree that he should question Watkins?"

"At the very least." Huff moved to an end table and knocked an ash off his cigarette into an ashtray. "Leave Red to me."

Before more could be said, Selma tapped lightly on the door, then opened it. "A package just arrived, Mr. Hoyle."

He motioned for her to give the Federal Express envelope to Beck. "Whatever it is, do you mind dealing with it?"

"Of course not."

Beck took the envelope from Selma and ripped it open. There was a single sheet of paper inside. Huff watched Beck's eyes as he scanned it quickly, then began again at the top and reread it, taking more time. When he finished, he cursed beneath his breath. Huff intercepted the worried glance he shot Chris.

"Bad news?" Huff asked. "Come on, come on, let's hear it."

Beck hesitated, which fueled Huff's temper.

"Goddammit!" he shouted. "Am I or am I not still in charge of this outfit?"

"I'm sorry, Huff," Beck said quietly. "Of course you are."

"Then stop fucking around and tell me what's in the letter."

"It's from Charles Nielson. He heard about Billy Paulik's accident."

Huff put his cigarette in his mouth and rocked back on his heels. "And?"

Beck sighed. "And then some."

Chris wasn't happy to see George Robson lurking around his office when he returned to it following a turbulent lunch with Huff, through which he had bitched about everything from Charles Nielson to Selma's menu.

"Can I have a minute, Chris?" George asked.

Chris could think of no plausible excuse to refuse the request, so he motioned him into his private office.

Physically, George had little to recommend him. His personality didn't particularly attract friends, either. His anxious attempts to please only made him annoying. He was an overgrown nerd who tried to fit in, and who might have even deluded himself into believing he had, without realizing that he never would.

It was his self-delusion that made him perfect for the position he held.

Chris found it amusing that George could be so blissfully unaware that he was being made a cuckold by the man who asked him to take a seat and offered him something to drink.

"No thanks."

"Then what can I do for you, George?"

"It's about that conveyor. I had someone here this morning to replace the belt."

"All right, so what's the problem?"

"He, uh . . . that is the technician, recommended that it remain out of commission until it undergoes a complete overhaul."

Chris leaned back in his chair and frowned. "Huff won't like hearing that."

"No, I don't suppose he will."

"So what's your recommendation?" Chris looked at him mildly.

George licked his lips. "Well, safety is my first concern."

"Naturally."

"And that machine has already cost one man his arm."

Enjoying the way George squirmed under his steady gaze, Chris didn't comment.

"But . . . but in my opinion," he stammered, "an overhaul would be unnecessary. I think she's ready to start back up."

Chris smiled at him. "I defer to your expertise on

matters of safety, George. So does Huff. You know that. If you say it's been repaired to your satisfaction and is now safe to operate, then we feel confident to do so. Anything else?"

"No, that's it." He got up to leave and was almost to the door when he stopped and turned back. "Actually there is something else. Lila."

Chris, who'd begun sorting through the message slips on his desk, stopped and looked up. What the hell was this about? Had the dumb bitch confessed to their affair, accidentally given them away, what? "Lila?" he said pleasantly.

George swallowed hard. "She mentioned to me not long ago that we ought to have you over for dinner one night. And Huff, too, of course. Would you like that?"

Relaxing, Chris replied, "Gee, I don't know. Is she a good cook?"

George gave a nervous laugh and patted his belly. "Speaks for itself." Then he ran his tongue over his lips again. "I had to fend for myself last night, though. She was out."

"Oh?" Chris returned his attention to the stack of pink message slips.

"She had to go see about a sick friend."

"Nothing serious I hope."

"I don't think so. But it was late when she got in."

Chris raised his head again and looked at Lila's husband. "A wife like Lila, you'd be crazy not to worry about her safety and well-being, George. Don't make us wait too long for that dinner at your house, okay?"

George nodded, hesitated as though uncertain

how to conclude the meeting, then turned and hustled out.

"Jesus," Chris muttered. Was it any wonder Lila screwed like there was no tomorrow?

"My husband died last year." As Mrs. Loretta Foster announced her husband's passing to Sayre, she crossed herself. "God rest his soul."

"I'm sorry. Had he been ill?"

"Not a day in his life. He just dropped dead right here in the kitchen while he was pouring himself a cup of coffee. Pulmonary embolism. The doctor told me he was dead before he hit the floor."

"Sudden deaths come as such a shock."

Mrs. Foster's overpermed gray hair moved as a unit when she bobbed her head in agreement. "It's good for the one who checks out. No fuss or muss," she said, snapping her fingers. "But it's hard on the ones left behind. Anyhow, it's only me and my boy now."

She gestured toward her son, who was sitting on the floor watching cartoons on a big-screen TV that took up most of the space in the diminutive living room of the small frame house. He was absorbed in the antics of Rocky and Bullwinkle.

Mrs. Foster had placed a bag of Cheetos and a glass of orange juice on a tray in front of him, admonishing him to be careful and not to spill on the carpet. He appeared not to have heard her and seemed completely unaware of Sayre, who was seated with his mother at the kitchen table, where they were sipping glasses of sweetened iced tea.

The "boy" was well into his forties.

"I guess you noticed that he's not quite right," Mrs. Foster said in a whisper that Sayre could barely hear above the manic sound track of the cartoon. "Born that way. Wasn't anything I did while I was carrying him. That's just the way he came out."

Sayre, at a loss over how to respond, said, "I appreciate your letting me interrupt your afternoon."

Mrs. Foster's laugh jiggled her generous bosom. "We don't go anywhere or do anything. Except for Sunday, when we go to mass, one day is the same as the next. As long as I get my boy's supper ready by five-thirty, he's content. This is about all we do with our afternoons, so I'm glad for the company and somebody to talk to. Except, I'm a little curious as to why you asked to come over."

Loretta Foster's name was on the list Sayre had obtained at the courthouse, thanks to Jessica De-Blance's contact.

"I know a woman who works in the parish tax office," she had told Sayre when she'd asked for a favor. "We're not close friends, but I think she would be willing to help. What is it you need?"

What Sayre had asked for was the list of jurors who had served during Chris's trial. Jessica placed the call to her acquaintance. The contact at the courthouse agreed to see if such a list could be acquired and asked for several hours in which to find out.

Sayre met her at the appointed time and was handed the list. "It was easier than I thought," the woman told her. "They keep track of people who're called to jury duty, because if someone is recalled within a certain length of time, they can ask for an exemption. When a juror is dismissed, the case number goes on their record of service for reference if it ever becomes necessary."

Last night, when she went to see Beck Merchant, Sayre had been holding that list of names like an ace up her sleeve. She hadn't had the opportunity to play it. This morning she had returned to the courthouse and, using tax records, had learned that ten of the twelve jurors still lived in the parish.

The first two she called told her straightaway they didn't want to talk about that trial and hung up on her. The third, she was told by his wife, was working his shift at Hoyle Enterprises. When Sayre stated the nature of her business, his wife's initial friendliness turned guarded, and when Sayre persisted, she got hostile. She said her husband would be too busy to see Sayre at any time in the foreseeable future.

It was on her fourth attempt that she succeeded in having Mrs. Foster agree to a visit.

She stirred her glass of iced tea. It was so syrupy with sugar it was opaque. "I wanted to talk to you about my brother Chris's murder trial. You served on the jury, didn't you?"

Suddenly Loretta Foster's smile showed signs of strain. "That's right. First and only time I was ever called, and I've lived in this parish my whole life. Why're you interested?"

Selling her explanation was going to be the tricky part. "I let my brother down by not being here during the trial. I regret not coming back to Destiny to lend him moral support. I hoped to talk

to some of the people who were involved in order
to gain a better understanding of what happened."

Mrs. Foster didn't buy it. At least, not entirely.
"What do you mean by that? Nothing *happened*.
We couldn't reach a unanimous decision, that's all.
Split right down the middle."

"Which way did you vote, Mrs. Foster?"

She left the table and moved to the stove. Lifting
the lid off a pot, she gave the simmering contents a
stir. "I don't see that it matters now. Your brother
got off."

"Did you think he was innocent?"

She replaced the lid on the pot, a bit too loudly,
and turned back to Sayre. "What if I did?"

"If you did, I owe you my thanks." Sayre gave
her a smile she hoped was convincing. "I'm sure my
brother and father properly thanked you."

Mrs. Foster returned to her chair across the table
from Sayre, watching her closely as she sipped from
her glass of tea. "They came around and shook our
hands after the trial. Other than that, I don't know
what thanks you're talking about."

Sayre looked into the living room. It was tidy,
but the furniture was dated and worn. Crocheted
antimacassars covered spots where upholstery had
become completely threadbare. The wallpaper was
faded, and the carpet Mrs. Foster had been so concerned about was already badly stained from
countless spills.

The television was by far the newest, most sophisticated, and most expensive thing in the room. It was
out of keeping with the rest of the decor, which
amounted to a crucifix hanging on the wall behind

the tattered sofa and a ceramic panther with green glass eyes on the coffee table.

Sayre had decorated rec rooms and dens around similar video units, so she knew the cost involved. It would be far beyond the widow's budget.

Since her arrival, Mrs. Foster's son hadn't budged from his spot in front of the large screen. He continued to sit Indian style on the floor, nibbling Cheetos and drinking orange juice, transfixed by the images on the TV. Content.

Sayre came back around and looked directly at Loretta Foster. At first the woman's expression was defensive. But when Sayre's stare didn't waver, she became nervous. Finally she looked ashamed.

"If you'll excuse me," she said, "I've got to get my boy's supper ready. He's prone to pitch a fit if it's not ready by the time *Wheel of Fortune* comes on. He likes to eat while he's watching that show. Don't ask me why 'cause he doesn't know his letters too good."

Then, addressing Sayre with a mix of defiance and appeal, she added, "As I told you, he's not quite right. Never has been. He depends on me for everything. I'm all he's got in the world, and when I'm gone, well, I've got to see that he's taken care of, don't I?"

chapter 20

Red Harper knocked lightly, then poked his head around the door of Huff's den. "Selma told me it was all right to come on in."

"I've been expecting you. Fix yourself a drink."

"Believe I will." He poured a bourbon and water and carried it with him to the sofa where he sat down, resting his uniform hat on his knee. Huff saluted him with his own glass, and they each took a sip. "You look good," Red remarked. "How're you feeling?"

"Like I'm twenty."

"I forgot what that feels like."

"I remember it like yesterday," Huff said. "I was working for old man Lynch in the foundry. My job was to charge the furnace. Backbreaking work, but I pulled a double shift every chance I got. Already I had plans for that place."

The orphanage school had been strict about studies, and that was the only thing Huff could thank it for. After only a few months there, he had more than caught up with children his age. He spent recesses in the classroom reviewing the lesson just taught, not playing ball and chasing girls as he had imagined when he was idealistic and innocent. He had higher goals in mind now, so he applied himself to learning as much as he could, as quickly as he could.

He read for hours every night by a weak night-light in the communal bathroom, sitting on the hard tile floor, sweltering in the summertime, shivering during the winter months. The food was tasteless, but he cleaned his plate at every meal, and by eating regularly he began to grow.

By the time he escaped at thirteen, he was far ahead of his contemporaries in size and had twice their knowledge. The rest of his education, and perhaps the most important lessons, were learned through experience. He was surviving on his own, living by his wits, providing himself with food and shelter when other teenage boys were stressing over pimples.

He'd been riding a freight train to an undetermined destination when it stopped in Destiny to unload several railcars of scrap metal at Lynch's foundry. He wasn't even sure what state he was in, but when he read the name of the town on the water tower it had seemed like an omen.

He decided in an instant that Destiny was where his future lay.

He had no experience in metal casting, but Lynch's foundry was the only industry in town and the only business hiring. Huff learned quickly and soon distinguished himself with Mr. Lynch.

"By age twenty-five I was his right-hand man,"

he told Red now. "Spent the next several years trying to pound some business sense into him."

The gentleman who had ultimately become Huff's father-in-law hadn't been a visionary. He had made what he called a "darn good living" out of his operation, and that was satisfactory to him. His limited ambition had been a constant source of frustration to Huff, who recognized an expanding market and a wasted potential for keeping that market supplied.

This was the basis of endless disagreements between them. Expansion and increased production were not on Mr. Lynch's agenda. He was pleased with his mediocrity. Huff had unlimited energy and grandiose ideas. Mr. Lynch had an ultraconservative approach to financial matters. Huff adhered to the economic tenet that one had to spend money in order to make it.

The one certainty they did agree on was that old man Lynch held the purse strings and Huff was penniless except for his weekly salary. Consequently Mr. Lynch's opinion was the only one that mattered.

It was his misfortune that finally provided Huff with an opportunity. When a stroke incapacitated the older man, Huff assumed control of production. Anyone brave enough to challenge his takeover was summarily fired. Though unable to speak legibly or ambulate for the last three years of his life, Mr. Lynch lived to see his business quadruple in size and net annual revenue, and his sole heir, his daughter, Laurel, marry the man who had achieved that growth.

"I was thirty when Mr. Lynch died," Huff said to Red. "Two years later I put my own name on the business."

"You've always had a healthy ego, Huff."

"Hell, I did the work. I had bragging rights."

Red stared into his highball glass. "Did you ask me out here to talk about old times?"

"No, you're here to tell me what the hell's going on. Chris is being pestered by this new detective on your staff, and you're allowing it. Why? Aren't I paying you enough?"

"It's not that, Huff."

"Then what?"

"I'm dying." He tossed back the remainder of his whiskey, then rolled the empty glass back and forth between his palms.

Huff was too stunned to speak.

Eventually Red raised his weary eyes and looked at him. "Prostate cancer."

"Goddamn you, Red." Huff released his breath in a gush and waved his hand as though dismissing the problem. "For a minute there, you had me good and scared. That's no life sentence these days. They can go in, get it—"

"'Fraid not, Huff. Didn't catch it in time. It's spread into my lymph glands. Bones. Practically everywhere now."

"Chemo? Radiation?"

"I don't want to go through that. It would only buy me a few months, if that, and I'd feel like shit for the short time I have left."

"Hell, Red. I'm sorry as all get out."

"Aw, well, if one thing doesn't get you, something else will," the sheriff stated philosophically as he set his glass on the coffee table. "Fact is, Huff, I'm tired. Plumb worn out. I'm not up to taking on Wayne Scott in any kind of fight. He's an honest man, trying to do the job he was hired to do. Me, I'm a reprobate. Like you."

Red raised his hand to stave off Huff's protest. "No sense in trying to put gilding on it, Huff. This arrangement we've had, no matter how we want to color it to make it prettier, is damn ugly. I've done more crooked things than I care to think about.

"Nothing I can do about what I've done in the past. But now, Chris has got himself into another jam, and I don't think I have the time, or the energy, to get him out of it."

It was quite a speech, especially coming from a man of few words, as Red had always been. However, the underlying importance of it went beyond the words. "How long before you leave the job?" Huff asked.

"A month. Give or take a few weeks."

"That soon?"

"I'd like to spend some time with my family before the worst of it sets in."

"That's understandable, Red. But your retirement is coming at a damn inconvenient time."

"I can't help that. This thing with Chris could drag on for a while."

"This thing with Chris," he mimicked angrily. "He's no choirboy. Hell, I wouldn't have any use for him if he was. He's committed more than his fair share of mischief, and he would be the first one to admit it." Huff leaned toward his guest. "But he did not kill his brother."

Red was slow to respond but finally said, "I don't think so, either."

"He thinks he's being framed."

"Beck told me that. Was he serious when he mentioned Slap Watkins?"

"Goddamn right, he was." Huff shared what he had discussed earlier with Beck and Chris. "Now, I don't know if this Watkins cretin is capable of planning and executing a gumbo cook-off much less a murder he frames someone else for, but it's an idea worth thinking about. I'm sure you agree." Huff's stare warned the sheriff that agreement was his only option.

And lest there be any misunderstanding of his meaning, he continued. "Watkins is a criminal with three years of prison under his belt. I seriously doubt he spent his time there getting reformed and rehabilitated. I bet if you looked hard enough, Red, you'd find him breaking laws right and left, and one of those crimes might include doing away with Danny, out of revenge or just pure meanness."

Huff always conveyed what he wanted done without having to come right out and say it. Sheriff Harper read the message loud and clear.

Reluctantly he nodded. "I'll bring him in for questioning."

"That'll be a good start and maybe all you'll need to get a confession. The boys said he's acting real cocky. You come down on him hard enough, and he may boast his way right onto death row."

"I'll put out an APB right away." Red was about to stand, but Huff motioned him to remain.

As he lit a cigarette, he said, "There's something else I want you to do. In New Orleans."

"Huff—"

"No, this should be relatively simple. You could even delegate it to somebody there you trust. You've got contacts in the city, right?"

Huff explained what he wanted. Red listened carefully. "I'll make it worth your effort," Huff added as enticement. "You know how well I pay for solid information. This is important. It would be worth a lot to me."

"All right. I'll put out a few feelers, see what turns up. I can't promise anything."

"Nielson. Spelled with an *i e*. Any little tidbit could be helpful."

Red nodded and stood up. "Take care of yourself, Huff. Do as Selma tells you. Shouldn't fool around with the ticker. Better throw away those coffin nails, too."

"When you do."

Red tried for a smile but didn't quite make it. He walked to the door, his gait that of a man much older. He looked reduced, infirm, utterly defeated. Huff, liking none of what he saw in his confederate, called him back.

"Are you still my man, Red?"

"What do you mean?"

"I have to spell it out?"

Red's woebegone eyes turned angry. "After forty-something years, you've got the gall to ask me that?"

Huff wouldn't be put off by Red's indignation. At this juncture, he didn't care if he was affronted. "When you're lying on your deathbed, do I have to worry about you making some soul-cleansing confessions to your priest?"

"This late in the game, confession wouldn't do me any good, Huff. I'm gonna burn. And so are you."

"I'd better be getting back to town," Lila said, reaching for her hat.

"No rush. George is having to deal with that conveyor. He's going to be busy for hours. Besides," Chris said, holding up the bottle of white wine, "there are at least two more glasses left, and one of them has your name on it." He took the hat from her hand and replaced it with a refilled wineglass.

The picnic had seemed like a good idea. Had *seemed* like a good idea. But all Lila had done since her arrival was whine. About the heat. The bugs. You name it.

They'd driven out to the meeting place separately. It was one of their usual rendezvous. The grassy picnic area overlooked a bayou and was heavily shaded by mature trees. On weekends it was crowded with families, but on weekdays it was deserted.

He had given her only an hour's notice, calling her just after her husband left his office. She arrived a few minutes late, alighting from her convertible wearing a wide-brimmed straw hat and a wisp of a sundress through which he could see nearly all of Lila.

But when she saw the picnic he'd laid out, her expression turned sour. "What's this?"

"What does it look like?"

"Why don't we stay in your car so we can have air-conditioning?"

He wasn't partial to picnics himself. But if they stayed inside the car, they would have sex and then she would leave. He needed more time than that. Today he needed time to smooth talk and woo her.

He had thought that the romance of alfresco dining would appeal to her. He'd taken her hand and drawn her down onto the quilt beside him. Gently he'd removed her hat. He'd stroked her neck and décolletage.

"I've been feeling so claustrophobic, Lila. Because of Danny. The walls seem to be closing in on me. When I'm indoors, all I think about is his death, and the horrible way he died." Sliding his hand up into her hair, he whispered, "I wanted to lie down with you, not wrestle in the car. Help me forget for a while. Please?"

The sweet talk appealed to her, and she applied herself to eradicating his sorrow. After some sweat-inducing foreplay, she straddled his hips, impaling herself on him with such vigor, his breath left his lungs in an audible whoosh.

For the next several minutes, Lila seemed intent on erasing from his mind all thoughts of anything except their slippery coupling. She focused strictly on restoring him emotionally. Or killing him in the process.

But afterward, she began to complain. She didn't

like the outdoors. "There's never a bathroom around when you need one," she'd said. "Like now, for instance."

"Go behind a bush."

"And get a rash on my privates? I don't think so."

Two glasses of wine improved her outlook somewhat. So did Selma's delicious chicken salad and crispy cheese biscuits. But after swatting away a bothersome fly, she reached for her hat and announced that it was time she went home.

Now that he had forestalled her leave-taking with another glass of wine, he said, "Come on, drink up." He pressed the glass to her lips and tilted the bottom of it to such a sharp angle that the wine dribbled over her chin.

His eyes followed the trickles down her throat and chest until they disappeared beneath her dress. He winked at her, then moved the fabric aside and licked the wine from her breast. "Excellent vintage," he said.

Sighing with pleasure, she reclined on the quilt and adjusted her bodice to accommodate him. By the time his lips found their target, she was moving against him restlessly. "Ah, God, that drives me crazy."

He flicked his tongue. "What, that?"

"God, yes."

He kept her nipples pinched between his fingers while his mouth traveled to more exotic terrain. Before it was over, he feared she would tear his hair out by the roots.

She was an obliging and fair lover, taking him

into her mouth, which she cooled first with pinot grigio. On the brink of release he got on top of her and thrust himself into her roughly. She responded in kind, and each enjoyed a crashing orgasm. But the instant it subsided, she gave his shoulder an ungracious shove. "Get off me. It's hot and you're heavy."

With her hair and makeup mussed, her dress twisted around her body in a way that revealed more than it covered, she was the picture of debauchery. Poor George didn't stand a chance of keeping her satisfied.

Smiling at her and lazily trailing his finger down the outside of her thigh, Chris said, "You're the sexiest woman I know, Lila, but sometimes you outdo even yourself. Like just now. Like last Sunday."

"Last Sunday?" She checked her wristwatch, cursed beneath her breath, and sat upright.

"You remember. When I went over to your house."

"Lord, I bet I'm a sight." Hastily she straightened her dress and searched the rumpled quilt for her underpants. "If George is home when I get there—"

"He won't be," Chris said, trying to curb his impatience. "He's busy. He'll be at the foundry for hours yet."

"But he might come home unexpectedly." Finding her underwear, she stood up and stepped into them, then bent down to retrieve her hat. "He's been acting weird lately. Watching me. I think he suspects something."

"That's your imagination."

"At first, I thought so, too. But the other night after we got home from the wake, he asked me where I'd disappeared to."

He chucked her beneath the chin. "Bet you didn't tell him."

She wasn't amused. "I've been all lovey-dovey ever since, to try and throw him off track, but I'm not sure he's convinced. He talks about you a lot and watches me when he thinks I don't know he's watching."

In light of his recent conversation with George, Chris wondered if she was right. But if George suspected them of having an affair, so what? He didn't really care if her husband knew. Right now he was interested only in Lila's cooperation should it be needed.

He followed her as she made her way up the incline to where she'd left her car. She tossed her hat into the backseat and opened the passenger door.

"Hold it." He turned her around and drew her close. "No good-bye?"

"I haven't got time, Chris."

"Are you sure?" he growled, nuzzling her ear.

She pushed him away, playfully, but meaning business. "I'm supposed to be waiting for my doting husband to get home from a hard day at work. You'll have to find some other girl to take care of this." She squeezed him playfully, quickly.

"I don't want another girl." He pushed his thigh between hers and rubbed it against her crotch. "I want a woman. You, Lila. And you want me, too, because I know how to make you happy."

It wasn't very graceful screwing. It certainly

wasn't comfortable. But he gave her another orgasm, which was all that mattered with Lila. When
he finally released her, she was panting and her eyes
were glazed.

Now was the time to ask, he thought. "If I ever
need you, you'll be there for me, won't you, Lila?"

"I'll try." She was attempting to straighten her
dress, but the lightweight fabric was clinging to her
sweaty skin. "Sometimes it's hard for me to get
away on short notice."

"I don't mean just for sex. What if I really
needed you?"

She pulled back and looked at him with misapprehension. "Needed me? Like for what?"

He smoothed his hands down her arms, a tender, affectionate caress. "Like, if your uncle Red
asked you whether or not I was at your house last
Sunday afternoon, you'd admit that I was,
wouldn't you?"

Her eyes cleared instantly, as though someone
had thrown cold water in her face. She no longer
looked drowsily satiated. In fact, she had never
looked more alert. "Why would Uncle Red ask me
something like that? Oh, Christ, George does
know."

"No, no, this has nothing to do with George."
He held her shoulders, massaging them gently. "It's
about me. Us. I'm trying to get a divorce, Lila.
When I do, I want to talk to you about the future.
Our future.

"I know it's too soon to ask you for a commitment. Especially with this mess about Danny hanging over my head. But that will be cleared up soon.

How soon will depend a lot on what you tell Red about last Sunday."

There, that had subtly placed their future together in her hands. He had gracefully shifted the responsibility for whatever happened onto her, and he had dangled the prospect of marriage to him.

To seal the deal, he leaned forward and kissed her on the forehead. "I can count on you, can't I?"

"Of course you can, Chris."

"I knew I could." He kissed her lightly on the lips, released her, and helped her into the car. She started the motor. Then she smiled up at him. "You can count on me to look after Lila."

He felt like he'd been slapped. "What?"

"You must really think I'm stupid. You're a great lay, Chris, but that's the only reason I can stand you. George isn't much, but he worships me. I'm the princess in my household. In yours, I'd be under Huff's thumb, and just be the wife you were cheating on. And this business about your brother's death? It's your mess, baby doll. Get out of it yourself."

chapter 21

*B*eck's cell phone rang as he was climbing the front steps of the Hoyles' house. He answered, listened, cursed, then asked, "When?"

Red Harper said, "'Bout an hour ago."

"Did he offer an explanation?"

"That was the problem. He couldn't."

"Okay, Red. Thanks for letting me know. I'll get back to you."

He disconnected and went into the house. The wide foyer was shadowed and hushed, as though the house was napping. There was no one in Huff's den. Beck found him in the most unlikely place—Laurel Lynch Hoyle's plant conservatory.

"What are you doing in here?"

"I live here."

"Sorry. I didn't mean that the way it sounded. I'm a little cranky."

"So I see. Go pour yourself a drink."

"Thanks, but I'd better not."

"You need a clear head?"

"Something like that."

"Sit down. You're wound up tighter than an eight-day clock."

Beck lowered himself into one of the rattan pieces that furnished the room. The western sky, as seen through the tall windows, had turned lavender with the dusk, the same color as several of the potted orchids that bloomed in profusion. The ferns were lush and deeply green, suggesting a coolness that was welcome after the heat outside. The room was like an oasis, inviting one to relax.

But it was going to take more than a tropical ambience to unwind him.

Huff was reclined on a chaise lounge, fringed throw pillows behind his back. He was holding a glass of bourbon, but he wasn't smoking, upholding his late wife's wish that he not smoke in her special room.

"Feeling okay?" Beck asked.

"Better than you, I think. If I were to bet on which of us has the highest blood pressure right now, I'd put my money on you."

"Is it that obvious?"

"Tell me what's going on."

Beck released a long breath and settled back against the cushions of his chair. "We're getting hit from all sides, Huff."

"Give them to me one at a time."

"For starters, there's the Paulik crisis. I spoke by phone to the doctor overseeing his care. Billy's prognosis for recovery is good. Physically he's doing as well as can be expected."

"But?"

"But he's severely depressed."

"That means a shrink," Huff said, looking none too pleased about it.

"Not even workmen's comp pays for that, even if the Pauliks filed a claim, which they haven't. I think we should offer to provide a psychiatrist."

Huff made a sound of disgust. "Those doctors drum up business for each other. It's a racket."

"In some instances I'm sure that's true. However, it stands to reason that Billy is having a difficult time coping mentally and emotionally. Beyond that, it would be a good PR stroke for us. Which we desperately need."

"All right. But a few sessions ought to do it," Huff said. "Nothing long term."

"Say five."

"Say three. What else?"

"Mrs. Paulik. The new SUV we sent over yesterday was in my parking space when I got to work this morning. I dispatched laborers to their house to do some repairs, repainting, et cetera. Mrs. Paulik wouldn't let them in. She sent them packing, then called and told me where I could stick our bribes. She's moving her family out of your house—your 'stinking house,' to quote—and said that if we thought a few play-pretties could shut her up, we could think again."

Huff took a sip of bourbon. "That's not all, is it?"

"No," Beck replied reluctantly. "She's going to sue us."

"*Dammit!* She said that?"

"She promised that."

Swirling the liquor in his glass, Huff thought it

over for several moments. "I'm betting she won't, Beck. She's grabbed us by the short and curlies with these threats. Okay, she's got our attention. Let's sweeten the pot."

"More gifts? I think that would only strengthen her resolve and give firmer footing to her allegations that we're using bribes to buy her compliance. And there's a furthermore." Beck paused, sighed. "Furthermore, she's threatening to talk to the Justice Department. She wants criminal charges to be filed."

Huff finished his drink and set the glass on an end table, his jerky movements attesting to his anger.

"She doesn't have a chance in hell of succeeding," Beck said. "It would have to be proved that we knew an accident was virtually certain to occur, and that would be damn near impossible to do even by the sharpest prosecutor.

"On the other hand, I know of companies who've had to contest charges of intentionally disregarding safety factors and purposefully endangering their employees. Customers of long standing suddenly take their business elsewhere. Employees, especially middle management, resign for fear of going down with a sinking ship.

"It can take years for these type cases to come to trial. A huge conglomerate with a billion-dollar budget and a phalanx of lawyers working the case might survive. Privately held companies like yours rarely do."

Huff scoffed at that. "It'll take more than one disgruntled, loudmouthed woman to shut down Hoyle Enterprises."

"Ordinarily I would agree with you. But Alicia

Paulik isn't acting alone. She's recruited Charles Nielson to lead the charge. I received a fax from him today. I won't bullshit you, Huff, it's your worst nightmare."

"Where's the fax?"

Beck opened the briefcase he'd carried in with him and took out a single sheet. He stood and handed it to Huff, saying, "Maybe I'll have a short one after all."

He went into the den, poured himself a bourbon and water, spoke to Selma, who came to inquire if he was staying for dinner, then returned to the conservatory. Huff was no longer reclining on the chaise. He was pacing the width of the windows. Beck noticed that the fax had been balled up and thrown to the floor.

"He's pissing in the wind. Our workers won't strike," Huff said definitely.

"They might."

"They won't."

"If they're rallied—"

"Rallied, hell!" he roared. "They're too afraid for their—"

"Things aren't like they were forty years ago, Huff," Beck shouted. "You cannot conduct business like you did when you first took over the plant. You cannot be autonomous."

"Tell me why the hell not."

"Because Destiny isn't some feudal burg without any connection to the outside world. The government—"

"Has no goddamn right telling me how to run my business."

Beck laughed shortly. "Well, federal law says they do. The EPA and OSHA are monitoring us and taking names. Now Justice might enter the fray. That's probably given Nielson a hard-on." He rubbed the back of his neck before taking a sip of whiskey. "He's called upon the labor unions to send—"

"Thugs."

"They'll be here by the first of next week. They'll organize a picket line and urge our employees to strike until . . . Well, you read the fax. There's a list of demands with the promise of more to come."

Huff made an impatient gesture. "Our employees won't listen to any outside agitators, especially if they're from up north."

"And what if they're homegrown southern boys? Cajun. Whites and blacks. Nielson's too smart to send men who would be dismissed out of hand. He'll send people from this area who speak the language."

"No matter where they hail from, our people will resent their interference as much as we do."

"Possibly. Hopefully. But Billy's accident has had a profound impact, Huff. You haven't been to the plant since it happened. The atmosphere is dismal, charged with resentment. Men are grumbling, saying it wouldn't have happened if we had maintained the machinery routinely and enforced safety rules."

"Paulik had no business trying to work on that belt. He hadn't been trained to."

"I wouldn't use that argument, Huff, because it's one of theirs. I've heard complaints that new employees are put on the floor without any proper training, and that a foundry is no place to get it on the job. If I were George Robson, I'd be watching my back, although they all know he's only a mouthpiece."

Muttering a stream of profanity, Huff turned toward the windows and looked out over his property. Beck let him have this time to mull over what they'd discussed.

Eventually, Huff wandered over to the piano and struck several of the keys. "You ever play the piano, Beck?"

"No. My mother went through a Pete Fountain craze and enrolled me in clarinet lessons. I went three times before refusing to go again."

"Laurel played." Huff smiled down at the keyboard, as though seeing her hands moving over it. "Bach. Mozart. Dixieland jazz. She could just sit down and look at the sheet music and play like a maestro."

"She must have had quite a talent."

"You bet your ass she did."

"Sayre told me she didn't inherit it."

"Sayre," Huff said around a snuffle. "Know what she's been doing today?"

Beck shook his head. He didn't want to talk about Sayre. He didn't want to think about Sayre.

"Well, let's just say she's kept herself occupied."

Beck wasn't sure how he was expected to respond, or even *if* he was expected to. Apparently not. Because Huff returned to the chaise and picked up their discussion.

"Here's what I think, Beck. I think this Nielson

character is all talk. Why did he give us advance warning that he's sending people in? Why not spring them on us?"

"Like a surprise attack?"

Huff's finger jabbed the air as though Beck had hit the nail on the head. "That would be my tactic. Why did he give us time to prepare? He's let us know he's gunning for us. That indicates to me either that he's a lousy strategist and not nearly as smart as he thinks he is."

"Or?"

"Or that he's raising a ruckus to drum up publicity for himself but doesn't really intend to follow through on his threats. I don't think he wants a fight. I think he's scared of us."

Beck thought it over for a moment. "He doesn't seem anxious to confront us. I placed several calls to his New Orleans office today after I received the fax. I was told he was out. I left word for him to call me back. He hasn't so far."

Huff smiled expansively. "See what I mean? He's avoiding us. That says coward to me. Call his bluff."

"Keep trying to contact him?"

"Pester the snot out of him. Let's see how he likes being the one who gets pushed and pushed again. Make a nuisance of yourself."

"That's actually a good idea, Huff."

"Don't let up until he's agreed to have a face-to-face meeting. That's the only way we'll get an accurate read on him. These faxes and FedExed letters are bullshit. I'm tired of littering my trash can with them."

"I'll get on it first thing in the morning."

"In the meantime, I want you to talk to some of our most loyal men. Fred Decluette for one. Men whose loyalty we can count on. We need to know who the rabble-rousers among our employees are."

"I talked to Fred this afternoon. He and some others will be keeping their eyes and ears open and reporting back who the troublemakers are."

Huff winked at him. "Should have known you'd already be on top of the situation."

"Another drink?" Beck got up and took Huff's glass. In the den, he poured each of them a refill, then returned to the conservatory.

As he handed Huff's drink to him, Huff said, "Now let's talk about something else."

Beck looked at him grimly. "I'm afraid there is something else. Red Harper called just as I was coming in and—"

"That can wait. Let's talk about Sayre."

"What about her?"

"Why don't you marry her?"

Beck stopped short of the rattan chair and turned quickly to look back at Huff, who was placidly sipping his fresh bourbon. He laughed at Beck's astonishment.

Beck collected himself and resumed his seat. "You must be feeling the effects of mind-altering drugs. What did Doc Caroe give you, and should you be mixing it with alcohol?"

"I'm neither drugged nor drunk. Hear me out."

Beck pretended to relax against the chair's back cushion. "This ought to be good. I'm all ears, Huff."

"Don't be a smart-ass. I'm serious."

"You're delusional."

"Do you like her looks?"

Beck merely stared at him, schooling his features to remain impassive.

"I thought so," Huff said around a belly laugh. "I saw the two of you together down by the bayou after the wake. Even from that distance, I sensed some heat."

"Heat? Right. She was telling me in so many words that I'm the lowest life-form on the planet."

But even as he dismissed Huff's matchmaking as lunacy, Beck wondered if Huff had been talking to Chris. Had he told Huff about the scene he'd interrupted in Beck's kitchen? And just how long had Chris been standing there? How much of their conversation had he overheard?

With as much nonchalance as he could muster, he asked, "Where did you get this harebrained notion?"

"You're practically a member of the family already. Marrying Sayre would make it official."

"There's a major hitch to your plan, Huff. Even if I were dying to marry Sayre—and I'm only playing devil's advocate here—she despises this family."

"You could bring her around."

Beck smiled crookedly. "She doesn't strike me as being that pliant. In fact, she's about as flexible as one of our iron pipes."

"You don't think you're man enough to handle her?"

"Not even close." Beck laughed. "Anyway, I wouldn't want a woman I could 'handle.'" Too late he realized he'd talked his way into a trap.

Huff's eyebrows shot up. "Then it sounds like a perfect match, doesn't it? Chemistry, sizzle, all that. Sayre's a handful, and you don't want a doormat."

Beck finished his drink and set the empty glass on the dainty end table, nearly knocking over a lamp. "It's not going to happen. Let's forget you ever mentioned it."

"If you're worried about the nepotism angle, don't. I married the boss's daughter. Look how well it turned out."

"This is different."

"Damn right it is. You bring a hell of a lot more to the table than I did. I was a penniless, uncouth nobody without a pot to piss in. You've got a lot to offer Sayre."

"She wouldn't even let me pay for her cheeseburger the other night at the diner."

"What about out at the fish shack? Did she let you pay then?"

Beck felt his ears turn hot with embarrassment. Just how much did the cagey old bastard know? He tried to maintain an inscrutable expression. "For a thin girl, she sure can pack it away. Cost me fifteen bucks to feed her that night, counting the change I left in the tip jar."

Huff chuckled, but he didn't let Beck's joking divert him. "I've worked all my life for one thing, Beck," he stated seriously. "You might think money. No. I like having money, but only because it buys you power. I'd rather have power than any material possession money can buy. Respect? Shit no. I don't give a damn what anybody thinks of me. Whether they like me or despise me, it's not my problem."

Holding up his index finger, he said, "I've worked for this and this alone—for my name to outlive me. That's it. Does that surprise you?" He waved his hand as though clearing away a pest. "You can keep your money and fancy thingamajigs, your honorary plaques for doing good deeds, your polite society bullshit. None of that matters to me. No, sir.

"All I want for my time and trouble is for the name Huff Hoyle to be remembered and repeated for a long time, even after I'm dead and buried. That means grandchildren, Beck. So far, I don't have any, and I mean to remedy that."

All joking aside now, Beck said, "You'll have to rely on Chris."

Huff frowned with annoyance and reached for the pack of cigarettes in his shirt pocket before he remembered they were forbidden in this room. "Chris isn't going to be a father anytime soon." He then told Beck about Mary Beth's tubal ligation.

"I didn't know. Chris hadn't said anything to me."

"Well, that's the sad state of affairs in that camp. So you see the problem? Chris has got to get that divorce by fair means or foul. But even if Mary Beth granted it to him tomorrow, he hasn't got a future bride waiting in the wings. But you," he said, fixing his gaze on Beck. "If you got down to business, I could have a grandson in ten months."

Beck shook his head with incredulity. "This conversation gets more bizarre by the moment. First you have me married to a woman who can barely tolerate the sight of me, and now you have me fathering her child?

"Speaking for myself, I'm flabbergasted. But can you even imagine Sayre's reaction to this idea? She'd either laugh the house down or scream it down. Either way, even to have a discussion with her about it, you'd have to approach her with a chair, whip, and muzzle. Now, can we drop this? It's out of the question."

Unfazed, Huff said, "Sure, there are some obstacles, but I can find a way around every one of them."

"Not every one, Huff."

"Name one."

"Conflict of interest. I'm Chris's lawyer."

Huff furrowed his brow. "So? What's that got to do with it?"

"So . . . Sayre thinks Deputy Wayne Scott may be on to something."

He watched Huff's face gradually evolve into a mask of rage. "She thinks Chris killed Danny? How could she? Why would she? Because of Iverson?"

"There's the specter of that, certainly."

"And?"

Beck looked down at his clasped hands. "She mentioned Sonnie Hallser." Huff took so long to respond that eventually Beck raised his head and looked over at him. "She said that killing runs in the family."

Huff's face had turned so red that Beck had a fleeting fear he was about to go into cardiac arrest again. "Should I get you some water?"

Huff ignored the offer. "The Hallser incident happened a long time ago."

"Not long enough apparently. Sayre has vivid recollections of it."

"Does she recollect that I was never charged?"

"She does. But she wonders if maybe you didn't . . ." He shook his head, unable to finish. "It doesn't bear repeating."

"She wonders if maybe I didn't leave the shop floor until *after* Hallser stepped into that sandpit and was pulled into the machine? That maybe I even pushed him into it and left him there to bleed to death?"

Beck merely looked at him, offering no comment. Those had been the allegations leveled against Huff. They were never proven, were never even presented in a court of law. They'd been only marginally investigated.

"Sayre has always thought the worst of me," Huff said. "When all I ever wanted was to make damn certain that I provided the best of everything for my family." He came off the chaise and began to pace again. "When I was just a skinny little kid with Mississippi mud between my toes, I determined that nobody was ever going to walk over me, that I was never going to duck my head or grovel to anybody. I haven't and I won't, goddammit. If somebody questions my methods, that's their problem, and that includes Miss Sayre Lynch Hoyle!"

"I didn't mean to upset you, Huff. But you asked."

Huff waved off the apology. "She's going to think what she wants. Why she'd want to dredge up something that happened when she was just a mite, I can't even begin to guess. She had run out of reasons to hate me, I suppose, and had to go scraping the bottom of the barrel to find another. Who the hell knows why she does anything? But she doesn't have to feel kindly toward me to marry you."

Then he drew himself up short, looked at Beck shrewdly, and gave a low chuckle. "You got me going, didn't you? You thought, 'I'll raise the old man's hackles, sidetrack him.' You're putting up smoke screens, boy. What's really bothering you? Is it that Sayre's been married twice before?"

"I'm in no position to judge her."

"She was young," Huff said, as though Beck hadn't spoken. "Rash and impulsive and headstrong. She made bad choices."

"That's not quite accurate, is it, Huff? Weren't her bridegrooms *your* choices?"

His eyes narrowed. "She tell you that?"

"No. Chris did."

Huff moved his lips around an imaginary cigarette, as he was wont to do when he wasn't actually smoking one. "The girl was out of control. Her life was a shambles and she seemed bent on making it worse. I was her only parent and saw it as my duty to step in and try to avoid total disaster. I'll admit, it may have been a bit drastic to lay down an ultimatum that either she get married or else, but the situation called for me to be tough.

"I'll tell you, Beck, you may be thinking 'Poor Sayre,' but don't. She made the lives of those two men sheer misery. Oh, they asked for it. They wanted her. The second husband just as much as the first, even knowing the first marriage had gone south before the ink was dry on the marriage certificate. But they considered her worth the hell she put them through. She was a beauty, a firebrand. Wild and . . . well, you know."

Yeah, he knew, all right. She was all of that. His hands had felt it. His lips had tasted it. But better not to linger on thoughts of it. "When the first marriage ended, why did you insist on the second?"

"She wasn't straightened out yet."

"Was she still in love with Clark Daly?"

Huff's scowl deepened. "You know about that, too?"

"Not much. Some."

"I was right to bust up that little romance, wasn't I? Look how he turned out. Do you think Sayre would be happy with him now? He's the town drunk. Living hand to mouth. A failure. Now tell me I was wrong to prevent that match."

Beck withheld further comment. Obviously it was a touchy subject to both Huff and Sayre.

Huff gave Beck a calculating look. "I bet it's crossed your mind."

"What?"

"What she's like between the sheets."

"For godsake, Huff." He shot to his feet. "I'm not listening to any more of this."

He turned toward the door and nearly collided with Chris as he strolled in. "You're not listening to any more of what?"

"I'm trying to persuade Beck to marry Sayre," Huff said.

Chris looked at Beck, his dark eyes dancing with

amusement over the secret they shared about the interlude he'd interrupted. "Should I be airing out my tux?"

"I told Huff he was delusional. And apparently you're living in a dreamworld, too."

His tone caused Chris to take a step back. "What's got you so steamed?"

"What the hell were you doing out at the fishing camp?"

"What?" Huff exclaimed.

"That's what Red called me about earlier," Beck explained. "He was giving us a heads-up. Seems Wayne Scott returned to the sheriff's office a while ago, barely able to contain his excitement because he'd caught Chris inside the cabin at the fishing camp."

"So fucking what? I'm going to get a drink."

As he turned to leave, Beck reached out and caught him by the arm. Chris angrily shook off his grip, but he remained where he was. Beck said, "What were you doing out there?"

"It's my cabin."

"It's a crime scene. Do you know how that makes you look?"

"No. How?"

"Guilty."

The two glared at one another, each as angry as the other. Chris was the first to back down. "It's nothing for either Scott or you to get worked up about. I took Lila on a picnic this afternoon, mistakenly thinking it would be romantic. I wanted to soften her up in case I need her as an alibi for Sunday afternoon. I thought if I acted needy, emotionally fragile, her nurturing instincts would kick in."

"How'd it go?"

"Turns out Lila doesn't have any nurturing instincts," he replied dryly. "But I'm still working on her."

Beck wasn't satisfied with the evasive answer, but he didn't take issue with it now. "You still haven't explained why you went to the camp."

"It was on the way as I drove back into town. I saw the turnoff and acted on impulse. I hadn't been there since . . . it happened, and I wanted to see the cabin for myself.

"I went inside and looked around. It's been cleaned up, but you can still see bloodstains. I stayed no more than a few minutes. When I came out, there was Scott, leaning against his squad car with this stupid smirk on his face."

"What did he say?"

"Something clever about criminals always returning to the scene of the crime. I told him to go screw himself. He asked me what I was doing in there and if I'd removed anything."

"What did you tell him?"

"Nothing. You told me not to answer any questions without you present."

"What happened then?"

"I got in my car and left him standing there."

"Chris, *did* you remove anything from the cabin?"

He looked like he might tell Beck to go screw himself, too. But he only gave him a clipped no, then added, "The only thing I touched was the doorknob to let myself in."

Beck wasn't sure he believed that, but he asked no more questions. Although it would be helpful if Chris were completely honest with him, he wasn't required to be. A lawyer didn't always want to know his client's guilt or innocence.

"Hopefully no damage was done," he said with more confidence than he felt. "I just wish you had consulted me before you went out there."

"You're my lawyer, not my kindergarten teacher."

Using that as his parting shot, Chris left the room. A few moments later he reentered the conservatory with a highball glass in hand. As he sat down on a small settee, he looked around as though he'd never been in the room before. "Why are we in here?"

"I'd been in the den all day and needed a change of scenery," Huff said. "This is where Beck found me when he stopped by to talk over some matters."

"Like what . . . besides a pending marriage between you and Sayre? Which I find laughable, by the way."

"So do I," Beck said. "And any discussion of that ends here." He gave Huff a hard look, then turned back to Chris. "I stopped by to bring Huff up to speed on several issues." He enumerated the topics like bullet points on an interoffice memo.

"Those are hardly trivialities," Chris said. "You couldn't have waited on me to have this conference? It's becoming a habit of yours to cut me out of the loop."

"It wasn't intentional, Chris. Huff asked and—"

"He answered," Huff said, interrupting. "He can

fill you in on the details later, Chris. Right now, there's something else we need to discuss. It's serious and it concerns Sayre."

"I told you, the subject is closed."

"It's not about that, Beck. It's something else."

Chris sipped his whiskey. "I can hardly wait. What's my dear little sister up to now?"

chapter 22

It was Saturday night, and Slap Watkins had nowhere to go.

Since ten o'clock that morning, he'd been drinking in a honky-tonk located so deep in the swamp that unless you knew it was there, you'd never find it. The anonymity was intentional. The clientele seldom went by the names on their birth certificates and took exception to nosy questions.

He'd played a lot of pool and lost heavily on his gambles. Then a woman with a missing front tooth and a nose ring had turned down his offer to buy her a drink. She looked at his ears and laughed out loud. "I ain't that thirsty."

Following that rejection, he'd made his stumbling exit from the place, asking himself who needed that kind of abuse. Slap had never been a happy drunk. Instead, spirits tended to make him surly. The drunker he was, the nastier his disposition. Tonight he was extremely drunk.

His piss factor went off the charts when he returned to the buddy's house where he'd been staying. "They came looking for you, man." The guy—right then Slap was a little foggy on his name—was blocking the door with his bony body, talking to him through a rusty screen, which was uncomfortably reminiscent of the rare visits he'd had from friends while in prison.

"Who did?"

"Two deputies from the sheriff's office. 'Bout four o'clock this afternoon. My ol' lady wigged out."

She would. She operated a meth lab out of the bathroom. "They say what they wanted me for?"

"Naw. But as they were getting back in their squad car, I overheard one of them say something about Hoyle. Anyhow, my ol' lady says you can't stay here no more, Slap. Sorry, man, but fuck . . ." He raised his knobby shoulders in a shrug. "You know how it is."

Swell. So now he had nowhere to stay, and—this was the clincher—the sheriff's office was looking for him. He couldn't buy a break, could he? Story of his life.

He'd been initiated into violence by a father who beat him regularly and further coached by a passel of siblings who teased him about his ears. Their ridicule was merciless. He had learned to defend himself just as ruthlessly. He belonged to a clan of short-tempered, hotheaded brawlers whose sole resolution to even the slightest tiff involved some form of weaponry, even if it was one's own hands, feet, or teeth.

Those violent tendencies were percolating inside him now as he sped along a back road on his motorcycle. Everything he owned was packed in a roll tied behind the seat. He was trying to think clearly and calmly, but his brain was pickled in cheap alcohol, making his reasoning powers a bit dodgy, which was unfortunate because he had some serious decisions to make.

First off, where was he going to light? With kinfolk? He had them spread all over southern Louisiana, but he didn't like any of them much. His uncle reminded him of his late daddy, and Slap had hated that mean son of a bitch. Most of his relatives had whining kids who got on his nerves.

A few weeks ago a cousin had agreed to let him sleep on his living room sofa. But after only one night he'd accused Slap of entertaining impure thoughts about his wife. Slap had laughed and said she was so butt ugly that only a blind man could entertain impure thoughts about her.

Actually she wasn't *that* ugly, and he hadn't only entertained impure thoughts but had acted on them with her practically begging him to, and urging him to hurry up and finish before her old man got back from the store with the six-pack of Bud and a jar of mayonnaise she'd sent him after.

But in any case, the accusation had put an end to that. He'd moved out and started mooching off friends.

There were lots of them scattered around, too. But now he'd been kicked out of one place because the law was looking for him. Word got around. He'd be like a man with a contagious disease. None of his friends would want him bunking under their roofs.

And why had two deputies come around looking for him?

Well, duh.

He didn't want to think the worst, but he wasn't stupid. They'd mentioned Hoyle, and Slap would bet his left nut they were referring to the one recently deceased.

Afterward, he thought he must have been guided by a sub . . . sublim . . . sub-something thought. What did you call those messages deep inside your brain that made you do stuff before you were even aware of it? He didn't think he had a destination in mind, but he must have. Because he found himself on the pretty rural road where the Hoyles lived.

Yep, there it was, their mansion, sitting among oak trees so perfect they looked fake, like something in a movie. The sun was setting behind the house, outlining it in gold. It was large enough to house a whole cell block. One thing you could say about it, it was prettier and cleaner than their foundry. He drove past the estate, along a white rail fence that looked harmless enough, but Slap wouldn't trust it not to be wired with electricity.

The sonsabitches. Thought they were the lords of the land. They for goddamn sure lived like it, didn't they?

As he drove past the house a second time, he saw Chris Hoyle jog down the front steps and climb into his silver Porsche. Slap sped up so he wouldn't be seen spying on the house. Luckily, when Chris drove out of the lane, he turned in the opposite direction. Slap made a U-turn and followed at a safe distance.

Hoyle didn't go far before turning off the road and driving through an open gate. The house at the end of the drive was much smaller than the Hoyles', but it was a damn sight better than anything Slap had ever lived in.

Beck Merchant, Hoyle's trusty sidekick, came out the front door and got into the Porsche. Again, Slap sped up and went past Merchant's house so they wouldn't see him. He grinned into the hot air that whipped against his face. Whatever their plans were for this Saturday night, they were about to change.

Beck hadn't wanted to go out with Chris tonight.

He'd spent an idle Saturday at home. He'd washed his pickup and given Frito a bath and good brushing. These·were activities that he could do while trying to unravel the problems besetting him.

When Chris had called late that afternoon and invited him to go out, he'd declined. But Chris had been persuasive. "We haven't been out together since Danny died. We've been on edge with each other because of all the crap that's going on. Let's go out and forget about our troubles for a few hours."

"Where are we headed?" Beck asked now. Chris was driving away from town.

"I thought the Razorback."

"I don't want to go there. It's too boozy, noisy, and crowded."

Chris cut a glance at him. "You're getting old, Beck."

"I'm just not in the mood for it tonight."

"Thinking about my sister?"

Chris was heckling him, but he responded seriously. "In fact, that's exactly what I'm thinking about. What is she after?"

"I don't have a clue."

That was what Chris had said yesterday after Huff told them that Sayre had been making the rounds of the jurors on Chris's trial. "She's talking to anyone who'll talk to her."

When Beck had asked why she was doing that, both Huff and Chris had pled ignorance. They had shrugged as though befuddled by Sayre's activities and what had prompted them. But their worry over it was inconsistent with their claim to be clueless. Huff hadn't liked her talking to those jurors. Nor had Chris. That bothered Beck greatly.

Chris interrupted his reverie by asking, "What's this?"

"What?" Beck turned around to see what had attracted Chris's attention in his rearview mirror. A motorcycle was behind them, and it was roaring up fast.

"Wasn't he driving past my house as I came out?" Beck asked rhetorically. Then, "Oh, hell. That's—"

"Our friend Slap Watkins. I thought Red was handling that situation."

"Obviously he hasn't found him yet." Beck reached for the cell phone clipped to his belt, intending to call the sheriff. "You can outrun him in this, but try and keep him in sight. I'll give Red our location. Maybe we can keep Watkins busy long enough for Red to get here."

Just as he said that, the motorcycle rammed the back of the Porsche.

Chris cursed lavishly. He sped up, then shouted, "Hold on!" Less than a second later, he stamped on the brakes. Beck hadn't had time to brace himself before the tightening seat belt caught him hard across his chest.

Averting a total disaster, in which Chris and Beck would probably have been decapitated as the bike sailed over the Porsche, Watkins managed to cut his front wheel sharply to the left. It clipped the left rear fender of the Porsche before skidding across the road on its side, Slap's left leg beneath it. He pulled himself free, got to his feet, then came at them in a hopping-running limp while shaking his fist and yelling obscenities.

Beck's phone had been jarred from his hand when Chris hit the car's brakes. Unbuckling his seat belt, he searched the floorboard for it.

"Call Red. I'll take care of this." Before Beck could advise against it, Chris got out of the car and immediately went on the offensive.

"You must want to talk to me real bad, Slap."

"You know what I want."

"More Hoyle blood, I assume."

Slap cut his eyes toward Beck, who'd just retrieved his phone from the floorboard. "Drop it, Merchant!"

"Not until you back down and cool off."

Suddenly looking nervous and indecisive, Slap licked his lips before swinging his gaze back to Chris, who said, "My brother's blood wasn't enough for you?"

"Is that why the sheriff's looking for me?"

"Unless you've killed somebody else."

He took one lurching step toward Chris. "You goddamn—"

That was all he got out before Chris bent double and head-butted Slap in his midsection, sending him reeling backward. Slap reacted with the reflexes of a habitual fighter. Beck quickly pressed 911 on his phone, then tossed it onto the seat, knowing that the emergency call would be traced to their location.

He clambered out the passenger door but hadn't noticed that the car had stopped on the shoulder of the road. He didn't anticipate the deep ditch and stepped into it hard, lost his footing, and fell. By the time he got back on his feet and climbed out of the ditch, Chris and Slap were standing on either side of the white stripe in the center of the road, frozen in a tableau that crackled with tension.

Chris was holding his arm against his side. Blood seeped through his fingers. Slap looked down at the knife in his hand, blinking at it stupidly as it dripped blood onto the hot tarmac. Lifting his head, he looked at Chris with an expression of stunned disbelief. Then he turned on his heel and ran back to the motorcycle.

Chris took several staggering steps after him.

"Let him go." Beck grabbed a handful of Chris's shirt and held him back. "They'll get him." Chris's knees buckled, and he dropped to the ground.

Slap righted his bike, hopped onto it, and as soon as the motor roared to life, he sped away. In the still night, the sound was deafening.

Beck helped Chris to his feet and ushered him around to the passenger side of the car. "Watch your step. We're on the edge of the ditch. Are you all right?"

Chris nodded, then muttered, "Yeah, yeah, I'm fine." Glancing down at his arm, he said, "Cocksucker cut me."

"I called nine-one-one." As he put Chris in the seat, Beck picked up his phone. "Shit! They've got me on hold!"

"I'm fine, Beck. It's only a flesh wound."

Beck looked at the arm Chris extended to him. A long cut ran from his biceps to his wrist. The wound didn't appear to be deep, but darkness had fallen and there were no lights by which to see. It might be more severe than it looked. "You don't know where that knife has been."

"Take me to Doc Caroe. He'll give me an antibiotic."

Chris wouldn't hear of being taken to the emergency room. Beck gave up trying to insist and called Red Harper instead. The sheriff wasn't available, but a dispatcher took down all the information. "Tell Red we're on our way to Dr. Caroe's house."

By the time Beck had completed his call, they had reached the neat brick home of the family physician. He had settled in for an evening of HBO, he told them when he answered the door in his pajamas. Like all his clothing, they were several sizes too large and made him look like a gnome as he led them down a dim and narrow hallway into a room at the rear of his house that was outfitted to serve as an examination room.

"This was where my father practiced medicine for over fifty years," he explained to Beck. "Even after I set up the office on Lafayette Street and renovated this house, I kept this room ready to treat emergencies."

He concurred with Chris that the knife wound, while ugly, wasn't deep enough to require stitches. He cleaned it with antiseptic that stung so bad it brought tears to Chris's eyes, then wound it in a gauze bandage. "I'm going to give you a buttful of antibiotic. Drop your pants."

Chris got the injection and as he was readjusting his trousers said, "Are we all agreed not to tell Huff about this?"

"Why not?" Caroe asked absently as he placed the disposable syringe into a hazardous waste container affixed to the wall.

"Hearing that his only surviving son was knifed may not be good for his heart."

Caroe looked at Chris blankly for several seconds, then said, "Ah, right, right. Good thinking. Too soon after his heart attack."

"He'll hear about it from Red anyway," Beck said. "If we don't tell him, he'll be mad as hell and his blood pressure will still go up."

"I suppose you're right," Chris said. "Let's at least hold off until tomorrow, though. I'll tell him over breakfast. Maybe by that time Watkins will be in custody and Huff won't get too upset."

As they were leaving, Red Harper arrived. "We've got an APB out on Watkins's motorcycle," he said as he got out of his car and approached them. "Officers are focusing on the roads in the vicinity of where you saw him. How's your arm, Chris?"

"It'll be fine. Just find Slap and be quick about it."

"Problem is, he's got kinfolk and cronies all over the place, in every surrounding parish. Lots of places to hide in the swamp, and those people don't rat each other out. You start asking questions, they clam up, and you can't pry information out of them with a crowbar."

"Do you know where he's been living since his release from prison?" Chris asked.

"He's supposed to be staying with his daddy's people. That's according to his parole officer. But I went to see his uncle today and he said Slap left weeks ago. It was his understanding he was staying with friends." He told them about canvassing several places that afternoon. "Everybody we talked to played dumb, but somebody's lying. We'll start making the rounds again tonight."

"Exercise caution," Chris said. "He knows you're looking for him."

"So he's been tipped?"

Beck said, "When Chris mentioned Danny, Slap immediately asked if that's why you were looking for him."

"Have search warrants handy," Chris suggested. "You might come across something linking him to Danny."

Red dashed that optimistic possibility. "I wouldn't count on Slap being caught with hard evidence. He's no Einstein, but he's not that dumb."

"You're probably right," Chris said grimly.

"But as sure as I'm standing here, he killed my brother."

Red promised to keep them updated, then returned to his car and drove away. Chris instructed Dr. Caroe to send him a bill, and the doctor told him he could count on it.

"Not quite the evening out I anticipated," Chris remarked once they were back in his car, which now sported a dented rear fender and busted taillight. Beck was driving.

"I knew I should have stayed at home."

"Well, thanks a lot for your concern," Chris said with feigned affront. "I hazard to think what would have happened if I'd been alone. Of course, you dillydallied long enough for him to gut and fillet me. It was over before you got there."

"I fell in the ditch," Beck admitted with chagrin.

"What?"

"You heard me."

"Is that what I'm smelling? Stagnant water?"

"I was up to my knees in it."

Laughing, Chris cradled his arm against his chest like a newborn. "This is beginning to hurt. I wish I'd asked the doc for some pain pills."

"It does sound like Slap was somehow involved with Danny's death, doesn't it?"

"I don't think he was *involved,* I think he murdered him out of revenge."

"Then . . . ? Never mind."

"No, what?"

Beck gave a quick shrug. "If he killed Danny, wouldn't he be trying to avoid us, particularly you? It strikes me as odd that he pursued us tonight."

Chris shook his head. "You're thinking like a rational, intelligent person, Beck. Watkins is a moron. He's itching to let us know that he killed Danny. He's taunting us. He can't resist the impulse to gloat. Before he went to prison, I could count on one hand the times we crossed paths. Now suddenly he's everywhere we are. You think that's coincidence?"

"I suppose you're right. He could've killed you, Chris."

"That crossed my mind," he said grimly. "But not until it was over. When I realized what could have happened, I got weak in the knees."

Beck turned into the Hoyles' drive.

"Oh, hell," Chris groaned. "It didn't even keep until breakfast."

All the lights in the house were on. Huff was standing on the gallery, smoking a cigarette, waiting for them.

Well, he'd gone and screwed himself but good.

Slap Watkins kept to the back roads, some of them little more than dirt trails that wound through the swampy terrain. Usually they ended at either a body of slimy, snake-infested water or a cul-de-sac of dense forest, forcing him to backtrack and possibly meet head-on a posse of badges who had picked up his scent. And, speaking of scent, he wouldn't put it past the Hoyles to sic a pack of search dogs on his ass.

He was no whiz kid when it came to book learning, but he had well-honed fighting skills. He knew how to deal with brute force. You fought back, and if you wanted to win you fought dirty.

When Chris Hoyle had charged him, he was momentarily startled. But his self-defense instincts instantly took over. Reverting to the lessons of a lifetime, forgetting about his tenuous parole and the three years of hard time he'd served prior to the conditional release, he'd slid the knife from his boot.

He berated himself now for not keeping a clearer, cooler head, for drinking too much, for letting that arrogant, rich bastard egg him on. His head was still fuzzy on the details of the fight. He didn't remember lashing out with his knife, but he must have, because Hoyle was the one who wound up bleeding.

Honest to God, Slap would later tell anyone who would listen, *I only meant to threaten him with the knife. I never intended to use it.*

chapter 23

Sayre phoned Beck at his office at five o'clock on Monday afternoon.

"Beck Merchant."

"Sayre Lynch. Are you free this evening?"

"Are you asking me for a date?"

"There's someone I want you to talk to."

"Who?"

"Calvin McGraw."

"My predecessor? What for?"

"I'll meet you at my motel at six."

The next thing he heard was the dial tone.

He knocked on the door of her room at precisely six o'clock, and she answered immediately. Her handbag was already on her shoulder. The room key was in her hand.

"I don't get to come in?"

She closed the door behind her. "I'll drive."

The top was down on the rental convertible. The wind played havoc with her hair as they headed out of town, but she seemed not to notice. The air conditioner was blowing at top speed, but it was having little effect on the temperature inside the car. It had been parked in the sun all day, and the upholstery was like a heating pad along Beck's thighs and back.

"I heard that you and Chris had an exciting Saturday night," she remarked.

"We tried to keep a lid on it, but news of it spread."

"How is his arm?"

"Not as bad as it could have been."

"I can't imagine Chris having a face-off with anyone in the middle of a public road. What was he thinking?"

"He was thinking that Watkins killed Danny."

She turned her head sharply. "*Slap Watkins?* Are we talking about the same guy?"

"Your would-be suitor. Danny passed when he applied for a job at the foundry." He gave her a condensed explanation of why Watkins was considered a viable suspect.

"Do you think that's credible?" she asked when he finished.

"Credible, yes."

"Likely?"

"I don't know, Sayre." He shifted in his seat, uncomfortable with both the scorching upholstery and her question. "The sheriff's office thought it had enough credibility to want to question Watkins."

"If you lined up everybody who has a grudge against the Hoyles, the line would stretch for miles. I can think of a hundred people with far more reason to hate them. What about all the employees over the years who've been fired? It's like Watkins's name was drawn out of a hat."

"I would tend to agree with you, if not for what he did Saturday night. I saw him cruising past my house. At the time, it didn't register with me who it was, only that it was a guy on a motorcycle. But it was Watkins. Clearly he followed Chris there, then deliberately tried to run us off the road.

"As of now, he's facing charges of assault with a deadly weapon whether or not he had anything to do with Danny's death. He's had a long and illustrious criminal career. He became visibly nervous at the mention of Danny's name. Any way you look at it, he's a dangerous man, and I don't think he'd get squeamish over committing murder."

Sayre still didn't seem convinced. "Because of his criminal record, he makes a convenient scapegoat, doesn't he?"

"He attacked Chris with a knife."

"Did you witness the fight?"

"Most of it. When I wasn't wading my way out of a ditch."

He told her about his mishap, but the humor of it escaped her. Instead, her lips formed an analytical moue. "If you were on the witness stand in a court of law, could you testify under oath that Watkins intentionally slashed Chris?"

"Isn't it obvious? Chris had a bleeding arm."

She pulled off onto the shoulder and stopped the car beneath a magnolia tree that provided shade. Leaving the engine to idle, she turned to him. "Once when we were teenagers—junior high or thereabouts—I was spending the afternoon in the bathroom, primping. Despite there being three other bathrooms available, Chris kept knocking on the door, bugging me for no other reason than that he was bored. Finally I opened the door and told him to get lost and leave me the hell alone.

"He pushed his way into the bathroom and we got into a tussle, slapping each other, kicking. Then suddenly he screamed bloody murder and went tearing out of the room in search of Huff. He claimed that I had attacked him with my curling iron, and he had a nasty burn on his arm to prove it."

She paused to let him know that she had reached the point of the story. "I wasn't even holding my curling iron when I opened the door to him, Beck. It was plugged in but lying on the dressing table."

"You're suggesting that he intentionally burned himself?"

"Yes. It was worth the pain to get me in trouble."

"What you're saying is that Chris may have let himself get conveniently cut by Slap Watkins's knife."

She gave him a long look, then steered the convertible back onto the road. "Your encounter with Watkins wasn't the only buzz today."

"Where do you hear your 'buzz'?"

"The beauty shop."

He tipped down his sunglasses and looked at her wind-wrecked hair.

"I had a pedicure," she said defensively.

That gave him an opportunity to lean forward and look down the length of her shapely calf to her right foot, which had kept the accelerator at a constant seventy miles an hour since they left the city limits. "Hm. Pretty. That's not really a color, though. Not like red or pink. What do you call a color like that?"

"Beige Marilyn."

"Like Monroe?"

"I suppose. I never thought about it. The point isn't the color of my toenails, Beck. The point is, a salon is the best source of local information. They may be iffy on the exact location of Iraq, but they know with absolute certainty who's sleeping with whom, who got slashed last Saturday night, and so forth."

"Is that how you tracked down the jurors of Chris's trial?"

She shot him an arch look but refused to be thrown. "Actually, no," she said coolly. "I got that information from the courthouse." After a short pause, she said, "I wondered if Huff knew about that."

"He knows. Did you think you could keep your meetings with these people a secret? You're high profile, Sayre. You may be outfitted in the best the local Wal-Mart has to offer, but you still look like 'city' to them. The fact that you're back after a ten-year absence is big news. But you're meddling in Huff's affairs, and that news is even bigger. As much as they're in awe of you, nobody wants to get on the bad side of Huff Hoyle."

"I knew when I started calling on those jurors that it would get back to Huff and Chris. And you," she added, glancing across at him. "I didn't care."

"What did you hope this scavenger hunt would yield?"

"An individual with a conscience. One who would admit to either accepting a bribe or knowing that others had."

She told him about a widow named Foster who had a mentally disabled middle-aged son. She described her meeting with a man who had begun to weep when she asked him about his jury service.

"When I pressed him for more information, his wife asked me to leave. Later I discovered that he was saved from declaring personal bankruptcy a month following Chris's trial. What a coincidence." She turned off the highway and drove through a pair of impressive iron gates. The walls on either side of the gates had artificial waterfalls cascading over faux stone with "Lakeside Manor" spelled out in wrought iron.

The retirement community was situated on a man-made lake and flanked by an emerald, eighteen-hole golf course. There was a clubhouse nestled in a grove of sprawling live oaks that had a swimming pool, state-of-the-art workout gym, restaurant, bar, and recreation center. Beck knew this because the amenities were listed on a discreet green sign with white lettering. The residential lots were compact, but the homes on them were elegantly appointed. Paved walkways meandered through the immaculately landscaped complex.

Sayre parked at the clubhouse in the lot designated for visitors but made no move to leave the car. "I hate places like this. They're so sterile.

Everybody is the same, and so is each day. Don't they get bored?"

"At least they don't have labor strikes to worry about."

She turned to him. "So that buzz was accurate, too."

"Unfortunately."

"Tell me about it."

"There's this guy named Nielson."

"His name was mentioned at the salon. You dropped it the other night. Who is he?"

"Trouble for companies like Hoyle Enterprises."

"Apparently Billy Paulik's wife has been in contact with him."

"And because of that," Beck said, "he's called in the heavy artillery. He's recruited union men to picket and incite our workers to strike."

"Good for him."

"It's going to get ugly, Sayre."

"It's already ugly."

"People will get hurt. No, don't say it," he said quickly when he saw that she was about to speak. "I realize you can't get hurt much worse than Billy was, but that was a tragic accident. Preventable perhaps, but still unintentional. A strike is a war."

"I hope your side loses."

He laughed ruefully. "You may get your wish." Settling his head on the headrest, he looked up through the branches of the tree under which they were parked. "The timing of it stinks. Danny died little more than a week ago, and his death was most likely a homicide. Red Harper is having the devil of a time tracking down a local reprobate who has a taste for Hoyle blood. Meanwhile a detective in his department is still putting his money on Chris as the most likely suspect.

"You're driving around hither and yon in your bright red convertible, reminding folks that this isn't the first time Chris has been implicated in a man's death. You're sending Huff's blood pressure into the stratosphere. You're rooting for the opposing side in a labor dispute. And then there's the other."

"What other?"

Without raising his head, he turned it toward her. "I'm having a hell of a time keeping my hands off you." He looked down at her right leg, where her skirt had ridden high above her knee. "I don't know which is worse. To be away from you and able only to daydream about touching you. Or to be this close, to see you, and still not be able to act on the impulse."

He dragged his gaze from her exposed thigh to her face, which he had mistakenly thought would be safer territory. Her turbulent expression disabused him of that. "Mrs. Foster was bribed with a large-screen TV that would keep her disadvantaged son 'content,' " she said tightly. "That man sold his soul to get out of debt."

Sitting up straight again, Beck sighed. "You know these things for fact? You can prove it?"

"No."

"You know that these two individuals were among the six who voted for Chris's acquittal?"

"No."

He looked at her with reproof. "Let's say, for the

sake of argument, that the widow with the retarded son and the man who barely escaped bankruptcy did accept bribes to vote for Chris's acquittal. Did it make you feel better to remind them of their malfeasance?"

She looked away and answered a quiet no.

"What edifying effect did it have on their lives for you to hold a mirror up to them, Sayre?"

"Nothing," she snapped. "You made your point."

"Then why did you bother these people? What purpose did it serve? Your beef is with Huff and Chris. Why don't you confront them directly?"

"Why don't *you*?" she fired back. "Or don't you want to know the truth about Chris's trial? You would rather not know that Huff bribed jurors so Chris could get away with murder. Isn't that right?"

Raising his voice to the level of hers, he said, "If Huff bribed those jurors, maybe it was to make damn sure that his son didn't get convicted of a crime he did *not* commit. This vendetta of yours—"

"It's not a vendetta."

"Then what are you looking for?"

"Integrity. They have none. I hoped that maybe . . ."

"What?"

She paused, took a breath, then said gruffly, "That maybe you do. That's why I brought you here." She nodded toward a row of lakefront homes. "Calvin McGraw lives in the third house from the corner. He consented to talk to me this morning. I was actually surprised that he agreed to see me. Until I arrived. I was shocked by his appearance. He's aged considerably since I last saw him."

"Ten years can take their toll."

"I think most of his aging has occurred in the last three, since he tampered with the jury and saw to it that Chris got off. He's been ravaged by guilt."

"He admitted that?"

"Yes, Beck, he did. That was his last big hurrah for Hoyle Enterprises. He signed on as legal counsel soon after Huff assumed control from my grandfather. McGraw did for Huff and the company what you do now. The last thing he did before Huff retired him in favor of someone younger and—"

"More unscrupulous?"

"I was going to say brighter."

He frowned skeptically but motioned for her to continue.

"After the jury was selected, McGraw looked for those with vulnerabilities."

"Like a retarded son."

"Precisely." She gazed toward the tennis courts, where two couples were playing a lackluster match. "Very perceptive of you to ask if I'd felt good after talking to these people. In all honesty, I felt rotten. Especially after visiting with Mrs. Foster.

"I don't blame her for seizing an opportunity to improve their life, even with something as vacuous as a television. In her situation, I would have grabbed at it, too. What she did wasn't selfish. She did it to benefit the son she loves."

When she turned back to him, her wistful smile

turned into a frown of distaste. "But Calvin Mc-Graw did Huff's dirty work for the most selfish of reasons. There wasn't any nobility behind what he did. He left Huff's employ financially fixed for life, able to afford a swank retirement community like this. But the man isn't living out his days peacefully. He welcomed the chance to unburden himself to me this morning. He admitted everything."

Beck looked at her for a long moment, then reached for the door handle. "Okay, let's go hear what Mr. McGraw has to say."

They took a footpath that followed the shoreline of the lake. McGraw's house had lacy ironwork grilles in front of the second-story windows, simulating the balconies in the French Quarter. Deplorably so, in Sayre's expert opinion.

She depressed the doorbell and stared at the peephole. The door was pulled open by the same nurse who had admitted her earlier. She wore a crisp white uniform and a sour expression. This morning she had been all smiles. Sayre couldn't account for the change in her attitude.

"Hello, again."

"You didn't tell me who you were this morning," the nurse said, making it sound like an accusation.

"I introduced myself by name."

She gave a grunt of disapproval.

Sayre, aware of Beck taking all this in, gathered herself to her full height. "As I told you this morning when I left, I hoped to bring someone back with me to see Mr. McGraw. Is he available?"

"Yes, ma'am," she said starchily, and stepped aside to admit them. "He's back there in the sunroom where you visited with him this morning."

"Thank you. Is he expecting us?"

"I believe so."

Despite her rudeness, Sayre thanked her again, then motioned for Beck to follow her. They moved down a hallway that was crowded with too much furniture, as were all the rooms they passed. The sunroom was at the back of the house overlooking the golf course.

Calvin McGraw was seated in the same chair he'd been in on her previous visit. It was facing the door. Sayre smiled at him and spoke his name. He looked at her without registering any recognition, and she felt a twinge of apprehension. "I've brought Mr. Merchant to see you. Is now a good time?"

"I'm afraid not, Sayre." Chris, seated in a wicker chair with a high, fanned back that had concealed him up till now, stood up and turned around to face her. "Beck told me you were coming out, and it reminded me that I've been neglectful of Calvin lately. I try to get out here every so often, check in on him. Unfortunately, he's not having one of his good days. His mind comes and goes, you know. I understand that's how it is with Alzheimer's."

He walked over to the old man and placed an affectionate hand on his shoulder. McGraw didn't flinch or show any reaction whatsoever but continued to stare blankly into middle space.

"He has days when he can't remember his own

children. Other times he claims to have fathered a baby with the seventy-eight-year-old widow who lives next door. Last week they caught him wading naked out there in the lake. It's a wonder he didn't drown. The next day, he was right as rain, in total control of his faculties. He beat his nurse in five straight games of checkers."

He squeezed the man's shoulder again. "It's tragic, isn't it? When you think about how eloquent he used to be in the courtroom. Mind like a steel trap." He shook his head with remorse. "Now he'll go for days without saying a word. Other days he's a regular jabberwocky. Of course at those times he talks crazy and doesn't make any sense. You can't put stock in a thing he says."

Her breath was coming hot and quick. Blood had rushed to her head. She wasn't on the verge of fainting, but she thought she might explode. She could ignore Chris. She would expect treachery from him. It was Beck's betrayal that she felt like a mortal wound.

He'd laid this trap for her, then had the gall to talk sweet talk about desire and daydreams. She wanted to scratch his eyes out for getting her to trust him even a tiny bit, for leading her to think that maybe he wasn't as despicable as the men to whom he owed his fealty.

Turning to him, she said, "You son of a bitch," which was a paltry epithet compared to what she was feeling.

She brushed past him, left the tasteless pseudo-home, and ran every step of the way back to her car. By the time she reached it, she was gasping for breath, partially because of the heat, but mostly from outrage and humiliation.

She pushed the ignition key into the slot and saw that her hand was bleeding. She had been squeezing her fist so tightly, the teeth of the key had punctured her palm.

chapter 24

Clark Daly left his house at ten past ten. That was a half hour before it was necessary for him to leave, the plant being less than a five-minute drive from his house and his shift starting at eleven.

But the atmosphere at home was so hostile, he'd just as soon be at the foundry. Luce was on his case about Sayre. She had known when she married him that he and Sayre Hoyle had once been involved and that even though they'd been in high school at the time, the relationship had been serious. No self-respecting gossip was going to let Luce miss out on all the juicy details of their romance.

Luce had broached the subject while they were still dating. He was candid with her about Sayre. He would rather she hear the story from him than from people in town who thrived on other people's misfortunes and loved to embellish them.

Luce had even wormed a confession out of him that he had loved Sayre. But he also had made it clear that their relationship was ancient history, and had reminded her that she wasn't coming to him a virgin either. The matter was dropped. Once they were married, there were more pressing issues to argue about.

Knowing about Sayre and him was one thing. Having Sayre in town, showing up at their house and looking like a million, was something else. Luce hadn't liked it one bit. No sooner had Sayre driven away than she had lit into him.

"I won't have it, Clark."

She'd spoken in the quiet but firm voice indicating she meant business. When she yelled at him, he knew the quarrel was spawned by anger, that it wasn't that serious, and that it would be short-lived. This wasn't one of those. When her voice was low, she was telling him he'd better sit up and take notice of what she was saying.

"On top of the drinking and the chronic depression, I will not have you sleeping around on me with Sayre Hoyle, or Lynch, or whatever her name is."

"I'm not going to be sleeping with Sayre. We're old friends."

"You were lovers."

"*Were.* When we were kids. Besides, do you think she'd want me now?"

Of all the things he could have said, that was probably the most ill-advised. Luce took it to mean that if Sayre would have him, he'd be willing. It also suggested that he was good enough for Luce but not good enough for Sayre Hoyle.

She'd been crying when she left for work that morning. By the time she returned that afternoon, the tears had dried, but the climate in the house was cool, downright cold in the bedroom, and here a week after Sayre's visit it still hadn't warmed.

The hell of it was, he loved Luce. She didn't have Sayre's polish and sophistication, but she possessed a beauty of her own. She loved her children and had provided for them alone when her first husband walked out on her. Most important, she loved him, and that was just shy of a miracle. He had given her few reasons to love him.

Lost in thought, he didn't notice the car behind him until it was right on his rear bumper. He pulled to the right side of the road, giving the other driver ample room to pass him. But the driver stayed on his tail and began blinking his headlights.

"What the hell?"

Immediately he checked for a light bar on the roof, thinking it might be a patrol car, but there was nothing to indicate that it was an official vehicle. Feeling a twinge of apprehension, he reached beneath his seat for the tire iron he kept there. When he binged, he typically did his drinking in places that had disreputable characters for customers. Occasionally he got crosswise with them. He saw only a driver in the car behind him, but that could be a trick.

The driver flashed his headlights again. Clark pulled his car to the curb and braked. The car behind him did likewise and turned off the headlights. Clark got a tighter grip on the tire iron.

He saw the driver get out, rush around to the passenger side of his car, and tap on the window.

"Clark, it's me."

Recognizing the face beneath the baseball cap, he

let go of the tire iron and leaned over to unlock the door. Sayre scrambled in and closed the door quickly to extinguish the interior light. She was dressed in blue jeans and a dark T-shirt, her hair stuffed under the cap.

"What the hell are you doing?" he exclaimed.

"I'll admit it's a little theatrical, but I had to see you without anyone knowing."

"I have a telephone and the bill is current. I think."

"Luce might have answered if I'd called. Unless I miss my guess, she wasn't too happy to see your high school sweetheart standing in her front yard."

"No, she wasn't."

"I don't blame her in the least. I would feel the same. But, Clark, I swear I don't want to complicate things for you. I would never do anything to harm your marriage or come between you and your wife. If you don't believe that, I must leave right now."

He studied her face for a moment, and while it was still lovely, her eyes no longer glowed with passion for him. Between Sayre and him there would always be an affection based on bittersweet memories, but their chance for a lasting love had died. Rather, it had been destroyed by Huff. Either way, it was dead, and he knew she was speaking the truth when she said that rekindling their romance wasn't the reason for this tryst.

"I believe you, Sayre."

"Good."

"So what *is* this about?"

He listened for a full five minutes, his amazement increasing the longer she talked. She finished by saying, "Will you do it?"

"You're asking me to spy on the men I work with."

"Because they're spying on you, Clark."

She propped her knee up on the seat so she could face him more easily. Leaning forward slightly, she continued. "Do you think Huff and Chris are going to let this strike happen without putting up a fight? Beck Merchant predicted it would get bloody. He referred to it as a war."

"I've heard the scuttlebutt about Charles Nielson," Clark said. "He's supposed to be sending union organizers here to talk to us. Secret meetings are being scheduled."

"So the employees are already talking about it?"

"Almost to the exclusion of everything else," he admitted.

"Well, you can be sure that Huff has spies who report to him everything that's being said, and who is saying it."

"Everybody knows Fred Decluette is Huff's man. He was shaken up the night of Billy's accident. I was there and saw the whole thing. Nobody tried harder than Fred to get him to the hospital before he bled out. But when push comes to shove, Fred's got six kids to feed, clothe, and educate. He'll protect his own interests first, and if that means sucking up to Huff, he'll do it. Others will, too, because it's a well-known fact that Huff rewards anyone who betrays his pro-union coworkers."

"Do you know who the others are?"

"Some, not all. Fred's obvious. Others aren't."

"You could level the playing field, Clark. Sniff out Huff's spies, feed them false information. At the same time, begin organizing men you know who would stand up against Huff if it comes to a show-down. You could help change things."

She spoke with such conviction, it made him pity her naïveté. "Sayre, changes won't come about as long as Huff Hoyle has a say-so."

"He may not have a say-so for long."

"The heart attack—"

"No, it wasn't that serious and he'll probably outlive us all. I was referring to the federal govern-ment. Whether or not a strike is successful, several agencies are breathing down his neck. If vast im-provements aren't made, he could be shut down.

"But that wouldn't exactly be a victory, would it, Clark? Without the foundry, what would happen to the economy of this town? Think of the terrible im-pact a shutdown would have on all the families who depend on the plant for their livelihoods." She paused to take a breath, then said earnestly, "Changes must be made, and soon. Otherwise, everyone loses.

"You could make Billy Paulik's accident count for something, Clark. I know what I'm asking of you won't be easy. You'll have to look sharp, be sharp. You'll have to earn the respect and trust of men."

He rubbed his jaw and felt the bristle sprouting from it. He was embarrassed because once again she'd caught him unshaven. But it also reminded him of how low he'd sunk. "That's a challenging assignment."

SANDRA BROWN

"I realize what I'm asking of you."

"I'm not sure you do."

"I went onto the shop floor, Clark."

"I heard about that."

"I knew it was bad, but frankly I was staggered by how bad. The working conditions are medieval. How do you stand it?"

"We don't have much choice."

"Now you do. It's imperative that changes—drastic changes—be made."

"I agree. But I'm not the man to do it, Sayre."

"You're a leader."

"I might have been a long time ago. Do I look like a leader of men now?"

"No," she snapped. "You don't. What you look like is a damn coward. Yes," she emphasized when he reacted with surprise. "The other day you told me that your life needed purpose, that you needed to get back on track, that you wanted to do right by your son. Well, I'm handing you a purpose, and you're backing away from it. Why? What are you afraid of?"

"Failure, Sayre. Failure. And until you're no longer making money hand over fist and driving fancy cars, until you sink so low that getting out of bed every morning is an effort that requires a sheer act of will, you won't know what failure feels like.

"You can't know what it's like until you walk down the street and know that people who used to cheer you from the bleachers are shaking their heads and whispering behind their hands about wasted lives." He stopped to compose himself, realizing that he was angry not with her but with himself. "You're goddamn right I'm afraid. I'm afraid to even *hope.*"

His speech had subdued her. When she spoke next, her voice was barely audible. "You're wrong, Clark. I know exactly what it's like when getting out of bed is an act of will." She drew a breath that caused her chest to shudder.

"But you're at a critical crossroads. You can do nothing, tell me no, and continue living as you are. Down on yourself and life in general, drowning your disappointment in whiskey, saying 'woe is me,' and making your wife equally miserable, until you finally die a useless, lonely alcoholic. Or you can start acting like the man you were when you were only a boy."

She took his hand and pressed it between hers. "I don't want you to do this to get even with Huff. Nothing could pay back what he took from you, Clark. Besides that, he's not worth it. Nor do I want you to do it for me." Squeezing his hand more tightly, she said, "I want you to do it for *you.* Now, what do you say?"

As she drove back to The Lodge, Sayre was cautiously optimistic that Clark would come through. Calling him a coward had been harsh, but it had given him the kick in the butt he'd needed. She had bet on him retaining some pride buried beneath the layers of defeat. Stung pride was a good motivator.

She didn't know for certain if her tactic had worked. He'd made no pledge of sobriety. He hadn't committed himself to the task she had asked of him. But whether or not he could influence the future of Hoyle Enterprises, she hoped that he would improve his life. When she returned to San Francisco, she wanted to leave knowing that at least in that endeavor she had been successful, that she had done some good.

At the door of her motel room, she pushed the key into the lock.

"You're out late."

Nearly jumping out of her skin, she spun around to find Chris standing close. It was as though he had materialized out of thin air.

"What do you want, Chris?"

"Can I come in?"

"What for?"

"I want to talk to my sister."

His disarming smile left her cold. "About what?"

"Invite me in and I'll tell you." He held up a bottle. "I brought wine."

He hadn't come bearing wine out of the goodness of his heart. Nor had he come merely to chat. Chris had an ulterior motive for everything he did. She just didn't know what it was tonight. She was loathe to be near him, but in spite of her aversion, she was curious.

Turning back to the door, she opened it and went in ahead of him to switch on the lamps. He followed her inside and took a look around the drab room. "I haven't patronized this place since high school, when I used to bring girls here. I didn't pay much attention to the decor then. Not much, is it?"

"No."

"Then why not stay at home? For ten years Selma has faithfully kept your room shipshape."

She removed her baseball cap and shook out her hair. "That isn't my home any longer, Chris."

He sighed over her stubbornness. "Do you at least have drinking glasses?"

She brought two tissue-sealed plastic cups from the tiny bathroom. He looked at them derisively as he opened the bottle of wine with the corkscrew he'd brought with him. "This is a nice Chardonnay from Napa."

"I've been to the vineyard. It *is* nice."

After filling their cups, he touched his to hers. "Cheers, Sayre."

"What are we drinking to? The coup you pulled off at Calvin McGraw's house?"

"Ah, that. Forty-eight hours later, you're still hacked." He chuckled. "Honestly, I can't say I blame you. You should have seen the look on your face."

"I'm sure you and Beck found it amusing."

He sat down in the shabby armchair and motioned her toward the bed. "Can you sit down and try to be civil?"

She hesitated, then moved to the bed and sat on the edge of it.

"I've been waiting for more than an hour," he said. "Where have you been? Destiny doesn't offer that much of a nightlife, and the way you're dressed—"

"What do you want, Chris?"

He sighed. "I can't be here simply to have a

conversation? You won't let me be a nice guy?"

"You're not a nice guy. You never have been."

"You know what your problem is, Sayre? You can't let things go. You wouldn't know what to do with yourself if you didn't have a bug up your ass."

"You came with wine to tell me that?"

He shot her a grin but continued. "You're not happy unless you're griping about something. I would have thought you'd outgrow that habitual discontent, but no. Now you're holding grudges for things I did to you when we were kids. Brothers are like that, Sayre. It's in the job description. Brothers tease and torment their sisters."

"Danny didn't."

"And that's why you were mad at him. His passiveness made you angry. Danny was born with a submissive nature, but you refused to accept that. You didn't want to concede that he wouldn't, possibly couldn't, stand up for himself."

She didn't argue that because it was true.

"You're still mad at Huff because of Clark Daly."

She looked down into her wine, hoping that he didn't catch her alarm at the mention of Clark's name. She hoped it was a coincidence that Chris had timed this unprecedented visit within minutes of their clandestine meeting.

"You shouldn't resent Huff for breaking off that relationship," he said. "You should be thanking him. But all that is water under the bridge." He reached for the wine bottle and refilled his cup.

"Your current grievance is Danny's death, and

that's what I want to talk about. You've taken it upon yourself to do some sleuthing into his apparent homicide."

"And you came here tonight to threaten me to back off, or else."

"Not at all," he replied evenly. "I admire and share your desire to get to the truth. What I'm having trouble with is the direction you've taken. Let me make this clear, Sayre, and save you a lot of time and trouble. My trial three years ago has nothing whatsoever to do with what happened to Danny.

"Your interest in the outcome of my trial is foolish and three years delinquent. You were welcome to return home when the case was being tried. You could have observed it all firsthand. I would have seen to it that you got a front-row seat in the courtroom. But, Sayre, it's over," he said, breaking the last word into two distinct syllables.

"You killed him, didn't you? Just like Huff killed Sonnie Hallser."

"No and no."

"Does anyone except me know that you saw Huff do it?"

His focus sharpened. "What are you talking about?"

"You sneaked out of the house that night, Chris. I caught you, remember? You threatened me within an inch of my life not to tell Mother. You said you wanted to surprise Huff at the foundry and stay with him until he came home.

"I remember being envious of your courage to walk all the way there by yourself after dark. And even more envious that Huff would be glad to see you. I knew he would think you were brilliant for having done it, that you wouldn't get into trouble for it." Lowering her voice, she said, "What did you walk in on that night, Chris?"

"How old were you?"

"Five."

"Right. So how could you possibly remember? I often sneaked out and went to the plant so I could ride home with Huff. You're getting your nights mixed up."

No, she wasn't. Some childhood memories were too sharp to confuse, and the days following the discovery of Sonnie Hallser's mangled body were one of them. It was also starkly fixed in her mind because it was the only time she remembered Chris behaving as though he was frightened.

"I believe Huff killed that man," she said. "And you killed Gene Iverson decades later over the same argument. But you learned from Huff's mistake. You disposed of Iverson's body so it would never be found."

"No one knows what happened to Iverson. Maybe Huff had put the fear of God into him, he got cold feet, and ran away."

"Leaving everything he owned behind?"

"Maybe he was kidnapped by aliens." He snapped his fingers. "I know. Colonel Mustard got him with the lead pipe in the library."

"This is no game of Clue," she said angrily. "How can you joke about a man's murder?"

"Which brings me to the next point. We don't even know that Iverson is dead, much less that he was murdered. My guess is that he's walking around hale and hearty, laughing up his sleeve at all the shit he threw at the fan for the Hoyles to clean up. What I know with absolute certainty is that I didn't kill him."

Unswayed, Sayre said, "You and Huff didn't trust a jury to acquit you, so you took matters into your own hands. Calvin McGraw admitted to me that he bribed those jurors."

"He has dementia!" Chris exclaimed. "If you had asked him if he'd blown up the Golden Gate Bridge, he would have confessed to that, too. He doesn't know which end is up. Sayre, for godsake, be reasonable. Why would you believe an Alzheimer's patient with limited mental capacity over your own brother?"

She left the bed and went to stand in front of the bureau. She set her untouched cup of wine on the chipped laminate top and looked into the mirror above it, barely recognizing herself.

Was this the interior design guru for the Bay City's rich and richer? Haute couture had been replaced with jeans and T-shirts. She'd given up trying to iron her hair into compliance and had let it do what it wanted to do in the humid climate, which was to swirl and curl in confusion.

Who was this person looking back at her, and what was she doing in this pathetic room, dressed like this, playing cloak-and-dagger games for causes that seemed to matter only to her? What business was it of hers if Clark Daly slowly killed himself with drink and despair? Why should she care about a labor strike and the future of Hoyle Enterprises, when, for decades, the people who worked there had tolerated maiming accidents, deaths, and deplorable working conditions?

If Chris had committed murder and gotten away with it, why not leave him to the devil? It seemed to bother no one except her that he and Huff had thumbed their noses at justice being done. Why had she taken up this mantle?

As for Danny's phone calls to her, they could have been about something major or something trivial. Statistically, people seriously contemplating suicide are rarely talked out of it. Had she taken one of Danny's calls, the inevitable might have been postponed, but that was all. It was egotistical of her to think that she could have been the one to keep him from doing it when his own fiancée couldn't.

Then she caught Chris's reflection in the mirror. He was watching her, as though he knew she was second-guessing not only her resolve but herself. Drawing herself up to her full height, she turned to face him.

"You asked a straightforward question, and that's how I'll answer you, Chris. Why would I believe even an unreliable source over you? Because Huff spoiled you rotten, and it shows. You're consummately selfish. You've acted on every self-gratifying impulse you've ever had.

"When you're caught doing something wrong, you rely on your charm or Huff's influence to spare you any backlash. You're self-absorbed, hedonistic, and amoral. You lie, sometimes simply for the fun of it, just to see if you can get away with it. You take what you want when you want it. You've never been denied anything in your life. Except, possibly, a divorce, which I'm sure you and Huff will find a way to obtain by fair means or foul.

"Do I think you killed Iverson?" she asked rhetorically. "Yes. You got away with it. But if you killed Danny, you will pay, Chris. I swear to you that I'll see to that."

He set his glass of wine on the nightstand. "Sayre, sit down. Please."

It was so unusual for him to say please that she returned to the edge of the bed and sat down, albeit reluctantly. He reached for her hands and held on to them tightly even when she tried to pull them back.

"Think about the way Danny died," he said quietly. "In order for me to have murdered him, I would have had to have taken down that old shotgun, loaded both barrels, pushed them into his mouth, and pulled the trigger.

"Now, despite all the character flaws you've enumerated, do you really think I could do that to my own brother?" Without waiting for an answer, he declared, "I did not kill Danny. I did not. To even consider that I did, you're making a fool of yourself."

"What difference does that make to you?"

"None whatsoever. I just don't want you to embarrass yourself."

His nonchalant explanation was so transparent, she saw straight through it. "No, that's not it, is it, Chris? I'm stealing his attention away from you, aren't I?"

"What are you talking about?"

"Huff. I'm causing a stir, and even though it's making him mad, his focus is on me, not you, and you can't handle that."

His eyes became shuttered, reflecting only an image of her in their ebony depths. The lips that had smiled so facilely moments ago were now compressed and barely moved when he spoke. "Go back to San Francisco where you belong, Sayre."

"Yes, I'm sure you'd like that."

"Not for my benefit, for yours."

She laughed and laid a hand on her chest. "I'm supposed to believe that you're thinking of my well-being?"

"That's right. You said it yourself, Huff's attention is on you these days. And do you want to know why? Do you want to hear what he has in store for you?"

His lips broke a smile then, but it was actually a triumphant sneer.

chapter 25

Charles Nielson's office was in a bank building on Canal Street in downtown New Orleans. He shared the twentieth floor with two dentists, an investment brokerage firm, a psychologist, and an entity of undetermined enterprise that went only by initials. His was the last office on the left at the end of a carpeted corridor. The name was stenciled on the door in unpretentious black block lettering.

The anteroom was small and furnished with basic waiting room issue—a pair of matching upholstered armchairs with an end table and lamp between them. Seated at the reception desk was a pretty, middle-aged woman.

She was in conversation with Sayre when Beck entered the office.

It would be difficult to say who was the more stunned to see the other there.

Peering around Sayre, the receptionist greeted him with a cordial "Good afternoon."

"Hello."

"I'll be with you in a moment. Please have a seat."

He didn't sit down but remained where he was, curious to hear what Sayre, who upon seeing him had become as wooden as a cigar store Indian, had to say.

The receptionist said to her, "Apparently there's been a breakdown in communication. Sometimes Mr. Nielson makes appointments and forgets to tell me so I can put them on the calendar."

"He didn't forget . . ." She stopped, cleared her throat. "He didn't forget to tell you about an appointment. I don't have one."

"Oh, well, what is the nature of your business with him? I'll be happy to pass along a message."

"My name is Sayre Lynch. My last name used to be Hoyle."

The receptionist's smile faltered. "Of Hoyle Enterprises? That Hoyle?"

"Yes."

"I see."

"I don't believe you do. I'm not here as a representative of my family."

The receptionist folded her hands on top of her desk as though ready to hear an explanation. "I'm sure Mr. Nielson would be interested to know that."

"When you speak with him, please impress upon him that I want to offer him my assistance."

"Yes, well, Mr. Nielson—" The receptionist was interrupted by the ringing of the telephone. She held up her index finger, signaling for Sayre to stay put while she took the call. "Charles Nielson's office. No,

I'm sorry, he's presently unavailable. May I relay a message?" She reached for a notepad and began jotting down information.

Sayre turned toward Beck. "Did you follow me here?"

"Don't flatter yourself. Unlike you, I have an appointment."

As soon as the receptionist concluded her call, he stepped around Sayre and approached the desk. All smiles, his voice like melting butter, he said, "You must be Brenda."

"That's right."

"We've spoken on the telephone several times. I'm Beck Merchant."

She reacted with obvious distress. "Oh, my goodness. You didn't receive my message?"

"Message?"

"Mr. Nielson was called out of town unexpectedly. I left word on your cell phone that he was unable to keep your appointment this afternoon."

Beck withdrew his cell phone from the breast pocket of his suit jacket and checked the LED. "So you did," he said. "Obviously I failed to retrieve it."

"I had hoped to catch you before you drove all this way."

"I wish your employer had paid me the courtesy of a meeting before he rushed out of town. When will he be returning?"

"He hasn't informed me of his plans."

"Is he reachable by phone?"

"I can give you his hotel. He's in Cincinnati."

"I suppose a cell phone number is—"

"Out of the question," she said. "Unless I want to lose my job."

"I don't want to be responsible for that."

"When Mr. Nielson calls in for messages, shall I reschedule your appointment, Mr. Merchant?"

"Please. If I don't answer, be sure to leave the date and time on my voice mail. I'll adjust my schedule accordingly. And this time, if you would be so kind, call my office and home numbers, too. I'd like to prevent a mix-up like this from happening again."

"Certainly, Mr. Merchant."

"Thank you."

"I'm sorry you were inconvenienced. Both of you," she said, including Sayre.

"I would also like to see Mr. Nielson at his earliest convenience," she said.

"I'll let him know that, Ms. Hoyle."

"Lynch."

"Of course. I'm sorry."

Sayre gave the receptionist her cell phone number and that of the motel switchboard, then turned to leave.

Beck was standing at the door and held it open for her. "Good-bye, Brenda," he said over his shoulder on his way out.

"Good-bye, Mr. Merchant."

They moved down the corridor in tandem. They waited together for the interminably slow elevator. They rode it down to the lobby level. When they stepped out of the elevator, he headed straight for the exit. Sayre followed the signs to the ladies' restroom.

All of this was accomplished in complete silence.

*   *   *

He was standing on the sidewalk in the shade of the skyscraper talking on his cell phone when Sayre emerged from the building five minutes later. She wasn't glad to see him, having given him ample time to disappear.

It was five o'clock, and the downtown sidewalks were crowded with people eager to get home. Motor traffic was already snarled. Exhaust fumes were trapped by the humidity and had nowhere to go, making the air even more cloying and difficult to inhale.

Beck looked frazzled. To block out the city noise, he had a finger poked in one ear while he squinted to concentrate on what was being said into the other. He'd removed his suit jacket and draped it over his arm, loosened his tie, and rolled up his shirtsleeves, looking much as he had the first time Sayre saw him at the cemetery.

When he spotted her, he ended his call and swam upstream of other pedestrians until he fell into step with her. "Nielson hasn't checked in yet," he said. "Save yourself a call to his hotel."

"I'll try later."

"You could have knocked me over with a feather when I saw you in his office. What prompted you to come?"

"As I told his assistant, I was there to volunteer my support. Why did you?"

"To meet Nielson in person," he returned smoothly. "I wanted to show him that neither I nor the Hoyles have horns and cloven feet and hope-fully to negotiate a peaceful resolution to our differences and avert a strike. I wanted to impress upon him how detrimental one would be, particularly to the foundry workers who depend on a weekly paycheck."

"You're all heart," she said, being intentionally droll. "How much?"

"How much what?"

She nodded down at his briefcase. "How much of a cash bribe did you bring with you?"

The light changed, and she rapidly crossed the street. When she reached the other side, Beck nudged her out of the tide of other pedestrians and forced her to stop. "Enough cash to cover dinner."

"You want to have dinner?"

"Customarily you insist on picking up your own tab, but I'd like to buy this time. Unless you eat too much, in which case I might need you to chip in."

His smile was teasing, his green eyes mischievous. But rather than feeling the desired effect, she was repelled. Instead of being swept off her feet by his flirtation, she was wondering how he could be so disingenuous. Oddly, she was crushingly disappointed in him.

"Chris told me about Huff's plans for you and me."

His heart-melting smile slipped.

"I'd hate for you to waste all that charm on seducing me when you don't stand a chance in hell of succeeding. Now, if you'll excuse me, I have another errand." She stepped around him and continued down the sidewalk. But he wouldn't be deterred and kept in step with her.

"Asking you to dinner has nothing to do with Huff's matchmaking."

"Get out of my way, Beck," she said when he stepped in front of her. "I'm going to be late."

"For what?"

"Visiting hours. I'm going to see Billy Paulik."

That took him aback, which gave her time to step around him.

"Wait, Sayre. I'll drive you."

"I'll drive myself. Besides, I don't think you'd be welcome."

"Actually, I've got something to deliver." He patted his briefcase. "Where's your car?" She told him. He said, "My truck's closer."

He'd parked his pickup in a ground-level lot nearer than the garage in which she'd left her car, and she was under a deadline to reach the hospital before visiting hours ended.

It wasn't that far, but because of rush-hour traffic and a shortage of parking places, it took them almost half an hour to get to the ICU floor where Billy Paulik was still recovering from surgery. During that time, they didn't exchange a word.

Alicia Paulik was in the hallway conferring with a young man in a white lab coat when Beck and Sayre alighted from the elevator. Spotting them as they made their way toward her, she glared at Beck with unmitigated hostility. "What are you doing here?"

"We came to see about Billy," he replied evenly. "This is Sayre Lynch."

She eyed Sayre up and down. "Lynch, huh?

You're Huff Hoyle's daughter. Can't say as I blame you for going by another name."

"How is your husband?"

Mrs. Paulik hitched her thumb at the young man in the lab coat. "This is his shrink. Ask him how he is."

The doctor introduced himself and shook hands with them. "Naturally I can't divulge what Billy confides to me during our sessions. Suffice it to say, he's extremely depressed. He's trying to heal physically, while also mentally and emotionally adjusting to the idea of living without his arm. Even with a prosthesis, he's facing difficult challenges. He's also fretful about the welfare of his family."

"I've told him we're gonna be fine," Mrs. Paulik said. "Better than fine. Because I'm gonna take your rotten company for every cent I can get." She addressed this threat to both Sayre and Beck, seeming not to draw a distinction between them.

The young doctor awkwardly interceded. "All of Billy's reactions are typical of patients who suffer traumatic injuries. It'll take time for him to come to terms with the permanent effects of it."

"Continue your sessions with him for as long as you deem necessary," Beck told him.

The doctor glanced uneasily at Billy's wife. "I was told I was limited to three."

"Mr. Hoyle has changed his mind," Beck said. "Continue the sessions. Call me if you have any questions." Beck gave a business card to the doctor, who nodded his good-byes and excused himself to see another patient.

Beck turned to Mrs. Paulik. "Is it all right if I go in to see Billy?"

"What for?"

He held up the manila envelope Sayre had seen him take from his briefcase before they left his pickup. "Get-well messages from his coworkers. I promise not to stay long."

She snatched the envelope from his hand. "I'll deliver it to him. It'd likely upset him to see you or anybody from Hoyle."

"As you wish, Mrs. Paulik." He told Sayre he would call the elevator, then turned and walked briskly down the hallway, leaving her alone with Alicia Paulik.

"How are your children coping?"

"They're scared. Wouldn't you be?"

Overlooking the woman's defensive tone, Sayre said, "Yes, I would. When my mother died, I remember being not only sad but very afraid that I would die, too. Traumatic events make all of us feel vulnerable, but it's especially true of children."

Mrs. Paulik ruminated on that, then muttered, "Shame about your brother Danny."

"Thank you."

"He was right decent."

"Yes, he was."

"Are you back in Destiny for good?"

"No, I'll soon be returning to San Francisco."

"Sooner the better. I's you, I'd leave town before the trouble starts. Wouldn't want to be a Hoyle when Nielson gets hold of them."

Before Sayre could form a response to that, Beck

called to her from the end of the corridor. "Elevator's here."

She touched Alicia Paulik's arm lightly. "I know you mistrust me, and your mistrust is understandable, but I'm deeply sorry for what's happened."

Then she turned and went to join Beck at the bank of elevators. "I had to let that one go," he said. "The people aboard were beginning to grouse about the holdup."

"I'm sorry I detained you, I just wanted—"

She was interrupted by a shriek that was out of keeping with hospital decorum. She looked back to see Alicia Paulik standing in the spot where she'd left her. But now, her feet were surrounded by cards and letters. The contents of the card she was holding in her shaking hands had obviously been so shocking she had dropped the others.

Sayre turned to Beck, aghast. "What was in that envelope?"

Another elevator arrived, and he motioned her toward it. "I don't want to miss this one, too."

But Sayre was moving away from him and the elevator, quickly making her way back to Alicia Paulik, who was hugging a greeting card to her breast and loudly keening.

chapter 26

He was waiting for her in his pickup outside the main entrance of the hospital. Leaning across the seat, he opened the passenger door, and she got in. He didn't mention Alicia Paulik or ask what had transpired after he left. "I was serious about dinner," he said. "I skipped lunch. Would you like to go with me, or not?"

It wasn't the most gracious invitation she'd ever received, but she accepted it. She was hungry, but her hunger could have been assuaged with a stop at a fast-food restaurant's drive-through. Her curiosity, however, couldn't be satisfied with a quick fix. The questions arising from what had happened in the hospital could be answered only by Beck, and getting him to address them might require some time.

They said little as he navigated his way through traffic back down Canal Street and then into the French Quarter. He parked in a public garage, and from there they set out on foot along Royal Street.

After they had strolled for a couple of blocks, passing several eateries from which wafted mouthwatering aromas, Sayre asked, "Do we have a specific destination?"

"I know a place."

The sun was low enough to cast long shadows of the buildings and create welcome shade, but the narrow street shimmered with heat captured throughout the day. It radiated off the pastel plaster walls of the ancient buildings and up from the uneven brick banquette.

Beck had left his suit jacket behind. He still had on his necktie, but it was loosely knotted beneath his open shirt collar. Sayre, who was wearing the black dress she'd worn to Danny's funeral, wished for shoes with heels more suitable for walking.

Conversation was kept to a minimum. They lingered at one corner for several minutes, listening to a solo saxophonist before continuing on. They were approached by a roving clown in a frizzy pink wig and polka-dot britches but declined to have their faces painted by him. A group of intoxicated young men eddied around them. One was brave enough to address a lewd overture to Sayre, but when he noticed Beck and interpreted his expression, his boozy grin, along with his courage, vanished and he hastened to catch up with his buddies.

The shops and galleries on Royal Street tended to be upscale. They boasted European antiques, estate jewelry, paintings, and sculptures for the most discerning collectors. One shop sold souvenirs, but the merchandise was several steps up from the ordinary junk found in the T-shirt shops on Bourbon Street.

Beck and Sayre walked past the store; then he

stopped and retraced his steps to go inside. "Be right back," he said over his shoulder.

Sayre wandered back to the display window to admire an array of Mardi Gras masks. They were decorated with faux jewels, spangles, lace, and lavish plumes. Some were ferocious, others exquisitely beautiful.

Beck came out of the shop carrying a strand of white pearl beads interspersed with smaller beads in metallic green, gold, and purple. "That dress is great, but it reminds me of the funeral. I thought this might help." He draped the strand around Sayre's neck, lifted her hair over it, then adjusted it to the neckline of her dress. "There. Better."

"Traditionally a man doesn't give a woman beads until she does something to earn them."

His fingertips lingered on the beads before he slowly withdrew his hands. "The evening's not over yet." Their gazes held until a group of laughing people bumped their way past on the narrow banquette. Beck started them on their way again.

She never would have found the place, nor would anyone else who didn't know it was there. The side street on which it was located was no more than an alley with a drainage gully running down its center. There was no sign to indicate a place of business. Beck stopped at an ivy-draped iron gate and worked his hand through the foliage to press a bell.

Through a concealed speaker, a disembodied voice said, *"Oui?"*

"It's Beck Merchant."

The gate unlocked with an audible click. Beck

ushered her through, then carefully latched it behind them. They followed a narrow exterior corridor that opened into a courtyard enclosed by
lichen-covered brick walls. Ferns the size of Volks-
wagens were suspended by chains from the
branches of a live oak tree that embraced the entire
enclosure.

Flowering plants peeked out from beneath gar-
gantuan philodendrons and elephant ears. The
twisted trunk of a wisteria vine, now in full leaf, had
climbed the wall of the adjacent building and spread
across the tile roof.

Beck directed her upstairs.

Sayre, entranced, went ahead of him up a circu-
lar staircase that led to a balcony with a railing of
iron fretwork. Ceiling fans circulated, causing gas
flames to flicker inside the hurricane lamps affixed
to the exterior wall. At intervals along the length of
the balcony, hibiscus shrubs grew out of china pots.
The bright blooms were as gaily colored as para-
sols, and nearly as large.

They were greeted by a dapper man in a tuxedo.
He clasped Beck's hands between his own. He
spoke rapid French, but Sayre understood enough
to know that he was exceedingly glad Beck had
come. Beck introduced her. The man's compliments
were effusive to the point of embarrassing her. He
kissed her on both cheeks.

Beck said, "It's presumptuous to show up without a reservation."

The maître d' shushed his apology and assured
him that there would always be a table for him.

Beck asked if they could be served drinks on the

balcony before going inside for dinner. "Champagne, please."

"*Certainement*. I guarantee your privacy," he said, bobbing his eyebrows at Sayre. "Take your time. Enjoy." He snapped his fingers, and a waiter appeared through a set of open French doors to take the order of champagne.

Beck motioned her toward a bistro table at the far end of the balcony. He held one of the dainty chairs for her, then sat in the other across from her. "Maybe I should have consulted you before asking to stay outside."

"I welcome it actually."

"Not too hot for you?"

"I like the heat."

"I remember."

Something about the way he said it, the way he was looking at her, made her heart knock lightly against her ribs. Changing the tenor of the conversation, she commented on his knowledge of French.

"My major required a foreign language."

He hadn't learned to be fluent in a university classroom, but his laconic reply indicated to her that his being bilingual was no big deal.

There one second and gone the next, the waiter appeared with a serving tray on which were two champagne flutes. Another waiter placed a wine cooler near their table. He poured from the opened bottle of champagne, then replaced the bottle in the ice and melted into the shadows along the balcony.

Beck raised his glass and clinked it softly against hers. "What are we drinking to?" she asked.

"Your departure."

"Oh?"

"Get the hell out of here, Sayre. Go back to your life in San Francisco before you get hurt."

"I got hurt."

"You had your heart broken over a high school romance. That was kids' play compared to what could happen to you now."

"Little do you know, Beck."

"Then tell me."

She shook her head. "What happened is between Huff and me. I left and swore I would never come back."

"Yet here you are."

"Yes, here I am."

"Why?"

She debated with herself for maybe thirty seconds before she said, "Danny called me."

His surprise was evident. "When?"

"The Friday before he died." She told him about the calls she had declined to take. "For the rest of my life, I'll chide myself for refusing to talk to him."

"I assume he didn't leave a message."

"No, but I doubt he was merely homesick to talk to me. I think he was calling for some fundamental reason, and I can't resume my life until I know—with a degree of certainty—what that reason was."

"It could have been anything, Sayre," he said softly.

"It could have been. Believe me, my conscience has tried to persuade me that it was inconsequential, a what's-new-in-your-life? call. But knowing what I do about the working conditions in the plant, and the ambiguity surrounding Iverson's disappearance, and Chris's recent quarrel with Danny, a more accurate guess would be that it was about something important."

She looked at him and sighed. "Beck, my family is corrupt if not lethal. They can't continue to destroy lives and livelihoods with impunity. Somebody must stop them. I was furious with you for taking me off that airplane, but I thank you for it now. I couldn't have lived with myself if I'd returned without some hard answers to difficult questions."

He tried one last argument. "What about your business? Won't it suffer while you're away?"

"I might lose some potential clients who are in a hurry, but the majority will postpone their projects and wait for me to get back. In any case, I can't return to my life there knowing that I didn't at least try to right the terrible wrongs here."

Looking down at the bubbles rising in her glass, she said thoughtfully, "Chris wants me out of the picture. I wonder why. His eagerness for me to leave raises speculation that makes it impossible for me to go." She looked again at Beck. "I'm staying."

He seemed to accept that he couldn't talk her out of her involvement. Sighing with resignation, he nodded at the crystal flute. "Drink up. No sense in wasting France's best."

After taking a sip, she said, "Is the champagne part of your seduction strategy?"

His eyebrow arched. "Would you rather I just cut to the chase? Our host would accommodate us with a room." Lowering his voice, he added, "And it would be my pleasure to accommodate you."

"So you could rush back to Huff, mission accomplished?"

"Sayre, you can't think that I considered his proposition as anything but ridiculous."

She smiled ruefully. "Chris delighted in telling me that Huff was trying to pawn me off again. He delivered it as the coup de grâce of his campaign to get me out of town."

A waiter appeared with a platter of complimentary appetizers. Beck said, "Can we forget all that long enough to enjoy our dinner?" When she nodded, he motioned for her to help herself to the appetizers. She bit into a pastry shell that virtually dissolved on her tongue.

"What's the filling?" he asked.

"I don't know, but it's delicious."

He tried one of the same and agreed. "Gruyère? Spinach?"

"Beck, at the hospital—"

"Minced onion," he said, still analyzing the filling in the pastry.

"The first card Alicia Paulik took from that envelope was from you. You heard her reaction."

He put the remainder of the canapé in his mouth and dusted his hands. "Scrumptious. I believe I'll have another." But as he reached toward the tray, Sayre stayed his hand and forced him to look at her.

"The check you sent them was extremely generous."

"That's relative, isn't it? How generous is generous? Huff suggested that we—as he put it—'sweeten the pot.'"

"Huff had nothing to do with that gift. It wasn't a company check. It was drawn on your personal account."

He removed the bottle from the wine cooler and poured each of them more champagne.

"Mrs. Paulik was overcome by your generosity," Sayre went on. "But it also left her conflicted. She was almost angry at you for making her feel so bad about the spitting incident. She deeply regretted it and wanted to apologize."

"She doesn't owe me an apology."

"She owes you her gratitude."

"I don't want that either."

"Then why did you do it?"

"Be thinking about what you want to eat. I recommend the oysters Bienville."

"Beck, dammit, answer me."

"Okay," he said brusquely. "Maybe I'm trying to buy myself a clean conscience. Does that make you think better of me, or worse?" He signaled a waiter and spoke to him in quiet French. The waiter disappeared inside and returned shortly with soft leather folders containing handwritten menus.

Sayre left hers unopened on the table. "Monday afternoon, why did you tip off Chris about Calvin McGraw? Did you think it would be fun to watch my reaction?"

He laid down his menu and looked her in the eye. "No, Sayre. But I thought it would be interesting to watch Chris's."

"Chris's?"

Beck placed his forearms on the table and leaned forward, narrowing the distance between them.

"Chris and Huff have been nervous over your talking to the former jurors. I've been asking myself why. Why didn't they scratch their heads in bewilderment and chuckle over your cockamamie notions? Why not leave you to make an ass of yourself? Why not let you play yourself out until you gave up and went back to San Francisco? That's what one would expect them to do."

Catching his drift, she said, "Unless they had something to hide."

"Unless they had something to hide." He looked down at the menu and toyed with the tassel at the end of the silk cord that divided the sheets inside. "I let you be embarrassed because I wanted to see what Chris would do if Calvin McGraw had been having a good day and giving a credible, lucid account of what took place during Chris's trial, like you said he'd done that morning."

"You believed me, didn't you?"

Raising his head, he looked across at her for a long time before saying anything. "How do you do that?"

"What?"

"Pair a strand of cheap Mardi Gras beads with haute couture and make it look so damn perfect. When I looked up at you just now . . . despite all this crap we're talking about, I'm thinking, Jesus, she's gorgeous."

Self-consciously, she touched the strand of imitation pearls lying on her chest. "You didn't answer my question. Did you believe what I told you about Calvin McGraw?"

He sighed and sat back. "If I believe that, I'm one

step away from believing that Chris killed Gene Iverson and disposed of the body where no one would ever find it."

"He learned from Huff's mistake," she said quietly.

"What mistake?"

"Chris was a witness to Sonnie Hallser's murder."

His eyes focused sharply on hers. "What?"

"Chris waylaid me when I returned to my motel room last night. We talked about more than just Huff's design for you and me." She recounted for him their conversation, specifically regarding Hallser's death. "He argued that I was too young to remember it, that I had merged two separate memories. But that's not true, Beck. I know I'm right. Chris sneaked out of the house that night and walked to the plant to surprise Huff.

"Whether he saw Huff push that man into the machine or saw him leave Hallser to die in agony after an accident, it would have had a profound effect on him. It would either have turned him against violence forever or enlightened him to its benefits. I think the latter. He realized its true value when Huff suffered no consequences for what he'd done."

Chris was Beck's client; he would have been a fool to respond to what she had just told him, and Beck was no fool. She understood the reason for his rigid silence and, in spite of herself, respected him for it.

She watched a bead of sweat trickle down his temple, then diffuse in the starburst pattern of faint lines at the corner of his eye. "I'm curious. How much am I worth, Beck?"

"What?"

"Huff would compensate you well for marrying me and fathering his grandchild. Was a dollar figure agreed upon, or are you leaving the amount to his discretion? Did he give you a down payment?"

"How do you think I'm paying for this dinner?" he quipped. Standing, he came around to help her from her chair. "But please limit your order to the left side of the menu."

Each of their three courses was sumptuous, but none outdid the chantilly-drenched chocolate soufflé they shared for dessert. The dining room had no more than a dozen tables, set with white damask cloths, sterling, crystal, and antique china. Above the wainscoting, the walls were covered with pink moiré, which matched the window drapes that pooled on the gleaming hardwood floor. The room was subtly illuminated by tapers on the tables and a crystal chandelier that hung from a plaster medallion in the center of the ceiling.

As they moved back outside to have their coffee, Sayre said, "My compliments to the chef, as well as to the interior decorator."

"I'll see to it that they're both commended."

"How did you find this place?"

"I didn't. My mother did. She brought me here to celebrate my graduation from law school."

"Is she from New Orleans?"

"Born and bred."

"Is she the one who taught you French?"

He smiled. "While I was still in diapers."

The waiter poured their coffee, then left them alone. Beck added a dollop of Grand Marnier to the coffee and passed a dainty china cup and saucer to her. "It's not quite the Destiny Diner, but they try."

Smiling, she carried her cup and saucer to the railing. Music from an unseen source could be heard above the rooftops. The courtyard below was meagerly lighted, most of it remaining deeply shadowed, creating an atmosphere of mystery and intrigue.

The fountain in its center burbled lethargically. The carved angel was missing part of one hand, and her feet were covered with moss. A flowering plant sprouted incongruously from a crack in the pedestal base. Like all the shrubbery and vines, the wayward little plant had been allowed to grow where it would.

Sayre liked these imperfections. The intimation of decay and neglect throughout the French Quarter contributed largely to its beauty and enhanced its mystique.

Speaking into the hush of the courtyard, she said, "Last night, Chris told me that he didn't kill Danny. His denial was quite earnest."

Beck came to stand beside her. "Maybe we've been chasing our tails. Danny may have pulled off the perfect suicide."

She finished her coffee, returned her cup and saucer to the silver tray on the table, then rejoined him at the railing. "What's sacred to you, Beck?"

"Why?"

"I want to tell you something, but you must swear to me that you won't divulge it. Because by telling you, I'm betraying a confidence."

"Then don't tell me."

"I think it's important that you know."

"All right. Hire me as your lawyer. I'll take a five-dollar retainer. Then I'm bound by professional privilege not to reveal anything you tell me."

"I thought of that," she admitted. "But you couldn't take my retainer. It would be a conflict of interest."

"So what you want to tell me concerns Chris?"

"Specifically Danny."

She looked at him closely, watching the flickering light from the gas lamps play across his face. The day they met, she had called him her father's henchman, and he'd done little to convince her that he was anything other. He claimed to have set her up at McGraw's place in order to watch Chris's reaction to the old man. But was that true?

Clark had cautioned her to be wary of him. Mere hours ago she had pondered how he could be so disingenuous. She even questioned the motivation behind his generosity to the Pauliks. Had he been grandstanding for her benefit?

But he hadn't known Sayre would be at the hospital when Alicia Paulik opened the packet of mail. Nor could he have planned for her to open his card first of all the cards in that manila envelope.

Taking a leap of faith, she said, "I'm going to tell you something that no one else knows."

"Remember, I'm Chris's attorney, Sayre. Be careful what you entrust to me."

Well aware of the risk she was taking, she said, "Danny was engaged to be married."

She could tell that he was genuinely stunned. "Engaged? To who?"

"I won't tell you her name."

"How . . . how did you—"

"I met her by chance in the cemetery. She was visiting his grave and introduced herself to me."

He relaxed a bit. "A woman walks up to you, Danny's well-to-do sister, and introduces herself as the dearly departed's fiancée, and you took her word for it? She could be someone trying to cash in—"

"Give me some credit, Beck. I'm a better judge of character than that. She isn't a gold digger. She loved Danny with all her heart. He loved her, too. She has a diamond ring."

"Which she could have got from the last guy she blackmailed."

"If she were an opportunist with extortion in mind, wouldn't she have contacted Huff by now? Neither he nor Chris knew about the engagement when Danny was alive, and she doesn't want them to know about it now."

"Why not?"

"Because they would jump to the immediate conclusion that you did. They'd think she wanted something from them."

He had the grace to look chagrined.

"She said they would make something ugly of the love she and Danny had for each other, when in fact it was beautiful."

"This could have been the news Danny wanted to share when he called you."

"My conscience would love to think so. And quite possibly that's right. In any case, I'm convinced they were devoted and terribly in love. He intended to marry her, create a future with her, which makes her absolutely certain that he did not take his own life."

"Maybe he wanted to break off—"

"No. I asked her that, as gently as I could. She denied even the possibility that he wanted to back out. But it was she who told me that Danny was going through a . . ." She hesitated to say the word *spiritual,* afraid that would be a dead giveaway that Danny's fiancée was someone in his church. "He was going through a personal crisis that he wouldn't share even with her."

"The matter of conscience he was wrestling with."

"Yes. She called it an emotional struggle that Danny felt must be resolved before he committed his life to her."

"It could have been anything, Sayre. He could have had a gambling debt, a bad habit he kept secret, a pregnant girlfriend in another town."

"Or knowledge of something he could no longer live with."

"Obviously you've thought about this and have an idea of what that something was."

"My first guess was that it was an illegal practice at the foundry. Now I'm thinking that Danny knew what became of Gene Iverson."

Beck slowly went to the table and set his empty cup and saucer beside hers. The waiter started toward them, but Beck gave a firm shake of his head and the waiter disappeared into the background.

Beck returned to the railing and placed his hands on it, leaning forward, letting it support his weight. His shirt was stretched tightly across his back, delineating each vertebra and emphasizing the musculature.

"Danny had become religious," she said. "Confession is part of it. Isn't it possible that he knew something about Iverson, and that it was weighing so heavily on his conscience, he had reached the point where he didn't think he could go on with his life until he had unburdened himself of the guilt?"

He turned only his head toward her. "Which is a solid reason for killing yourself."

"It's just as solid a reason for someone to commit murder. Especially if a damaging public confession was in the offing."

Looking forward again, he swore into the darkness. "You've just handed me what Wayne Scott's case against Chris has been missing."

"His motive."

He stared down into the courtyard for the longest time. Finally, he roused himself and turned around. "We should be going."

"It's a long drive back to Destiny."

"Yeah, and it just got longer."

The ubiquitous maître d' thanked them profusely, kissing Sayre on both cheeks again and urging Beck to bring her back very soon. Carefully they made their way down the spiral staircase.

Halfway across the courtyard, Beck stopped. Puzzled, Sayre turned and looked up at him. He didn't smile or explain why he'd stopped. He didn't have to. He began taking backward steps, drawing her into the shadow of the wisteria clinging to the wall. She let herself be drawn.

A sweet lassitude laced her blood as the orange liqueur had laced her coffee. She felt sleepy with satisfaction, yet never more alive. Her eyelids felt heavy, but her nerve endings tingled with awareness and anticipation.

As Beck drew her closer to him, she could see the blood vessels of his throat just beneath the damp skin. She wanted to feel his pulse beating against her lips but resisted the urge to place her mouth there.

He slipped his hand beneath her hair at the nape of her neck and brought her face to within inches of his. His breath was as soft and warm as a morning mist that hovers above the bayou.

"If I touch you, you'll think it's because of Huff's offer."

Going up on tiptoe, she whispered against his lips, "I don't care. Touch me anyway."

He kissed her. She reached for him with her entire body, pressing herself up into him as his arms tightly encircled her. His kiss was possessive and willful. On her hips, his hands were hard and insistent, holding her lower body firmly against his sex. Bending his head down, he nudged aside the strand of Mardi Gras beads with his lips and kissed her breasts through the cloth of her dress.

Then he clasped her to him again and, cupping the back of her head in his wide palm, pressed her face into his neck while he spoke directly into her ear. "There's not enough money in the world to shackle me to a woman I don't want. You must know that, Sayre. The hell of it is . . ." He moved against her intimately, provocatively. "The hell of it is, I do want you."

He could have had her. At that moment, she was tasting him with all five senses. She was drinking him up, wanting him with the same mad, blind, impossible passion that he wanted her.

"But damn the irony," he said, his voice rough. "Huff's green light to take you stops me." He began releasing her by slow degrees until he set her away from him and they were no longer touching. "I want you. But I'm damned if I'll have you doubting the reason why."

chapter 27

Huff's head was wreathed in smoke. Mechanically he puffed on the cigarette anchored in one corner of his lips. Feet planted wide apart on the loading dock, hands on his hips, he scowled at the pickets.

About forty men, carrying inflammatory signs, were marching slowly and silently in an oval pattern along the shoulder of the highway just outside the main entrance gate of Hoyle Enterprises.

"How long have they been at it?"

The group of men huddled around Huff included Chris, several plant foremen, and a few middle management personnel, all of whom had been called from the comfort of their homes, some from their beds, and alerted to this latest critical development.

Fred Decluette had had the misfortune of having to notify everyone when the pickets arrived, so answering Huff's question also fell to him. "They began assembling about ten o'clock and were in place by the time the shift changed."

"Get Red over here and have them arrested for trespassing."

"He can't, Huff," Chris said. "As long as they stay on that side of the fence, they're on public property. But unfortunately, everybody reporting to work, or leaving, passes through that gate. There's no way our employees can avoid seeing them. They practically have to drive right through them."

"Plus, they have a permit to picket." This from George Robson. "They've covered their bases."

"Will somebody please give me some good news?" Huff snarled.

"The good news is that their permit is valid only if the demonstration remains peaceful," Chris said. "I think our job is to see that it doesn't."

There were chuckles from the group. Huff looked over at Fred. "You got some boys ready?" He gave his boss an affirmative nod, but Huff sensed reservation behind it. "What, Fred? Talk to me. Do I have to pull information out of you?"

"We might meet with some resistance from our own men." Fred glanced around uneasily. "There've been rumblings that some of our employees might join them."

Huff threw down his cigarette and ground it out beneath his shoe. "I'll take care of that right now."

The group entered the plant and within five minutes had reassembled inside Huff's office. They lined up along the wall of glass that overlooked the shop floor. Work was continuing as usual, but not very energetically. A pervasive tension could be sensed.

"Is the sound system on?" Huff asked.

Chris flipped several switches on the public address system console. "It is now."

Huff picked up the microphone, blew into it to test it, then said, "Everybody, listen up." His voice boomed into every corner of the factory, reaching every worker on that shift no matter where they were. Some ceased what they were doing and stood still but kept their heads down. Others looked up, but it was difficult to gauge a man's mood when he was wearing safety goggles.

"All of you know about what's going on outside. By now you've probably heard the name of the man who sent those clowns to hassle us, and you're probably asking yourself, 'Who the hell is Charles Nielson?'

"Well, I'll tell you. He's a troublemaker who hasn't got a damn thing to do with Hoyle Enterprises. Those pickets are wasting their time and looking ridiculous in the process, but that's their choice.

"If we stick together and ignore them, they'll eventually give up and crawl back under the rocks they came from. We know their sort, don't we? We've had agitators like this before. They breeze into our town, poke their noses into our business, and try to tell us how to run it. Speaking for myself—and I think I speak for most of you—I hate like hell for somebody to assume they know more about what's better for me than I do.

"And that includes the federal government and the labor unions. Those folks can't even agree among themselves," he shouted. "So why would we want them voting on how we do things here in Destiny? I say we wouldn't."

He paused, took a breath, and continued in a

softer voice. "What happened to Billy Paulik was tragic. Nobody can argue that. He suffered and he's going to continue suffering for a long time. We could give him all the money in the world, and it still wouldn't make up for his loss, would it? We're going to do our best for him and his family, but at the end of the day, Billy's future is really up to Billy, because none of us can roll back the clock and undo what's been done.

"The truth is, the work we do is dangerous. Accidents happen. Men have been hurt and men have died, but I'd like for some bureaucrat from Washington, D.C., to show me how to melt metal and cast iron pipe without risk. It can't be done.

"And you can bet that when that same bureaucrat flushes his crap through his sewage pipes, he's damn glad that pipe is there, and he doesn't give a rat's ass who might've got hurt while making it."

He paused to measure the effectiveness of this speech. No one on the floor had moved. They could've been statues. He could envision those in the Center, sitting at tables, hunkered over bologna sandwiches, packages of Twinkies, and thermoses of coffee, listening.

He had their attention, all right. Their futures were at stake as much as his, and that was what he needed to impress upon them.

"Those nitwits out there will urge you to strike. You know, I wish I didn't have to work for a living. I wish all I had to do was parade around other places of employment and encourage men to walk off their jobs. Never mind about the work ethic or the paychecks that won't be there come payday.

"If I told hardworking men to leave their jobs, I would expect them to call me a damn fool. I've got bills to pay. Groceries to buy. A family that's depending on me to provide for them. Am I right?"

There were a few reluctant nods of agreement from the men below. Others looked around warily to see how coworkers were responding.

"Now, I know we're far from perfect here at Hoyle. We've had our share of mishaps over the years. George Robson and I are investigating the accident and why it happened."

He saw George react with surprise to that lie, but he hoped that no one else had noticed. "We see the need for longer and more thorough training periods before a new employee is put on the floor. It's also time you all had a pay increase.

"But, frankly, whining disgusts me. I remember a time when a man would willingly give up his right arm to have a job. Before I became boss of this outfit, I was one of you. Don't forget that I worked and sweated right down there on that floor, so I know about the heat, and the grit, and the danger."

He pushed up his sleeves to bare his arms and thrust them out in front of him. "I've got scars that remind me every day how hard and hazardous this work is." He replaced his sleeves and mollified his tone. "But I'm also reasonable. I'm willing to listen to your grievances. So make a list of things you'd like to see happen, and we up here in the offices will review them.

"But." He paused to emphasize the qualifier. "If any of you agree with this bunch of rabble-rousers outside, go join them. Hear me? Go! Leave right now. If you think this is a rotten place to work, you know where the door's at.

"Only thing, if you join their ranks, you'll never work for me again, nor will anybody in your family, and you've made an enemy for the rest of your life." He paused to let that sink in, then concluded by saying, "Y'all think about that. Now, we've wasted enough production time on this business. Get back to work."

He switched off the microphone and turned back into the room. Chris said, "Well, that should take care of any fence straddlers. It wouldn't surprise me if we've heard the last from union sympathizers, too. They won't have the balls to speak in favor of it now."

Huff didn't share Chris's confidence. "Fred, what do you think?"

Clearly uneasy with being the center of attention, the laborer shifted from one foot to the other. "Uh, I'm sure you did some good, Huff. But this is Billy's shift. Those men saw him bleed and heard him scream. The accident is still fresh in their minds. I know you're doing a lot for his family. Just today, I heard about Beck going to see him. Alicia said—"

"Beck went to see him?" Chris asked.

Casting a wary glance around, Fred said, "That's what I understood from Alicia. She called a few hours ago, said Beck came to the hospital and gave them a right sizable check."

Huff looked at Chris. With a shrug, Chris disavowed any knowledge of Beck's gesture. "What were you about to say before Chris interrupted?" Huff asked Fred.

"Well, I was saying that the men who work with Billy aren't going to be forgetting what happened to him anytime soon. Their memories of it were fading somewhat, then tonight there's little reminders all around."

"Like what?"

"Like a yellow ribbon tied to the padlock of Billy's locker. Like his name painted on that conveyor. Somebody's keeping memories fresh and stirring up resentment again."

"Who?"

"I don't know yet. Lots of conversations were stopped soon as I got close enough to overhear."

"Find out who's responsible."

"I'm working on it."

Huff pointed a blunt finger at him. "I don't want you working on it. I want you *doing* it. Keep your ear to the ground and your eyes open or I'll find someone who'll get me the names I want."

Fred swallowed hard. "Yes, sir. What do you want me to do about the picket?"

Huff lit a fresh cigarette. He didn't answer until he'd taken a few puffs. "What I'd like you to do is take a scattergun down there. That would clear the area quick enough."

"I'll load it," Chris said laconically.

Huff laughed and shook his head. "No, let's not do anything tonight. They may go away on their own. They'll get tired and thirsty, bit by mosquitoes, their backs will start hurting from carrying those signs. We may not have to lift a finger to see the end of them. So let's give it another day or so. See how it shakes out. See how our employees react. But, Fred, have some men ready to knock heads at a moment's notice."

"Just you give the word, Mr. Hoyle. They're ready and willing."

"Good. But remember if there's a fracas, it's got to look like it was the picketers' fault. They drew first blood and our men were only defending themselves. That'll be our line."

"Understood."

Fred left. To those remaining, Huff said, "I don't think there's going to be any fireworks tonight. To-morrow, we'll carry on business as usual. Don't be provoked by anything those pickets shout at you, or by anything printed on their signs, no matter how ugly it is. Ignore the sons of bitches.

"In the meantime, maybe Beck can make some headway with Nielson and he'll call off these jack-als before any serious damage is done. Okay?" He got nods from everyone. "Y'all go on home now."

George Robson hung back. "Huff?"

"What is it, George?"

"What you said about us investigating the cause of Paulik's accident—"

"Only giving them what they wanted to hear, George. Don't worry about it."

"What I was thinking," he said, his eyes nervously darting between Huff and Chris, "is that maybe we should shut down that conveyor until it has been overhauled. Then nobody could come along later and finger blame."

Huff turned to Chris. "I thought you'd already discussed this."

"We did."

SANDRA BROWN

George said, "That's right, we did. But on second thought—"

"Stop thinking so much, George," Huff said. "Chris is over operations, and he made his decision about that conveyor."

"Based on your recommendation, George, remember?"

George nodded, looking uncertain and unhappy. "Yes. Okay."

"Go on home and try to salvage what's left of the night," Huff said.

"All right. See you tomorrow." George turned to go.

"Give our regards to that pretty wife of yours."

George stopped and turned, gave Chris a measured look, then scuttled out.

Huff looked across at Chris. "Saying things like that, you're playing with fire."

Chris laughed. "I doubt George will challenge me to a duel. If he was worried about marital infidelity, he shouldn't have married a slut."

Beck came in. "I met George in the hall. He said I missed a hell of a speech."

As soon as they were notified of the picket line, Chris had called Beck's cell phone and caught him halfway back to Destiny from New Orleans. Beck had told them he would get there as soon as he could. Huff glanced at his wall clock, noting that he'd made record time.

Now Beck placed his briefcase on the floor and, looking out of breath, plopped down onto the short sofa. "I leave town for a few hours, and all hell breaks loose."

Huff motioned Chris toward the credenza where he kept a bar. "Whiskeys all around, Son."

"I had to drive through our visitors as I came in," Beck told them.

"That's the point, I think," Huff said from behind his desk, where he'd lowered himself into the high-backed leather chair. "They didn't pick that spot at random."

"Have you confirmed that they were sent by Nielson?"

"They make no bones about it," Chris said, passing Beck one of the three highballs. "I went out to talk to the guy who appears to be the leader. He's a meathead, probably on steroids, but smart enough not to say anything except that he has a permit, which he showed me, and that I should refer all my questions to Mr. Nielson."

"Well, Mr. Nielson is making himself scarce." Beck then told them about his unproductive visit. "His office isn't very impressive. Modestly furnished. Only one secretary. She's overly polite and earnest. Looked like she would bake you an apple pie or sew a loose button on your shirt if you asked her. But certainly no pushover. Not exactly a fount of information, either. She wasn't very forthcoming on when I'll get to see her boss face-to-face. She's been well trained."

Huff snorted. "The coward knew you were coming, so he ducked out. He might be in Cincinnati, or he could've been waiting in the bar across the street until the coast was clear."

"A distinct possibility," Beck conceded. "I've called his hotel several times. At first I was told he hadn't checked in. Now, he's requested a hold on all his calls. Either way I feel like I'm being played for a chump."

"He didn't want to confront you on the same day his hired pickets showed up at our plant," Chris said.

"You're probably right," Beck said. "There's more. I haven't got to the good part yet. Guess who was in Nielson's office, dressed fit to kill, and, despite the high heels, looking ready to take on all enemies, starting with me?"

"You've got to be kidding," Chris exclaimed. "Sayre?"

"Good guess."

"What was she doing there?" Huff asked.

"Same thing I was, wanting to see Nielson. Of course her agenda differed from mine. She was there to enlist and offer him her help."

Chris asked, "By doing what?"

"We never got down to the specifics."

"Was she with you when you went to see Billy Paulik?"

Beck reacted with surprise, looking first at Huff, then back at Chris. "How did you know about that?"

"Alicia Paulik called Fred Decluette."

"*I* wasn't going to see him, *Sayre* was," he explained. "I went along and used the cards and letters Billy has received from his coworkers as my calling card. I thought hand-delivering them might win points with Mrs. Paulik. Besides, I wanted to see what Sayre was up to."

"What was she up to?" Huff asked.

"Nothing that I could tell. It appeared to be no more than a courtesy call."

"When Mrs. Paulik talked to Fred, she mentioned a 'right sizable' check. How much did that set me back?"

"Nothing, Huff. I made the contribution without your authorization. You don't have to reimburse me if you don't want to."

"Hell, I'm the one who suggested we sweeten the pot. And just as I thought, the woman is weakening. She kept the check, right?"

"As far as I know."

"There you go," he said, raising his glass to toast their success.

Beck said, "Before you drink to it, you should know that I also told the psychiatrist to continue the sessions with Billy indefinitely."

Chris groaned. "Are you trying to bankrupt us?"

"I'll admit that it was a bold, spur-of-the-moment decision. I didn't have time to consult with either of you. But I think it scored points with Mrs. Paulik."

Huff winked at him. "You wouldn't be worth spit to me if you couldn't make some decisions on you own. I trust your judgment or you wouldn't be in the position you're in."

"But we're throwing good money after bad," Chris complained. "So we see to it that Billy Paulik gets as good as he can get. What good will it do us?"

"I don't imagine Beck was thinking in terms of Billy's productivity as the payoff of that investment."

"That's right, Huff. I saw it as a gesture of goodwill that could stave off a lawsuit which could cost us millions. Anything we can do to prevent litigation is a sound investment."

"I agree." Huff tossed back his drink, liking the sting of the bourbon at the back of his throat and the heat it spread through his belly. "What was Sayre's frame of mind when you left her?"

Beck shrugged, but Huff didn't think he was nearly as indifferent as he wanted them to believe. "We had dinner together. I bought her a trinket. We drank champagne."

Happily, Huff slapped his palms together. "How did it go?"

Beck raised a wry eyebrow. "It would have gone better if Chris hadn't told her about your attempted matchmaking."

Huff turned to Chris. "You told her?"

"What difference does it make?"

"You have to ask?"

"Sayre may have drunk his champagne, but Beck's not in her bed, is he? And she's not about to invite him into it as long as he works for us."

"She might have. Now . . . Shit. You know your sister. She'll balk."

"She would have balked anyway, Huff," Beck said. "She's too smart and headstrong to be seduced by a bottle of champagne. However, I hoped that the wine and a meal of fancy French food would loosen her tongue."

"About what?"

"Nielson. I'm uneasy with the idea of the two of them together. He would exploit having a Hoyle in his corner. If nothing else, he could use that as a media hook." He framed an imaginary headline with his hands. "Huff Hoyle's daughter sides with opposition. Complete story and photos on page three."

Huff belched. The whiskey didn't taste so good recycled. "I see what you mean."

"Beyond that," Beck continued with obvious reluctance, "she thought McGraw was the noose that was going to hang both of you, only to discover that the rope was frayed.

"But that didn't dampen her resolve. She's convinced that Chris did in Gene Iverson, that by finagling the jury he got away with murder, and that it's up to her to see that justice is done. Despite the setback with McGraw, she has no intention of letting the matter drop."

He first looked at Chris, then turned to Huff. "I wasn't your lawyer then, Huff. But I represent you now. I don't want to be blindsided by something that Sayre may uncover. Is there anything regarding the Iverson case that I should be made aware of?"

Huff knew how to keep a poker face. He'd been doing it since he was eight years old. He looked Beck straight in the eye and said, "If the state had been able to make a case against Chris, there would have been another trial. Sayre won't uncover anything."

"Did you hear anything from Red while I was in New Orleans?"

"Nothing except that Slap Watkins remains at large," Chris told him. "So far there's been no trace of him."

"Have they checked out all the places where he's stayed recently?"

"With warrants. His last-known residence had a drug lab in the bathroom. The couple who lived there were arrested, but they claimed not to know Slap's whereabouts since they kicked him out. Red said they took the place apart but found nothing belonging to Slap."

"I hope they find him sooner rather than later," Beck said. "And when he's brought in, I hope he confesses to killing Danny. Because of everything that's going on here," he said, nodding toward the wall of glass, "we're going to be viewed through a microscope. By OSHA in particular."

"Bastards," Huff muttered around a fresh cigarette.

"We had some play with them," Beck said, "but it was lost with Billy's accident."

"Can't we head them off?" Chris asked.

"I hoped to. I've tried several times to contact the regional rep. He won't return my calls. Which leads me to believe that he's planning a surprise inspection."

Huff said, "I thought you had bribed someone on his staff to warn us of any unannounced visits."

"I learned yesterday that she's out on pregnancy leave."

"Fucking wonderful," Chris said.

"Yeah, bad timing for us. My point is," Beck continued, "we've got to present a squeaky-clean image. We can't give them one iota of ammunition more than Billy's accident already has. They could shut us down pending a thorough inspection. And they would."

Chris expelled a long breath. "Well, on that happy note, I think I'll go get drunk."

"Chris—"

"I'm joking," he said. "Christ, I'll be glad when everyone around me lightens up. Can't we look on the bright side for once? Paulik's wife is backing down. The pickets? When the sun comes up tomorrow and it gets hotter than hell out there, they'll break ranks and go home.

"OSHA? We'll beg forgiveness, promise to do better, pay their frigging fine, then go on about our business. As for Mary Beth, with any luck she'll piss off her pool boy and he'll drown her in the shallow end.

"It shouldn't be too difficult for me to find wife number two. I'll sow enough seeds to people China—and believe me, I've got the swimmers to do it—and deliver the first Hoyle grandson to Grandpa Huff. Last but not least, I'm innocent of murdering my brother. See? What's so terrible?"

Huff laughed. "All right, you've made your point. Get out of here. I'm right behind you."

Still smiling, Huff watched Chris saunter out. But when he glanced at Beck, his lightheartedness disappeared. Beck was staring at the open doorway through which Chris had just passed.

It troubled Huff that Beck looked so troubled.

It had taken Sayre a long time to fall asleep.

After the eventful trip to New Orleans and the long drive home, she had thought she would fall into an exhausted sleep the moment her head hit the pillow. But to her aggravation, she tossed and turned for hours.

The air-conditioning unit was noisy. When it was running, the room became frigid. When it cycled off, the room grew stifling, and the odors left by every previous occupant, embedded in the carpet, drapes, and bedcoverings, were resurrected.

But the lack of creature comfort was only partially responsible for her insomnia. Her conversations with Beck continued to replay inside her head. Had it been a mistake to entrust him with the secret of Danny's engagement? And knowing that her father was contriving a match between them for his own selfish purposes, why had she let Beck get anywhere close to her? Why had she wanted him close?

It wasn't until the wee hours that she managed to drift off. That was why she groaned unhappily when she awakened before daylight. She was lying on her stomach, face half buried in the lumpy pillow. She opened one eye and lay very still, willing herself to go back to sleep before she became too awake.

The air conditioner, she noticed, was silent, so the room was warm. She kicked the covers off her legs, thinking it was the mugginess that had awakened her and that if she got comfortable with the temperature again, sleep would reclaim her.

But removing the covers didn't help.

Maybe a champagne headache was coming on. She was dehydrated from drinking the champagne and the red wine she'd had with her meal. She needed a large glass of water. And now that she thought about it, her bladder needed attention, too.

Cursing under her breath, she rolled onto her back and pulled herself into a sitting position on the side of the bed. Automatically she reached for the lamp on the nightstand but then decided against turning it on. If she kept the room dark, it was more likely she would go back to sleep sooner.

Coming off the bed in a half crouch, she groped her way around the end of it, moving in the direction of the bathroom. By now she was familiar with the layout of the room, so she might have made it to the bathroom without mishap . . . if she hadn't stumbled over the pair of heavy boots that blocked her path.

That they had feet in them with legs attached brought her wide awake.

chapter 28

*H*er scream was trapped behind a grimy hand while another gripped a handful of her hair and pushed her facedown onto the bed. He fell on top of her, effectively pinning her down. But she didn't stop struggling.

"You fight me, I'll rip it out by the roots. Swear to God, pretty as it is, I'll tear it out and take it as a souvenir." He gave the handful of hair a sharp tug that brought tears to her eyes.

She stopped trying to twist away and lay still.

"That's better." He squirmed against her buttocks. "Now ain't this cozy? How'd you like a taste of some of the things I learned in prison?"

Behind his hand, she cried out in fear and outrage. He laughed at the muffled sounds. "Relax, Red. Your ass is awful tempting, but I ain't got time for romance. I came here to talk, but you can bet your life I'll hurt you if I have to. Do we have an understanding?"

Between the hand clasped over her mouth and the rumpled bedcovers beneath her face, she couldn't find sufficient air. She didn't believe that he had sneaked into her room merely to talk, but she nodded to keep herself from smothering.

"Okay, then. I'm gonna take my hand off your mouth. If you scream, it'll be the last sound you ever make."

Gradually he withdrew his hand. Sayre resisted the impulse to lick her lips, because tasting any residue of him would be repugnant. He gave her butt a hard squeeze as he climbed off her. When she was free, she turned onto her back, then sat up. She wiped her mouth with the back of her hand.

The light came on suddenly. She blinked away the sudden glare and saw Slap Watkins, his hand still on the switch of the bedside lamp. It projected harsh light up through the top opening of the lampshade, which shone eerily on his face. The shadow of his head on the wall was the sort that children's nightmares were made of.

His looks hadn't improved while he'd been on the lam. If anything he'd grown uglier. His teeth looked longer, yellower. His goatee was more scraggly. His face had become so lean that each bone of it was grotesquely pronounced, almost skeletal. His skinny neck was vulturine, and his large ears looked like attachments that had been stuck on the sides of his head for comic effect.

"Hi, Red."

Her heart was pounding and her mouth had gone dry, but she tried not to show any fear. She glanced at the door. "Don't even think about it," he said around a nasty-sounding laugh. "You couldn't make it out before I got to you, and that'd force me to break my promise not to hurt you." Grinning, he slid a knife from his boot and tapped the flat side of the blade against his palm.

"How did you get in?"

"I'm a criminal, remember? Picked the lock in no time flat. Silent, too. Shame on you for not using your chain lock. A lady all by herself, you ought to know better."

She didn't want to think about how long he'd been in the room with her before she woke up. It made her flesh crawl to think of him sitting in the chair near her bed, watching her sleep, listening to her breathe. Maybe it was his smell that had awakened her. It had been days at least since he'd washed, and his body odor was nauseating.

"Are these real?" She had left her diamond stud earrings on the nightstand. He was holding them up to the light, turning them this way and that, appraising their value.

"Yes. You're welcome to them if you'll leave."

"Thanks. Believe I will." He put the earrings in the pocket of his filthy blue jeans. "But I can't leave till we've had ourselves a little chat."

"What do you and I have to chat about?"

"Do you know I got the law looking for me?"

"You assaulted my brother with a knife."

"That's bullshit. I's only gonna scare him with it. He caused me to cut him. Did it deliberate."

Although she had advanced that theory to Beck, she posed the question to Slap now. "Why would Chris do that?"

"'Cause he wanted to make me out a killer."

"Chris believes you murdered our brother. Did you?"

In lieu of answering he opened the nightstand drawer, removed the Gideon Bible, and tossed it to her. "Genesis, chapter four."

Leaving the Bible where it landed beside her, she asked coolly, "You're a Bible scholar?"

"Up at Angola, I went to worship services every Sunday. Passed out the songbooks and everything. Looked good on my record."

"I suppose it balanced the sodomy."

His eyes turned flinty. "You calling me a fag? I'll teach you different."

Her sarcasm had been a dreadful mistake. She'd given him something to prove.

When he came at her, she tried to scramble to the far side of the bed, but again he grabbed a handful of her hair and yanked her back. He placed the tip of his knife against her cheek and laughed when she fell perfectly still.

"I thought that'd get your attention. Don't want to mess up that pretty face, do you?" Roughly he pushed her knees apart and moved to stand between her thighs, thrusting his hips toward her face. "You got a real sassy mouth, but I can think of one real good way to shut it up."

"You'd have to kill me."

"That might be fun, too."

Just then the air-conditioning unit came on with its customary clatter and knock. He reacted with a start to the sudden noise and whipped his head toward it. When he realized what it was, he was visibly relieved, but it had spooked him nonetheless. He released her hair and nervously backed away from her.

"Much as I'd love to take full advantage of this situation, I've spent too much time here already." He picked up the Bible and shook it at her. "You tell Sheriff Harper to read his Bible. The part about Cain and Abel. And you'd better be convincing when you talk to him, 'cause if I'm a wanted man for killing a Hoyle, then I'd just as soon kill me one."

He dragged the tip of the knife across her nipple. "And I've always had a real sweet tooth for red-heads."

She was waiting with Sheriff Harper and Deputy Scott in Red's office when Beck arrived. Like her, he looked a little worse for wear.

She had seen the picket line when she drove past the foundry, although it was no surprise to her because she had spoken to Clark Daly the night before. He had called shortly after her return from New Orleans. He was on his coffee break in the Center, he explained, using a buddy's cell phone. There had been excitement in his voice for the progress that had already been made.

"I've isolated some of Huff's stoolies and warned men to be careful of what they say around them because it goes straight to Huff." He and some men he trusted were also doing what they could to keep Billy Paulik in the forefront of everyone's mind.

"Nielson's got the picket going. Huff made a speech against it, but it didn't put the scare into us he intended. Things are looking up, Sayre. I'll give you progress reports when I can."

He'd sounded upbeat. His voice had had a ring of confidence that validated her getting him involved in

something important. She'd received no more up-
dates, but evidently the discontent among workers
had escalated through the night, despite Huff's efforts to squelch it. Some of the picketers this morning were Hoyle employees.

That explained Beck's haggard appearance as he
entered Red's office and said grimly, "Morning."

They chorused a good morning, although none
sounded like he meant it. Beck sat in the unoccu-
pied chair next to hers, facing Red's desk. Wayne
Scott remained standing.

"How are things over at the plant?" the sheriff
asked.

"Hot."

"We're supposed to have a heat index around
one hundred today," Scott remarked, and Sayre
wondered if he actually thought that Beck had been
referring to the outside temperature.

Beck ignored him and addressed his answer to
Red. "Another couple dozen pickets showed up in
time to greet the day shift when they reported at
seven. Some of our men took the pamphlets they
were handing out, and even joined in the march,
which made Hoyle loyalists angry.

"Tempers are high. I don't know how long we
can contain them. I'm trying like hell to reach Nielson, see if we can cap this thing, but he won't return my calls." Suddenly turning to Sayre, he asked,
"Have you heard from him?"

This was the first time they'd made eye contact
since his arrival, and it was like a physical jolt.
"No."

He held her gaze, as though searching for an indication that she was lying, then he turned back to Red. "I can't be away long. Why did you want to see me?"

Red motioned toward her. "Sayre had a visitor this morning. She thought you should hear what he had to say."

"Visitor?"

"Slap Watkins broke into my motel room early this morning."

Beck stared at her with shock, then he looked toward Red as though for confirmation.

"This office got the call a little after five this morning. A man was dispatched immediately. Of course by the time he got to The Lodge, Watkins was long gone."

Beck turned back to her. He looked her over, from the top of her head to her feet, then back up to her eyes. "Are you hurt? Did he . . ."

She lowered her head, shaking it as she responded to Beck's unfinished question and all that it implied. "He threatened to hurt me, but he didn't. The only damage he did is this." She touched the spot on her cheek where his knife had nicked her when the air conditioner cycled on. "He flinched at a sudden sound. I don't think he meant to do it."

"Wayne and I have read the statement Sayre gave the deputy who went to the motel, but we haven't heard about it firsthand. She thought you should be here."

Beck nodded absently. "What did Watkins do, say? Did he force his way in?"

"He picked the door lock. I hadn't put the chain

on, which was foolish. I woke up to find him in the room with me."

"Jesus."

"I don't suppose he told you where he'd been hiding," Scott said.

"No. He didn't volunteer that information."

"Did you happen to see which way he was headed when he left the motel?"

"No, but he must have left on foot. I didn't hear a motor."

"How did he know where you were staying?"

"It wouldn't have been that hard to locate me. There are only two motels in town. Process of elimination."

She noticed Beck's growing impatience with Scott's inane questions. Turning to the deputy, he said, "Why don't you let up on the stupid questions and give her a chance to tell you what happened?"

Before the deputy could address Beck's putdown, Red said, "Good idea. Sayre, start at the beginning. We won't interrupt until you're finished. What did he want?"

"He wanted me to deliver a message to you." She recounted the incident, leaving out only Slap's sexual innuendos, which had no bearing on the message he had wanted her to impart to the sheriff. As Red had stipulated, no one interrupted her. "That's it. Almost word for word."

After a short silence, Scott asked, "Did you make any attempt to escape?"

"I was afraid that if I ran toward the door I'd get a knife in my back. I couldn't have opened it and got out before he reached me. He's skinny, but in any kind of physical struggle, I would have lost."

"You never screamed?"

"I couldn't while his hand was over my mouth. Once he released me, I didn't scream because I didn't want to provoke him into using the knife. Besides, what good would screaming have done?"

No one had an answer.

Red was rubbing his sunken eye sockets. His skin had a gray cast, and he seemed to have lost weight since she'd last seen him, which had been only several days ago. She wondered whether he was ill, or just beleaguered.

Beck was loosening his tie and working his collar button out of its hole. He looked like a man losing ground against the demons he was battling.

Only Deputy Scott appeared to have been galvanized by this development. He hitched up his gun holster and said, "Well, let's go get him."

"I hope you're referring to Slap Watkins," Beck said. "Surely you don't mean to arrest Chris."

"The hell I don't," Scott retorted.

"Not so fast, Wayne," the sheriff said. Then to Beck, "Maybe we ought to talk to Chris again."

"Based on hearsay?"

Sayre looked at him with dismay. "Are you accusing me of lying?"

"No. Watkins is just stupid enough to pull a stunt like this. But until he's in custody, we've got only your word for what he said."

It took an act of will for her not to strike him. "Go to hell."

"Sayre," Red said sternly.

She turned toward the sheriff. "I quoted my conversation with Watkins verbatim. That's what he said. Genesis chapter four."

"I believe you," he said. "And probably Beck does, too. But he represents Chris, don't forget."

She turned and looked Beck in the eye. "I never do."

"And remember that Watkins is fresh out of the pen," Red continued. "He'd say anything to try and keep his sorry self from having to go back. He was throwing up a smoke screen with this Bible story reference, getting us all excited, wanting us to think that Chris killed his brother, take the pressure off himself, maybe long enough to make his way down to Mexico."

"I think that's precisely what he hoped to achieve," Beck said. "He's running scared. He's desperate and feeling the heat. He wanted to transfer it to somebody else, and we all know how he feels about the Hoyles."

"Don't you think I considered his self-interest?" she said angrily. "Of course I did. I'm not stupid."

"No one's accused you of being stupid, Sayre," Beck said.

"No, just a liar."

"Calm down. I'm not refuting your word. I'm only trying to make sense of it. Let's suppose that Watkins was speaking the unvarnished truth. Let's suppose he has firsthand knowledge that Chris killed Danny. Why wouldn't he contact the authorities with this information? Why risk getting captured by breaking into your motel room and threatening you with a knife? Why would he go to all that bother and risk to tell you?"

"Because he knew that I wouldn't sweep it under the rug."

"No one in this office will either, Ms. Lynch," Scott said staunchly. "We have to act on this, Sheriff Harper. We've already placed Chris at the scene."

Beck scoffed. "With a matchbook?"

"And we've established that he had opportunity during the two hours that he can't account for his time."

"Unless he produces an alibi."

"He doesn't have one," Scott said.

"He hasn't *produced* one," Beck said, correcting him. "That doesn't mean one doesn't exist."

While Scott was mulling that over, Red asked, "Where's the motive, Wayne? You've failed to establish a reason for Chris to kill Danny."

It was on the tip of Sayre's tongue to blurt out Chris's motive. She wanted to, if for no other reason than to pull the slats out from under Beck Merchant.

But she couldn't say anything without betraying Jessica DeBlance's confidence. If it ever reached a point where justice hinged on that, she would have to reveal what she knew about the engagement. But if she could avoid it, she would.

"I still think we've got enough for another round of questioning at the very least," Scott argued.

Red sighed. "Bad as I hate to say it, Beck, Wayne's right. Any other suspect, we'd bring in and see what he had to say about this allegation.

We can't exempt Chris just because of who he is."

Beck thought it over for a moment, then said, "We've got a powder keg at the foundry. God only knows what kind of chain reaction it would set off if you picked up Chris in a patrol car. I don't see what purpose it would serve, and in fact, it could cause a panic."

"Then I'm making you responsible for getting him in here voluntarily," Red said.

"Once he hears about this, he'll welcome the chance to respond."

"It's still mandatory that he come in today," the sheriff said.

"I'll have him here after lunch."

"Okay then."

Wayne Scott didn't look too happy with the arrangement, but he didn't have any choice but to accept it. "Are you afraid, ma'am?"

Sayre looked up at him. "Afraid?"

"Watkins threatened to kill you."

"He had an opportunity to kill me. He didn't."

"Just to be on the safe side, I'll post a squad car outside your motel room."

"No, Red. Please don't."

"If Huff finds out about this, you can bet—"

"And I'm sure you'll tell him," she said. "But I don't want watchdogs outside my door. I won't have them, so don't bother sending them."

"Well . . . be careful," he said lamely.

"I will." She stood up. "Is that all?"

"For the time being."

She nodded a good-bye to Red and Deputy Scott but ignored Beck completely. She exited the building and had almost reached the red convertible when she heard him call her name. She kept walking. He caught up with her as she was unlocking the car door.

When he laid his hand on her shoulder, she rounded on him. Before she had a chance to speak, he said, "I know you're mad."

"*Mad* doesn't come close."

"And I know why. But listen to me, Sayre. Take Red up on his offer of protection."

She gave a bitter laugh. "You believe my story? You didn't think my encounter with Watkins was a fabrication?"

"Of course I believed you."

"You just enjoy making me look like an idiot and discrediting me in front of other people. In fact, it seems to have become your favorite pastime."

"I'm Chris's counsel."

"So you've made clear."

She opened the car door and got in, but he prevented her from closing the door. Leaning in close, he spoke quickly and angrily. "Chris has placed his trust in me to act on his behalf. I couldn't betray that trust any more than you could betray the trust of Danny's fiancée.

"You had a perfect opportunity to venture a motive for murder, Sayre. You didn't. You couldn't. Because you had given that woman your word not to say anything. Now, why should the rules of confidentiality apply only to you?"

Technically, he was right. It would have been a breach of professional ethics if he had failed to argue on his client's behalf. But his being right didn't prevent her from being mad as hell.

"Let go of the door."

"Where are you going?"

"Anywhere I damn well please." She tugged hard on the door, but to no avail.

"Listen to me, Sayre. Forget that you're angry at me and focus on Watkins. You must pay attention to his threats. He's not that bright, but that only makes him more dangerous. Maybe he didn't intend to hurt you this morning, but now that you've delivered his message to Red, you've served your purpose. Maybe he'll come back and make an example of you. Watkins hates the Hoyles. You're a Hoyle, Sayre, like it or not, and . . ." His eyes moved over her. "You're conspicuous."

"Good. Then I'll be easy to spot on the picket line."

For the second time that day, Beck wheeled his pickup into a parking slot in front of the sheriff's office, pulling in next to Chris's Porsche. They had agreed to meet there after Chris went home to have lunch with Huff.

He left the windows of his truck down when he got out, although that wouldn't help much to prevent the cab from becoming suffocating during the time he was inside. There was no relief from the stifling heat. Even the air-conditioned sheriff's office felt dank and close.

"Hoyle's in the last room on the right," he was informed by the deputy manning the desk, Pat something.

"Thanks."

Beck knocked once, then opened the door to the

room, which was barely large enough to accommodate a table and two formed fiberglass chairs. Chris was seated in one of them. "Hi."

"Hi. Have you seen Red?" Beck asked.

"No. Only that Neanderthal at the desk. He showed me in here. Told me Red and Scott were still at lunch and to make myself at home."

Beck instantly sensed a change in his friend's demeanor. Notably absent was Chris's sarcastic derision, which was part of his character. Beck sat down across from him. "Want to tell me what's the matter?"

Chris smiled but not with humor. "If I tell you, I'll have to kill you."

Beck's heart did a flip-flop.

Chris's wry grin widened. "No, I'm not about to confess. At least not to murdering my brother."

"Then what?"

Leaning forward, he placed his elbows on the table and massaged his forehead with the fingers of both hands. "I'm scared. There. That's my big confession, Beck. This room feels an awful lot like a jail cell, and it scares me shitless."

The tightness in Beck's chest relaxed. "That's to be expected. That's what interrogation rooms are designed to do, Chris. To rattle you. Make you begin to doubt your own innocence.

"When I worked in the DA's office, I spent a lot of time in rooms like this with real badasses. Gangbangers, rapists, killers, thieves. But no matter what their rap sheet looked like, you got them in an interrogation room, and left them long enough, and they started wanting their mamas."

Chris reacted with a smile, but it was short-lived. "I'm beginning to fear they might just pin this thing on me."

"All they've got is conjecture and circumstantial evidence. Nothing hard. I doubt a DA would even present what they've got to a grand jury. Especially not in this parish."

"Yeah, but all this circumstantial evidence is stacking up. What's the legal term I'm searching for?"

"Preponderance?"

"Right. A preponderance of evidence is sometimes enough. Slap Watkins and his Bible story," he said scornfully. "It's probably the only one he knows. Hell, even nonbelievers like me have heard of Cain and Abel. Danny was a murder victim. He was my brother. Suddenly that adds up to my being the one who killed him."

He got up and made a slow circle around the small table. "Why would my own sister buy into the lunacy of a crazed career criminal, and then share it with this hotshot deputy who's looking for anything to use against me?"

Beck didn't tell him about the secret engagement that only he and Sayre were aware of, or about Danny's telephone calls to her. Either might have been extremely relevant. But in the likelihood that they were totally irrelevant points, he would keep them to himself.

"Sayre wasn't exactly jumping up and down with glee the last time I saw her, Chris." Thoughtfully, he added, "God knows what that sleazy bastard said and did to her that she didn't tell us."

"I know she must've been frightened, but why didn't she report the theft of her earrings and leave it at that? Why give any credence at all to Watkins's red herring?"

Beck frowned. "I can't explain anything Sayre does."

Chris stopped and looked down at him. "So it's true then?"

"You heard?"

"Somebody called the house while we were having lunch and told Huff. He went ballistic. She's really on the picket line?"

"Leading the parade."

Chris returned to his chair and looked at Beck expectantly.

"She showed up about eleven-thirty with burgers from Dairy Queen and ice chests of cold drinks," he told Chris. "As soon as she saw to it that everyone was fed, she picked up a sign and started marching with them. She was still there just now when I came through the gate."

Chris hung his head, shaking it in disbelief. "I never thought I'd live to see the day when a member of Huff's family would stand against the others. Of course some believe that I shot my brother in the mouth with a shotgun." Back to massaging his forehead, he said, "Who would think I could do that?"

"That's just it, Chris. They've yet to establish a motive. Unless you're holding something back."

His head came up. "Like what?"

"Have you told me everything about your argument with Danny?"

"About a hundred times."

"Was Danny keeping any secrets from us?"

"Secrets?"

"I just thought maybe there was something he had shared with you that the rest of us didn't know about."

"No. Nothing."

Beck peered into Chris's eyes, searching for even a flicker of a giveaway, but Chris's gaze was steady and guileless. "Just a thought. Never mind. What about Lila?"

"I went to her house yesterday when I knew George was out. She wouldn't even open the door."

"A hostile alibi. Terrific." Beck got up and moved to the window. There were iron bars across it, he noticed. He looked out at a sky that was so hot all the blue had been leached from it. The only thing whiter than the sky was the drifting smoke from the foundry. "I won't bullshit you, Chris. We've got to come up with some kind of solid defense."

"I did not kill my brother."

Beck turned around. "Something in addition to your denial."

Chris looked at him for a long moment, then said quietly, "Beck, this is one of the toughest things I've ever had to do. I'm firing you."

He laughed shortly. "Firing me?"

"This is no reflection on your ability or legal acumen. They're not at issue. You've wrangled Hoyle Enterprises out of scrapes that could have cost us plenty, and not just financially. Huff and I need you on the job there, running interference for

us with the federal agencies and now, thanks to
Nielson, our own employees." He smiled
crookedly. "And I need a criminal lawyer."

Beck returned to the table and sat down. "Actually, I'm relieved."

"You're not angry?"

"Chris, criminal law isn't my field. I was the first
to suggest that you retain a criminal lawyer. I
wanted to insist on it, but I was afraid you'd think I
was bailing out on you. I wasn't sure how Huff
would react, either."

"He won't like it. He wrote the book on keeping
things in the family, but I'm hoping you'll help me
persuade him that it's the right decision."

"I'll talk to him. Who'd you get?"

Chris told him, but Beck wasn't familiar with the
name. "He's from Baton Rouge and comes highly
recommended."

"Good luck with him."

"You swear you're not angry?"

"I swear. So where is this legal whiz? You need
him here now."

"That's the thing. He's not free until Monday.
What should we do about this interrogation?"

"I'll see if Red will postpone it until your new
lawyer arrives."

"Do you think they'll put me in jail over the
weekend?"

"If it's even suggested, I'll raise a hue and cry.
This is flimsy bullshit anyway. I think Red only
wanted to question you to pacify his deputy. He
doesn't believe in Bible stories any more than you
do."

They shook hands, but when Beck tried to withdraw his, Chris gripped it tighter. "I don't want to take the fall for something I didn't do, Beck. And I did not kill Danny."

Beck returned the pressure to Chris's hand. "I believe you."

chapter 29

When Sayre got back to her motel room that night, she opened the door with the key belonging to the new lock, which had been swapped for the one Slap Watkins had picked.

She stood at the threshold and surveyed the room. All traces of his stench had been eliminated. Not trusting the motel housekeeper to clean as thoroughly as she wanted, she had donned rubber gloves and given the room a sanitizing cleaning herself before she left for the foundry. She had insisted that the motel manager bring in another chair to replace the one in which Watkins had sat. The bedspread had also been changed.

Satisfied that all remnants of him were gone, she locked herself in, making certain also to secure the chain. Wearily she moved to the dresser and looked at herself in the mirror. Her skin was scorched from sun exposure, while at the same time so sweaty that her clothes stuck to it. She eased off her sneakers and inspected a crop of painful, angry-looking blisters that detracted from her Beige Marilyn pedicure.

She was almost too tired to eat the grilled cheese sandwich she'd picked up at the diner, but she was also ravenously hungry. After the first bite, she devoured the rest of it.

She stayed a long time in the shower, her second of the day. She had scoured herself that morning, trying to rid herself even of the memory of Watkins's touch.

Now she let the spray pound the achiness from her muscles. When she stepped from the tub, she felt almost human again. Too tired to bother with a blow-dryer, she rubbed her hair with a towel and let it go at that. Her only nod toward a beauty regimen was to apply moisturizer to her sunburned nose. The spot on her cheek had scabbed over. In a day or two it would be unnoticeable.

She put on a pair of panties and the short cotton nightie she had bought to replace the one she'd slept in last night. It had gone out with the trash that morning. She would never have worn it again no matter how many times it was washed.

She told herself to forget the incident. Nothing terrible had happened. She was vesting that imbecile with way too much influence over her.

Even so, as she pulled back the bedcovers, she decided to leave the bathroom light on, on the outside chance that she would wake up in total darkness again and have to relive those horrifying moments when she had discovered him in the room.

Her thoughts were interrupted by knocking on her door. "Sayre? Open up."

It was Beck. He had tapped lightly so as not to frighten her, but his voice was stern.

"What do you want, Beck?"

"I want you to open the door."

She unlocked it and opened it only as far as the brass chain would allow, looking at him through the crack. "I'm not dressed."

"Let me in."

"Why?"

His fractious mood was apparent in his expression. He didn't even deign to answer, just stared at her. She relented, mostly because she didn't want their conversation to have spectators. The bowling leagues must have been at the lanes, because The Lodge's parking lot was full and she had neighbors in the next room.

She unlatched the chain, and he came in, closing the door soundly behind him. His eyes dropped immediately to the hem of the short nightgown and her bare legs and feet. She crossed her arms over her middle, and the self-protective gesture caused him to look away.

"In light of what happened this morning . . . Put some clothes on if it'll make you feel more comfortable."

"You won't be here that long. What do you want?"

"Clark Daly is in the hospital."

"What?"

"He's in the emergency room."

Her hand went to her throat. "Another accident at the plant?"

"Hardly. He was beaten."

"Beaten?"

"To a pulp. His condition is serious. Whether or

not it's critical remains to be seen. He's got visible injuries. Loose teeth, a split lip, black eyes, torn eyelid, a gash on his scalp. Beyond that, he may have a skull fracture. Broken ribs, they're nearly certain. Possible internal bleeding. He's being X-rayed and such to determine all that."

Covering her mouth, she released a slow breath and sat down on the edge of the bed. "Wh . . . who?"

"Names haven't been named, but yours has been circulated as the person responsible." His eyes speared into hers.

She swallowed the gorge that filled her throat. "What happened?"

"I was staying at the plant tonight. In case any real trouble broke out, I wanted to be there."

Soon after the graveyard shift had reported for work, he'd sensed that something was amiss. "You work there long enough, you begin to pick up vibes," he said. "You feel it when something isn't right. I went down to the floor and started asking what was wrong. No one wanted to talk to me. Particularly in the climate we've got there now."

"You're Huff's main man."

His jaw clenched with anger, but he didn't address the remark. "Finally I wormed it out of a guy that Clark hadn't reported for work. One of his friends called his wife, who freaked out. She said he'd left in plenty of time to get there. This alarmed his buddies, who wanted to leave right then to look for him. I ordered them to stay on the job, but I picked a couple of them and we went looking for him. We spotted his car on the side of the road no more than two blocks from his house. Clark was lying facedown in the ditch, unconscious. He's in a bad way."

Sayre stood up and stumbled toward the bureau. "I'm going." She took a pair of jeans from a drawer, only to have Beck snatch them out of her hand and toss them aside. "Mrs. Daly wouldn't like that, Sayre."

"I don't care what—"

"Listen!" He took her by the shoulders. "When Luce Daly got to the hospital, she saw me and bared her claws. She let me know in no uncertain terms that I was persona non grata and yelled at me to keep away from her husband.

"I would have expected that from her if Clark had been hurt on the job. Like Alicia Paulik. But I was shocked, considering that I was the one who had found him and rushed him to the ER.

"It soon came out, however, that he wasn't the victim of a random mugging. Nothing like that. Clark had the crap beat out of him because you recruited him to finger Huff's spies and start rousing the men to strike."

He was breathing hard, barely keeping his voice at a moderate volume, and holding on to his temper by a thread. As though realizing how tightly he was gripping her shoulders, he released her suddenly. He turned away, ran his fingers through his hair, then came back around. "Tell me that Mrs. Daly was wrong, Sayre. Tell me that this isn't true."

She raised her chin defiantly. "You're the one who called this a war."

"It's not *your* war. Why are you fighting it?"

"Because somebody has to. Because what has been standard operating procedure in that foundry is wrong. Somebody has to set things right."

"Do you honestly think that your participation is going to help matters? Do you think it's beneficial to anybody that you're marching in that picket line?"

"I think it might be."

"Well, you're wrong. Dead wrong."

"I'm making a statement to the employees."

"You don't even speak their language," he shouted. "That was demonstrated to you the other day when you came to the plant. Carrying a picket sign does not put you in league with people who could eat for a month on what you pay for a pair of shoes.

"Your heart may be in the right place, Sayre, but your thinking is skewed. You haven't won the trust of the workers and their families. Not yet. Until you do, you're incendiary. Thanks to you, Clark Daly nearly got his brains knocked out tonight, and you're goddamn lucky it wasn't you we found in a ditch."

Stung by his accusation, but more so by its merit, she turned away from him, her shoulders slumping with the weight of her blame. "The last thing I wanted to do was cause more trouble for Clark."

"Then you should've stayed away from him. And that's the message I was sent to deliver."

She raised her head and looked at him in the mirror above the dresser. "From whom?"

"Luce Daly. Pretty smart lady. She nailed it. She predicted that you'd want to make a mad dash to the hospital, rush to Clark's bedside. Well, sorry. His wife doesn't want you anywhere near him. She told me about your visits with him and sent me to tell you to go back where you came from and to leave her husband alone."

"She's thinking like a jealous wife. I have no romantic designs on Clark. I was only trying to help him."

"Big help you were. His wife said you were like a sickness he had caught a long time ago and could never shake."

From Luce Daly's perspective, she probably did represent a sickness with which Clark had been afflicted for a long time. It was an unflattering analogy, and hurtful. She wanted to defend herself, but pride prevented her.

Instead she put Beck on the defensive. "Do you know who did it?"

"I could guess."

"But you won't have them arrested, will you? Because they're Huff's bullies. And you're their ringleader."

"A word of advice, Sayre, which I'm sure you'll ignore. Stay off the picket line. When word gets out about Clark, tempers are going to flare. There's bound to be a showdown of some sort, and you could get caught in the cross fire." He glanced toward the door. "At least you're using the chain now."

"After this morning, I'll never neglect to."

He came toward her slowly. "Did he hurt you, Sayre?"

"I told you—"

"I know what you told us. But I also know you left things out. Did he touch you?"

She shook her head, but to her chagrin, tears filled her eyes. "Not much."

"What does that mean?"

"He . . . he said some vulgar things, but he didn't act on them."

He reached for her, but she staved him off with a stiff arm and a shake of her head. "I'm fine. You should go now."

"All right," he said with a terse nod. "I only came to tell you about Daly and to convey his wife's wishes that you stay away from him. But I'm going to leave you with this question, Sayre. Why are you getting involved in all this?"

"I gave you my reasons last night."

"Because your conscience is bothering you for not taking Danny's calls. The ambiguities surrounding Iverson. To improve working conditions at the foundry. I know what you *said*."

"Well then?" she asked tightly.

"Are those the real reasons? I don't think so. There's only one reason behind every decision you make and everything you do." He pulled open the door and stepped out. Turning back, he said, "Huff."

"Sayre! Are you by yourself? Good Lord, girl, what business do you have driving around alone this time of night?"

"I hope I didn't disturb you, Selma."

She motioned Sayre into the house. "What if that white trash Watkins boy is stalking you?"

"I imagine he's halfway across Texas by now on his way to Mexico. Is Chris at home?"

"He left after dinner and hasn't come back. You want me to try and call him?"

"Actually I came to see Huff. Is he still up?"

"He's in his room, but I've heard him moving around up there, so I don't think he's asleep yet."

"How is he feeling? Does he seem to have recovered?"

"I can't tell if he's any different from before the heart attack. I make sure he takes his blood pressure medicine. With all that's gone on since Danny's parting, it's a wonder to me he hasn't blown a blood vessel clean out his neck."

Sayre patted her hand. "You've always taken good care of us, Selma, and I for one am grateful. Go back to your room. I'll let myself out after I've seen him."

The housekeeper's slippers slapped lightly against the hardwood floor as she retreated down the central hallway toward her apartment on the far side of the kitchen.

Taking Beck's parting words to heart, Sayre had dressed quickly and driven fast to get here. But now she was second-guessing her spontaneous decision to come. She wished she had asked Selma to summon Huff from his bedroom. This was no longer her house, her home. To be here in the middle of the night, creeping up the staircase, made her feel like an intruder.

The silence was unsettling. The staircase was so dark she could barely see the landing at the top. She hadn't been on those stairs in ten years. The last time, she'd been coming down them, carrying a suitcase, leaving for what she had thought would be forever. She had been apprehensive about her immediate future but resolved to face it.

She was no less apprehensive or resolute now as she set her foot firmly on the first tread. The going was easier after that. At the landing, she paused to gaze at the portrait of her mother and felt a familiar tug of homesickness. But was it for this individual who smiled down at her from the canvas, or did she miss the idea of a mother, someone to go to for comfort, advice, and unconditional love?

The upstairs hallway was illuminated by two night-lights plugged into wall outlets on the baseboard. Her footfalls were muffled by the carpet runner that had been one of Laurel's prized possessions. It had been an heirloom from her maternal great-grandmother's plantation house.

The door to Danny's room was closed. She hesitated but moved past without opening the door, feeling that going inside would be a violation similar to walking on his grave. It was still too fresh to disturb.

The door to Chris's room was standing ajar. According to Selma, he had moved back home, into his old room, after Mary Beth had taken up residence in Mexico. "We outfitted it a bit different than when he lived here before he got married."

Sayre peered into the room and, in spite of herself, recognized the good taste with which it had been decorated. The pieces were of good quality, but not ostentatious. The color scheme was neutral. It was masculine and uncluttered, much the way she would have decorated the quarters of a recently single male.

Light was showing beneath Huff's bedroom door. Before she could talk herself out of it, she rapped the door twice. It was opened instantly, creating a vacuum in which they stared at each other.

He removed a smoldering cigarette from his mouth and looked at her speculatively. "I was expecting either Chris or Beck."

"I want to talk to you."

His eyebrows lowered into a scowl. "By your tone of voice, sounds more like you want to chew my ass."

"Did you sic your thugs on Clark Daly?"

He stuck the cigarette back in his mouth and turned into the room. "Come on in. We'd just as well have this out now as later."

She followed him into the room, which also had undergone a redecoration. While Sayre had lived here, the master suite had remained much as it had been when her mother was alive. But at some point during her absence, Laurel's frills had been replaced with more tailored drapes and bed-coverings.

Huff motioned toward a small serving cart. "Pour yourself a drink."

"I don't want a drink, I want an answer. Did you give the order to have Clark beaten?"

"I didn't know it would be Clark."

"But you turned your dogs loose."

He sat down in a large easy chair and inhaled deeply on his cigarette until the tip smoldered red hot. "I have some boys who're loyal to me. I told them to stop any talk of a strike, and I wasn't particular about the way they did it."

He pointed the cigarette at her. "I won't have men taking my money and picketing me at the same time. If they want to join ranks with that Nielson character and his agitators, fine. But not on my clock and not on my dollar," he said, raising his voice.

"They almost killed him."

"But they didn't, and I've been told he'll recover." He ground out his cigarette. "Frankly, I'm surprised Clark Daly had the guts to inspire a spelling bee, much less a labor strike."

"He might not have . . . if I hadn't urged him to."

He reacted with a start. Then after several seconds of stunned silence he began to laugh his wheezing chuckle. "Well, I'll be goddamned. Should've guessed that. Clark Daly hasn't got the balls to undertake a project like that himself. He's been on the skids for years. Spineless as they come."

"That's what you thought, Huff. But you were wrong. Clark was a leader. You beat him down, robbed him of his scholarship, and consequently any chance of a college education. You trampled his hope and his confidence."

"Oh, Jesus, sing me another song. Haven't you gotten tired of that one? All the bad that's happened to that boy, he's brought on himself."

"He's not a boy any longer, Huff, he's a man. And he's proven again that he's a natural leader."

"Yeah, he could lead you straight to every bar in the parish."

"Men listened to him, Huff. Beck said Clark's friends were ready to walk off the job tonight in order to go find him. That sounds like a person who inspires the confidence of others."

Huff came out of his chair angrily. "What did Clark Daly ever inspire you to do except disobey me?"

"I was eighteen. We didn't need your permission to get married."

He went to the serving cart and sloshed whiskey from a decanter into a glass, then drank it down in one swallow. "Damn good thing I got word of your elopement and stopped it."

"Oh, yes, you were quite the hero, Huff. Chasing us down like criminals and then threatening to fire Clark's father if we went through with the marriage. You terrorized his parents, terrorized me and Clark. Very courageous."

"Would you rather I have shot that kid?" he bellowed. "I had a right to shoot him stone dead."

"The *right*? What right?"

"The boy defied me. He deserved—"

"None of it, Huff! The only thing he did to you was love me."

"He was wrong for you."

"Only in your selfish, self-serving opinion."

"He was fine for a high school sweetheart, but when it came to marriage material, you needed somebody from a family more like ours."

She threw back her head and gave a bitter laugh. "Huff, there *is* no family like ours."

"Don't play word games with me, Sayre. You know damn well what I'm talking about," he said querulously. "You needed to marry into a family with clout. Money. Not a family of wage earners."

"That's crap. It was crap when you used that excuse to separate Clark and me, and it's crap now. Money wasn't the issue, Huff. The only reason you didn't like Clark was because you didn't choose him."

"I'm tired of getting blamed for every goddamn thing," he said, making a broad sweep with his arm. "What did I ever do except want the very best for my children?"

"No, what you wanted was your way," she said, matching his voice for volume. "It had to be *your* way. You would not tolerate a single idea or a solitary plan that wasn't of *your* devising." She took a deep breath, and when she released it, her voice was lower and gruff with emotion. "Otherwise, you destroyed it."

He glowered at her as he poured himself another shot of whiskey. He carried it with him back to the chair, where he lit a fresh cigarette. He was breathing with effort. She could smell the whiskey fumes of his breath even from the distance that separated them.

"Yell at me all you want, girl. Rant and rave and stamp your foot, you'll never get an apology or an excuse out of me. When I was just a kid, this high, Sayre," he said, holding his hand parallel to the floor, "I swore I was going to begin a line of Hoyles where the name meant something. Where nobody was going to ignore or forget the name Hoyle." He wagged his cigarette at her. "And that line of Hoyles was not going to include Clark Daly's bastard baby."

She drew a shaky breath. "So you had it cut out of me."

"I did what any father would do who—"

"Who didn't have a soul."

"Who saw his daughter destroying—"

"*You had my baby cut out of me!*" Crossing the room in three strides, she struck him as hard as she could across the face.

He shot to his feet. His drinking glass fell from his hand and rolled across the carpet. He threw down his cigarette and balled his hands into fists, raising them threateningly.

"Go ahead, Huff, strike back. You hit me in the face the night you dragged me out of your den, kicking and screaming and begging you not to do it. Did you know that the floor still shows dents where my heels gouged it while I was trying to stop you that night? Go look at them. They're a testament to just how evil you are.

"When you couldn't get me in the car, you knocked me unconscious. I woke up in Dr. Caroe's back room. My feet had been tied into the stirrups, and my arms were bound to the table." She extended her arms from her sides, feeling again the restraints that had held her immobile.

Her face, she realized, was wet with tears. She licked them from the corners of her lips. "And that unscrupulous bastard scraped my baby out of me. How much did you pay him to end that sweet little life, Huff? How much did it cost you to prove your dominance over me?"

She was sobbing now on every word, but she pressed on. "It was put in a plastic bag and thrown out with the garbage." She flattened her hand on her chest and screamed, "My *baby*."

Following the outburst, the room became as quiet as a tomb, save for the ticking of the clock on Huff's nightstand. She wiped the tears from her face and shook back her hair.

"It's recently been observed that you're the motivation for everything I do. That's true. Hating you sustained me through depression and two unwanted marriages. And to this day, to this moment, I thrive on hating you for what you did to me that night.

"But . . ." She laughed lightly. "But, the joke is on you, Huff. You and your fucking dynastic ambitions. All your scheming to marry me off to Beck? Funny. Hilarious. And futile. Because, see, when your inept friend Dr. Caroe took my baby, he also ruined any chance of my having another."

He staggered back a step. "What?"

"That's right, Huff. I can't perpetuate your goddamn line of Hoyles, and you've only yourself to thank."

She turned and ran from the room, drawing up short when she saw Beck standing in the hallway.

chapter 30

Sayre faltered when she saw him, but without a word, she walked swiftly down the hallway and disappeared into the shadows on the landing. Seconds later he heard the front door close behind her.

He didn't go after her. She wouldn't have wanted him to. He was tainted by his association with Huff, and now he understood the reason for her animosity.

He knocked once on the bedroom door. "Huff, it's me."

Huff was sitting down, although Beck got the impression that he'd dropped into the chair without consciously deciding to. He was balanced on the edge of the cushion, staring at the floor, oblivious to the cigarette that was burning a hole in the carpet inches from his feet.

Beck picked it up and ground it out in the ashtray on the end table beside Huff's chair.

Huff seemed to notice him for the first time. "Beck. How long have you been here?"

"Long enough."

"You heard what Sayre told me?"

He nodded. "Are you all right? Your face is flushed."

"I'm okay. She hasn't killed me. Yet." Frowning down at the spilled bourbon, he added, "Could do with another drink."

Beck poured him a glass of water and brought it to him. "Start with this."

Huff made a face of displeasure but drained the glass. Then, leaning back in his chair, he released a sigh. "This has been a pissy twenty-four hours. Started last night with a picket line outside my foundry. Fine way to end it is learning that Sayre's barren."

"That's what's bothering you?"

"Pardon?"

Beck sat down on the ottoman that matched Huff's chair, facing him. "With everything the two of you talked about . . . I mean, when your only daughter . . ."

Huff gazed back at him as though waiting for him to stop stammering and get to the point.

If Huff didn't comprehend his point by now, he never would. "I don't know what I meant. It's a private matter between you and Sayre."

"Yeah, it's been a *matter* between us since the night it happened."

" 'Happened'? She didn't lose her baby by happenstance, Huff. You forced an abortion on her."

"She was just a girl," he said, gesturing impatiently. "I wasn't about to let her ruin her life before it got started, especially by saddling herself with a kid sired by Clark Daly. You know why she got pregnant, don't you?"

Although Huff didn't really expect a reply, Beck said, "To ensure the marriage."

"Exactly. I had stopped the elopement. Daly's parents folded quick enough, once I put his daddy's job on the line. They sent Daly to spend the summer with relatives in Tennessee. I thought distance would put an end to the romance.

"But Sayre defied me again. Sneaked off and met up with Daly for a weekend, then sashays in one day about a month later and announces that she's pregnant, says now I can't stop them from getting married."

"Only you did."

"You're damn right I did. No baby, no marriage." He snapped his fingers loudly. "I took care of two problems in one night."

It was such an appalling statement, Beck could think of nothing to say in response. "What about Daly? Did he know about the baby?"

"I don't know. I never asked Sayre, and even if I had, she wouldn't have answered me. She went for months without speaking to me. I thought she'd snap out of it, forget it in time."

Beck remembered the shattered expression on her face when she left Huff's bedroom. She'd looked as though she had lived through the experience only days ago rather than years.

"I don't think she'll ever forget it, Huff," he said quietly.

"Doesn't appear that way, does it? She's picketing, you know. Carrying a sign denouncing me. And she's the one behind this business with Clark Daly. Stood right there and admitted it. If he doesn't pull out of this, there'll be hell to pay from her, and you can bet I'll catch most of it."

"He's going to pull out. I called the hospital as I was driving over. No skull fracture, but several broken ribs. They're still looking for internal bleeding, but it's a good sign that none has been detected so far."

Huff rubbed a hand over his flattop and laughed with chagrin. "Guess the boys went a little overboard."

"It was a dumb move, Huff."

His laughter abruptly ceased. He looked at Beck sharply and angrily, which was rare.

"Don't get your back up," Beck said calmly. "You pay me to counsel you. If you don't appreciate my candor, get a new attorney. I'm telling you that drawing first blood was a bad idea. You said so yourself last night."

"I didn't know things were going to get out of hand as fast as they did. I wasn't going to stand around and do nothing."

"Attacking one of your employees was the wrong thing to do. All you accomplished was to prove our opposition's argument and provide them with more ammunition to use against us."

Grumbling, Huff levered himself out of his chair and went to the serving cart. "Everybody's on my case tonight."

"I realize my timing is bad," Beck said. "Having just gone through the meat grinder with Sayre, the last thing you want to hear from me is how badly you're handling the situation at the plant. But you are, Huff.

"I tried to impress upon you the other day that you cannot solve labor problems now like you did in the past. Nielson isn't as easy as Iverson. He isn't going to retreat." He paused strategically, then added, "And you can't make him disappear."

Correctly inferring his meaning, Huff came around slowly, holding an empty glass in one hand and several ice cubes in the other. He seemed unaware that they were dripping through his fingers onto the carpet.

Beck didn't flinch from Huff's quelling stare. "I'm not going to ask you, Huff, because I don't want to know. But I would be stupid to think that you, and probably Chris, had absolutely nothing to do with Gene Iverson's disappearance. A subtle suggestion to some of your men, with a word or even a look, would have been all it took to solve that problem.

"Chris must have played at least a small role in it. Logically, if there was no truth to the charge against him, you wouldn't have been worried about the outcome of his trial. You wouldn't have ordered McGraw to bribe those jurors.

"And despite that little song and dance Chris and I put on for Sayre at McGraw's place, we all know he did it and that he was well compensated for doing it. Whatever happened to Iverson, you and Chris walked away clean. History repeating itself."

"Meaning?"

"Sonnie Hallser."

"Irrelevant."

"Is it, Huff? I didn't know until recently that

Chris was at the foundry the night Hallser died."

Huff cursed beneath his breath as he finally plunked the dripping ice cubes into the glass, then turned back to the cart to finish pouring his drink. "He wasn't supposed to tell anybody he was there that night. He swore to me he wouldn't."

Beck didn't correct Huff by informing him that it had been Sayre, not Chris, who had told him. "What did Chris witness that night?"

"An argument between me and Sonnie."

"And?"

"And nothing," he said, raising his voice. "That's all there was to see. The man and I had an argument."

"A *heated* argument."

"That's the only kind I know how to have. We each blew off steam. I went home with Chris. Later that night Sonnie had a fatal accident."

"Terrible coincidence."

"That's right, it was. Why bring it up now?"

"To illustrate a point." Beck stood up and circled the ottoman, then turned to face Huff again. "You have a reputation for solving your labor problems with brute force. Short of outright violence, you've been known to apply muscle. Those tactics are as obsolete as doctors using leeches to cure patients."

Huff took a gulp of whiskey. "All right, maybe I've bent rules and crossed lines, but I never hesitated to do what was necessary to protect myself, my family, and my business. You gotta be tough—and I'm talking as nails—if you want to come out on top.

"Chris understands that. I don't think Danny ever did, or Sayre ever will. I took a mediocre foundry and turned it into a thriving one," he said, clenching his fist. "You think that would have happened if I'd been a pushover, pandering to labor unions and granting every demand put to me by my employees? Hell, no!

"I wore big boots and I kicked ass when I needed to, and I'm going to keep on doing it that way until they're shoveling dirt over me. Nobody is going to shut me down. Not Charles Nielson, not even the government agencies. And it'll become a union shop over my dead body." He finished the speech by shouting the last three words and punctuating them with a jabbing index finger.

"Let's avoid dead bodies if we can," Beck said quietly.

Huff relaxed his stance. He even laughed. "I'd prefer it. Especially if it's mine."

"Sit down before you blow a gasket." Once Huff was back in his chair and some of the color had receded from his face, Beck said, "Huff, please, no more rough stuff until I can at least try to negotiate a peaceful resolution to this mess. The Pauliks might reconsider filing suit if we offer them a significant cash settlement."

"How significant?"

"Significant enough to pacify them, not so significant that you'll have to start drinking cheaper bourbon. And I strongly urge you to shut down the conveyor that injured Billy."

"It's been repaired and is running fine now."

"Repaired, not overhauled like it needs to be,"

Beck argued. "It's another disaster waiting to happen. Do you think we can afford another accident right now?"

"George has given it a green tag. So has Chris. Those are their departments, Beck. You stick to keeping us out of a lawsuit."

Beck conceded, albeit grudgingly. "I'd better leave before Selma comes up here and throws me out for keeping you up so late."

"Are you on your way home?"

"Actually, I'm spending the night on the sofa in my office. One of us should be there in case of real trouble."

"Where's Chris?"

"He no longer has to confide in me. I'm not his attorney anymore."

"You talked Red out of keeping him in lockup over the weekend."

"That was my last official duty for him."

"So I was told. Can't say as I'm happy about this new lawyer."

"With all that's going on at the plant, it's best, Huff. I've got my hands full."

"The guy Chris has retained, is he any good?"

"I made a few calls today, asked around. He's reputed to be usurious, ambitious, egomaniacal, and obnoxious. Everything you'd want in a criminal lawyer."

Huff smiled wryly. "Let's hope Chris won't need him. That detective, that Scott, is drilling a dry well. Bible stories." He snorted. "As told by Slap Watkins, no less."

"He frightened her." Beck didn't even realize

he'd spoken his thought aloud until he noticed Huff looking at him strangely. "Sayre."

"Oh, right. Watkins breaking into her motel room. Serves her right for staying in that rathole."

"She was more disturbed by it than she let on. I don't think she told us everything that he said or did to her."

But Huff's mind was moving down another track, and it didn't include concern for Sayre's safety. "In light of her barrenness, you're off the hook, Beck, my boy," he said with a light chuckle. "The pressure is back on Chris to father me a grandchild. He's my one and only shot at immortality now."

"Knock knock."

Beck pried open one eye and saw Chris grinning down at him. With every muscle protesting, he sat up. "What time is it?"

"Going on seven. Have you been here all night?"

Beck swung his feet to the floor and painfully stood up. "Most of it."

"You look like hammered shit," Chris remarked. "Something the matter with your back?"

"I slept on a sofa two thirds my height. My back feels like a herd of buffalo has stampeded across it. While you . . ." He looked askance at Chris. "Fresh as a daisy."

"Huff ordered me here early this morning. I reminded him that today is Saturday and how I feel about working on weekends, but he was adamant. He wanted us to be here by the shift change. So here I am. Hungover, but showered and shaved, which is more than I can say for you."

"Give me five minutes." Beck took a Dopp kit from a drawer in his credenza and a change of clothes from the closet. "I brought these from home a few days ago in case I had to pull overnight duty."

Together they left his office and walked toward the men's restroom, where they'd had the foresight to install a shower. "Where were you last night?" Beck asked.

"Back at the club in Breaux Bridge. It's a happening place. You should go with me next time."

"If you can go nightclubbing you must not be worried."

"About what?"

"Well, for starters, about a pending labor strike. And if that isn't enough, how about being a prime suspect in a homicide investigation?"

"Huff says you're going to negotiate us out of the threatened strike. As for the other, I talked to my new lawyer yesterday afternoon. We were on the phone for over an hour. I told him everything, starting with the day Danny's body was discovered.

"He said I didn't have anything to worry about. They've got nothing linking me to the scene except a lousy matchbook, which for all they know could have been carried there by a raccoon."

"That would've been my first guess."

Chris shot him a look. "Pessimistic *and* droll. You're becoming no fun at all. Anyhow, this lawyer is going to make hash of Wayne Scott. Any news of Slap?"

"Not that I've heard."

"The attorney said that Cain and Abel nonsense was a desperate move by a desperate fugitive."

"I agree."

They went into the restroom together. Chris moved to a urinal, Beck stood at a sink and inspected his reflection in the mirror above it. His eyes were red from lack of sleep. He had a heavy scruff, and his hair was standing on end, but at least all his features were intact and in place, which was more than could be said about Clark Daly. He asked Chris if he'd heard about that incident.

"Huff was still up when I got in last night. He told me about it."

Reaching into the shower stall, Beck turned on the faucets, then began to undress. "Daly was worked over pretty good."

Chris flushed the urinal. "In my opinion he got exactly what he deserved. How many times has he had his pay docked for being late, or not showing up, or reporting to work drunk? Dozens that I can remember. But we always gave him another chance.

"And how does he thank us for not firing him all those times? By sowing seeds of discontent. Anybody who sides with those pickets out there doesn't get any sympathy from me, and that includes my own sister."

Beck pulled his face from beneath the spray and poked his head around the corner of the shower stall, looking toward Chris, who was washing his hands at a sink. "Oh yes, she's out there," Chris said, reading the question in Beck's bloodshot eyes. "Passing out coffee and beignets. Huff and I saw her when we drove in."

"Shit."

"I'm going to get some coffee," Chris called back to him as he went out.

Beck finished showering. He had to shave with bar soap but luckily had remembered to bring toothpaste and a toothbrush in his Dopp kit. He dressed quickly and had just reached his office when the seven o'clock whistle blew.

Beck, watching from the windows in his office, waited expectantly. The shop floor cleared quickly of those whose shift had ended. But after five minutes, only a handful of men had replaced them. "Damn," he muttered, knowing this boded ill.

He turned and was crossing his office when Chris appeared in the open doorway. He was carrying a two-way radio, which was making an awful racket. "We've got a problem outside," he said.

"I guessed."

"Fred Decluette says some of the men on his shift joined the picket line as soon as their shift ended," Chris told him as they jogged down the hallway toward Huff's office. "They're recruiting men as they report to work. Clark Daly's become their poster child."

Beck wanted to ask about Sayre, but by then they had reached Huff's office. Hearing them rush in, he turned away from the wall of glass overlooking the shop floor, his expression fierce. "Where the fuck is everybody?"

Chris summarized the situation for him in a couple of terse sentences.

"You two get out there," Huff said. "I want this thing capped. Now! I'm going to call Red, then I'll come down myself."

"No, you stay here," Chris said. "You had a

heart attack last week. You don't need this stress."

"Screw that. It's my foundry and my property," he yelled. "I won't cower up here like a goddamn invalid while they're being overrun!"

"I can handle it, Huff."

"I agree with Chris," Beck said. "Not because I think you're infirm, but because if you enter the fray, you appear worried about it. Stay away from it and its importance is automatically reduced."

Huff's expression remained truculent, but he relented. "Dammit, you make a good point, Beck. Okay, I'll stay and run the show from here. You two go. But keep me informed."

They left in a hurry, preferring to take the staircase rather than wait on the elevator. "Good thing he listens to you," Chris said, breathing hard as they rounded the last landing at a run.

Beck glanced over his shoulder. "I had to say something to keep him inside."

The metal exit door was already as hot as a griddle. Beck put his entire weight against it and pushed it open. The rising sun hit him like a spotlight. His eyes adjusted to the glare barely in time to see the beer bottle hurtling toward him.

chapter 31

Sayre was standing on the hood of her rental car. From that vantage point, the exit door was in her sights when Beck barreled through it with Chris close on his heels.

Apparently others had been anticipating their appearance, because no sooner had they cleared the door than a beer bottle was thrown at them. Beck saw it coming and deflected it. He and Chris ducked behind a large Dumpster where Fred Decluette was speaking into a bullhorn.

"We want this area cleared immediately. Any employee of Hoyle Enterprises who doesn't report to work by seven-thirty will be docked a full shift's wages."

This was met with jeers from the picketers sent by Nielson and those townsfolk and workers who had joined them outside the chain-link fence. The majority of Hoyle employees, who were either quitting their shift or reporting for work, loitered between the two camps, clearly weighing their decision of which to join.

One of Nielson's paid agitators was also speaking into a bullhorn, urging the Hoyle employees not to return to work until demands were met and their workplace was brought up to OSHA's standards.

"Is safety equipment too much to ask?"

A roared "No!" went up from those backing him.

"Hoyle Enterprises has made repairs—"

Whatever else Fred said was drowned out by boos and protests. One man grabbed a portable microphone and shouted into it, "Ask Billy Paulik about your lousy repairs."

That generated more shouting and name-calling. When it subsided, Chris took the bullhorn from Fred. "Listen, you men, we're compensating the Paulik family."

"Blood money!"

Despite hoots of laughter, Chris continued. "We're willing to work things out, to listen—"

"Like you worked things out with Clark Daly?" one of the pickets shouted. "No thank you!"

"What happened to Daly last night had nothing to do with us," Chris shouted into the bullhorn.

"You're a damn liar, Hoyle. Just like your old man."

Sayre watched as the agitator with the microphone turned and opened a car door, extending his hand down to the passenger inside. Luce Daly stepped out.

"Oh, Lord," Sayre murmured.

So far a violent outbreak had only been threatened, limited to the bottle thrown at Chris and Beck. But Luce Daly's presence and anything she said could spark violence and bloodshed. Sayre scrambled off the hood of her car and began elbowing her way through the press, hoping to reach Clark's wife and dissuade her from participating.

Unfortunately, she saw Luce take the microphone extended to her. It was an inexpensive sound system, probably part of a child's toy or a karaoke machine, but she made herself heard through the scratchy speakers.

"I'm here speaking for my husband. He can't talk this morning because his mouth is full of sutures. But he wrote down a list of names he wanted me to read to you."

She started reading from the list, and after the second name, the crowd began to react angrily. The man nearest Sayre cupped his hands around his mouth and booed loudly.

"Who are they?" Sayre asked, shouting to make herself heard above the din.

"Huff Hoyle's attack dogs," he shouted back.

Clark had named the men who'd beaten him. They were probably the men taking cover behind the Dumpster with Beck, Chris, and Fred. One of them snatched the bullhorn from Chris and yelled into it, "That bitch is lying!"

Sayre continued to fight her way through the mob toward Luce Daly, who was rereading the list, but workers who had previously been indecisive were now joining the throng of picketers.

It was growing into a moving mass with a will of its own, making it a struggle for Sayre to keep her footing. Surges of outraged people were pressing on her from all sides.

And then she heard someone near her shout, "You'll get yours, too, Merchant."

Coming up on tiptoe, she saw Beck moving through the chain-link gate that was the demarcation line between the hostile groups. He walked purposefully toward Luce, who continued to repeat the list of names in a deliberate monotone.

When Beck reached the fringe of the picketers, he stopped, looking straight into the eyes of the men forming a human barricade. The shouting was suddenly replaced by a dense silence that pressed upon the eardrums as solidly as the heat.

Beck held his ground. Gradually men began to shuffle aside. Some were more reluctant than others to yield ground, but eventually they opened up a path for him. The crowd closed behind him once he'd passed. In that eddying fashion, he made his way through the throng.

When he reached Luce Daly, she lowered her microphone and looked at him with patent animosity.

"I understand your outrage." He spoke quietly, but the mob had remained silent and his voice carried on the heavy, humid air. "If Clark has identified these men as the ones who attacked him last night, they'll be held accountable and dealt with legally."

"Why should I believe you?" she asked.

"I give you my word."

"Your word don't count for shit," said a voice from the crowd.

Gaining courage, another shouted, "You're Huff Hoyle's whore!"

"Yeah, he says bend over, you ask how far."

Others joined in until the epithets overlapped, but the pervading message was clear: Beck was more despicable than the enemy he represented.

He turned away from Luce to address the crowd, but before he could say anything, a rock struck him in the face. Then a man jumped him from behind and pinned his arms behind his back. Another punched him in the stomach.

Sayre, knowing that help could come from only one source, looked toward the Dumpster and saw that Chris and the men with him had stepped out from behind their cover.

"Chris!" Trying to make herself heard above the noise was futile, but she shouted to him again and again, waving her arms overhead.

Then she saw Fred Decluette step forward, prepared to rush to Beck's defense.

But her brother's arm shot out and caught Fred in the chest, halting him. She saw Chris shake his head and say something. Fred looked anxiously toward the spot where angry men had encircled Beck, then reluctantly he returned to his place at Chris's side.

Cursing her brother to hell, Sayre barged forward, shoving aside anyone in her path. A ring of cheering onlookers had formed around the men who now had Beck on the ground, taking turns kicking him.

"Leave him alone!" She grabbed the shirt of the man nearest her and hauled him back. He came around, hands balled into threatening fists, but when he saw her, he froze.

She fought her way forward until there were

only two men standing over Beck. "Stop it!" she screamed as one pulled back his foot to deliver a vicious kick. The man halted and turned. Taking advantage of his stupefaction, she shoved him aside and knelt beside Beck.

His face was streaked with sweat and blood, but he was conscious. She looked up at Luce Daly. "Call them off. This isn't accomplishing anything."

"It's making me feel better."

Sayre sprang to her feet, bringing herself face-to-face with the other woman. "Will it make Clark feel better?" Seeing a flicker of uncertainty in Luce's eyes, she said, "Beck carried him to the hospital last night."

"He's still one of them."

"I'm not."

Scornfully Luce said, "The hell you're not."

"Only by birth, Luce, and there's nothing I can do about that. But I'm not one of them, and I don't think you really believe that I am." When the other woman didn't dispute it, Sayre continued. "I know why you don't like me. I even understand it. But I swear to you that I am not your rival. Clark is your husband. He loves you, and I know you love him.

"Make the attack on him count for something, Luce. Something bigger than retribution for what happened last night. Something bigger than retribution for what happened a long time ago, before Clark even knew you."

She and Luce held each other's gaze, and Sayre detected a gradual relenting in the other woman's eyes. Finally Luce said, "Those men who beat up Clark, am I supposed to take Merchant's word that they'll be punished?"

"You don't have to take his word for it. I give you mine."

Luce stared at her for a moment longer, then turned to the man who had given her the microphone. She nodded brusquely. With a motion from him, the men surrounding Beck withdrew.

Sayre knelt again and slipped her hands under his arms. "Can you stand up?"

"Yeah. Just not too fast."

She lost the argument about taking him to the hospital. "Lately I've been to the emergency room more times than I care to count." He grimaced with the effort of talking.

"You've probably got broken ribs."

"No, I know what that feels like. Had two. Football. This isn't that bad. Just take me home."

He was gritting his teeth and holding his side as she pulled off the main road onto the lane leading to his house. "When you leave, lock the gate behind you," he said. "Media."

She hadn't thought about the media in relation to the events of the morning, but of course they would make news. Someone from Hoyle Enterprises would be sought for a sound bite. And no doubt Nielson, too.

She didn't stop in front of the house but drove around to the rear.

"What are you doing?"

"No one will see my car back here."

"Just drop me at the door, Sayre. You don't have to walk me in."

"No, but I may have to carry you," she said

under her breath as she got out and rushed around to the passenger side.

She helped him out, and together they limped up the back steps. "As long as you're here, would you feed Frito before you leave?" he asked.

"Of course."

The dog greeted them with such exuberance that Sayre had to admonish him. "Be nice," she said sternly, remembering the command Beck had used to settle him down at the diner. The dog obeyed, but he was crestfallen.

"Sorry, boy, I'll play with you later."

"I'll explain everything to him as soon as I've tended to you," she said as she guided Beck toward the bedroom.

"You don't have to do this."

"Yes I do. It's my fault."

"You didn't throw that rock at me." Turning his head to look at her, he said, "Did you?"

"No, but I was on the side of the individual who did. You warned me that the picket would turn violent and that people would get hurt. I didn't listen."

"I've noticed that about you. Bad habit."

"Beck, those ribs of yours that aren't broken?"

"Yeah?"

"I could change that."

He grunted in pain. "Please, don't make me laugh."

When they got to the master bedroom, she propped him against the footboard of the sleigh bed and quickly folded down the covers. Then she came back to help him sit on the edge of the mattress.

"Can you sit up long enough for me to get some antiseptic on your cheek?"

He was clearly in pain. He'd broken out in a sweat, and his lips were rimmed with white. "First-aid stuff is in the bathroom."

She searched the various drawers and cabinets until she located Band-Aids, cotton balls, peroxide, and ibuprofen tablets. When she returned to the bedroom, Frito was sitting at Beck's feet, whining pitifully. Beck was stroking his head. "He's worried about me."

"He's smarter than you. Besides the rock, did you receive any blows to the head?"

"No."

"Did you ever lose consciousness? Are you dizzy? What did you have for breakfast?"

"I didn't have breakfast."

"Okay, dinner last night."

"Sayre, I don't have a concussion."

"How do you know?"

"Because I've also had that before."

"Football?"

"Baseball. Caught one in the head."

"Is that what made it so hard?"

"Look, I'm not dizzy. I'm not nauseous. I never lost consciousness . . ." He sucked in his breath as she dabbed peroxide on his cheek.

"This may need to be stitched."

"It doesn't."

She wiped the blood away and saw that it was a long gash but not too deep. "I still recommend stitches."

"I'll live. I just need to lie down for a while."

He unbuttoned his shirt, but when he started to take it off, he caught his breath.

"Let me help." She eased the shirt off his shoulders. Moving slowly and gently, she helped him pull his arms from the sleeves, then stepped back to evaluate the damage. His torso was already discoloring where he'd been kicked and pummeled. His back looked equally bad.

"Oh, Beck," she whispered. "You really should be X-rayed."

"For this?" Groaning with the effort of moving, he lay down and settled his head into the pillow. "This is nothing."

"Please let me call paramedics. You could be at the hospital in fifteen minutes."

"I could be asleep in fifteen seconds if you'd shut up and get out of here. But first, could I have a few of those pills?"

She uncapped the bottle and shook three tablets into her hand. He asked for a fourth and she shook out another. Then she held his head while he swallowed them with a glass of water she brought from the bathroom.

He returned his head to the pillow and closed his eyes. "Before you leave, take the phone off the hook, please."

"All right."

"Pour some dry food into Frito's bowl and make sure he has water. Let him out to do his business."

"Don't worry about anything."

"The gate . . ."

"I'll remember."

She closed the shutters to dim the room and

turned on the ceiling fan. Then she waited until the rhythmic rise and fall of his chest indicated that he'd fallen asleep. Moving toward the door, she motioned for Frito to follow.

Instead, the retriever lay down on the floor at the end of Beck's bed, rested his head on his paws, and looked up at her with soulful eyes.

Quietly, she backed out of the room alone.

Midafternoon, Beck emerged from a sleep that had been restless for the last half hour. Disoriented, he focused on her. "Sayre?"

"You've been groaning. I think your ibuprofen has worn off."

He glanced at the clock on his nightstand. "Why are you still here?"

"Take three more tablets." She pushed them into his mouth and held the water glass for him.

He swallowed the pills, then asked, "Any media?"

"About one o'clock a news van from a New Orleans station pulled up to the gate and two men got out. They stared at the house for a while, then got back in the van and drove away."

His eyes had closed again; he only nodded.

"There was a brief mention of the fracas on the noon news, with promises of more to come on the evening newscasts. Nielson's office issued a statement. He regrets the violence, claims it wasn't his people but Hoyle employees who jumped you."

"He's right. I recognized them."

"Your cell phone has rung several times. I didn't retrieve messages, but I checked the caller ID and recognized Nielson's office number on two of the calls."

"Call back. See what that's about. If you don't mind."

"Not at all. I knew Huff would be worried about you, so I called him. I told him that you were all right, that you were resting at home, and that if anybody, including him, tried to come up the driveway, I'd shoot them."

He smiled at that. "I believe you would. Heard anything from Chris?"

"I'll tell you about Chris. He isn't your friend, Beck."

He opened his eyes.

Slowly she shook her head, saying softly, "He's not."

He continued looking at her for several seconds, then his eyes closed and he fell asleep again.

She placed another call to Huff at six-fifteen. After his snarled hello, she said, "It's Sayre. I just saw it on the six o'clock news."

His breathing was audible. She could imagine him gripping the telephone receiver so hard his knuckles were white. He would be furiously smoking a cigarette, his eyes black pinpoints of fury. "Did you call to gloat?"

"I called for Beck. When he wakes up, he'll want to know your reaction."

At first she hadn't believed what the TV anchorman reported, and would never have believed it if there hadn't been video to prove it. The Occupational Safety and Health Administration had moved in on Hoyle Enterprises that afternoon and shut down the plant, from the smelting of scrap iron to the shipping of new pipe.

"It's a sad day when a man can have his business taken over by a bunch of bureaucrats who push pencils for a living and have probably never broken a sweat in their whole lives," Huff ranted. "Were you behind this?"

"No, *you* were. You brought this on yourself, Huff. You'd been warned time and again. If you had complied with previous mandates—"

"If I'd tucked tail, you mean."

Arguing with him was an exercise in futility. He would never concede his own culpability. Hoyle Enterprises would not be allowed to resume operation until a thorough inspection had been conducted on every aspect of the plant. The agency was demanding total compliance with recommendations made as a result of that inspection as well as full payment of any fines assessed for cited violations. It was expected there would be many.

"What do you plan to do?" she asked.

"I plan to stay on those bastards like flies on stink. They've got another think coming if they think I'm going to turn my plant over to them to be redesigned."

According to an OSHA spokesperson, their "redesign," as Huff called it, included mandatory installation of kill switches on each piece of machinery, guardrails, adequate fall protection, and a ventilation system to improve the air quality.

"When Beck wakes up, what do you want me to tell him?"

He gave her the message he wanted delivered, then launched into another diatribe against the federal agency. "These Yankee D.C. bastards don't realize who they're fucking with."

"Oh, I'm sure they do, Huff. That's why they're giving you no quarter."

"You're enjoying this, aren't you? You're getting your revenge."

"It wasn't revenge I wanted, Huff."

"You carried a picket sign against your own father. If that's not revenge, what would you call it?"

"I wouldn't call you a father."

She hung up before he could respond.

"Hello?"

Chris smiled into the telephone receiver. "Well, at least I've gotten you to speak to me," he said to Lila Robson.

"Hi, Chris." Her tone was as frosty as it had been when she drove away from their less than idyllic picnic.

"Miss me?" She waited too long for the answer to be no. He laughed softly. "I thought so. Have you run down the batteries in your vibrator? Why don't I come over and let's test them?"

"I don't want to see you again until that business about your brother is cleared up. Understand? I won't get involved in that. I mean it, Chris. If you tell my uncle Red that you were with me that afternoon—"

"George will be fired."

He could hear her quick intake of breath through the phone line. He thought he even heard her swallow. "What?"

"These OSHA inspectors are looking for liability. The plant's safety director is the first person to come to mind, don't you agree? If George had done his job properly, he would have known that conveyor needed attention. He would have put a lockout on it until the drive belt was repaired by a qualified maintenance man. Billy Paulik wouldn't have lost his arm, we wouldn't have Nielson picketing in our backyard, and we would still be in operation instead of shut down."

"You can't blame George," she exclaimed. "You never want him to lock out a machine. He only does what he knows you and Huff want him to do."

"Then what you're saying is that he's superfluous. We won't miss him once he's gone."

"Chris, please."

Hearing the tremor in her voice, he smiled and mentally gave himself a thumbs-up for thinking to use this tactic. "Firing George would be my last resort, Lila. My first choice would be to back him when those inspectors start grilling him. I want to keep him in his present position. And you can guarantee that."

"How?"

"Come Monday morning, I want you to trot yourself down to the sheriff's office and tell your uncle Red that I was with you on the Sunday afternoon that Danny was killed. That'll serve a dual purpose, Lila. You'll be doing your duty as a law-abiding citizen by telling the truth to an officer of the law and saving an innocent man from further hassle. And you'll be saving your husband's job.

"See, I was thinking about this new attorney I've retained and how expensive it's going to be just to avoid an indictment. I asked myself why I was going to the time and expense, when all I have to do to put a stop to this mess here and now is produce my alibi."

He paused, then said, "I won't even ask if you'll do it because I know you will. Oh, and by the way, until I'm tired of you, whenever I call for you, you'll show up, looking gorgeous and hot to get laid. Understand?" he said, repeating the word with the same inflection she had used earlier. "I'm the one who'll end this affair, Lila, not you."

George watched Lila disconnect the cordless phone. She dropped it on the kitchen counter and covered her mouth with her hand, visibly upset.

"Lila?"

She spun around, her eyes wide and fearful. She splayed a hand over her chest. "I didn't hear you come in. I thought you'd be at the plant for hours yet. Are there any new developments?"

"You tell me."

"What?"

He nodded toward the phone. "You were talking to Chris, weren't you?"

She opened her mouth to speak but closed it before saying anything. Then she lowered her head, and her face crumpled as she began to cry. "Oh, George, I've made such a mess."

George crossed the room as quickly as his short legs would allow and took her in his arms. "There, there, baby. Tell me about it."

She told him everything, starting with the first time she'd been with Chris. "It was in a shower stall in the women's locker room at the country club. I guess part of the turn-on was the danger of getting caught. I just sorta lost my head, you know?"

He could understand that. He lost his head every time he looked at her.

Lila held nothing back. Some of it was so painful for George to hear that he actually groaned, but he encouraged her to continue, right up through the phone call he'd partially overheard.

"If I don't do what he says, you'll lose your job. And I heard on the news that criminal charges could be filed against some of the management personnel. That's you, George, especially if the Hoyles lay the blame with you. You could go to jail." Her eyes began streaming again. "I'm sorry, George. This is all my fault. I'm sorry. Can you still love me?"

Love her? He adored her. She was his sun and moon, the air he breathed. "I don't blame you, honey," he said repeatedly as he held her close, kissing her lips, her wet eyes, her tearstained cheeks.

She would not go to the sheriff's office on Monday morning. He didn't want everybody in town to know that Chris Hoyle had fucked his wife. He wouldn't be able to withstand the humiliation of everybody knowing that, when most people already looked upon him with derision.

He didn't blame Lila for her infidelity. She had to live with him, and for a vital, beautiful young woman, that couldn't be very exciting. Chris had provided her with a thrill that he was incapable of providing.

No, Chris was the one George blamed. And Chris was the one who had to be punished.

chapter 32

Sayre was roused from a light sleep by the sound of running water coming from Beck's bathroom. She'd lain down on the living room sofa, intending only to rest, but apparently she had dozed off. Knowing that he was awake, she got up and felt her way through the darkness into the kitchen.

By the time she entered his bedroom carrying a serving tray, he was coming out of the bathroom, a towel around his hips, his hair wet.

"You showered?" she asked, surprised.

"I woke up in a puddle of sweat."

She glanced up at the ceiling fan, which was still turning. "I guess I should have had the thermostat set lower."

"Wasn't that. I was dreaming."

She set the tray on an ottoman in front of the love seat that was positioned diagonally in the corner. "About what?" When he didn't say anything, she glanced at him over her shoulder.

"I don't remember."

"You're standing upright. How do you feel?"

"The hot shower actually worked out some of the soreness. Why are the lights off?"

"I closed all the blinds at sunset and have been using candlelight. From the road it will look like no one's here."

"Good thinking." He switched off the light in the bathroom.

Sayre struck a match to the candle on the tray she'd carried in. "I fixed you some supper. Tomato soup. Cheese and crackers."

"You shouldn't be waiting on me, but I'm too hungry to scold."

She motioned him toward the love seat, and he sat down, modestly tucking the towel between his thighs, then taking the tray onto his lap. She sat on the ottoman. He picked up the spoon and dipped it into the bowl of soup, then remembered his manners. "Have you had anything?"

"A while ago."

He took a sip of soup and bit into a slice of cheddar. "How's Frito?"

"He feasted on bacon and eggs and is presently sleeping it off."

"Bacon? Thanks a lot. Now he'll never settle for eggs alone."

"I felt he deserved a treat. He kept vigil over you most of the afternoon."

He stopped eating and looked across at her. "Apparently so did you."

Suddenly the room seemed too dark, too hushed, and Beck was too naked. She stood up quickly and, despite his protests, stripped the damp sheets off the bed and remade it with fresh ones. By the time she had finished, he was washing his supper down with a glass of milk.

She carried the tray back into the kitchen and returned with several Hershey's Kisses. "I thought you might want a sweet."

"Thanks." He removed the foil from a chocolate and popped it into his mouth. "What did you mean earlier when you said that Chris wasn't my friend? Or did I imagine that?"

She resumed her seat on the ottoman. "No, I said it. He stood by and did nothing while you took a beating."

"There wasn't much he could do, Sayre."

"I don't believe that," she said heatedly. "Even if he didn't want to fight, he held back Fred Decluette from helping you. I saw him do it."

"I volunteered to go out and talk to Luce Daly. Chris advised against it. He told me to wait until Red arrived with reinforcements. I guess he thought I got what I asked for. I was trying to be a hero."

His explanation didn't change her mind. It had some basis, she supposed. But she had seen the look on Chris's face, and it hadn't been the anxious expression of someone watching his friend being overpowered by a mob.

"If the situation had been reversed, could wild horses have held you back?" she asked. "Wouldn't you have leaped to Chris's defense?"

"I don't know."

"Yes you do. You joined him and Danny in the fight three years ago at the Razorback."

"Which, in hindsight, was reckless. And we weren't up against a mob, only Slap Watkins."

At the mention of his name, chill bumps broke out on her arms. She chafed them.

"I'm sorry," he said. "I shouldn't have reminded you of him."

"Doesn't matter."

"I don't suppose he's been captured while I was sleeping the day away."

"Not that I've heard." She noticed how neatly he had diverted the subject away from Chris, but she allowed it. "I rather imagine the sheriff's office had its hands full with the situation at the foundry."

"Did you call Nielson back?"

"I talked to his receptionist. She thanked me for returning her call. Word had reached them about what happened to you this morning. They regretted it, said violence wasn't Nielson's style, and asked how you were faring."

"Maybe he'll feel sorry for me and keep our next appointment."

"Maybe. However—"

"Uh-oh. There's a however?"

She nibbled at one of the chocolates. "Nielson is a moot point, Beck."

"Since when?"

Uncertain how he would receive the news, she broke it to him as gently as she could. "OSHA shut down Hoyle Enterprises today." She related to him what she'd heard on the newscasts and later from Huff.

"And," she added after taking a deep breath, "the agency spokesperson hinted that in addition to the fines that will almost certainly be assessed, probably into the millions of dollars, the Justice Department is conducting its own investigation. Hoyle may yet face criminal charges."

"I've got to get down there."

He attempted to stand up, but she laid a hand on his shoulder and pressed him back down onto the love seat. "Huff doesn't want you there."

"Doesn't want me there?"

"After I heard the news story on TV, I called him. He was in quite a state, so furious he was barely coherent. But on one point—well, two actually—he was emphatic. He wants you to stay away until the smoke clears."

"Why?"

She looked down at her hands as they rolled the foil candy wrapper into a tight ball. "He said you could do more harm than good. That you knew too much and . . . and that it would be best if you were indisposed by the injuries you received today and therefore unavailable to answer the questions put to you by the prying sons of bitches. I quote."

Beck thought it over for several moments, then said, "He's right, Sayre. I'd be placed in the position of either incriminating my employer or equivocating to the federal boys and consequently incriminating myself."

Sayre didn't say anything, but it disappointed her to hear him admit his culpability.

"What was the second point Huff was emphatic about?"

"That I should be ashamed for picketing against

my own flesh and blood, and that I'm no doubt gloating over the shutdown."

He opened another candy and put it in his mouth. "*Are* you gloating?"

"No. I'm glad Huff is being forced to make improvements. Whether the pressure was applied by the government, or Nielson and the labor unions, or by me, it had to be done, Beck. Things had to change."

She smiled sadly. "I just wish it could have been accomplished without anyone getting hurt. I was responsible for the attack on Clark and, indirectly, for the one on you. I refused to heed your warnings, and both of you suffered injuries because of it."

"I'm not sure major change can come about without conflict, Sayre. Progress usually has a price tag attached. Maybe not physical injury, but some form of strife."

"But you suffered physical injury. Does it still hurt?"

Just below his heart there was a bruise on his rib cage as wide as her palm, visible even in the flickering light of the single candle. She reached out and touched it with her fingertips.

She meant only to examine it briefly but found herself reluctant to break contact with his warm skin. In that spot it was smooth, although the rest of his chest and stomach were dusted with light brown hair.

Barely touching him, her fingertips moved across his stomach to a similar bruise on the other side. Several inches below that, there was another on his hip bone, half hidden by the towel around his waist. She touched it gently, then returned to the first bruise beneath his left breast.

She kept her hand there, watching her fingertips as they lightly rubbed the discolored spot. Then acting on impulse, she leaned across his lap and replaced her fingers with her lips. She kissed the bruise several times with pecks almost as light as air.

Tilting her head, she kissed the one on the other side of his rib cage, her lips scarcely glancing his skin. She nuzzled her way down to his hip bone and kissed the bruise there. Once. Then lifting the towel, she touched her lips to it a second time.

Beck made a low sound. Taking her head between his hands, he pulled her up. He searched her face, his eyes lighting briefly on every feature. He combed his fingers through her hair, holding it away from her head, then letting it drift back into place. He spoke her name on a ragged sigh.

A heartbeat later his mouth was on hers. Being careful of the cut on his cheekbone, she placed her hands against his face and gave herself over to the kiss.

Passion was so explosive and so well matched, it was almost competitive. Their mouths became fully engaged with each other, and the more each tasted of the other, the more they both wanted.

He drew her up to straddle his lap and fit himself into the notch of her thighs. He was surprisingly hard, his erection imperative. She tore her mouth away from his and looked at him with shock.

"My dream," he said breathlessly, ". . . the one

that made me sweat . . . I was making love to you. I'm not dreaming now."

"It could be painful."

"I'm already in pain."

Then he reclaimed her mouth and, if it was possible, kissed her even more urgently than before. They broke apart only long enough for him to pull her top over her head. Reaching behind her, he unhooked her bra and removed it, then pressed his head between her breasts and rested there for a time to catch his breath.

She folded her arms around his head, rubbed her cheek against his hair, which was still damp from his shower. The scent of his skin and the soap he'd used, the chocolate flavor of his breath, were intoxicants.

She rocked her hips forward, rubbing herself against him. "God, yes, again," he groaned, and she did.

When she felt his tongue against her nipple, she thought she would dissolve with pleasure. Encouraged by her involuntary murmurs, he kissed it sweetly before sucking it into his mouth and pressing it against his palate with his tongue.

He unfastened her slacks and slid his hands inside the back of them, kneading her, pressing, separating, making her thrill to her feminine vulnerability, making her ache with wanting him to exploit it.

"Beck, let me . . ." She eased herself off his lap and began undressing. When she was down to her lace bikini, she hesitated, afflicted with a sudden and uncharacteristic bashfulness.

He looked at her imploringly. "You're killing me."

She removed the panties. He pushed aside the towel at his waist. His sex was full, beautiful, and Sayre felt a primal reaction to it deep inside her own body.

He brushed his fingers through the gingery patch of hair between her thighs, then placed his hands on either side of her waist and pulled her forward. On her knees, she straddled his legs. He pressed his face into the giving softness of her belly and kissed it, then lower, and lower still until he was tasting her, and she was melting against his lips and tongue, quivering to have him inside her, and she told him so.

Given his recent injuries, the coupling wasn't vigorous . . . and was better for it. She sank onto him by degrees, because each sensation was new and exciting and too remarkable not to be savored. If he was impatient, he hid it well and seemed to enjoy her self-indulgent lack of haste.

When it seemed to her that they couldn't possibly be more intimately joined, he cradled her hips between his strong hands and held her in place as he pushed himself higher, making her softly cry out in surprised delight.

Their movements were subtle and slow, but so intense they held their breath through most of it, gasping for air only when reminded that they must. Their kisses were a carnal commingling of mouths. His fingers made deep impressions in the flesh of her hips and held her tightly to him, but her hands were never idle. They moved over his shoulders and arms, the back of his head and neck, his chest. Arching her back and reaching behind her, she ran her hands along his thighs, then caressed him between them. He groaned inarticulate ecstasy.

When he came, he wrapped his arms around her and laid his fevered cheek on her breast. His lips moved against her raised nipple. She couldn't understand the words he whispered, but they were spoken in such a sexy undertone and with a desperation for release so intense, they induced her own.

Later, they lay facing each other in his bed.

"What did you say?" she asked.

"When?"

She looked up at him and raised her eyebrows meaningfully.

"Oh. A string of dirty words, I think."

"Very erotic," she murmured, nudging his sex with her knee.

"Then I'll say them out loud next time."

He felt his nipple tighten at the touch of her fingertip, then to his supreme pleasure, she placed her open mouth over it and stroked it gently with her tongue. Keeping her lips against him, she said, "You knew I wanted this all along, didn't you?"

He was slow to find his voice but finally said, "I thought you might."

"You knew from the start?"

"From the piano bench."

She looked up at him. "On the piano bench, I thought you were one of the most arrogant bastards I'd ever had the misfortune to meet." Drawing her finger vertically down his chin, she added, "Also one of the most attractive."

"On the piano bench I was wondering how I was going to keep myself from groping you just to see if you were real. You were the sexiest woman I'd ever laid eyes on. Also one of the snootiest."

She laughed softly. "I wanted so badly to hate you." Then her expression changed and her tone became serious. "I want so badly to hate you now."

"You want to hate me for all the dirty work I do for Huff."

"Yes."

"I admire your integrity."

"Do you, Beck?"

"Yes. But can we leave your integrity and my shortage of it outside for a while?" he whispered. "At least until morning."

"You want me to stay?"

He hugged her closer. "Just try to leave."

They kissed long and leisurely while his hand moved from her breast to the soft, humid mystery of her sex, back to her breast and its hard tip. Since he'd met her, he'd entertained a thousand fantasies of her lying naked with him. But the reality far surpassed even his most arousing daydreams. Now that it was happening, he couldn't get enough of merely touching her.

When they pulled apart, he looked down the length of her. "You're beautiful, Sayre."

"Thank you."

"Not a single flaw."

That comment caused her drowsy smile to fade gradually. He felt her emotional withdrawal even before she sat up and pulled her knees to her chest, propping her chin on them.

"I'm flawed, Beck. You'd have been better off never to have met me."

"Not true."

"It is. I leave destruction in my wake. We Hoyles are notorious for that. It's our specialty. We leave people broken, irreparably damaged."

He placed his hand on her back. Her skin was incredibly smooth, pale compared to his. Her hips swelled gracefully out of her waist. On each side of her cleft was a shallow dimple, and that feminine trait made him ache with a tender longing he'd never felt before. He'd experienced desire too many times to count. Lust, shamefully often. But never this yearning to possess a woman's body, to know and have the entirety of her.

"What have you done that's destructive, Sayre?"

"I married two men I didn't love. I spent their money. Slept in their beds. And I barely remember what they looked like."

She turned her head to read his reaction, but he kept his features carefully schooled. He wanted her to elaborate on that period of her life. He wanted to know all the ugly details of it.

Turning away again, she spoke slowly and with seeming difficulty. "I wrecked their lives. Deliberately and with wanton self-interest. I had nothing against them personally, but I used them without regard or mercy. I was trying to punish Huff for taking Clark and my baby from me.

"I no longer cared about my own life, so long as I could make Huff's miserable. When he said marry,

I married, with the sole intention of wreaking havoc that would ultimately affect him. Those two men were victims of the infamous Hoyles and our talent for ruining lives."

"I don't feel a bit sorry for your so-called husbands," he said bitterly. "They married you knowing you didn't love them. They begged to be used. In return for their trouble, they had you in their beds. How old were you?"

"Nineteen when I married the first. Just turned twenty-one when I married the second."

"And how old were they?"

"Older. Much. Closer to Huff's age than to mine."

Two horny acquaintances of Huff's had known a good thing when they saw it. They'd grabbed at the opportunity to marry Sayre, even knowing it would probably be a temporary arrangement.

"They got to spend every night with a beautiful young woman. Unless you withheld . . ."

"No. I wish I could tell you I did," she said in a voice so low he could barely hear her. "But access to me was part of the bargain."

"Then you were used, too, weren't you?"

She rested her forehead on her knees. "Not a pretty past, is it?"

Although it cost him a jabbing pain to the rib cage, he sat up and placed his arms around her, pulling her back onto the pillows with him as he reclined. He brushed her hair away from her face and forced her to look at him. "Who could blame you for anything you did after what was done to you?"

"Last night, you overheard Huff and me. Everything?"

"Enough so that I now understand why you hate him so much."

She buried her face in his neck. "What they did to me was a carefully guarded secret. Not even my brothers knew. Not Selma. No one. I didn't have anyone to talk to about it, no one to share the grief."

"Clark?"

"He never even knew I was pregnant. I made the mistake of flaunting it to Huff before telling Clark. After the abortion, what good would it have done to tell him? The baby was gone. Knowing about it would only have made him as miserable as I was."

"You loved him too much to tell him."

"Something like that. I still hold him dear. Our courtship will always be a sweet memory, first love. But I anguish . . ." She stopped, and it was several seconds before she continued. "I anguish for my child. It was the only thing in my life, in the whole realm of the Hoyles, that was innocent. Clean. Pure. And Huff destroyed it."

Placing his hand beneath her chin, he tilted her face up. As tears rolled down her temples toward her hairline, he kissed them away.

Huskily she said, "I couldn't stand it if you pitied me."

"All right. Pity me."

He took her hand and folded it around his penis. As he kissed her deeply, his hand stayed on hers, guiding it, until she turned. She kissed all the bruises on his chest and stomach and lower.

"This was your fantasy, wasn't it, Beck? That day at the foundry, you said you didn't want a man distracted by my hair and—"

"And imagining it sweeping across his stomach. I gave myself away."

"You gave yourself away long before that," she whispered. Then she bent to him. Her mouth was by turns shy, provocative, and bold. But wet. And hot. Very.

He gasped her name, pulled her up and kissed her, tasting himself, tasting them on the kiss. Holding it, he separated her thighs and moved between them, stretching out on top of her.

"Doesn't that hurt?" she asked.

"Like bloody hell."

"Wouldn't you rather—"

"No. This is what I would rather." He thrust himself into her.

"Yes," she moaned. "Yes."

She surrendered completely. Her arms were bent at the elbows, her hands lying palm up on either side of her head. He aligned his palms with hers, then tightly laced their fingers. And when he began to move inside her, they were looking directly into each other's eyes.

"You don't want pity, so tell me what you want to hear, Sayre, and I'll say it."

"You don't have to say anything. Just . . ."

"What?"

"Go deep."

"I am deep. I'm so deep into you, I'm lost. What else?"

"Please . . ."

Her throat arched up. She clamped her teeth over her lower lip, and he felt her body closing around him like a fist. He watched the orgasmic blush spread across her breasts, her nipples harden. He gauged her rapid breathing, and when he knew she was close, he ground his pelvis against hers in small, rhythmic circles.

"Please what, Sayre?"

"Oh, God!"

"What?"

"Cover me," she cried helplessly.

He did. He let her absorb his weight, and they clung to each other as their bodies pulsed together and their hearts drummed in unison.

Later, she lay sleeping in the crook of his arm, her hand lying trustfully on his chest, her breath warm against his skin. He rested his chin on the top of her head and stared at the ceiling.

He'd wanted to fuck all that heartache out of her—Huff, the abortion, Clark Daly, all of it. He'd wanted to obliterate it, so she would realize one moment of peace and contentment, perhaps even joy. He'd wanted to give her one blinding instant of life without the taint of anger and regret.

And for those splendid, heart-stopping seconds of sexual abandon, he thought maybe he had.

But as he lay watching the revolving blades of the ceiling fan, he questioned exactly who had delivered whom.

chapter 33

*H*uff was on the front gallery having his morning coffee when Red Harper drove up in his official car. He got out, tucked a bundle of some sort under his arm, and approached the house in his plodding gait.

"You're out early for a Sunday morning," Huff remarked.

Climbing the steps seemed to require all Red's strength. His face was gray beneath his uniform hat, which he removed as soon as he reached the gallery. "No rest for the weary, Huff."

"Holler at Selma to bring you some coffee."

"No thanks. I can't stay that long. Just came to give you some news."

"I hope it's good news. That would be a change."

"Can't tell you how sorry I am about the goings-on at the plant."

"More to the point, there's nothing going on, thanks to those government sons of bitches."

Huff was in a truculent mood. He had slept in bouts, waking up frequently to find himself wound in sheets that reeked of his own sweat. As yesterday's events had gone from bad to worse, he'd kept on a good face for everyone. If he'd given the slightest indication that his confidence was shaken by OSHA's intrusion, or that his will was weakening, it would have been disastrous for the future of Hoyle Enterprises. He had appeared undaunted and optimistic, and would continue to.

But the performance was taking a toll on him.

Because in his most private self he was experiencing twinges of fear. He was riddled with uncertainties he hadn't felt since that evening his daddy had been bludgeoned to death before his eyes. From that day forward, fear had been his enemy. For decades he'd been convincing people that he was immune to it.

But as he watched Red Harper creakily lower himself into the other rocking chair, he wondered if he had fooled himself into believing that his fear was undetectable. Was it as apparent as the ravages of Red's cancer? Did everyone secretly regard him as aged, decrepit, even terminal?

Until only recently, a single word from him, one meaningful look, could shrivel the most pugnacious of men. Without that ability to instill fear, he would no longer be Huff Hoyle. Without his power to intimidate, he would be just another old man, impotent and stripped of dignity.

He looked toward the horizon where ordinarily smoke would be billowing from his blast furnaces. He had always fancied those streams of smoke as his signature that he'd written like a skywriter above his town.

Today there was no smoke, and he wondered if he, too, would disappear that quickly and completely. The thought brought him close to panic, which he tried to conceal with querulousness. "What's your news, Red?"

The sheriff winced as though he was in pain, which he probably was. "It's good news. And it isn't."

"Don't keep me in suspense. What's in the sack?"

"Evidence. I can't show you without risking contamination, but it pretty much nails Danny's killer."

"Well?"

"Slap Watkins."

"Good news, my ass," Huff bellowed, loudly smacking his hands together. "That's great news. I knew all along that swamp rat was involved." He motioned toward the sack. "What'd you find?"

"One of his biker friends called me before dawn this morning. He was letting Watkins stay at his place this weekend while he went up to Arkansas for a bikers' rally. By the time he got home late last night, Watkins had split. But he'd left behind a boot. When the guy saw that it was bloodstained, he called me."

"Danny's blood?"

"I don't know for certain yet, but that would be my guess. I'm going to send it to the crime lab in Orleans Parish for the tests. This biker was willing to give Watkins a place to hide so long as he was only wanted for questioning. But when he found this," he said, holding up the sack, "well, he wanted no part of aiding and abetting a murderer.

He cooperated completely. We searched the house high and low, but this is all we found belonging to Watkins. Looks to me like when he cleared out, he accidentally dropped this boot.

"And that brings me to the bad news. We still haven't located him. When he realizes he left behind his boot, he'll know his goose is cooked and that he's got nothing to lose by taking out another Hoyle."

"He could have killed Chris the other night on the road."

"Naw, he wanted to prick with him first. That's like a Watkins. One of his half brothers, I believe it was, stalked his ex-girlfriend for months, threatening to kill her, before he actually got around to it.

"Besides, Slap wouldn't have done anything too drastic with Beck as a witness. As for his coming into Sayre's room . . . Well, let's just say I'm real glad we found this evidence after Watkins paid her a visit and not before, else he might have really hurt her.

"He'll go to death row for Danny. He might figure they can't give him the needle twice, so he'd just as well go all out. That said, want me to station a deputy over here?"

"I can take care of myself."

"I was afraid you'd say that."

"I wish he would come here. I'd like a crack at him."

"I was afraid you'd say that, too, and that's the main reason I wanted a deputy here. As much for Watkins's protection as yours. Be careful, Huff. This is no wayward boy we're dealing with. Slap was mean and violent before Angola, and he only came out meaner. Not too smart, though. Can't figure why he didn't destroy the clothes he was wearing that Sunday."

"No Watkins I ever knew was any too bright."

"Stupidity is probably what'll do him in. I figure if we give him enough rope he'll hang himself." Then he said, "I truly am sorry about what's happened at the foundry, Huff."

The way one thought had segued into the other made Huff wonder if, somewhere in between, Red had stopped referring to Slap Watkins and had started referring to him. Was even this sick old man losing confidence in him?

"It'll be back up and running in no time," he said. "Nothing can keep me down, Red. You ought to know that by now."

Red stared out across the lawn. "I'm glad to have this evidence against Watkins," he said after a prolonged silence. "If this blood turns out to be Danny's, it seals the case against him. I can tell you this now, Huff, I was a little worried that maybe Chris . . . Well . . ."

The two men exchanged a long look. Finally the sheriff said quietly, "There's also this." From the breast pocket of his shirt, he withdrew an envelope and laid it on the small table between the two rocking chairs.

"What's that?"

"The information you asked me to get on Charles Nielson."

"What have you learned?"

"It's all in there."

"Good stuff? How much is it going to cost me?"

Red didn't return his grin. "Nothing, Huff. This one's on the house."

"That's a first."

"Actually it's the last." Red used the arms of the rocker to lever himself out of it. "We had a good run. For a long time, we made sure things went your way. But this finishes it. I'm out of it now. I'm washing my hands of it. You understand? I'll never betray you, but I won't help you with this." He pointed down at the envelope. "Whatever you do from here on, you're on your own."

Red didn't look like he had enough stamina to make it back to his car, much less execute the duties of his office, or carry out his extracurricular duties for Huff. At least he recognized his weakness and had the good sense to relinquish his responsibilities. Anyone afflicted with either a physical ailment or moral uncertainty was of no use to Huff Hoyle.

"Take care of yourself, Red."

"Too late for that." Then he hitched his chin toward the house. "Better warn Chris that Watkins is still at large and probably more desperate than before. Sayre, too. Tell them to keep an eye out."

"Sure thing."

Red replaced his hat and hobbled down the steps. He didn't look back. He didn't wave as he drove away.

Huff retrieved the envelope the sheriff had left on the table and went into the house, calling loudly for Selma.

She came from the kitchen, wiping her hands on her apron. "Need more coffee?"

"I'll get it myself." He peeled back the flap on the envelope. "Go upstairs and wake Chris. Tell him I need to talk to him."

"He's not here."

Huff stopped what he was doing, realizing now that Chris's car hadn't been out front. "Where'd he go this early?"

"He didn't spend the night here, Mr. Hoyle. He called late last night, told me not to disturb you, but wanted you to know that he was staying the night at the fishing camp. I forgot to mention it to you—"

Huff left Selma apologizing for not telling him sooner and went quickly to the nearest telephone, in his den. He called Chris's cell number. It rang four times before it was answered by his voice mail. "Come on, Son, answer."

His fingers had turned clumsy. The muscles of his chest clenched around his heart, which was beating like a son of a bitch, as though he'd actually suffered a recent heart attack. He punched in the sequence of numbers again, but the result was the same.

Wasting no more time, Huff dropped the phone and went to the gun cabinet.

At some point during the night, the antique air conditioner had shut itself off and failed to recycle. Chris lay on the hard, narrow bed amid a jumble of damp and dingy sheets that smelled of mildew. He was wearing only his boxer shorts, and even that much clothing was cloying in the stifling heat.

It was almost as hot this morning as it had been

on that Sunday two weeks ago when Danny had been shot to death in this very room.

Had it only been two weeks? It seemed like ten years.

The old wood floor had soaked up Danny's blood like a sponge. Chris doubted the discoloration would ever come out, no matter how much chemical scouring it underwent.

He'd come here to escape the pressures of yesterday. One good thing that had come out of it: he had settled that matter with Lila. He would be cleared of all suspicion of Danny's murder as soon as she talked to Red, which she would do in order to save George's job.

But the plant was silent. Which had caused Huff to rant like a madman.

Unable to stand any more of Huff's ravings, in addition to the reporters who kept calling him for a comment, Chris had isolated himself at the fishing camp, the last place anyone would look for him.

It guaranteed him privacy, which he needed, but the place had lost its allure. He used to have fine times out here with buddies, drinking, fishing, playing poker marathons that lasted for entire weekends, guys enjoying the rusticity of the camp.

But both he and the camp had gotten older. He'd matured; the cabin had become derelict. Maybe it was time to sell it. With those bloodstains on the floor, how could he and Huff ever enjoy it again?

They could buy a boat instead. Or a beach house. Biloxi maybe. Although Huff hated Mississippi for reasons known only to him. He—

Chris actually smelled him before he heard the

planks on the porch squeak beneath his weight. Seconds later he came crashing through the door.

Chris sat bolt upright.

"Don't move, Hoyle. I'd hate to have to kill you right off. Before I slit you open from gullet to gonads, I got some things to say to you."

In one hand, Slap Watkins was wielding his knife. In the other he held several articles of clothing, which he threw at Chris. They landed in his lap. He took one look at them, then recoiled and frantically flung them off.

Watkins laughed. "That's right. That's what come from your baby brother's head. It splattered like a pumpkin that fell off a tall truck."

Chris glowered at him.

"What's the matter, Hoyle? Are you too prissy to hear the grisly details? Too bad, 'cause I'm gonna tell you anyway." He propped one foot on the end of the bed as though they were old friends about to have a casual conversation.

"Danny boy told me he was expecting to meet you here. He warned me that you could show up at any time, so why didn't I just take whatever I wanted and leave before you got here and called the cops.

"Ain't that a hoot? He thought I'd come to rob the place." He gave the surroundings a scornful glance. "As if I'd want anything. This place makes my prison cell look like a palace."

Chris inched closer to the edge of the bed.

"No you don't," Slap warned. "You're gonna sit there and listen, and if you so much as blink, I'm gonna pop your eye out with the tip of this knife and then you won't need to blink no more, will you?"

He paused to let the threat sink in and assure himself that Chris was going to comply, then he said, "Where was I? Oh, yeah. Brother Danny. When I took the shotgun off the rack, he commenced to praying. The prayers got louder as I loaded the thing. I have to tell you that it came as a relief to shut him up when I poked the barrels into his mouth." He paused a second, then leaned slightly forward and in a stage whisper said, "Bang!"

Slap laughed again. "Messy as all get out, but almost too easy. He didn't even fight me. Oh, he put up some token resistance, but nothing that a little intimidation didn't put a stop to, and right quick."

"You're a moron for saving those clothes. Why didn't you get rid of them?"

"I wanted you to see what Hoyle brains and blood look like. Surprise! Ain't no different from anybody else's."

"Why did you break in on Sayre?"

"Yeah, I thought that might yank everybody's chain." He winked and smacked his lips. "I'd sure like her yanking something of mine, know what I mean?"

"Very clever, the Bible story."

"I thought so. Thought that up all by myself." Then he scowled. "But you only got me to talking about that to distract me from the business at hand. Ain't gonna happen. No sir." Leering, he leaned in closer and said, "I get to kill my second Hoyle. Am I lucky or what?"

*   *   *

Beck was framed in the back door, watching Frito tree a squirrel, when Sayre entered the kitchen. He was wearing only a pair of cargo shorts. His back was a patchwork quilt of bruises. Moving up behind him, she slid her arms around his waist and kissed a mean purple bruise on his shoulder.

"Good morning."

"Good and getting better." He turned around and pulled her against him, kissing her lips tenderly. When they pulled apart, he took in her dishabille and smiled.

She had put on one of his old college T-shirts, which had been laundered so many times the LSU logo was almost unreadable. "Very fetching," he said.

"You think so?"

"Hm." He rubbed his knuckles across the V of her bikini panties. Sayre reached for the fly of his shorts and began undoing the buttons. Putting their foreheads together, they laughed softly at the absurdity of their desire, which a night of lovemaking had failed to quench.

But Frito wasn't happy. Simultaneously they became aware of him scratching at the screened door and whining for being excluded.

Beck looked at her and arched his eyebrow. "What do you think?"

"I don't think I could live with my guilty conscience."

"Me neither, dammit." He released her and opened the screened door for the dog, who bounded in, grabbed one of his discarded tennis balls, and carried it over to them.

The ball landed soggily on Sayre's bare foot. She made a face of distaste but patted his head and thanked him for the gift.

Beck poured each of them a cup of coffee and sat down at the kitchen table. Sayre took the chair opposite his and began idly scratching Frito behind the ears.

"He's got a huge crush on you," Beck remarked.

"He told you that?"

"He didn't have to. Look at his face. He's dotty."

The dog was indeed looking up at her with unabashed adoration. She took a sip of her coffee. Setting her cup down slowly, she said, "I'm going to hate myself for this later."

"For last night?"

"No, I have no regrets about last night."

"My only regret is that it didn't last long enough," he said. "And that I wasted an hour of it sleeping."

"Barely an hour."

"Much too long."

"And even during that hour you were . . ."

"Yes. I was," he said huskily. "And you were so . . . snug."

They shared a long intimate look, then he asked what she was going to hate herself for.

"For asking the morning-after question."

"The 'where do we go from here' question?"

"So you've been asked that before?"

"Asked, but I've never honored it with an answer."

"I've never asked before."

He hesitated, then got up and moved to the back

door again. Frito picked up his tennis ball and padded over to him, hoping that it was playtime. But Beck didn't move, only stared through the screen.

"If you have to think about it that long, I suppose that's answer enough." She scraped back her chair and stood up.

He came around quickly. "Sayre."

"You don't owe me any explanation, Beck. Certainly no promises. I'm not a silly girl with stars in my eyes. Last night we responded to an emotionally charged situation, along with a mutual physical attraction. We did what we wanted to at the time, and it felt great in the dark. But it's daylight now and—"

"Can you doubt for one instant that I want to eat you alive?" His tone so closely bordered on anger that it took her aback and checked anything else she was about to say. "Sayre, I wanted you the minute I met you. And every time I've been near you since. And last night. And right now, this moment. And I'll want you tomorrow and each day after that from now on. But—"

"But between Huff and me, you choose Huff."

"It's not that simple."

"Isn't it?"

"No."

"I think it is."

"There are things at play that you don't know about and I can't tell you," he said. "I must finish what I started."

"Will there ever be a finish to your protecting Huff and Chris? How far will you go for them, Beck? You took a beating for them yesterday. You got spat on because of them. People scorn, mistrust, and revile you. And for their sake, you take it. Don't you ever get tired of it?"

His eyes speared into hers. "You have no idea."

"Then leave them!"

"I can't."

"What's stopping you?"

"I made a commitment. My life is inextricably bound to them. I don't want it to be, especially after the night I just spent with you, but it is. It is a fact of my life."

His jaw was set and his mouth a stern line of resolve. The bottle-green eyes that had looked at her with such smoky desire only a few minutes ago had turned guarded and cold.

"So it is," she whispered. "God help you."

His telephone intruded with a shrill ring. She held his stare through the second ring, then he cursed softly and answered. "Hello?"

As he listened, his expression changed like the mercurial transitions of a kaleidoscope. "When? Where?" Obviously distressed by what he was hearing, he dragged his hand down his face. "Aw, Jesus, it was fatal? He's dead?"

chapter 34

By the time Beck and Sayre reached the fishing camp, he had to jockey for a parking space among squad cars and other emergency vehicles. Law officers, paramedics, and a photographer from the local newspaper were milling around in the yard between the cabin and the bank of Bayou Bosquet, talking among themselves.

As the photographer backed up to take a shot of the cabin, he accidentally stepped on the stuffed alligator in the yard and jumped in fright, to the amusement of those around him.

The mood was more grim inside the cabin, where the parish medical examiner was supervising the removal of Slap Watkins's body.

Beck and Sayre stood aside as the gurney carrying the black plastic body bag was wheeled past them toward the waiting ambulance. After the door had closed on it, they joined the group huddled around the front steps of the cabin.

Red Harper, Wayne Scott, and Huff were there with Chris, who was seated on one of the treads.

He was dressed only in a pair of slacks, his torso and feet bare and streaked with blood. He was holding a cigarette, which he had smoked halfway down.

He glanced at Sayre, then greeted Beck with a weak smile. "Thanks for getting here so soon."

"Are you all right?"

"Shaky." He raised the hand holding the cigarette. It was trembling.

"What happened?"

Beck posed the question to the group at large, but Deputy Scott was the first to respond. "According to Mr. Hoyle, Watkins barged in, taunted him with the clothes he'd worn when he killed Danny in that very room, and then threatened to kill him, too."

Chris addressed Beck. "The other night, on the road, maybe because you were with me, I wasn't afraid of him. He was just being an asshole. But this morning, he was . . . I don't know, psychopathic. He meant to kill me, and if I hadn't been damn lucky he would have."

In a bolstering gesture, Huff squeezed Chris's shoulder. Beck wondered if he was the only one who had noticed the pistol stuck in Huff's belt.

"Watkins had the clothes he was wearing when he killed Danny?" Sayre asked. "He brought them here?"

Sheriff Harper pointed to a brown paper sack, which Beck recognized as an evidence bag that would better preserve DNA evidence. "A boot belonging to him was turned over to us earlier this morning." He told them the circumstances. "I warned Huff that when Watkins realized we had this evidence, he would be even more dangerous to y'all. I told him to keep his guard up. We couldn't alert Chris in time."

"I didn't have my cell phone on," Chris explained. "I got tired of media people calling me for a statement about the shutdown. I turned off my phone when I got here last night. I didn't know to be on the lookout for Slap."

"How did Watkins know you were here?" Beck asked.

"Obviously he's been surveilling us. Driving past your house. Meeting us on the road. Breaking into Sayre's motel room. If he was watching this place, my car would have been easy to spot." He nodded toward the Porsche. "Maybe he came to leave those clothes just to mock us. They're caked with . . ." He glanced at Huff and amended what he was about to say. "Who knows why he did anything? He didn't think like a normal person. This morning he was maniacal."

"How did you defend yourself?"

"The old-fashioned way. He was being a smartaleck, propped one foot on the bed, which left his crotch vulnerable. I kicked him in the balls as hard as I could. However, I must have missed the sweet spot because it didn't completely disable him. He fell backward but managed to hold on to his knife.

"When I tried to get it away from him, he took a slash at me, missed, tried again, but this time I managed to catch his wrist. We fought for control of the knife. He lost, fell on the blade. I think it must've severed a major blood vessel in his gut because blood poured out of him. I tried to stop it, but he was dead within minutes."

Beck looked at Deputy Scott. "Clearly it was self-defense."

"Sure looks like that." He offered his hand down to Chris. "I owe you an apology, Mr. Hoyle, for all the inconvenience and embarrassment I've caused you. Mostly I'm sorry I suspected you in the first place."

Chris shook his hand. "You were only doing your job. We Hoyles need a man like you to protect our town, right, Huff?"

"Right."

Blushing over their approval, the deputy retrieved the evidence bag. "I'll get this back to the office and log it," he said to Red. "If you'd like, I can drive it to New Orleans."

"Thanks. Soon as I get back to the office, I'll type up a statement for Chris to sign."

The deputy touched the brim of his hat and nodded at Sayre. "Ma'am." He left, taking the evidence bag with him.

Chris inhaled deeply on the cigarette one final time, then ground it out on the step. "I'll be glad to put all this behind me. Being a suspect in a murder case is no party. It's also distracted me from the plant and the mess we've got there." He shot a dirty look toward Sayre but didn't address her participation in the events leading up to the shutdown.

The ambulance bearing the body had already departed. Gradually others began to leave. Red Harper was the last to drive away. "He looks worse than Slap," Chris remarked of the sheriff.

"He's got cancer."

Shocked, they all turned toward Huff.

"Bad?" Chris asked.

"Let's just say it's a good thing we now have Wayne Scott playing on our team."

"He hasn't signed a letter of intent yet," Chris said.

"Contrition can make a man agreeable. I think now would be an ideal time for you to send him a thank-you note with a little gift inside."

Chris returned Huff's conspiratorial grin. "First thing tomorrow."

"I'm going down to the water," Sayre said stiffly. "Call me when you're ready to leave, Beck."

Chris, looking amused, watched her stalk away. "I think we've offended Sayre. Or is she just pissed off that she was so wrong about me?"

Beck didn't have an answer for him, and Huff was only half listening. He was appraising the facade of the ramshackle cabin. "I should sell this camp."

"I was thinking along those same lines this morning, even before Slap arrived," Chris said. "None of us will want to come out here after this."

"Handle the sale, will you, Beck?" Huff said. "I don't want anything more to do with this place."

"I'll take care of it." Beck motioned at the pistol. "What did you intend to do with that?"

"I couldn't reach Chris to warn him about Watkins. Panicked a little, I guess. But as it turns out, with good reason. When I got here, saw all those squad cars that had converged on the place, I suffered several minutes of pure hell, thinking I was too late." Again he clamped his hand on Chris's shoulder. "When I think of what could have happened . . ."

"Now, Huff," Chris chided. "Don't go soft on us."

"And put the pistol away before you hurt somebody or shoot off your own manhood."

Huff laughed. "Will do, Beck." He motioned toward the road behind the cabin. "I had to park down the road a piece. I'm on my way to the plant. We need to talk about how we're going to handle these OSHA inspectors."

"Handle them?" Beck said.

Huff winked at him. "They might be more obliging if we threw them a bone in the form of somebody expendable."

"I'm way ahead of you, Huff," Chris said. He told them about the bargain he'd struck with Lila. "As it turns out, we don't need her to clear me. But that's not to say that George won't come in handy as a fall guy."

"Okay then, that's the plan," Huff said. "Y'all coming?"

Chris looked down at the blood spatters on his chest and frowned with disgust. "I'll be along as soon as I wash off."

"I'll stay here with Chris until he leaves," Beck said.

Huff raised his hand in a wave, then disappeared around the corner of the cabin.

Chris went inside only long enough to retrieve his shirt and shoes. "I put my clothes in the closet when I undressed last night," he told Beck when he came out. "Good thing, too. It looks like a slaughterhouse and smells like a meat market in there."

Beck followed Chris down to the edge of the fishing pier, where there was a water faucet and several yards of rubber hose they used when they cleaned fish. A porcelain basin and several bars of soap were also left there for washing up afterward.

Sayre turned at the hollow sound of their footfalls on the pier. Chris said to her, "Unless you want your eyes opened to what a real man looks like, you'd better turn your back because I'm about to strip."

"You're in an awfully chipper mood for someone who just knifed a man to death."

"Would you have rather he knifed me? No, don't answer. It might hurt my feelings."

"How can you be so blasé, Chris? Does nothing affect you?"

He thought about it for a moment, then gave an indolent shrug. "Not much, no."

She looked at him with disgust. "You're a bastard, Chris. You always have been."

"No, what I am is Huff Hoyle's favored firstborn son. And always have been. And always will be. And that's always stuck in your craw."

"I'm sure it stokes your colossal ego to think that, but you couldn't be more wrong."

Beck, seeing that nothing would be gained by this brewing quarrel, played the diplomat and stepped between them. "Take my pickup," he told Sayre. "I'm going to the plant for a meeting with Chris and Huff, but I'll catch up with you later. Where will you be?"

When she looked at him, he realized that even though Chris's phone call had interrupted the discussion about the future of their relationship, the discussion was in fact over. In her eyes he saw disillusionment. Disappointment, perhaps. Disdain, certainly. "I'll be in San Francisco."

She sidestepped him and walked briskly up the pier. Beck watched her climb into his pickup, execute a three-point turn, then drive away without another glance in his direction. Staying behind and watching her leave was the most difficult thing he'd ever had to do.

He wanted to run after her, but even if she stopped, which he was certain she wouldn't, what would he say that hadn't already been said?

"Well, that was certainly . . . ah, poignant," Chris said, tongue in cheek. "If you need to take a moment to collect yourself—"

"Shut up, Chris."

Snuffling a laugh, he took off his trousers. His boxer shorts, Beck noted, were saturated with blood. After removing them, Chris turned on the faucet and washed vigorously with a bar of soap, even his hair.

When he finished, he sluiced water off his skin and shook it out of his hair, then dressed, leaving his undershorts behind. Together they walked to his car and headed for the foundry. They were almost there when Chris noticed Beck tentatively dabbing the cut on his cheekbone.

"It could have been worse," Chris remarked. "Think about Clark Daly."

"I have," Beck said somberly.

Entering the plant, now silent and empty except for the security guards, was a surreal experience. They went up to the executive offices. All were empty, even Huff's.

"He must have stopped somewhere along the way," Chris said. "But let's wait for him in here. I need a drink. Want one?"

"It's ten o'clock in the morning."

"But it's been that kind of morning."

While Chris was pouring his drink, Beck moved to the window and looked out over the shop floor. The OSHA inspection would begin on Monday. For now, the place was deserted. It was still dark, still dirty, still hot even though the furnaces had been turned off.

What was Sayre doing? Was she at The Lodge now, packing, making travel arrangements to California? Would he ever see her again?

Chris carried his drink with him to the sofa. Sinking into the cushions, he tilted his face toward the ceiling and closed his eyes. "Some two weeks, huh?"

"Some two weeks. Sort of symmetric that it started and ended at the fishing camp, on a Sunday."

"Maybe that's what Watkins had in mind."

"I don't think he had in mind to get a knife in his belly."

"No, but he wanted to put one in mine." After a short silence, Chris said, "Did Sayre spend the night at your place?"

"Yes."

"No contraceptives necessary."

Beck turned and looked at him sharply.

"Huff told me. He said Sayre had a female problem that had made her sterile. That put an end to his scheme for you to marry her and beget offspring."

"She wouldn't have me anyway." Beck crossed the room and leaned against the edge of Huff's desk, too restless to sit down.

"Too bad it didn't pan out. It would have been convenient to have a lawyer in the family. On the other hand, I'm glad Huff's plan went awry. Want to hear a confession, Beck?"

Chris finished his whiskey in one swallow and set the empty glass on the end table. "Of late, I was becoming jealous of you. True," he said, sensing Beck's surprise. "When Huff won't listen to anybody else, he'll listen to you. He's vested you with authority he hasn't given to anyone outside the family. Now if, on top of all that, you had sired his first grandchild out of my sister, I would not have liked it."

Chris's engaging smile was still in place, but Beck heard the echo of Sayre's warning: *I'll tell you about Chris. He isn't your friend.*

"Nobody could replace you in Huff's affection, Chris. In any case, I wouldn't even want to."

"Glad to hear it, Beck. Glad to hear it." Sighing, Chris leaned back and stacked his hands on the crown of his head. "But you know what this means, don't you? The responsibility of giving Huff an heir falls to me after all. I've got to father a child in order to keep Huff's dynasty alive. Actually, I wouldn't have it any other way. That's how it should be.

"Sayre abandoned the family. It would have been unfair if no sooner than she reappeared she gets pregnant with Huff's desired grandchild. Danny couldn't stop praying long enough to have a baby with that titmouse he was about to marry. That leaves me. Huff will be on me to—"

"What?" Beck's lungs and heart seized up. He could barely breathe. "What did you say?"

Chris looked at him blankly. "What?"

"About Danny. About the woman he was going to marry."

Chris's expression remained impassive for several seconds, then gradually a sly smile appeared, and finally he laughed. "Son of a bitch. I'd come close to slipping so many times, but until now I always caught myself."

"You knew Danny was engaged?"

He gave Beck a derisive look. "No matter how clever Danny thought he was being by sneaking around to see her, he should have known Huff would find out."

"Huff knew, too?"

"And evidently so did you. When did Danny tell you?"

"He didn't. Sayre did."

"How did she know?" Chris asked.

"She met his fiancée at his grave site."

"Was she singing?"

"Singing?"

"That's what she does, sings at that Holy Roller church. She's the one who influenced Danny to join the congregation. Convert. Confess. Get baptized. The whole nine yards.

"Huff and I let it go for a while, thinking it was an infatuation that would soon wear itself out. But when we realized how serious it had become, the engagement ring and all, we pinned him down about it.

"We said we were glad he'd finally shown some inclinations toward romance, even marriage, but we disapproved of his choice. Huff ordered him to break the engagement, never see her again, and never return to that church."

"The fiancée didn't know you and Huff were aware of their engagement."

"I guess Danny didn't want to tell her. He hoped to win our approval. Beck, the guy was completely brainwashed. He started *praying* for us. Can you believe that? Dropped to his knees right there by Huff's recliner and started praying out loud for our salvation. He went on for ten minutes about how we needed to be washed clean of our sin and iniquity. I thought Huff was going to have a stroke."

Beck's heart was thudding. "Danny wanted to come clean about Iverson, didn't he?"

"Pardon me?"

"That was the obstacle, the cause of his emotional turmoil. Danny couldn't marry this woman he loved until he had purged his conscience and confessed his sin against Gene Iverson. Except he couldn't do that without fingering you and Huff. Danny knew that Huff had killed Iverson and—"

"Huff did no such thing." Chris got up and poured himself another drink. "If I keep this up, I'll be drunk by lunchtime. Can't see that it matters, though." He motioned toward the windows. "It's not a workday."

He sat back down and looked at Beck. Beck stared back at him. Finally, Chris broke a slow smile. "You're just itching to know, aren't you? Okay, I'll tell you. It was an ac-ci-dent," he said, emphasizing the syllables.

"You?"

Chris made an offhand gesture. "I followed Iverson out of the meeting that night. I confronted him in the employee parking lot. I had taken a hammer with me, just to give some punch to my warning that he keep his mouth shut about the union and stop making trouble.

"The fool charged me like a bull, forcing me to fight back. I was only trying to protect myself. I don't remember hitting him that hard, but next thing I know, I'm holding a bloody ball-peen and he's got a hole in his head the size of a half-dollar.

"*Shit*, I'm thinking. *Shit!* I panicked. I ran back into the plant and got Huff. I was scared somebody was going to come along and see Iverson lying there, but it was between shift changes, so no one was in the parking lot.

"Huff calmly assessed the situation. He believed me when I told him that it had been self-defense, but who needed an inquest, he asked. No, he said, the fastest solution to the problem would be to make the body disappear. Which was a smart decision. If the DA had seen that hole in Iverson's skull, he might have been able to make a more convincing case against me.

"Anyhow, Huff told me where to bury the body,

and how to do it, and recruited Danny to help me. Meanwhile he and Red Harper cleaned up the mess in the parking lot and took care of Iverson's car. You know, now that I think on it, I never asked what happened to it. Hm."

"Where did you bury him?"

Chris chuckled. "You're my lawyer, Beck. You can't divulge anything I confide in you. But some things I'm not completely comfortable telling you." He gazed at Beck with a mix of amusement and vexation. "Stop looking at me like that. It's not like I meant to kill him. He was dead and nothing was going to change that. I got on with the rest of my life. Of course I had to go through the trial, which was a pain, but it worked out all right."

"You never really feared any consequences, did you, Chris? Because you'd seen Huff get away with killing Sonnie Hallser."

"Hallser?" He frowned as though trying to place the name. "I was just a kid. I barely remember that."

"You're lying, Chris. You were there. You saw what happened, and it made a lasting impression on you."

He leaned back and placed his arms along the top of the sofa as though inviting Beck to talk.

Beck got up and began to pace. "Those days, employees worked two ten-hour shifts, with a four-hour break in between for maintenance and so forth. Huff was about to change that. Go to three eight-hour shifts, eliminating that important time for inspections and repairs. That was the substance of his quarrel with Sonnie Hallser."

"He was the workers' appointed spokesperson," Chris said. "He was a stand-up kind of guy. Everybody liked him, even Huff. The problem with Mr. Hallser was, he took his role of employee representative too seriously. He was close to sounding prounion. I think he might have been working as a spy for the union all along."

"Huff had made up his mind about changing the shifts and nobody was going to talk him out of it," Beck said, thinking out loud. "The shop floor was deserted except for Hallser, who was working on that machine above the sandpit. Huff confronted him. They quarreled. Huff pushed him into that machine and started it up, and you saw it. That man got crushed so severely he was cut almost in half. You saw that, didn't you, Chris?"

"How could I have seen that, when I wasn't even there?"

"Huff told me you were."

Chris was taken aback by that. "Really? Well, even if I was, I didn't see anything." He tilted his head and gave Beck a long look. "Why are we talking about this? And why do you seem upset?"

"Every attorney wants his client to be innocent."

"Oh, I doubt that. If everyone was innocent you'd be out of business. Actually I'm relieved that you finally know about Iverson. We shouldn't keep secrets from each other. Otherwise, how will there ever be any trust between us?"

"You didn't trust me with the secret of Danny's engagement."

"True. I hate that I let that cat out of the bag."

"Because your and Huff's problem wasn't just

the young woman's piety. It was Danny's determination to confess."

Chris swore beneath his breath. "He was going to blab to Jesus and the whole world what happened to Iverson."

"Do you realize what this means to your case?"

"Case? What case? There's no longer a *case*, Beck. Remember Wayne Scott's humble apology for suspecting me? If I'd been wearing a ring he would have kissed it."

"You had a powerful motive for killing your brother."

Chris shook his head and laughed softly. "You think *I* killed Danny?"

"Did you?"

"I had an alibi. Sweet Lila, remember."

"*Did you?*" he shouted.

"No, Beck. I didn't."

Chris was smiling when his cell phone rang. He answered it, his smile turning into a frown. "What is it, George?" He listened. "Right now? How long will it take? All right," he said reluctantly. "I'll be right down."

Chris disconnected. "He's nervous about the inspection on Monday and wants me to look at the drive belt on that conveyor while it's running, see if I think it'll pass muster. His ass is on the line because he signed off on the repair of it. He's afraid he's going to be left holding a bag of shit, and he's right. But until we fire him I guess I'd better humor him. I've got the only key to that machine, so I'm the only one who can restart it. I knew this lockdown-tagout nonsense would be a pain."

"We were talking about your motive for murder," Beck said.

"No, *you* were. Slap Watkins was the culprit. It's a dead subject. Get over it, Beck."

And to Beck's consternation, Chris walked out.

chapter 35

*P*arked at the Dairy Queen, eating a Blizzard with peanut M&M's, Huff laughed with self-derision as he pulled the .357 pistol from his belt and carefully laid it on the passenger seat.

He supposed toting the weapon had made him look a bit ridiculous, but he would have had no compunction about shooting Slap Watkins right between the eyes. It was a foregone conclusion that he had to die.

Now that he was in the morgue, the whole mess was over and done with.

Huff thought that maybe a visit to Danny's grave would be appropriate. He hadn't been to the cemetery since the funeral. Yes, he would go today and take flowers.

Wouldn't be too long, he would be attending Red's funeral, he thought sadly. He was going to miss—

And that was when he remembered the envelope Red had left with him that morning. He'd stuffed it into his pants pocket when Selma informed him that Chris was at the fishing cabin. In his haste to warn Chris, and with all that had come afterward, he hadn't thought of it again until now.

With Slap Watkins no longer a worry, and Chris in the clear, he could confront the issues at Hoyle Enterprises with singular concentration and renewed energy. The OSHA inspection had supplanted Charles Nielson as his main concern, but Nielson had been integral to the shutdown, and by God, he was going to pay for that.

Huff removed the envelope from his pocket. Inside was a single sheet of paper, folded like a business letter. This morning when he'd asked Red what he'd unearthed about Nielson, he had replied, "It's all in there."

But if this was all the information Red and his contacts in New Orleans had obtained, it was precious little. To Huff's disappointment, there were only a few typewritten lines on the sheet.

"Dammit." Red was old and sick, and his work had become sloppy.

Huff had hoped for more to work with, a character flaw or bad habit that would leave Nielson vulnerable to attack. Was he a gambler, tax evader, drug user? Did he like kiddie porn? Did he have multiple DUIs? Huff was searching for something in the man's life that, if exploited or exposed, could destroy his credibility.

Huff put on a pair of reading glasses, which he used only when no one was around, and read what Sheriff Harper had uncovered about his nemesis.

Seconds later, a family van was nearly driven off the road by Huff Hoyle as he sped out of the Dairy Queen parking lot. He had dropped the paper cup with what was left of his Blizzard onto the floorboard. As it rolled with the erratic motions of the speeding car, it slung a sticky, melting goo onto the floor mats.

By the time Huff reached Hoyle Enterprises, that goo had turned to milky liquid. Huff didn't think twice of it. But he remembered to get the pistol from off the passenger seat.

Sayre was latching her overnight bag when someone knocked on the motel room door. She pushed aside the window drape and looked outside. "Red?" Alarmed, she opened the door. "What's happened now?"

"I didn't mean to scare you, Sayre. Nothing's happened, far as I know." He removed his hat. "Can I come in?"

She waved him inside and indicated the packed bag. "You just caught me. I've booked a flight this afternoon out of New Orleans."

"You're going back to San Francisco?"

"That's where I belong now."

"I thought maybe you and Beck . . ."

"No."

This morning she had drawn a line in the sand. He had remained on the opposing side of it with Huff and Chris. As she was packing, she had vacillated between tossing the strand of Mardi Gras beads he'd bought her into the nearest trash can or taking it with her. Ultimately she had wrapped it in a T-shirt and placed it in her bag. One memento. She allowed herself that.

"I won't be seeing Beck again before I leave."

"Huh. Well." Red looked around the room as though at a loss as to what to say next. When his eyes finally reconnected with hers, she noticed the pinched look of pain at the corners of them. "Have you talked to Huff this morning?" he asked.

Rather than explaining what he was doing here, his questions were becoming more perplexing. "Only at the fishing camp." Again, he seemed to zone out. Several moments ticked by. Finally she said, "I haven't got much time, Red. What did you want to see me about? Is it something to do with Danny? Watkins?"

"No. That's pretty much wrapped up."

"Which is why I can go home. I vowed to stay in Destiny until I knew what had happened to Danny. I can return to my life now."

He nodded, but it was an absentminded motion, as though he really hadn't heard her and didn't really care what her plans were. He cleared his throat. "Sayre, I take full responsibility for my own actions and won't lay blame for them on anybody else's doorstep. I would never double-cross Huff. I want you to understand that."

She indicated that she did, when in fact she didn't have a clue what he was trying to say.

"We colluded on lots of things I'm not proud of. At first it seemed harmless enough to bend a few rules, then, I don't know, I just got caught up in it. Like in a net. I couldn't find my way out." He raised his hands helplessly as though asking for her understanding and absolution. "But what's done is done. I can't go back and fix things.

"But the future is something else," he continued. "I'm telling you this because I want somebody else to know the way things are in case . . . well, in case something bad happens and I'm not around to give the truth of it."

"Truth of what? Tell me what?"

"Beck Merchant is Charles Nielson."

The room seemed to tilt. "What?"

"I had some guys I know in New Orleans—private investigator types—checking Nielson out for Huff. Fact is, there is no Charles Nielson, just somebody made up by Beck."

She lowered herself to the arm of the chair, the nearest place to sit down.

"Now, I don't know why he worked up such an elaborate charade," Red said. "Don't really want to know. But my last official duty to Huff was to give him that information this morning."

"Oh my God."

"Out at the fishing camp, Huff didn't let on like he knew yet. But anytime now, he could open the envelope I left with him and read what's inside. When he does, I don't know how he'll react."

She shot to her feet. "Like hell you don't, you gutless old bastard."

She shoved him out of her way and ran for the door. The tires of the rental convertible smoked on the hot asphalt as she pulled onto the highway. She leaned on her horn if another motorist dared to get in her path as she sped toward her old home, thinking that was where Chris would probably want to go once they left the camp.

She couldn't even consider the implications of Beck's being the elusive Nielson, or his reasons for scamming them all. Her only thought was to prevent Huff from finding out before she could warn Beck.

She shook the contents of her handbag into the passenger seat and rifled through it in search of her cell phone, before remembering that she had left it charging after placing a call to her office to alert her assistant of her return.

Her foot pressed harder on the accelerator. She almost spun out in loose gravel when she took a corner too fast, nearly ran over a flock of buzzards that were picking at the carcass of an opossum on the road, and jarred her teeth when she crossed a railroad track doing eighty-five.

Still, it seemed to take forever to get there, and when she did, she moaned as she saw no car parked out front. She stopped the car so suddenly, she smelled the scorched rubber of the skidding tires. She alighted at a run, without bothering to cut the engine or close the car door.

As she raced up the steps to the gallery, the toe of her shoe caught on one and she tripped, catching herself on her hands, painfully scraping her palms. She stumbled up the last couple of steps and lunged across the deep porch. The screened door was unlatched and the front door unlocked. She barreled through them. Selma was coming downstairs with a laundry basket under her arm.

"Have you seen Beck? Where's Huff?"

"Last I knew, Huff was on his way to the fishing camp. Haven't seen Beck at'all. What's happened?"

"Do you think they're at the plant?"

"I—"

"Call Beck on his cell phone," Sayre shouted over her shoulder as she raced back to the door. "Tell him Huff knows about Charles Nielson. Have you got that, Selma? Huff knows about Charles Nielson."

"Got it, but—"

"Tell him, Selma."

Then she was off again, driving like hell toward the dormant smokestacks.

Beck ignored his ringing cell phone as he clambered down the stairs to the shop floor.

It had taken him only a few moments to put all the fragments together. When he did, the whole picture became stunningly clear.

Chris's earnest claims that he hadn't murdered his brother were true. He wasn't guilty of loading the shotgun, sticking it into Danny's mouth, and pulling the trigger.

That didn't mean he was innocent.

When Beck reached the conveyor, George Robson was standing close behind Chris, who was leaning into the machine, inspecting the faulty drive belt in operation. Neither had on a hard hat or safety glasses. Neither had learned a damn thing. But then Chris believed himself invincible—with reason.

Beck had to speak loudly to make himself heard. "Chris!"

George jumped as though he'd been shot and spun around. His pink jowls were flabby with shock. He looked like he'd seen a ghost.

Chris straightened up and dusted off his hands. His eyes were on Beck, but he spoke to George. "We can always blame the maintenance man for a lousy repair job, George. In any case, there's not much we can do about it today. Go on home."

George seemed to be gulping for oxygen like a fish out of water. He was sweating copiously and wringing his pudgy hands. Without a word, he turned quickly and left them. Beck watched him climb the metal staircase to the Center and disappear through the door.

"Poor George." Chris hit the machine's kill switch, and it stopped. "He's more nervous than I've ever seen him. He sees the handwriting on the wall."

"You had Slap Watkins kill Danny for you," Beck said without preamble. "While you were with Lila, creating an alibi, Watkins went to the fishing camp, where you had told him Danny would be, and he killed him. You weren't lying when you said you hadn't done it. You had somebody else do it for you."

Huff checked Beck's office first. Always conscientious Beck. Always working overtime Beck. Always looking out for the interests of Hoyle Enterprises Beck.

Fucking Beck. Cheating Beck. Lying Beck.

Beck's office was empty. So was Chris's. But hearing machinery running in the otherwise silent plant, Huff went to the windows above the shop floor. He looked down and saw the two of them in conversation, his son and the Judas who had betrayed them. Huff didn't think about the irony of using a biblical metaphor. His single thought was of destroying the person who had tried his damnedest to destroy him.

Hefting the pistol, he left the office and headed for the back stairs, but when he reached the shop floor, he cautioned himself not to lose his head, not to go out there with pistol blazing.

As he had told Beck the week before, Nielson was a lousy strategist. The best attack was a surprise attack.

Chris laughed softly. "Slap was very upset with Danny for not hiring him, you know. He took it up with me one night in the parking lot of the Razorback."

"Where you told him you had a job for him."

Chris regarded him impassively.

"You told Slap to make it look like a suicide. It might have been convincing, except that Watkins forgot to remove Danny's shoe. That one mistake made Deputy Scott question that it was a suicide. Never thinking that you would be implicated, you were desperate to do something, so you advanced the idea that Slap Watkins was the culprit and was trying to frame you."

Beck's mind was skipping across the events of the past two weeks like a stone over water. "What I can't figure is why Watkins didn't hightail it out of town the moment the deed was done. Why did he stick around? Why would he force that encounter with you on the road, and that night at the diner . . ."

He looked at Chris as though willing him to fill in the blanks, but Chris's implacable eyes gave away nothing.

"Wait," Beck said, "I just remembered something. When Watkins came into the diner, I remember him looking surprised to see us there. But it was only me he was surprised to see, wasn't it? He said he was there for a business . . . Ah," he said with sudden enlightenment. "The payoff. He was meeting you there to get his money.

"That was the night of Billy's accident. I'd just come from the hospital. Our unscheduled meeting in the diner prevented you from conducting your transaction with Watkins. No wonder he was so angry that night on the road. He still hadn't been paid. He was getting antsy. The heat was shifting from you onto him. In desperation, he went to Sayre and got Scott focused on the fratricide angle. That brought things to a head, so you arranged for a meeting with Watkins at the camp this morning."

Chris grinned. "I bet you aced law school, didn't you? You're actually very sharp. But, Beck, the only thing I would swear to under oath is that Slap Watkins came crashing through the door of the cabin, waving a knife and telling me he was going to kill his second Hoyle and how giddy he was at the prospect."

"I have no doubt that's what happened, Chris. He just arrived earlier than you expected. He wanted to get the jump on you because he didn't trust you. Justifiably. Even Watkins was smart enough to realize that you weren't about to hand over money and let him walk away from that last meeting. He signed his own death warrant the minute he agreed to kill Danny."

"Please, Beck. Let's not get sentimental over Slap. A double cross was his plan from the very beginning. Why do you think he left that matchbook in the cabin?"

Beck mentally stepped back from himself and considered his options. He could leave now. Simply turn around and walk out. Go to Sayre. Live out the rest of his days loving her, and to hell with Chris and Huff, their treachery and corruption, to hell with their stinking, maiming, life-taking foundry.

He was so damn weary of the struggle and the pretense. He longed to throw off this mantle of responsibility, to forget he ever knew the Hoyles and let the devil take them—if he would have them. That was what he *wanted* to do.

Or he could stay and do what he had *committed* to do.

As appealing as the former option was, the latter was preordained.

"Slap Watkins didn't plant the matchbook in the cabin, Chris." He held Chris's stare for several seconds, before adding, "I did."

George Robson's eyes stung from unmanly tears. He wanted to weep with a mix of frustration and fear. When he left the building, the heat slammed into him, making him feel even weaker and more dizzy. Shaken to the core, he stumbled to the exterior wall and vomited bile into the dry weeds growing there. Spasms racked him while the sun beat down on his sweating back.

When he realized how close he'd come to committing a deadly sin, when he recognized how disappointed he was that he'd failed, he was assailed with another bout of nausea.

His stomach finally emptied, and the dry spasms stopped. He wiped his mouth with a damp handkerchief that he took from his rear pants pocket. He blotted his perspiring palms and mopped his neck.

He had planned to kill Chris. He had figured it out in his mind, how he would make it look like an accident. He had weakened that belt so it might break as soon as the machine was restarted, causing it to fly off, which might have resulted in a terrible death to whoever was inspecting it while it was running. But the belt had held.

In hindsight, he thanked God it had. He thanked God that even in that he'd been inept.

Had he succeeded, had he been found out and sent to death row, he would have lost Lila anyway. At least now he had another chance to make her happy. He had more time with her. If she left him for Chris, or someone equally charming, next month, or a year from now, well, at least she would be his in the meantime.

Yes, he thanked God for averting a disaster.

"Mr. Robson?"

He pushed away from where he'd been leaning

against the wall and blinked at Sayre Hoyle, who looked out of breath and shaken. "Have you seen Beck Merchant?"

"Uh, yes. He's . . . he's here."

"In his office?"

"On the shop floor with Chris."

She didn't even thank him but pulled open the door and disappeared inside.

George hurried to his car. He was anxious to get home, where Lila was waiting for him.

"I planted the matchbook in the cabin," Beck repeated.

Chris looked at him like he was waiting for the punch line. When it didn't come, his expression changed. His features hardened like setting concrete. "My, my. That's quite a bombshell. Why would you do that, Beck?"

"Because I knew you did it."

"I didn't."

"Stop splitting hairs. If not for you, Danny would be alive. I was afraid you'd get away with it unless I pointed the sheriff in the right direction. The moment Deputy Scott questioned how Danny had pulled the trigger, I was ninety-nine percent sure you had killed him. Add another half of a percent to that when you suggested a frame-up and named Slap Watkins.

"The only nagging question was your motive. You didn't seem to hate Danny. If anything you were indifferent toward him. As for Huff's affections, there was no contest as to who was the favored son, who would assume control of the foundry when he died. So what threat did Danny represent to you? Why did he have to die?

"I didn't know the answer until I learned about his engagement. His fiancée had told Sayre that Danny was wrestling with a moral issue. Then I had it. Your motive was the Iverson case. Danny knew where the body was buried—literally. And he was going to tell."

Chris took a deep breath and released it slowly. "It was the single time in his life that Danny wouldn't back down. He insisted on making a public confession. Huff and I couldn't let that happen. He told me to take care of it."

"So you took care of it."

Chris spread his arms as though Beck's statement summed it up. "If Iverson's body had been disinterred, it would have raised all sorts of pesky questions and added to the charges, namely obstruction of justice. Nasty stuff all the way around."

"You won't escape justice this time."

"But, you see, Beck," he said, smiling pleasantly, "I have."

"Not yet."

"Are you out to get me? Why? Because of Iverson?"

Beck laughed. "Ah, Chris, here's the zinger. You Hoyles are so damn arrogant it makes you gullible. You never once questioned my showing up the night your trial ended in a hung jury. You took me in, set me up with a sweet position in your company, made me one of the family. And that was right where I wanted to be, ensconced in the bosom of the family, a trusted ally and confidant."

Chris's eyes narrowed to slits as he asked softly, "Who are you?"

"You know who I am. You knew me from college." Beck flashed a grin. "That wasn't happenstance, either. I attended LSU because that's where you attended. I pledged the fraternity because it was your fraternity. I put myself in your path, brought myself to your attention, so that when the time came for me to join Hoyle Enterprises, I'd be a shoo-in. And it worked. Better than I anticipated. I had instant credibility. You accepted me without a blink, and so did Huff."

"You're union, aren't you?"

"No."

"A state prosecutor? FBI maybe."

"Nothing that grandiose."

"Then who the fuck—"

"I'm Beck Merchant. But Merchant was my stepfather's name. He adopted me when he married my widowed mother. I took his name because, even as a boy ten or twelve years old, I was plotting your downfall, and I knew that my real name would be a tip-off."

"I can hardly wait," Chris said caustically. "What's your real name?"

"Hallser."

Chris gave a start, then nodded as though commending Beck for his cleverness. "That's certainly enlightening."

"Sonnie Hallser was my father."

"Then it's really Huff you want revenge on, not me."

"It goes deeper than revenge, Chris. I want you and everything you represent destroyed."

Chris shook his head, and in a tone that bespoke pity, he said, "It'll never happen."

"It's already begun. Hoyle Enterprises has been shut down."

"Are you in cahoots with Charles Nielson?"

"I *am* Charles Nielson. Or rather, there is no Charles Nielson. He's just a name on a letterhead, the subject of a few press releases that I wrote and distributed myself. His name is an anagram of my dad's name with his middle initial, C."

"Clever boy."

"I've waited years for this day, Chris. My father's life was cut short by decades. And why? Because he stood in Huff's way, so Huff eliminated him. Everyone knew it. But Huff got away with it. The same as you did with Iverson. Well, guess what, Chris?" he said, lowering his voice to a menacing whisper. "It's over."

"What are you going to do, Beck? Tattle on me? You're our lawyer. You can't tell a thing I've said to you or you'll be disbarred."

"Good try, but the fact is, I don't care if I'm disbarred. I never wanted to practice law and only did so in order to get close to you and be privy to your dirty secrets. I'll be bad-mouthed, called a traitor and worse, but I can live with that. Representing you and Huff, I've grown used to people thinking I'm shit. It'll be nothing new."

"You've covered all the bases."

"Yes."

"Is this where I'm supposed to faint or something?"

Beck knew Chris well enough to recognize his flippancy as a bluff. He was sweating, and not just figuratively. "Huff will atone for my father. You learned from him, and he coached you well because you even exceed his depravity. You killed your own brother. And for that you're going down, Chris."

Chris's gaze moved beyond him. "It's about time you joined us, Huff."

Beck slowly turned around to confront the man who had been his adversary for almost as long as he could remember. If ever, during all those years, his resolve had weakened, he needed only to remind himself that he never got to tell his father good-bye. Neither he nor his mother even got to see him in his casket. It would be too gruesome a sight, the funeral director had told her.

Because of this man's greed, his mother had been widowed, he had been orphaned, and his dad had been dissected. As Beck faced him now, animosity coiled inside him as sharp and deadly as razor wire.

"Beck and I have been having the most interesting conversation," Chris said.

"I heard."

Apparently he had. His face was flushed. His eyes were burning like coals. In the hand held stiffly at his side he was clutching the pistol. His voice sounded like steel against a whetstone.

"I heard," he repeated as he raised his arm and extended the pistol straight out in front of him.

Defensively Beck put up his hands. "Huff, no!"

But Huff pulled the trigger anyway.

In the vastness the .357 sounded like a cannon. The reverberation lasted several seconds, and

Beck realized that it was followed by another noise, a terrible racket, really—the conveyor restarting.

Huff dropped the pistol. It fell heavily from his hand and landed on the concrete floor. Then he shoved Beck aside and, releasing a feral wail, rushed past him. Beck turned in time to see Chris sliding to the floor in front of the conveyor. A chunk of metal was stuck in his neck. The wound was gushing blood.

Huff's knees hit the floor directly in front of Chris, and he pressed his hands against the wound. As the color rapidly drained from Chris's face, he stared at Huff with profound bewilderment.

Beck peeled his shirt over his head and wadded it into a ball, then pried Huff's frantic hands away from the wound and tried in vain to staunch the fountain of blood.

Sayre materialized beside him. "Oh my God!"

"Call nine-one-one," Beck told her tersely, and felt her yank his phone off his belt.

Huff clasped Chris's head between his hands and shook it hard. "Why'd you do it? You had Danny murdered? Son, why? *Why?*"

"You shot at me?" A horrible gurgling sound issued from Chris's throat and along with it a geyser of blood that showered his father's face. "You said Danny had to be stopped, Huff. You said . . . take care of it."

Huff threw back his head and howled like a wounded animal. He yanked Chris forward and held his head against his chest, wrapping his arms around him tightly, protectively. "Danny was your brother. Your *brother*." He was sobbing, keening, rocking back and forth, making Chris's arms flop against the gritty shop floor, as lifeless as a rag doll's. "How could you do it, Son? How?"

Chris wheezed wetly. "You told me to take care of it." His words were barely audible now, mere filaments of sound, but they conveyed his confusion and incredulity over Huff's disapproval.

Huff bent his head down and placed his lips against Chris's temple. On Huff's face, Chris's blood mingled with the tears. "I loved you best. You know that. But Danny was my son, too." He moaned in anguish. "He was my flesh and blood. He was my daddy's flesh and blood. And you killed him. Why, Chris? Why?"

Beck looked up at Sayre, who had made the emergency call and was standing by helplessly just as he was. When their eyes met, he saw his own thoughts mirrored in hers. Chris had only done what he had learned to do by Huff's example.

Huff continued that heartrending lament for what seemed to Beck like hours while Chris's blood drained from his body to form a lake around them. Huff held his favored son against his chest and rocked him like an infant. He stroked his hair and kissed his cheeks, unmindful of smearing blood and tears and mucus over Chris's still face. He told him again and again that he loved him more than life and repeated a thousand times that chastising refrain, "But, Son, how could you kill your own brother?"

Eventually an ambulance arrived. When the

EMTs tried to separate Huff from Chris, he fought them like a madman. Covered with Chris's gore and the sweat of his own torment, he screamed until he was hoarse that no one would take away his firstborn . . . who was long past hearing.

epilogue

"You look exhausted."

"Then looks aren't deceiving," Beck replied as he came up the steps of his gallery, where Sayre and Frito had been waiting on him. "It was a grueling six hours."

That was how long it had been since Chris had been pronounced DOA at the parish hospital and Huff had been taken into custody. He was being held for manslaughter, since his firing the pistol at Chris had caused the accident.

Huff was incapable of making a decision, so Beck, acting on his behalf, immediately called the reputable defense attorney previously retained by Chris. He'd agreed to represent Huff instead and had arrived in Destiny as soon as his jazzed-up Lexus could get him there.

An assistant prosecutor from the DA's office had been summoned by Wayne Scott to question Sayre and Beck. They had told their stories several times. Beck's was by far the most revealing. He'd omitted nothing, explaining in detail how their overheard conversation had led to Chris's demise.

"I've no doubt Huff was coming to shoot me for my deception," he'd told the ADA. "I knew that in order to beat them, I had to think like them, act like them. I had to become one of them."

Sayre had listened with mounting dismay. Out of love for his father and his sense of duty toward him, Beck had become the reviled advocate for the Hoyles.

"But when he heard Chris admit to conspiring to have Danny killed, I guess he just lost it. He fired the pistol out of rage. His shot missed. But as Chris recoiled from disbelief, his arms windmilled. He hit the unguarded start switch on the conveyor. The faulty drive belt flew apart. It scattered pieces of metal like shrapnel. One of them found Chris."

Eventually Sayre had been excused from the proceedings, but Beck was asked to stay and give his account one more time. He was reminded that he was violating attorney-client privilege and what that would mean to his legal career. He talked anyway.

Once excused, Sayre wasn't sure what to do with herself. Unwilling to return to the house, which was no longer her home, or to the dreary motel, she had followed her instinct and come here to wait for Beck's return.

Now he sat down in the spare rocking glider and scratched a happy Frito behind both ears. "We should all have his life," Beck remarked. "Each day is a new day. Whatever happened yesterday is forgotten, and he doesn't worry about tomorrow."

"What will happen tomorrow?"

"Huff will be arraigned. You and I will probably be deposed. We'll be witnesses for the prosecution at his trial."

"I gathered that."

"Unless he pleads guilty."

"Do you think he will?"

"Wouldn't surprise me. He told them where they could find Iverson's remains. Red Harper admitted his complicity. He's got a lot to answer for, too. If he lives long enough."

Beck leaned forward and planted his elbows on his knees, tiredly massaging his eye sockets with his fingers. "Huff's a broken man, Sayre. Before I left, I went back to the jail cell to check on him."

"How did he react to seeing you?"

"He didn't. He was lying on the cot in the fetal position, crying his heart out. Huff Hoyle, reduced to that." He spoke softly and sadly. "I think he would have forgiven Chris anything except killing one of his own. If Chris had shot the president, Huff would have covered for him, protected him with his last breath. But to kill his own brother? Huff couldn't allow that. It was incomprehensible to him. It violated his intense sense of family."

"I wonder where that came from," Sayre said. "It's not like he grew up surrounded by a slew of kinfolk. He never mentioned his parents other than to say that both had died when he was young."

Beck reflected on it for several moments, then said, "Late one night, Chris was out, Huff and I were alone, and he'd consumed a lot of bourbon. He was rambling drunkenly, but he said something about when his daddy died. And he didn't call him Father, he called him Daddy. He said, 'The bastards got his name wrong.' "

"Who was he talking about?"

"He didn't elaborate. That's all he said. It could have been a random, meaningless statement. Or very profound."

She gazed out across the lawn and sighed. "When I think what it cost him to pull that trigger. . . . He was trying to destroy what he loved most."

"Chris was also his last hope of a grandchild to carry on his name. He destroyed all chance of that, too. But I don't pity him, Sayre. He made Chris into what he was. He cultivated him."

"And he killed my baby. I guess he didn't think of it as one of his own."

Beck reached for her hand and squeezed it tightly.

"Are you hungry?" she asked.

They went inside. She had picked up an order of fried chicken on her way there. Together they began to put food and place settings on the table, dodging Frito, who tracked their footsteps as though afraid they soon would leave him alone again.

"I spoke to Luce Daly," she said. "Clark will be released from the hospital tomorrow or the next day. His coworkers have asked him to represent them to the OSHA inspectors. He won't be able to do much until he makes a full recovery, but this vote of confidence should speed that. His spirits are also raised by knowing that the men who attacked him are in jail. Luce thanks you for keeping your word to her about that."

"Reporting them to Wayne Scott was the least I could do."

"I also called Jessica DeBlance and told her what had happened today. I beat the newscasts by only a half hour, and she thanked me for letting her know before she learned about it through the media. She's very kind, Beck. When I owned up to Danny's telephone calls to me, she urged me not to dwell on it. She said Danny wouldn't want me to bear any guilt over that. She also said her prayers were with all of us, including Chris. I'm glad Danny knew that kind of forgiving love, even for a little while."

"Me, too."

"I think you would enjoy meeting Jessica."

"She may not enjoy meeting me," he said. "I'm still the enemy to most of the people around here."

"You could identify yourself as Charles Nielson."

"No, he needs to fade back into the woodwork from which he came. Public attention is fleeting. In a few months, no one will remember him."

"What about the men and women who picketed? And the Pauliks."

"Nielson will refer them to another labor lawyer. A better one."

"What will you do?"

"What's in my future, you mean? That's up to you, Sayre. For all practical purposes, Hoyle Enterprises is yours now. I work for you. What do you want me to do?"

"Can you grant me power of attorney?"

"With Huff in the condition he's in, that won't be a problem."

"Once that's done and I'm making all the deci-sions, I want you to put Hoyle Enterprises on the market. I don't want it, but I can't just shut it down and leave this town without an economy. Once OSHA's demands are met, sell it to a responsible company. Top-notch in terms of safety and labor relations, or it's no sale."

"I understand and agree. I have some excellent prospects. Companies that have approached me. I always told them Huff would never sell. They'll be glad to know otherwise."

"For as long as the plant is closed for the OSHA inspection, I want the employees to receive full pay."

"All right," he said. "I'll stay on until every-thing's resolved."

"And then?"

"Consulting, maybe. I could be a knowledgeable liaison between labor and management for large operations like Hoyle. God knows I've had the ex-perience, and I'm well acquainted with both sides of the coin."

They had believed they were hungry, but when they began to eat, they discovered they had little appetite. Sayre picked at a buttered biscuit. "You told me your mother was alive. Is she?"

"Very much so."

"I'd like to meet her."

"You did. In Charles Nielson's office."

"Brenda?" she exclaimed.

"When I walked in and saw you there, it threw me completely, but Mom didn't miss a beat."

"No, she didn't. I never would have guessed."

"She thought you were gorgeous. Chic. Smart. Let's see . . . I can't remember all the adjectives, but she gave you a glowing review. Remember when you came out of the building and I was supposedly trying to track down Nielson in Dayton?"

"Cincinnati."

"Well, I was actually talking to her. She was giving me an earful about how rude I'd been to you."

"She must have been frantic yesterday after you were beaten. No wonder she called here to inquire about you on Mr. Nielson's behalf."

"I talked to her while I was driving home just now. Told her what had happened today. We've been preoccupied with toppling the Hoyles for more than two decades. She's very relieved that it's finally over. Even more relieved that I survived. She always feared that Chris or Huff was going to discover who I was and that I'd disappear like Gene Iverson or get *accidentally* killed like my father."

"What about Mr. Merchant?"

"He died several years ago. He was a decent man. A widower with no children. He was crazy about my mother and raised me like his own son. I was fortunate to have two good fathers."

She stood up and began to clear the table. "Yes, you were. I didn't have *one*." She set what she was carrying on the counter and returned to the table to get more.

Beck clasped her around the waist and pulled her between his legs. "When I'm done here, after I've tendered my resignation, I'll be looking for a place to relocate, set up my consulting firm."

"Any ideas about where?"

"I was hoping you might have a suggestion." He searched her eyes meaningfully.

"I do know a lovely city," she said. "Great parks. Good food. The weather can be dicey, but Frito wouldn't mind a little fog, would he?"

"I think he'd love it. I know I would. As long as I could come back here every so often and have a bowl or two of gumbo."

"Want to know a secret? I have it shipped to me frozen."

"No!"

"Yes." She ran her fingers through his hair, but her affectionate smile faltered. "We've only known each other for two weeks, Beck. And it's been a rather tumultuous two weeks."

"That's an understatement."

"Yes. So isn't it too early for us to be making permanent plans along these lines?"

"Possibly," he said. "To be fair to ourselves, maybe we should give it more time, see how things go, before making any kind of commitment."

"I think so."

"How much time do you need?"

She glanced at the clock. "Till half past?"

He smiled, then laughed softly. "I don't need nearly that long." He encircled her waist, buried his face between her breasts, and sighed heavily. "Destroying the Hoyles has been my driving force to the exclusion of everything else. Since my dad was killed, I didn't make a single decision that didn't relate to bringing this day about. But now that it's done . . . I'm just so tired of it all, Sayre."

"I've grown tired of being angry, too. I don't

even feel much satisfaction over Huff's being broken. I mean, I'm glad he's finally having to account for his crimes, but he's a tragic figure. There's no joy over it, is there?"

"No. Not joy. Peace perhaps."

"Perhaps."

He splayed his hand over her abdomen and rubbed it gently. "Of all the things he did, I hate most what he did to you."

She laid her hand over his, stilling it. "I'm a Hoyle, Beck. We're not always truthful, and we can be cruelly manipulative."

He raised his head and looked up at her.

"I lied to Huff. It was a cheap shot, admittedly, but I was irate and wanted to pierce him to his soul." Lowering her voice almost to a whisper, she said, "Dr. Caroe didn't do any permanent damage."

His eyes dropped to her middle, then snapped back to hers. "You can have a child?"

"There's no physical reason I can't. And I'm thinking that maybe . . . maybe I'll tell Huff."

He came to his feet slowly and pulled her to him. "That's what separated you from them, Sayre. They had no mercy. You do. I saw that, and loved you for it."

"No, Beck," she said, laying her cheek against his chest. "That's what I saw in you."

SANDRA BROWN IS BACK
WITH MORE HEART-STOPPING
TWISTS AND TURNS
IN HER NEW THRILLER,

THICK AS THIEVES

AVAILABLE NOW!

Turn the page for a preview of
Thick as Thieves . . .

prologue

That night in 2000

"Talking about it is the surefire way to get caught."

He let the statement settle, then looked each of his three companions straight in the eye one at a time, using the deliberation rather than additional words to serve as a warning.

The huddled quartet was coming down from an adrenaline high. It hadn't been a crash landing but a gradual descent. Now that they were no longer in immediate danger of being caught red-handed, their heartbeats remained stronger than normal, but had slowed to a manageable rhythm. Breaths gusting into the humid air were just as hot, though not as rapid as they'd been.

However, what hadn't let up, not by a single degree, was the tension among them.

They couldn't risk being seen together tonight, but before going their separate ways, they must forge an understanding. If, during the process of creating that bond, a threat was implied, so much the better. It would discourage any one of them from breaking the pact to keep their mouths shut. One stuck to the vow of silence, or else.

"Do not talk about it." The speaker's hair was a paprika-colored thatch that grew straight up out of a sidewall. A freckled scalp showed through the bristle. "Don't tell any-damn-body." He made five stabbing motions toward the ground to emphasize each word.

Somewhat impatiently, the oldest of the group said, "Of course not."

The one vigorously gnawing his fingernails spat out a paring while bobbing his head in assent.

The fourth, the youngest of them, had maintained an air of cool detachment and remarkable calm throughout the evening's endeavor. A laconic shrug conveyed his unspoken *Goes without saying*.

"One of us boasts about it, or drops a hint, even joking, it'll have a domino effect that could—"

"You can stop going on about it," the oldest interrupted. "We got it the first time, and didn't need a lesson from you to start with."

The ditch in which they were hunkered was choked with weeds, some thriving, some lying dead in the mud, having drowned during the last hard rain. The ravine was four feet deep and made for an ugly scar that cut between the narrow road and a listing barbed-wire fence demarcating a cow pasture that reeked of manure. Without a breeze to disperse the odor, the sultry atmosphere kept it ripe.

At the center of the circle formed by the four was the cause of the resented lecture: a canvas bag stuffed with stolen cash.

It was a hell of a lot bigger haul than they had anticipated, and that unexpected bonus had been both exhilarating and sobering. It made the stakes seem higher, which wound the tension tighter.

Following the rebuke about unnecessary lessons, no one moved or said anything until the young, aloof one reached up and ground a mosquito against the side of his neck, leaving a smear of blood. "Nobody'll hear about it from me. I don't cotton to the idea of jail. Already been there."

"Juvie," the redhead said.

"Still counts."

The older one said, "Only a fool would blab about it. I'm no fool."

The redhead thought it over, then nodded as though reassured. "All right, then. Another thing. We see each other on the street, we act the same as always. We don't go out of our way to avoid each other, but we don't get chummier, either. We recognize each other on sight, maybe we're well enough acquainted to speak, but that's it. That's why this will work. The only thing we have in common is this." He nudged the canvas bag with the steel-tipped toe of his boot.

The other pair of cowboy boots in the circle weren't silver-toed. They weren't worn for show but lived in. This wasn't the first time they'd been caked with mud.

The pair of brown wingtips had sported a shine before sliding down into the ditch.

The navy blue trainers had some mileage on them.

"Six months is a long time to wait to divide it up," the eldest said, eyeing the carrot-top. "In the meanwhile, why do you get to keep the money? We didn't vote on that."

"Don't you trust me with it?"

"What do you think?"

If the one with the gingery thatch took offense, he didn't show it. "Well, look at it this way. I'm the one taking all the risks. Despite our pledge not to talk it up, if one of you lets something slip, and somebody who wears a *badge* gets wind of it and starts snooping, I'm the one holding the bag."

The other three hadn't missed the emphasis he placed on that certain word. They exchanged glances of patent mistrust toward the self-appointed banker, but no one argued with him. The youngest gave another one-shouldered shrug, which the redhead took as consensus.

"Once you get your share," he said, "you can't go spending cash like crazy. No new cars, nothing flashy, nothing—"

The older one cut him off again, testier than before. "You know, I could well do without these instructions of yours."

"No call to get touchy. Anything I tell you is a reminder to myself, too." The redhead fashioned a placating smile, but it wasn't in keeping with his eyes, which reflected the meager moonlight like twin straight razors. He then turned to the nail-biter, who was running out of fingers on which to chew. "What's the matter with you?"

"Nothing."

"Then stop with the nervous fidgeting. It'll single you out like a red neon arrow."

The older seconded that. "He's right. If you come across as nervous, you had just as well confess."

The nail-biter lowered his hand from his mouth. "I'll be okay." His Adam's apple forced down a hard swallow. "It's just . . . you know." He looked down at the bag. "I still can't believe we actually did it."

"Well, we did," the redhead said. "And when you report for work on Monday morning and are informed that the safe was cleared out over the weekend, you've got to pretend to be as shocked as everybody else. But don't overreact," he said, raising his index finger to underscore the point.

"Just a soft 'holy shit' will do. Something like that to show disbelief, then keep your trap shut. Don't do anything to call attention to yourself, especially if detectives start interviewing all the store employees, which it's certain they will. When your turn comes, you stay ignorant and innocent. Got that?"

"Yeah."

"*Got that?*" demanded the older.

"Sure. I know what to do." But even as he acknowledged his responsibility, he dried his palms by running them up and down his pants legs, a gesture that didn't inspire confidence among the other three.

The older sighed, "Jesus."

The nervous one was quick to reassure the other three. "Look, don't worry about me. I've done my part, and I'll continue to. I'm just jumpy, is all. Out here in the open like this." He made a sweeping motion with his arm that encompassed the pasture and deserted stretch of country road. "Why'd we stop out here, anyway?"

"I thought we should come to an understanding," the redhead said.

"And now we have." The oldest one started up the embankment and gave the nervous one a warning glare. "You had better not screw this up."

"I won't. By Monday I'll be okay." He wet his lips and formed a shaky grin. "And six months from now, we'll all be rolling in clover."

As a group, they climbed out of the ditch, but the adjourning optimistic prediction didn't pan out.

By morning, their plan had been shot to hell.

One of them was in the hospital.

One was in jail.

One was in the morgue.

And one had gotten away with the haul.

chapter 1

Present day

"Lord, Arden. I had counted on it being run-down, but . . ."

Lisa expressed her dismay with a shudder as she stepped through the back door into the kitchen and surveyed the conditions in which Arden had been living for the past five months.

Arden trailed her sister inside and pulled a chair from beneath the dining table. As she took her seat, she noticed that the tabletop had defied the recent polishing she'd given it. Before yesterday, she had fretted over those nicks and scratches. Today, she couldn't see what possible difference they made.

Lisa was rattling on. Arden tuned back in. "Have you had that stove checked for a gas leak? It could be a safety hazard. Is there a functioning smoke or fire alarm?"

"They're called Braxton Hicks. Think of them as practice contractions. But it'll be a month or so before you start to experience them. And when you do, they're no cause for alarm."

That's what the OB had told her on her last prenatal checkup.

But yesterday's contractions weren't Braxton Hicks. They'd turned out not to be a rehearsal, and they'd caused a great deal of alarm in the produce section of the supermarket.

She forced her thoughts away from that and back to Lisa, who stood in the center of the kitchen, elbows tucked into her sides as though afraid she might accidentally make contact with a contaminated surface.

"You told me you were occupying only a few of the downstairs rooms. What about in here?"

Lisa went over to the open doorway and looked in at the formal dining room and, beyond it, the living room. Two decades ago, they'd been emptied of all furnishings except for the upright piano that stood where it always had. Arden had been surprised to find it still here, but she supposed that it had remained for the same reason Lisa hadn't taken it with them when they vacated. How does one cart off something that large?

"I suppose the rooms upstairs are as empty as these," Lisa remarked. "Doesn't appear as though you've been in here at all." She gave the staircase a sweeping glance, then turned back into the kitchen. "Where are you sleeping?"

Arden nodded toward the room off the kitchen. Lisa gave the partially open door a push with the knuckle of her index finger.

It was a square and featureless space with a square and featureless window. Their mother, Marjorie, had used it as a catch-all to store Christmas decorations, castoff clothing bound for Goodwill, their dad's rarely used golf clubs, a portable sewing machine, and such.

When Arden moved in, she'd decided to set up a temporary bedroom in here rather than use her old room upstairs, saving herself from having to go up and down the stairs as her pregnancy advanced and she grew more ungainly.

That was no longer an issue.

When the first pain gripped her, Arden dropped the apple she'd been testing and splayed her hands over her distended abdomen. Although the sharp and unexpected contraction robbed her of breath, she gave a cry of fright.

"What's the matter, honey?"

She turned toward a voice filled with concern. She registered a pleasant face framed by gray hair, a blue-and-white-striped blouse, and kindly eyes. Then another pain seized her, meaner than the one before. Her knees buckled.

"Oh, goodness. Your water broke. You're going into labor."

"No! I can't be. It's too early."

"How far along are you?"

"It's too early!" Her voice went shrill with panic. "Call 911. Please."

Lisa was commenting on her drab, makeshift bedroom. "I simply don't understand why you chose to come back here and live like this."

Arden had furnished the room with a twin bed, a nightstand and lamp, and a chest of drawers that she had assembled herself over the course of two days. She remembered feeling a great sense of accomplishment and had imagined herself assembling a crib soon.

The mirror that Arden had mounted on the wall above the chest reflected Lisa's dismay as she came back around, shaking her head slowly and regarding Arden as she would an indecipherable ancient transcript.

"Is there anything to drink?"

Without waiting for an answer, Lisa returned to the kitchen and checked inside the refrigerator. "Good. Diet Coke. Or would you rather have something else? Does the ice maker work?"

Arden tried to keep up with Lisa's brisk thought processes, but her mind was fettered by vivid recollections.

"You'll be all right. Lie back. Take deep breaths."

A young woman in yoga attire had responded to the older lady's shout for help. She eased Arden down until she was reclining in the supporting arms of another stranger who'd taken up position behind her. Kneeling at her side, the young woman continued to speak to her in a calm and soothing manner. But nothing she'd said helped, not with the pain that assailed her, not with the despair that was equally intense.

Desperate, she shoved her hands between her thighs in an effort to hold inside the life that her body was prematurely trying to expel.

Lisa located the drinking glasses in the cabinet in which they'd always been and poured them each a drink. Bringing them to the table with her, she sat down across from Arden.

She sipped from her glass, then reached out and covered Arden's hand with her own. "Baby sister."

Lisa whispered the endearment with affection, caring, and concern. All of which Arden knew to be genuine. Lisa was as baffled by her life choices as she was annoyed.

She said, "From the moment you called me yesterday, I've been in a tizzy. I don't know how much you remember of last evening, but when I got to the hospital, you were in hysterics one minute and near catatonic the next. I was beside myself. Then this morning, trying to get you out of there . . ."

"What's your name?"

At her side and bending over her, the EMT had replaced the yoga-clad woman. He was young and fresh-faced.

"Arden Maxwell."

"Arden, we're going to take care of you, okay? How far along are you?"

"Twenty-two weeks."

His partner, who looked like a career body-builder, was taking her vitals. They asked everyone who'd congregated around her to move aside, then lifted her onto the gurney, and rolled her out of the store.

The midday sun was directly overhead. It was blinding. Her vision turned watery.

She blotted tears from her eyes now.

Lisa must have noticed, because she stopped enumerating the aggravations associated with being discharged from the hospital. "What I'm leading up to is that this is the first chance I've had to tell you how sorry I am. Truly, truly sorry, Arden." She stroked Arden's hand.

Fresh tears welled up in Arden's eyes. She looked into her untouched glass of Coke where bubbles rose in a rush to the surface, only to burst upon reaching it. Something vital and alive, extinguished faster than a blink.

In the ambulance, her jeans were cut away. She was draped. When the young-looking medic examined her, his smooth brow wrinkled.

She struggled to angle herself up in order to see what had caused his consternation, but the body-builder kept her pressed down, a hand on each of her shoulders, not unkindly, but firmly.

"My baby will be all right, won't she?" Arden sobbed. "Please. Tell me she'll be okay."

But, thinking back on it now, she believed she'd known even then, on a primal and instinctual level, that her girl child would never draw breath.

"You probably won't believe this," Lisa continued as she rubbed her thumb across Arden's knuckles, "but I admired you for electing to have the baby. Oh, don't get me wrong. I was appalled when you told me about it and what you planned to do. Coming back here to live and raise the child. *Here* of all places?"

She took a look around as though seeking to find an explanation for the inexplicable written on the faded wallpaper.

"It's masochistic. Does this self-inflicted punishment have to do with the baby's father?"

Arden picked up her glass and tried to hold it steady as she took a sip of Coke. The glass clinked against her lower teeth. She set it back down.

In a hushed tone, Lisa said, "Is he married, Arden?"

She cast her eyes downward.

Lisa sighed. "I figured as much. Did he even know you were pregnant?"

She took Arden's silence as a no.

"Just as well," Lisa said. "You're under no obligation to tell him now. If he didn't know about the child, he doesn't need to know about its fate. That episode of your life is behind you. You can start afresh. Clean slate."

Again she covered Arden's hand and pressed it affectionately. "First thing on the agenda is to get you away from here. I want you to move in with me until you figure out what you want to do with your life." She gave Arden time to respond, but when she didn't, she continued. "Since Wallace died, the house seems so empty."

Lisa's husband, who had been much older than she, had died two years earlier. No doubt their huge, rambling house in an elite neighborhood of Dallas did feel empty.

"I'll give you all the privacy you wish, of course, but Helena will be delighted to have you there to fuss over. She and I will pamper you until you're completely recovered." She smiled and patted Arden's hand again before checking her watch.

"You can't have much to pack. If we get away soon, we'll be there by dark. Helena will have dinner waiting." She was about to leave her chair, when she paused. "And, Arden, you're not under a deadline. Give yourself time to think things through. Really think through an idea before you act on it. Don't rush headlong into something.

"In all honesty, I had a bad feeling about your move to Houston, and, at that point, I didn't even know about your relationship with this married man. Granted, the job held promise, but your pulling up stakes and relocating seemed impulsive and doomed from the start."

The attending physician in the ER clasped her hand. "Ms. Maxwell, I'm sorry."

"No."

"Your daughter was stillborn."

"No!"

"Don't blame yourself. Nothing you did caused it. It was an accident of nature."

Doomed from the start.

Feeling as though her breastbone was about to crack open, Arden pushed back her chair and went over to the sink. Opening the blinds on the window above it, she looked out at the backyard in which Lisa and she had played.

The fence was missing slats. The grass had been overtaken by weeds. Her mother's rose bed, to which she'd given so much tender loving care, was a patch of infertile dirt.

She sensed Lisa moving up behind her even before her sister encircled her waist and rested her chin on her shoulder so she could share the view through the window. "I remember the day Dad brought the swing set home for you."

It was still anchored in the ground with concrete blocks, but it was rusty, and the chain was broken on one of the swings.

"I was around twelve years old, so you would have been two. There was a little seat for you with a bar across your lap."

Lisa rubbed her chin against the knob at the

crest of Arden's shoulder. "You were too young to remember that, but surely you remember when I taught you how to skin-the-cat."

Lisa had been almost too tall by then, but she was athletic enough to demonstrate how easy it was. She'd spotted Arden on her first fearful attempts, then had challenged her to do it on her own.

Her palms damp with nervous sweat, she'd braced herself on the crossbar, taken a deep breath, and somersaulted over it. But she fell short of making the full rotation. Her hands slipped off the bar, and she'd landed hard on her butt.

Pride smarting as much as her bottom, she'd fought back tears. But Lisa had insisted that she try again.

"Tomorrow," Arden had whined.

"No. Right now."

On the second try, she'd succeeded. Lisa had practically smothered her in a bear hug. She recalled now how special Lisa's approval and that congratulatory hug had been.

The family had celebrated her feat with dinner out at the restaurant of her choosing: McDonald's, of course.

That had been a happy day, one among the last happy family times that Arden recalled. Their mother's fatal accident had occurred within months.

But losing her hadn't been as sudden and unexpected as their father's abandonment.

This past March marked twenty years, twice the age she had been when Joe Maxwell left his two daughters, never to be seen again. His desertion remained the pivotal point around which Arden's life continued to revolve.

It did no good to speculate on how differently Lisa and she would have turned out as individuals, or what kind of futures they would have had, if he hadn't forsaken them. He had.

Softly, sympathetically, Lisa said, "You've been through a terrible ordeal, and I don't want to pressure you when you're so vulnerable. But, Arden, this isn't the place to recover. Believe me, it isn't. You were younger. You can't appreciate how bad it was after Mother died. Or maybe you can, but you've blocked it from your memory. I haven't. I remember.

"When Dad disappeared, and I moved us away from this town, I swore it would be forever. People who lived here then will remember us. Why subject yourself to gossip and speculation? To say nothing of the fact that this house is literally falling down around you." She flipped her finger over a chip in the Formica countertop.

"So many times, I've thought about selling it, but I would get sentimental, think of Mother in these rooms, cooking in this kitchen, humming as she folded laundry, and I couldn't bring myself to let it go. Though God knows we could have used the money, selling it would have made severance with Mother seem so final. Besides that, the house belonged to you, too. Selling it wasn't a decision I felt comfortable making for both of us."

She took a deep breath. "But now I wish I had gotten rid of it, so you wouldn't have made this dreadful mistake of moving back. You've deluded yourself into seeing this place as *home*. It isn't. It hasn't been for twenty years, and, without your child, it never will be.

"I'm your only family. I'll nurture you until you decide what you want to do from this point forward."

She gave Arden a quick, hard hug and held on for a moment longer before letting go.

Arden turned to face her. She kissed her sister's cheek, then crooked her pinky finger, and Lisa linked hers with it. After their father's desertion, they'd begun doing this often. It symbolized that they had only each other, and that their bond was unbreakable.

They kept their fingers linked, smiling wistfully at each other, then Arden pulled her hand free. "Are you finished, Lisa?"

"Finished?"

"Finished telling me where I'm going to live and what I'm going to do with my life from this point forward. If you're done, please leave." She took a bolstering breath. "If not, leave anyway."

Arden was still awake when she heard the car approaching on the road.

She glanced at the clock on her nightstand. It read a few minutes past one a.m. The drive-by was a little later than usual tonight.

Immediately after learning she was pregnant, she'd made plans to leave Houston. Within a week, she had resigned from her job, paid out her lease, emptied her condo, and made the move back to her hometown.

Although Penton was a county seat, most of the

county was rural, so the "city" itself was small, and it had a thriving grapevine. Anyone familiar with the Maxwell family's history would naturally be curious about the recent occupant of the house that had remained uninhabited for so long, and it hadn't taken long for word to get around who the resident was.

She had grown accustomed to motorists slowing down and coasting past the house.

She wasn't bothered by the daytime gawkers.

But one came at night. Every night. By now she recognized the sound of his car's engine. She even found herself listening for it. Too often, she didn't fall asleep until he, or she, had driven past. It wasn't the kind of close to each day that she wished for. It didn't feel like a benediction.

Of course she hadn't breathed a word of this to Lisa, who had predicted that Arden's taking up residence would resurrect the suspicion, rumor, and speculation about their father and the crimes he was alleged to have committed before disappearing.

As usual, Lisa was right, but Arden sensed that this particular passerby wasn't motivated strictly by curiosity and the hope of catching a glimpse of the infamous Joe Maxwell's youngest daughter. These nightly rounds had a predatory quality that made her uneasy.

But just today hadn't she determined she would no longer yield to intimidation?

She threw off the covers, got out of bed, and went to the window, keeping well behind the wall so she wouldn't be seen. It seemed sensible and cautious not to let the person in that car know that she was aware of him.

The house was set too far back off the road for her to make out more of the vehicle than its headlights. As it came even with the house, it slowed to a crawl, as it did every night, and didn't resume its speed until having driven past.

As she watched the taillights go around a bend and out of sight, she told herself that maybe she was letting her imagination turn something innocent into something ominous. That purring motor could belong to a night worker who was making his way home after his shift.

But she didn't know of any businesses out this way, and what kind of job would require a seven-day workweek? He came past the house on weekends, too. He hadn't missed a night in months.

The regularity of it felt compulsive and sinister.

Trying to shake off her uneasiness, telling herself that she was being silly, she returned to bed. But turbulent thoughts kept her awake.

Lisa hadn't gone quietly.

For half an hour after Arden had made her declaration of independence, Lisa had argued with her. "If Wallace were still alive, he would side with me."

Arden had no doubt of that. She'd liked her brother-in-law, who had been a good surrogate father—more like a grandfather, actually—after he and Lisa married. A successful commercial real estate developer, the even-tempered Wallace Bishop had routinely negotiated deals that left both sides feeling they had come out favorably. Numerous times he had mediated disagreements between the sisters, but, in order to maintain marital harmony, he had leaned toward Lisa's side.

But even though Lisa had invoked his name, Arden had remained steadfast in her decision to stay, giving Lisa no choice except to ultimately relent. As she left, she'd said, "I only want you to be happy, Arden."

"I want me to be happy, too."

Now, as she lay in the dark, staring at the ceiling, she conceded her sister one point: For most of her adult years, she'd been moving at a frenetic pace but getting nowhere. She hadn't discovered her path. She'd been directionless and without purpose.

Reflexively, she ran her hand over her abdomen, missing the small mound that had been so wonderfully new, yet had soon become endearingly familiar.

The baby had given her purpose.

"As it is . . ." she whispered.

Grief suffused her, but she refused to give it a foothold. She couldn't let her mind, her heart, center on the loss of the baby. If she did, bereavement would immobilize her.

She had to get on with her original plan. Just like learning to skin-the-cat, she must do it, on her own, and now.

Exhausted as her body was, her mind continued to churn, busily mapping out a plan of attack on a house that had stood neglected for twenty years.

Until her own dying day, she would mourn the daughter she had lost, but she felt a sense of urgency to act, to move, to *live* before it was too late.

That last thought gave her pause.

Too late for *what*?

chapter 2

The name "L. Burnet" was stenciled on the metal mailbox mounted on a post at the entrance to a gravel driveway. Although the road to get here had been bumpy, narrow, and roundabout, Arden had arrived at her destination.

Up to this point, the two months since the loss of the baby had been busy, but discouragingly unproductive. She hoped this call on L. Burnet would change that.

She turned into the driveway, pulled up behind a dually pickup truck, and let her motor idle as she assessed the house. The architecture was Acadian, which was unsurprising since the state line with Louisiana bisected Caddo Lake, and the lake was within shouting distance.

The white-frame, one-story structure had dark green shutters and a matching tin roof. It was scrupulously tidy and aesthetically pleasing. A porch with a low overhang ran its width. The only thing on the porch was a varnished wood rocking chair with a tall slat-back and wide armrests. Landscaping was limited to dwarf evergreen shrubs that bordered the edge of the porch on either side of a set of recycled redbrick steps.

She turned off her car. When she got out, her ears were assaulted by a high-pitched whine coming from behind the house. She walked around the tank-size truck and followed a footpath worn into the grass. It led her around the left side of the house to the backyard, which was studded with tall pine trees.

A sizable outbuilding matched the house's white exterior and green tin roof. Its double garage door was raised. She made her way over to the opening and looked inside. The source of the racket was a buzz saw. The man operating it had his back to her. The noise was earsplitting.

"Excuse me?"

He gave no sign of having heard her and remained bent over the worktable, ably cleaving a length of lumber down the middle.

She raised her voice. "Mr. Burnet?"

When he didn't respond, she decided to wait until he'd finished. When he did, he straightened up, surveyed his work, then, much to Arden's relief, switched off the saw.

"Mr. Burnet?"

As he came around, he pushed a pair of safety goggles up to his forehead. Upon seeing her, he reacted in a manner she couldn't quite specify, and it had been so fleeting that if she had blinked, she would have missed it.

She said, "I hope I didn't startle you. I called out, but you didn't hear me above the racket."

He held her gaze, gave her a slow once-over, then turned away to set the saw on the worktable. He pulled off the goggles and a pair of suede work gloves and placed them beside the saw before facing her again. "I heard you."

She didn't know what to say to that. If he'd heard her, why hadn't he acknowledged her presence?

"My name is Arden Maxwell." She walked toward him and stuck out her right hand.

He looked at it as though a handshake was a new experience for him, then reached for a faded red shop rag and used it to wipe sawdust off his forearms before shaking hands. He did so economically, almost curtly. "What can I do for you?"

She gave an uneasy laugh. "A lot, I hope."

He didn't return her smile, only cocked his eyebrow.

And somehow that added an unintended innuendo to what she'd said. She was quick to explain. "I saw your ad. On the internet. I Googled local contractors, and you were listed."

"Um-huh."

That was all he said, displaying no particular interest in whether or not he could secure her as a customer. She plunged on. "I called yesterday and left a voice mail, asking that you return my call. I guess you missed it."

"I got it. I've been busy."

She looked beyond him at the newly halved board. "Yes, I see. Well, I had another errand to run in town, so I decided to try and catch you here, since it was on my way."

"On your way?"

She gave another light laugh. "A *winding* way. Granted, you are off the beaten path, and I almost missed the turnoff. But I found you."

"Lucky I was here, or you would have come all this way for nothing."

"I consider it a stroke of luck, yes."

"Well, now you're here, what do you need?"

"I have a home project, a rather extensive one. It will require considerable time and a lot of hard work."

Finished with the rag, he tossed it down onto the worktable. "How many contractors did you call before me?"

Abashed, she ducked her head. Then, realizing she owed him no explanation, she again met his gaze, which was cobalt blue and unwavering behind an unfriendly squint. He was younger than the image she'd formed in her mind, but she figured that the threads of gray in his dark hair, the squint lines, and the unsmiling mouth added years to his actual age.

His physique certainly wasn't that of a man settling comfortably into his middle years. No paunch overlapped the waistband of his jeans. Well-defined biceps stretched the short sleeves of his black t-shirt. He was tall and lean and, overall, looked as tough as boot leather and as cuddly as a diamondback.

"He was a soldier, you know."

"No, I didn't know."

"Afghanistan. Iraq before that."

"He was in combat, then?"

"Oh, yeah. He saw action, all right. Might have spent a little too much time at war, if you know

what I mean. But he's all right. Not dangerous, or crazy, or anything."

In the ad, a former client of Mr. Burnet's had left his name as one to call for a reference. Arden had. In addition to his endorsement of Burnet's craftsmanship and trustworthiness, he'd volunteered the information about his military service.

In truth, she *hadn't* known what he'd meant by his comment on Burnet's spending too much time at war. Now, she wished she had asked him to elaborate.

Maybe war had left L. Burnet taciturn and borderline rude. Or perhaps he was standoffish by nature. But, as long as he could do the work, she didn't care whether or not he had an engaging personality. She wasn't hiring someone to entertain her.

His stare was piercing, but she didn't detect any madness behind it. Quite the contrary. She sensed intelligence, acute attentiveness, and a perceptiveness sharper than an average person's. Little would escape him, and that was a bit discomfiting. However, she was willing to take her chances that he was of reasonably sound mind.

But—and this was the bottom line—what really recommended him was that over the course of the past two months, she had interviewed many contractors, and he was the last on her list of candidates for the job.

Thanks to the trust fund her late brother-in-law had established for her, she could afford to hire anyone. However, as a matter of principle, she wanted to finance this project using money she had earned, which put a ceiling on how much she could comfortably spend.

In answer to his question, she said, "Honestly, Mr. Burnet, I've consulted several others who were qualified."

"They couldn't fit your project into their schedules?"

"I couldn't fit them into my budget."

"So you called me."

"Please don't take offense. The comments posted online said that you do good work, that you're dependable, and that you're a one-man operation. At first, I didn't see that as an advantage."

"Now you do?"

"Yes. Because you don't have a crew, I thought perhaps you would be a good choice."

He propped his butt against the worktable and hooked his thumbs into the front pockets of his jeans. "You thought I'd work cheap."

So much for diplomacy. His stance was challenging if not downright belligerent. The placement of his hands was a none too subtle assertion of masculinity. He seemed set on being blunt. To all of the above, *Fine.* "All right, yes, Mr. Burnet. I thought you might work cheap. *Er.*"

"No doubt I would. But I'm not the guy for the job."

She gave a short laugh. "Before you determine that, couldn't you at least hear me out?"

"Waste of time."

"How do you know?"

"An extensive project that would take considerable time? Lots of hard work? Sounds like what you have in mind is a complete overhaul of your house."

"More or less."

"I don't do complete overhauls."

"Would you at least come and see—"

"I've seen it."

Her heart gave a bump of alarm. She had identified herself by name on the voice mail but had said nothing about the location of her house. The vehicle that came past her house each night sprang to mind. "You know where I live?"

He bobbed his square chin.

She studied him for a moment, then said slowly, "When you turned around and saw me here, you recognized me, didn't you?"

Another brusque nod.

"How?"

"Somebody had pointed you out to me."

"Where?"

"I think it was in the fried pie shop."

"I didn't even know there was a fried pie shop."

"Oh. Well, then it must've been somewhere else."

"Why was I being pointed out to you?"

He pulled his thumbs from his pockets and pushed away from the table, then glanced aside for several seconds before coming back to her. "You're the lady who had the . . . emergency . . . in the grocery store."

Her breath hitched, and instinctively she took a step back.

"Oh."

The recollections swarmed her, blocking out light and sound, everything. Her mind unreeled the memories at warp speed, but they were as distinct as though it had happened yesterday instead of two months ago.

She recalled being jerkily conveyed from the ambulance into the ER, the rapid-fire questions of the medical personnel, the pervasive antiseptic smell, the biting coldness of the stirrups against the arches of her bare feet, the kindly voice of the nurse asking if she would like to hold her daughter. Her lifeless daughter.

She didn't know how long she stood there, remembering, but, as the kaleidoscope of memories receded, she realized that she was slumped forward, hugging her elbows. Her skin had turned clammy. Self-consciously, she straightened up and swiped a strand of hair off her damp forehead with the back of her hand.

She became painfully aware of him, standing motionless and silent, watching her. To avoid eye contact, she looked around and took stock of the workshop. Fluorescent tubes augmented the natural light pouring in from four skylights. Two ceiling fans as large as airplane propellers circulated from the ends of long rods. She could identify some of the tools of his trade, while the purposes of other apparatus and pieces of machinery were unknown to her.

A large draftsman's table occupied a far corner. A light fixture with a perforated metal shade was suspended above it. Next to it was a desk with a computer setup. Except for the sawdust on the floor beneath the table where he'd been working, everything was neatly arranged and appeared well maintained.

Finally her gaze returned to him.

He shifted his stance slightly, the soles of his

boots scraping against the floor and disturbing the sawdust. "Sorry about . . ."

He made a small hand gesture in the general direction of her midsection.

"Thank you." She didn't dwell on that. "So when you listened to the voice mail yesterday, you recognized my name."

"Yeah. Rumor had been circulating for months that the youngest of the Maxwell girls was back. Living out there alone. Expecting a baby."

In all the time she'd been back, this was the first time she had come face-to-face with the gossip about her. "Do you know the rest of it?"

"Don't know who or where the baby's father is."

She ignored the implied question. "Are you acquainted with my family's history?"

"I grew up here." He said it as though that were explanation enough, and it was. Everybody knew her family history.

"You ever learn where your dad went, what happened to him?" he asked. "Did the money ever turn up?"

She didn't address those questions, either. "Are you open to discussing my project, Mr. Burnet?"

"I told you. Discussion would be a waste of time."

"You won't even consider it?"

"Don't know how plainer I can make it."

"Are you afraid that being associated with the youngest Maxwell girl will dent your reputation?"

The corner of his stern mouth twitched, but it couldn't be counted as a real smile. "My reputation is already dented. The thing is, your project would involve more work than I take on at any one time. I specialize in small jobs. Ones with a short shelf life. That way, I'm not overcommitted or overextended. I don't like being tied down. I'd rather keep my work schedule flexible."

She crossed her arms and looked him up and down. "That sounded like bullshit."

"It was."

SANDRA BROWN is the author of seventy *New York Times* bestsellers, including *Mean Streak*, *Friction*, *Sting*, *Seeing Red*, and *Tailspin*, the latter two debuting at number one. Since the launch of her career in 1981, Brown has published eighty novels, most of which remain in print. Her books have been translated into thirty-four languages. She lives in Arlington, Texas.

ISBN 978-1-9821-3216-3   **$9.99 U.S./**$12.99 Can.

THE #1 *NEW YORK TIMES*
BESTSELLING AUTHOR OF *SEEING RED*
IGNITES CRACKLING SUSPENSE AND
FIERY EMOTION IN AN UNFORGETTABLE
NOVEL OF PASSION AND VENGEANCE.

When her younger brother, Danny, commits suicide, Sayre Lynch breaks
her vow never to return to her Louisiana hometown and gets drawn
back into her tyrannical father's web. He and her older brother—who
control the town's sole industry, an iron foundry—are as corrupt as
ever. Worse, they have hired a shrewd and disarming new lawyer, Beck
Merchant . . . a man with his own agenda. When the police determine
that Danny's suicide was actually a homicide, Sayre must battle her
family—and her passionate feelings for Beck—as she confronts a powder
keg of old hatreds, past crimes, and a surprising plan of revenge.

"A MASTERFUL STORYTELLER."
—*USA TODAY*

INCLUDES AN EXCERPT FROM THE NEW
SANDRA BROWN NOVEL, *THICK AS THIEVES*

SimonandSchuster.com

POCKET
BOOKS

COVER DESIGN BY PATRICK KANG
COVER PHOTOGRAPHY © GETTY IMAGES

ISBN 978-1-9821-3216-3   **$9.99** U.S./$12.99 Can.

50999

9 781982 132163